Found and Destroyed

The Sara Martin Mystery Series
Lost and Found
Found and Destroyed

Found and Destroyed

Danelle Helget

NORTH STAR PRESS OF ST. CLOUD, INC.
Saint Cloud, Minnesota

Copyright © 2012 Danelle Helget

ISBN 978-0-87839-609-2

All rights reserved.

This is a work of fiction. Names, characters, places, and incidents are the products of the author's imagination or are used fictitiously. Any resemblance to actual events or persons, living or dead, is entirely coincidental.

First Edition: June 2012

Printed in the United States of America

Published by
North Star Press of St. Cloud, Inc.
P.O. Box 451
St. Cloud, Minnesota 56302

www.northstarpress.com

Dedication

For my Mom, who always told me that I could do anything I put my mind to. You are truly cherished. Thanks for the support, encouragement, and love.

With love,

Nell

1

Regular or decaf? That's easy. Cash or check? Again, easy. Paper or plastic? Easy. Deciding whether to live in the Twin Cities close to friends, family, and lots of great restaurants and shops, or in a cabin on a lake with acreage and only three neighbors way up north where dirt roads outnumber paved . . . that's harder. So I decided, since I couldn't decide, that I would just buy more furniture to fill up the cabin in Nisswa and keep my apartment in the Cities too. A perfect scenario for the indecisive!

I'm Sara Martin and ya know what? I'm kind of a mess. There, I said it. Ahhh, it's like free therapy. Just saying it makes me feel tons better. The last six months of my life have been a train wreck, to say the least.

Late last summer I went on a vacation at a cabin with my husband of four years, Jake, and a couple we'd been friends with since grade school, Mark and Lily. While on that vacation, I found out that my husband and Lily were having an affair. That gave me a migraine, so I went to lie down. I woke up to find out that Lily was gone. Turns out that, while I was asleep, she and Mark went on a walk in the woods to talk about things when she slipped on a rocky patch, hit her head, and died instantly. Mark and Jake stupidly decided to cover up her death because it looked suspicious, and they were sure people would believe they killed her because of the affair.

Well, it all got figured out by my new friend, Detective Derek Richards . . . with a little help from me and some weird dreams. I don't like the word psychic, so I don't talk about that part. Jake is my ex now and is serving time for his crime. Mark, as it turns out, had a past and that all came out too. Unbelievably, he had been involved in the death of a childhood friend as well . . . and on the same piece of rocky ground!

My dreams included her and Lily's ghost. Both cases were solved and now the people of Nisswa have closure and seem to think they need to thank *me* for it.

It was awkward and I didn't enjoy the attention from it, but I dealt with it. When everything settled down, I had fallen in love with the area, so I used the very large inheritance I had gotten from my grandmother to purchase the cabin we'd stayed in. Almost all of the property around the lake and a boutique in town called Lost and Found came along with it. The lake was a smaller one, but was big enough for me. It was clean and stocked with fish, and did not have a public access. Another plus was that the only other homes on the lake were the three on the other side, which are all next door to each other.

Lost and Found, a cute little store on Main Street, got a lot of out-of-town visitors and traffic in the summer. The store came turn-key and the staff wanted to stay when I purchased it, which worked out great for me since I'd never run a business and they knew the ropes. It was nice to have a trustworthy staff that enjoyed their jobs. As soon as I purchased the store, I remodeled it and stocked it with everything including home decor, t-shirts, gifts, souvenirs, candles, and handmade jewelry. The older couple who owned it had it open during tourist season, but I wanted it open year round, with shorten the hours in the cold months. It had been a learn-as-you-go adventure, but I enjoyed it, and worked very part time, coming and going as I pleased.

The last couple of weeks, I'd been repainting the inside of the cabin and moving in a few things from the Cities. Yesterday I brought in all of the big furniture I'd ordered for the cabin. I guess driving for hours and hauling heavy items was not a good idea. My back was killing me by the end of the day. I'd had Detective Derek's help, but there was still a bedroom full of furniture, new kitchen table and chairs, and a new couch for the living room. It was a lot. After we'd gotten all of that loaded up in the Cities, we drove all the way to Nisswa, unloaded the stuff, then reloaded the trailer with the old stuff from the cabin and brought it to the Goodwill and unloaded it there. It was a long day.

On Monday morning I woke up an hour before I had to open Lost and Found. I had taken three Tylenol before I'd gone to bed, but it wasn't working. I rolled myself out of bed and into a hot shower. I took my time and did my exfoliate and shave routine. By the time I got out, the heat and meds were doing their thing and I could move again, pain-free. I quickly dressed and did a simple hair and makeup routine. I'd recently cut my hair really short into an inverted, tapered bob. I loved the ease of it. My hair was thick and normally dark brown, but I'd had it dyed a blonde-caramel.

I walked into the kitchen and tossed some Kitty Krunchies into Faith's bowl. She came bounding over from her favorite chair and started to eat. She was four months old, and I couldn't imagine not having her in my life. She had been a gift from my BFF, Kat, after everything that had happened with Lily. Faith had become my best friend when Kat couldn't be there.

Kat lived in the Cities. We worked in the same law office. She was in family law doing mostly divorces, and I did living wills, trusts, and estate planning. I dropped back my hours when I bought the cabin to taking a case here and there, when I wanted one. She and Lily and I used to meet for drinks a couple of nights a week before the affair and Lily's death. Kat was always single and loved to go out dancing. I tried to keep up, but she was always more of a free spirit than I was. She was a great friend though, and had always been there for me when I needed her. She made me laugh and forget my problems when I was with her. I always felt so blessed to have her.

With Faith happy, I made toast for my breakfast, filled a travel mug with coffee, and threw my shoulder bag on. I gave Faith a pat on the head.

"Keep an eye on things for me, girl. I'll be back later."

I shut and locked the door and headed out to my Jeep. I noticed that Derek had unhooked the trailer for me. *I'll need to return that to Kat's dad sometime this week.* Derek was great about doing stuff like that for me, even when I didn't ask him.

I had about a twenty-minute drive to town. I was ten minutes late. It wasn't a big deal since I was the only one scheduled 'til eleven, and I was the boss. I threw the Jeep into park behind the store and walked around to the front. In the store, I flipped on the lights, turned the sign to open, and walked back to the office. I took off my coat and put it and my purse on the hook behind the door. It was early fall so the traffic in the store was slowing for the season. I went through the place and lit a few scented candles—they sold better when people could smell them burning, plus it gave the store a great scent.

My cell phone rang, so I ran across the store to grab it out of my purse. It was Derek.

"Good morning, beautiful," he said.

"Good morning!" He had a way of putting an instant smile on my face.

"Just checking in. Are you at the store already?"

"Yup, just got here."

"I wanted to tell you thanks for a great weekend. I had a lot of fun," he said sweetly.

"Thank you for all of your help. I couldn't have done it without you," I said.

"I also wanted to let you know that my sister called this morning to say she's getting married. I'm excited for her, but she just met this guy and it's kind of bothering me, so I wanted to talk to someone about it."

"Oh, wow," I said, "which sister?"

"Kelly."

"Ohhh. When? Do they have a date set?" I asked.

"Yes, December 2nd," he said reluctantly.

"Wow, that's soon! Is she . . . pregnant?"

"I . . . I . . . I don't know. I guess I didn't think to ask," he said, sounding even more concerned.

"Well, there's not a whole lot you can do about it either way. Why don't you call and ask her to lunch so you can talk to her? Maybe she'll put your mind at ease," I told him, not really knowing what to say.

"Yeah, I'll have to do that. Anyway, I just needed to vent to someone. I'll let you go for now. I've got a call on my work line, but I'll talk to you soon."

"Okay, bye."

I disconnected and took a deep breath. I'd never met anyone in Derek's family, but I knew that he was close to his family, and he seemed really upset.

The morning went by quickly. When Ginger got in at eleven, I took a break and went two doors over to Morning Glory, a little diner that was open all day long. They served everything from breakfast to broasted chicken dinners, and they had a great bakery selection.

I sat in a corner booth with the *Minneapolis Star-Tribune*. Nisswa had a paper, but it was just a weekly that came out on Thursdays. I looked towards the counter area and noticed a large woman in her late thirties headed in my direction with a coffee pot and cup.

"Coffee, sugar?"

Was she calling me sugar, or offering it with the coffee?

"Sure, thanks," I said with a smile at the sweet hospitality.

"Do you need sugar or creamer?"

There's my answer. I nodded and she grabbed both out of her apron pocket.

"You're not from around here. You coming through town on business or pleasure?" she said leaning back on the booth behind her.

"Actually, I'm new in town. I just bought the store two doors down, Lost and Found, and some property on Lake Hawsawneekee," I said.

"No shit? You that woman that found the bones of the little Sander's girl?" she asked. She straightened up and leaned forward. Her face was lit up with excitement and she looked eager to hear more. "You're the hot topic in this place these days. Small town gossip spreads fast in these parts. People say you're psychic and talk to ghosts. They say a ghost told you where to look," she said, awaiting my response.

"Umm, gosh, people have big imaginations . . . don't they? " I responded, not wanting to get into the details with this . . . stranger.

"Yeah, they sure do," she said, noticing my unwillingness to carry on with the conversation. "Well, sugar, can I get you something to eat?"

"Yes, I'll take a caramel roll, and just the coffee is fine."

She took a pen out of her ponytail and wrote it down on a receipt pad, then spun around and walked off. I wondered if I'd annoyed her by not offering any more information. I opened my newspaper and ran my eyes across the headlines. *Nothing exciting happening.* I sipped my coffee and was pleasantly surprised when it tasted really good. *They even have little flavored creamers.*

The waitress returned with my roll, which she'd warmed up. *This is no good for my diet. I have such a weakness for caramel rolls. I'll have to go for a run later,* I thought. The waitress topped off my coffee and leaned back on the booth again.

"Sorry if I seem nosey. It's just this town doesn't have a lot going on, so news like that is huge. It's nice to actually talk to the source rather than just hear the stuff from the customers, and the newspaper didn't do a very good job on the article. It just left all of us with more questions," she said, seeming much friendlier now. "I'm Tannya by the way," she said with a smile, extending her hand.

"Hi. Sara Martin," I said shaking her hand.

We talked a few more minutes about my owning Lost and Found. She knew the old owners, not well, but she said they came in for breakfast on Sundays. She worked full time, mostly Monday through Friday 5:00 a.m. to 1:00 p.m., but occasionally she helped out on weekends or in the evening.

Tannya had grown up in the area and informed me that she had been divorced after a year of marriage and now lived in a small fixer-upper about a mile from town. She was taking some online college classes, but wasn't really sure what she wanted to do. When another customer came in, she excused herself.

She's a chatty one, I thought. *Seems nice. Nosey, yes, but friendly.* Tannya had long, bleach-blonde hair with dark roots, and really bright makeup. Her lips and cheeks were very pink. Her build was large, not obese, exactly, but she had me by about sixty pounds. She was dressed in too-tight khaki pants and a blue polo shirt that said Morning Glory on the upper left side in gold. I watched her until she started talking to the new customer, then returned to my paper.

Finishing the last bite of my roll, I began to feel the guilt rush in. *That was so unhealthy. Never again!* I promised myself. *I'll run when I get home and eat salad the rest of the day.*

"Good to meet ya, hun," Tannya said, as she placed the bill on the table.

"It was nice meeting you, too," I said with a smile and placed a five on the table and walked back to work.

When I got back, Ginger was checking out a customer. Two others looked around. I was excited to see people in my store. Every time the door opened, I got excited. It was fun owning my own business, especially in my case because I didn't have any money pressure. If my business didn't make money, I'd be fine and could still pay the bills and staff. I did want the business to do well though. And I enjoyed the tasks: stocking shelves, getting new stuff in, decorating areas, setting up displays . . . all of it, even the paperwork. It was pure bliss.

I finished up some paperwork in the back and said goodbye to Ginger. She was scheduled until close, so I had the rest of the day to myself. The first thing I did was stop at the First National Bank of Nisswa and open checking and savings accounts for me, and a business account for Lost and Found. It was a nice bank. It was clean but seemed a little old-fashioned with all the women dressed in matching business suits. Still, they had all of the services I needed, and there was only one other bank in town, which was smaller and didn't offer Internet banking. The experience was pleasant and seamless.

Next I stopped at Schaefer's Foods and picked up some much needed groceries. My cupboards at the cabin were bare. That was the one hang up in floating between the two locations. It was hard to transfer perishable foods back and forth and to determine what you would need for each stay. I didn't really have a schedule, and never really knew how long I'd be gone when I left each place. It was a good thing that Faith liked car trips. I took her with me every time I headed to the Cities, just in case I wouldn't be back for a while. I loaded up my cart with healthy foods, since I still felt the guilt of the caramel roll, and checked out.

At home, after I put the food away, I grabbed a cup of hot chocolate and went out to the patio. I returned to the cabin and grabbed a heavy sweatshirt and threw it on. I was bummed that summer was over, even though the cabin was very cozy and I loved the fireplace. The fall colors around the lake were well past peak and the trees where getting very thin. It made me think about raking leaves, which didn't sound like fun to me, so I made a mental note to call a landscaper.

I took my phone out of my purse and called my mom, Jan. She was retired now, thanks to my grandmother's inheritance. She and my dad, Will Lewis, had been married for thirty-two years and seemed still very much in love. My mom said that she wanted to come up the next day to help me finish painting the kitchen. Everything else was already pretty much done. I told her I'd buy her dinner at Morning Glory as a thank you. I gave her the directions, again, and we agreed on meeting at 11:00 a.m. She'd been at my cabin once before when I first bought it, but she was really bad with directions. I was scheduled to open the store in the morning, so I'd be home after that to meet her. I put my phone down on the little glass-topped table and my feet up on the chair next to me. I had begun to feel my back tightening up again.

When I had finished my hot chocolate I went back inside. I was bored. I wasn't used to having so much free time. When I worked as a lawyer I was up at 6:00, out the door by 7:30, and in the office at 8:00. My hours were long. Most nights I was there until seven, and some nights I even had to bring work home. That, plus trying to have a life with my husband, took up all of my time, so now, minus such strenuous work and the husband, I didn't know what to do with myself.

I changed into workout clothes and laced up my tennis shoes, determined to run off the caramel roll and hot chocolate. I threw my inhaler in my pocket and grabbed my iPod from my room. I left the door unlocked, knowing I wouldn't last long. I headed down the driveway, took a left on the county road, and picked up the pace. An hour later I was home. Most of the time had been spent walking. I'd made it only about a third of the way around the lake. I'd thought about stopping at the Sanders' place and letting them know I was living at the cabin now, but I couldn't make it that far.

They lived in one of the cluster of three houses across the lake. Their daughter had been the other ghost in my dreams. She had been missing for many years when we found her remains on the property where Lily died. Her parents were very grateful to me for finding them. I wanted to get over there and let them know that I'd bought the cabin and the store before they heard it from the town's people. *This small town living is going to take some getting used to.* My phone rang. It was Derek.

"Hey, sweetness," he said.

"Hey. Did you talk to your sister yet?" I asked.

"No, but I did talk to my mom. She wants to have all of us kids to dinner tomorrow night to talk about things with Kelly. She asked Kelly to come alone."

"Oh, really? That's sounds like a drama-filled evening."

"Yeah, not looking forward to it, but hopefully we can talk some sense into her."

"Well, good luck," I said. "I'm painting the kitchen with my mom tomorrow, then taking her to dinner at Morning Glory. Too bad you're busy. You could have joined us," I said with as much sarcasm as I could fit in.

"Oh gee, now I feel torn. I don't know which sounds better."

"Well, I hope it goes well. Let me know," I said.

"Thanks, I will. I'll call you Wednesday sometime. Take care, sweetness." He disconnected.

Our relationship was new, but deep because of what we had gone through together. I had met Derek in college one night at a party. We had stayed up all night talking. I was with Jake at the time, so it was just a conversation, but there was still chemistry there. I was attached to his hip throughout the entire investigation and things just kind of moved from friendship into . . . something. I was not really sure what, but we'd been on a few dates, and kissed a lot. He'd spent the night at the cabin a couple of times, but had always slept in the other room. He was an old-fashioned kind of guy and didn't want to move too fast. His words, not mine. But, I was thinking the same thing. I hadn't known him that long, but he had become a very important part of my life. I liked him a lot. But I was newly divorced and wasn't sure I was ready for another relationship yet. But I definitely knew I liked him. A lot.

I'd lay down and watched a movie, then made a quick dinner. I really didn't like eating alone, or living alone for that matter. I mean, sure, it was nice because there was no one to answer to, or worry about, but it was too quiet, and a person can only talk to a cat so much before it starts to feel crazy.

After dinner I took a long, hot bath and went to bed early. I needed the extra rest for my back.

The next morning I woke up startled. Faith had been climbing on my dresser and knocked my phone to the floor. It was time to get up anyway—already seven. I got ready for work in a rush, grabbed my purse and coat, and scooted out the door. I opened the store and avoided getting too involved in any big projects, knowing that right after I got off I was supposed to meet my mom at home.

The morning went by quickly as usual. When Ginger arrived a little before eleven, I ran for the door. Before I left town, I spun into the hardware store to pick up some new paint rollers. I was just on my way out the door when my mom called.

"Hey, I'm about twenty minutes away," she said.

"No problem. I'll see you when you get here," I said and disconnected.

I beat her home and started gathering all the painting supplies. I moved all of the items off of the counter and began the taping process.

I was about half done when my mom walked through the front door with her arms loaded with more paint supplies, as if I didn't know what we needed. She sang hello.

"Hey, I brought some items from home in case you didn't have them," she said putting the bags in the entry and slipping off her shoes.

"Hi, I have a bunch, but thanks," I said and walked over and gave her a hug. She handed me a Danish roll from one of the bags.

"A snack for break time," she said with a wink.

"Looks good," I said and put it down. "I'm almost done taping. If you want to you can start doing the brush work, or rolling, and I'll join you when I get done with the tape."

"Sure, I'll brush," she said rolling up her sleeves and reaching for the tray and paint.

I'd picked out a burnt orange that, I thought, went great in the room. We talked the whole time we painted. It was good to catch up. My mom was very good about listening to me and not trying to run my life. She was a great friend, but still offered advice like a mom should. She always let me make my own choices, but warned about mistakes she could foresee and always praised my success. It was a good mother-friend balance.

My father was pretty quiet and straight to the point. He was loving, but a man of few words. He was retired and spent most of his time on the couch. Once in a while he'd meet his guy friends for breakfast and take the boat out, but in Minnesota boating season was short. Mom had tried to get him involved in other stuff, but he wasn't interested.

"So, how are the neighbors?" Mom asked.

"I don't really know. I haven't met any yet, I mean, besides Carrie's parents who live on the lake. I haven't met the people who live in the other two houses. You can see their houses pretty well from here now that the leaves are gone," I said pointing out the patio door. Mom went over and looked out across the lake.

"Oh, yep. The homes seem well taken care of, so they can't be that bad, right? I mean crazy people don't rake leaves, paint their homes, or garden right?" she said seeming a bit concerned.

"Riiiiight," I said raising my eyebrows and smiling. "I did meet a waitress at the restaurant this morning. Turns out I'm the big talk of the town. She was very interested in my story, but I didn't give her much. She seems to know all the gossip though. She was nice, nosey but nice," I added.

"Oh, good, you're making friends already."

"I don't know if I'd go that far," I said with a snort. "She was a great waitress, and if her food doesn't lift your spirits, her makeup will."

A couple of hours later we were finished with the painting. It looked really nice. We cleaned up, changed our clothes, and fixed our hair and makeup. We hung out on the porch for a bit, and drank some coffee and had the rest of the Danish. After a while, I gave Faith strict instructions to stay away from the walls and served her a handful of kibble. We locked up and sauntered out to the Jeep. Mom pointed out the fact that I had a lot of trees, and a lot of leaves. That was a fat hint.

"I know. I'm going to call a landscaper to take care of that after they all fall. Sometime in the next couple weeks," I told her.

Pulling up to Morning Glory, I noticed it was kind of busy. I wasn't expecting that on a Tuesday evening in such a small town. When we got inside, it smelled like Mexican food. I noticed that the decor had changed a bit, and there were two buffet bars full of Mexican food. There were all kinds of things hanging from the ceiling, and the booths and tables all had brightly colored tablecloths on them. There was also a big note on the special's chalk board that read: HOLA! IT'S MEXICAN BUFFET NIGHT, AMIGOS! The hostess walked up to us in a white shirt with a lacey, rounded collar and puffy sleeves and a brightly colored skirt to complete the outfit. It was cute. Loud Mexican music filling the room too. It was louder than one normally found in a restaurant. It was actually very uplifting. It made me feel as if a party was going on. I smiled.

"Two?" the hostess asked.

"Yes," I answered.

"Do you want menus or the buffet?" I looked to my mom.

She was smiling looking around the room. "Buffet," she said.

"Right this way, please," the hostess said. She took our drink order, which was virgin margaritas. They had to be virgin since the Morning Glory didn't have a liquor license. "Help yourselves when you're ready, ladies," she added.

"This is super fun!" Mom said with a smile.

"I know, right? So cute and apparently the customers like it too," I said looking at all of the people bustling around. Everyone seemed happy. I didn't see Tannya anywhere. *She must have gone home for the day.*

We went and got our food. It looked really good. The buffet had everything Mexican a person could ever want, and a bunch of Mexican desserts that I couldn't wait to check out on my next trip up there. We ate and talked a little about the differences between living in the Cities and Nisswa. There were lots of things that I liked, and a few I didn't. After we finished our meals and desserts, we drove back to the cabin. Mom left for home as soon as we got back, she had a long drive and didn't like driving at night. I cuddled up with Faith and went to bed early. My back was still sore.

2

I'm not sure what I was thinking when I put myself on the schedule to open. At night I always had big plans to get up early, go for a run, and then go into work. But, then morning came, and the alarm went off, and I hit snooze. Then I hit snooze nine minutes later, and again after nine more minutes. When it went off for the fourth time, I'd look at the time and leap out of bed, angry with myself and running behind. It was a vicious cycle. I'd always promise myself I wouldn't do it the next day, but I'd do it anyway. And, of course, it happened again, so I had to rush through getting ready, feeling exhausted and scatter-brained, which lasted for hours afterwards.

After pulling out of the driveway, I went as fast as I could on the dirt, back-county road to make up for lost time. A mile or so later, I noticed lights in my rear-view mirror. *Shit! A cop. Dang it. Now I'm going to be even later.* I pulled over to the side of the road and put my hazards on. *Dang it. Dang it. Dang it.*

I looked in my side mirror and saw a uniformed male get out of the car and saunter up to my door. He was gorgeous. *Oh, my gosh, drop dead gorgeous!* His skin on the tan side, and he had a great body. It was usually hard to tell in the unflattering uniforms the cops had to wear, but he made it work. His eyebrows and day-old beard were dark. He had his hat on, so I couldn't see his hair, but I could imagine it being just as dark.

He smiled. "Hey there, speedy," he said stepping up to my window. I mentally face-slapped myself to snap myself out of dreamland. I noticed that I was suddenly two degrees warmer. I didn't care anymore what this was going to cost me. I just wanted to hear his voice again. His teeth were white and straight, and he had a great smile—*Oh, gosh even a dimple in one cheek.* It was just too much. I could see the area women speeding regularly just to get him to stop them and talk. It was worth a ticket.

"You in a hurry?" he asked again, with a sexy, velvety voice.

"Um . . . I . . . ah . . . yeah," I finally answered, feeling like an tongue-tied fifth grader. I wondered if my jaw had been hanging slack when he'd walked up. I shook my head slightly to refocus. "Yes, officer. Sorry. I was going a bit fast. I'm running late for work . . . again." I said with a wince, hoping he'd go easy on me.

"Ah, yes, the late for work excuse," he said slyly, looking like he was sizing me up. "And where is it that you work?"

"Lost and Found, the little boutique in town," I answered.

"Really?" he asked confused. "Are you the new owner?"

"Yes, I am." I smiled proudly, and realized that I must have looked really dorky as soon as I did it.

"Oh, so you must be Sara Martin," he said extending his hand. I took it and shook.

"Yes, hi," I said, with a small giggle. "Nice to meet you Officerrr . . . Dalton," I said spotting his name badge.

"Rex, Rex Dalton," he corrected. "Nice to meet you, too. You've been very popular conversation topic around here lately. I was on leave with a leg injury when the case was being handled, so I never got to meet you. But I heard all about it from the guys. Interesting story, to say the least."

"Yeah, tell me about it," I answered.

"So you decided to stick around? Bought the store?"

"Well, actually, I bought the cabin. The store was sort of part of the package," I answered. "I still have an apartment in the Cities, so I've been floating back and forth."

"Oh, okay. So tell me, what do you think of our little town so far?" he asked.

"It's nice. The people so far have been great, and I love the cabin and Lost and Found."

"That's good to hear. And if the people are ever not great, you let me know. I'll take care of that for you. And since you own the store you won't get in trouble from the boss if you're late. So, you can slow down a little, right?"

"Right," I said, biting my lower lip and smiling like a kid getting scolded.

"All right," he said. "Take it easy. I'll see ya around. Nice meeting you." He tapped the top of the door twice, winked and walked away.

"Okay, thank you." *Wow, he's . . . nice.* I pulled out onto the road with a huge grin on my face. He reminded me a lot of Derek. I took a deep breath and a sip of my water to cool my body down while I tried to concentrate on my driving.

I kept it at the speed limit the rest of the way and got to work fifteen minutes late. No one was standing outside the door when I got there, so it was fine that I was late, I just didn't want to make it a habit. *In fact, starting tomorrow, I'm going to start that running routine.*

I was starving by the time Ginger got there. I not only missed breakfast, but I didn't bring any snacks with me, so as soon as she was ready and punched in, I went to the Morning Glory for brunch. Tannya was waiting on a table near the door. I walked past her, and she looked up at me. "Hey, girl!" she said with a big smile.

"Hi," I said taking a seat a few tables over. I took a quick peek at the menu.

"Well, look what the cat drug back as a treat for us!" Tannya said, walking up to the table. *I've never heard it said quite like that, but it seems to work for her.* She had her blonde hair pulled back into a pony again with a pen stuck in there, and the blue Morning Glory polo shirt and too-tight black stretch pants to boot. Her makeup was neon-blue eyeliner with ruby-red lipstick and bright pink cheeks. My fingertips ached to rub it in to blend it better. It was tacky to say the least, but she made me smile. I giggled at the comment and set the menu down on the table.

"Yup, I'm back," I said, smiling. "I'll probably be a regular here, since I can't seem to get my butt out of bed to eat a good breakfast before work."

"Great, you'll keep us in business, and give me something to do."

"I was here last night with my mom. It looked a lot different," I told her, noticing that the Mexican decor was all gone and the music was on quiet radio tunes.

"Oh, geez, ya got to see Taco Tuesday, huh? I avoid working Tuesday nights like the plague. What can I get ya today?"

I ordered the two-egg omelet, whites only with the veggie mix, and a side of whole wheat toast dry.

"Kind of a change from the caramel rolls," Tannya said, grabbing the pen from her hair and writing the order on her pad. She reached for the cup on my table and flipped it up, then grabbed the carafe she'd set on the table behind me and filled it up.

"Yes, that was a moment of weakness. I've had a lot of those lately," I said.

A few minutes later, Tannya brought over my order and glass of ice water. "So I hear you got pulled over this morning by Officer McHottie."

I almost spewed out my coffee. *Seriously? That was hours ago, news really does travel fast.* "Um, yeah . . . Officer McHottie?" I said, in obvious shock.

"Yeah, McHottie! Or don't you agree?"

"Oh, no, I completely agree. He's a very nice looking man."

"Honey, nice looking is my brother. Rex is far from nice looking. One look in my direction from him and I melt like butter on a hot tin roof," she said, fanning herself. "He comes in here a couple times a week on his break, and I can't stand the wait between visits. He looks good and smells good, *and* he's single."

I laughed at her enthusiasm. "Are you single too?" I asked.

"Yes, but I don't stand a chance, sweet thing. He likes those cutzie wootzies like you. You're single, right? I think you should give him a call. Maybe ask him to dinner. Maybe you ask him to dinner and you come here. I wouldn't mind at all waiting on your table. I could look at him all day long."

"Well, thank you for the advice, but I'm kind of seeing someone right now."

"Really. Is this other guy your 'kind of seeing' as hot as Rex?" she asked.

"I guess it's a matter of opinion but, yes, I think he is. And he's a cop too," I added, hoping to close the conversation.

"Yeah, well I heard the way Rex talked about you," she said suggestively. "So, if you can get through your day and not think about him, then maybe it ain't meant to be. Enjoy your lunch, love," she said then spun on her heels, tipped her chin up, and marched away.

Great, so now I'm the talk of the town again. I took a deep breath and started to eat. When I was almost done, Tannya came back and filled my cup again. "So, how are things at the store going?" she asked.

"Good so far. Thank goodness for the staff. They really know what they're doing and have been very helpful."

"Yeah, Ginger and Maureen are good people. You lucked out there. So, getting back to this crime solving, psychic ability of yours . . . do you take on new cases?"

"What? Ah, no. I'm not psychic, and I'm certainly not a crime solver at all," I said, with an awkward giggle.

"Well, I think you are, and so do the people of this town. You solved the biggest crime this town has ever seen, and they think it's good to have you around," she informed me.

I laughed out loud. "That's not really my cup of tea. The situation was very strange, and I'm glad it worked out, but I don't normally do that. I'm a lawyer, or, well, I used to be. I don't really do it that much anymore either. I really just run the Lost and Found. That's it."

"Huh. Well that's too bad 'cause I heard a local talking today about . . ." she looked around, lowered her voice, and dipped her head closer to me, ". . . a problem of sorts that you could probably help her with. She said she was looking for a private investigator . . . of sorts and was willing to pay a lot for the service, but there's no one around here who does that sort of thing, and Miss Kitty has a lot of money.

You could help her out and maybe make some cash too," she said quietly.

"I don't do private investigating," I said, incredulous at the idea. "I simply helped out on a case that involved me. I got lucky. I don't have any training or skills in that kind of work. Sorry, but I'm not interested, or qualified for that matter."

"All right, well it doesn't hurt to ask," she said as she set a piece of paper and the bill on the table, then sashayed back to the counter.

I looked at the paper. On it was Tannya's name and cell number, and Miss Kitty's name and cell number, and the words: *Just in case you change your mind.* After I read it, I looked up at Tannya. She was trying her best to appear busy behind the counter and didn't look back at me. I put the paper in my purse and money on the table and walked out.

All the way home I thought about the conversation, and my curiosity was churning at full speed. I wondered about Miss Kitty. *Who is she, and what does she want me to do?* I wondered about Tannya, and who she really was. *She's a hoot, and very down to earth. Her energy is contagious.* I also wondered about Rex, the cop, then remembered what Tannya said about trying not to thinking about him, *and here I'm thinking about him again. Dang it.*

When I pulled into the driveway I tried to refocus. I walked out to the end of the dock and sat in the chair. I inhaled the fresh air and tipped my head up towards the sun. A moment later, I got up and went inside, it was getting too chilly to sit outside. It was a nice thought, but I couldn't do it without shivering. It did make me think about winter prep for the yard and dock though. I knew that the dock had to come out before winter, and that I needed a pontoon trailer. Reggie, the previous owner, never had one. He had paid a service for the moving and storage of the pontoon. I needed to figure that out soon, so I went inside and called my dad.

"Hey, Dad," I said when he picked up.

"Hey, Sara. What's up?" he answered. There was no small talk with him, he was a straight-to-the-point kind of man.

"I need your help. I have a pontoon and dock out here, and I don't know what to do with it this winter. When do I need to take them out, and how do I do that?" I asked in a sweet voice.

"Well, the dock needs to come out soon. Someone's going to have to get into the water to do that, and the water's getting colder, so the sooner the better. But, before you do that, you need to get the pontoon out. I'd suggest buying a pontoon trailer. You'll want one if you ever want to take the boat to another lake, or if you go camping, or it needs repair anyways."

"That's kind of what I was thinking too."

"You should shop for one now. The stores will be trying to get rid of their inventory before winter. You'll also need to build a large shed out there for your pontoon and Jeep to fit in. This is Minnesota. It's gonna be a long, hard winter," he added.

"I've thought about that too." I said, mentally adding that to my list of things to do.

"When can you get Derek out there to help us?" he asked.

"How about this weekend?"

"That's fine here. Check with him, and I'll tell your mom."

"Okay, great! Thanks, Dad. I'll get some beer in the fridge, and we can grill one last time before it gets too cold."

It was Wednesday. I hadn't heard from Derek yet and wondered if I should call him, but I didn't want to seem too clingy. We were in a strange stage of the relationship. I knew he liked me, but I didn't want to be too needy and scare him away. I did want to keep him close at hand though. I decided to call. He picked up on first ring.

"Detective Richards."

"Hey, detective," I said with an instant smile at the sound of his voice.

"Hey, sweetness, how are you? It feels like forever since I've seen you," he said with a sigh.

Aww, he melted my heart. "So how did the dinner with the fam go?" I asked.

"Ugh, don't ask. It's a bigger issue than I thought. I'll fill you in when I see you . . . When am I going to see you?" he asked. "Can you come to dinner with me tonight?"

"Ah, maybe . . . I need to check with Ginger and Maureen to see if they can cover my shifts for me. I'll call you back in a bit okay?" I said.

"Okay. Talk to ya soon," he said and disconnected.

I called Lost and Found. Ginger and Maureen were both there, so we changed the schedule. They were both happy to get more hours, and I got the rest of the week off. I called Derek back and told him that he had me for the rest of the week. He seemed happy, and said that we had reservations at Fogo De Chao, a Brazilian Steak House, downtown at 7:30. *Man he works fast!*

I disconnected and jumped into the shower. It was two. By the time I showered, shaved, got ready for the hot date, and drove almost three hours to get there, I'd be right on time. I told him I'd meet him at the restaurant. I cleaned the cat box and packed Faith's stuff into the Jeep, hooked up Kat's dad's trailer, then got ready.

At 4:15 p.m. I was out the door and programing my GPS for the restaurant. I knew the Cities pretty well, but the one-ways downtown could turn me around in a heartbeat. *Best to trust the machine.* I dropped the trailer off at Kat's parents' home, quickly thanked them, and headed to the restaurant.

3

At 7:35 p.m. I walked in and saw Derek at the bar, tall beer in hand. He looked gorgeous. Even from the back.

"Hey, handsome," I said sliding onto the stool next to him.

He turned to look at me and gave me a quick kiss, then scanned me head to toe. I was wearing a dark-blue, satin shirt with long sleeves and a high-waisted black mini-skirt. My black heels were strappy all the way up the top of my foot and high on the ankle. My legs were bare except for the tan-in-a-bottle I sprayed on them before dressing.

"Wow! You look amazing. You clean up fast." He looked into my eyes. I could see him relax when he exhaled. "Ah, it's good to have you here. I missed you," he said and kissed me again, this time a second longer.

When I'd finally caught my breath, I asked, "Tough week so far?"

"Yeah. Work's busy, and the family is crazy and falling apart."

We both looked down at the bar and noticed the table pager blinking and buzzing. He picked it up and put his hand out and motioned for me to go first. We walked to the hostess podium, and he handed her the pager.

"Right this way," she said and led us to a table.

"So, tell me about the family," I said after we were seated and my wine was delivered.

"Oh, gosh. Where do I start?"

"We don't have to talk about it, if you don't want to," I offered.

"No, it's fine. It just bothers me. I know when to trust my gut, and this is one of those times I feel I need to trust it." He took a drink and continued. "Okay, so I have two sisters Kelly and Kendall. Kelly is twenty-one, and Kendall is twenty-three. They are really close and are both going to school in Morris. Kelly's in nursing, and Kendall's in teaching. They live in an apartment together and both waitress at Applebee's. So, I get a call from my mom on Sunday night, after I left your place. She's in tears. She's all upset and telling me that Kelly's engaged and going to ruin her life and on and on."

"Ah, nice, just what you need—more drama queens in your life," I said with a wink.

"I know!" he said with a huge grin. He took a big gulp of his drink and a deep breath, then continued. "So the story goes that Kelly just met this guy, Cory, at Applebee's two months ago. She was his waitress and they exchanged numbers. The next night they went out together and she hasn't been back to the apartment since. Kendall said that the guy's a creep and she doesn't approve. Kelly won't even return Kendall's calls anymore. She's completely heartbroken and hurt, and just when she thought it was bad, it got worse. Kelly came back to the apartment on Friday night at about midnight with Cory on her arm. Kendall was asleep and heard her come in. She came out into the living room to find Kelly loading up a bag with a few of her things. Kendall asked Kelly what she was doing. Kelly told her that she was just getting a few things and then she was leaving. Kendall said that both of them were drunk and high. She could smell pot on them. Kelly had never touched the stuff until then. Kendall tried to get her to talk, but Kelly wouldn't even make eye contact with her. When Kelly went into the bedroom to get her clothes, Kendall went into the kitchen to introduce herself to Cory. She extended her hand, but he just looked at her and said, 'Hey,' and kept rooting through the cupboards."

"What?"

"She said he was in his thirties, had a three-day-old beard, and was dirty. His clothes were old and tattered and looked 'kinda like a sexy, drug addict'—her words, not mine," Derek said and took another big drink. "He grabbed a bunch of snacks, a can of corn, and the three beers that were left in the fridge and shouted at Kelly that they were leaving. Kelly said she'd be right there. Then he yelled, 'Now Kelly! Let's go!'

She apparently came running out of the bedroom still stuffing clothes into the bag."

"Oh, geez," I said with a wrinkled brow.

"Yeah. So, they just walked out. Cory looked at Kendall, gave her a creepy body scan, licked his lips, and winked, then said, 'Later,' and shut the door. Kendall called my mom right away and told her what happened. Later that day, Kelly called my mom to announce her engagement. Then I got the call from Mom."

"Wow, Derek, I'm so sorry."

"My sisters are both beautiful, smart, and morally grounded women. I think that Kelly has herself in a really bad situation right now, and I think that drugs and alcohol are big players in it. The worst part is that Kelly said she doesn't want a big wedding. She just wants my mom and dad to give her money to elope."

"Your folks said no, right?" I asked.

"They didn't say anything yet. They just said that we should all get together and meet Cory and his parents and talk about the details and dates."

"Did she agree?"

"She hung up. So my mom and dad had me, Kendall, and my brother, Travis, over instead. We ate and spent the night talking to Kendall about what she knew. We tried to call Kelly, but she wouldn't respond to any of us. No one has talked to her in over a week, except for Kendall briefly that night at the apartment."

"So now what?" I asked taking a sip of wine.

"I don't know. I ran a check on him and there's nothing on record, criminally anyway."

"Does he have a job?"

"We don't know. Kendall doesn't know him, and Kelly never talked about him. She just left for a date and never came back." I tried to absorb what I'd just heard.

"What about his place? She must be with him somewhere."

"His address is listed as Morris. That's all I have right now. It's an apartment. I'm thinking maybe this weekend I pop in for a visit."

"Has Kelly been attending classes?"

"No. Kendall checked with a couple of her professors, and they haven't seen her in a week, and she's not turning in her work either. She's shown up for work when scheduled, which was a few nights last week, so money is important enough, I guess."

"Great, so she still needs money, but is dropping out of school?" I asked, now even more concerned.

I started thinking that this was a bad conversation to have at a Brazilian steak house. My stomach was sensitive to stress. An hour ago I really wanted a big slab of red meat, now . . . not so much.

After the first mouthwatering bite, I got over it. After we ate our dinner, I followed Derek back to his apartment. I got Faith all settled in and showed her where I'd put the litter box. We put on an HBO movie and curled up together on the couch in pajamas. We drank some water to help the meat settle. When the movie was over, Derek got up and went to the linen closet. He said I could sleep in his room and he'd take the couch. He didn't seem like he wanted to discuss it, so I agreed and thanked him. He seemed tired and stressed, and had to be into the office by 8:00 a.m. He gave me a short, but sweet, kiss and padded over to the couch with a pillow and blanket in tow. I closed the door halfway and climbed into his bed. It was amazing. The sheets were soft and fresh, but still had his cologne scent in them. I inhaled deeply and sank deeper into the plush, pillow top mattress and fell right to sleep.

I heard a door close quietly in the distance. I opened my eyes. It took me a second to remember that I was at Derek's. I stretched and sauntered sleepily into the living room. The couch was empty with the blanket and pillow Derek had used neatly stacked on the floor next to the coffee table. I looked around the apartment and didn't find Derek, but saw a half-folded piece of paper propped up on the counter with my name on it: *Good morning, beautiful. Off to work . . . didn't want to disturb you. Please make yourself at home. Call ya later. Derek*

Sweet. I checked the coffee pot. It was programmed to start in an hour, so I figured that was a sign to go back to bed. I dragged my feet to the bedroom and slid back in bed. It was so awesome, *so soft and still warm*. I closed my eyes for a second and opened them when I smelled coffee. *I have to get up now.* I padded into the kitchen and a poured a cup, and prayed that he had a good flavored creamer. Inside the fridge I found Hazelnut and Fat Free French Vanilla. *Yummo!* I took a few sips then sat in front of the TV and watched *Good Morning America*.

At nine, when *Live with Kelly* started, I headed to the shower. It was weird taking a shower in Derek's apartment. I could smell his products in the steam. It filled the room and made me miss him. My tummy got butterflies. *It's funny, no matter how old you get, love makes you feel like a kid again.* I had no idea what I was going to do with myself all day. After I was all prepped and ready, I called Derek and thanked him for the coffee.

"You're welcome. Did you sleep well?" he asked.

"Like a baby. I love your bed! I took a shower too, and now I'm bored. What time are you off?"

"Not 'til five."

"Okay . . . I'll make sure to be here then. I think I might see if I can meet Kat for lunch. Maybe visit my parents for a bit too."

"Have a fun day. I'll bring home something for supper, okay?"

"Sounds great. See ya later," I said.

"Bye, sweetness," he said and disconnected.

I called Kat and we agreed on Applebee's in Bloomington, near the law office, at noon. Noon was a ways off, so I popped two slices of bread in the toaster and searched for some peanut butter and honey. I couldn't find honey, so I sliced up a banana instead. Faith was bounding around the place like a lion on the hunt. She had been quiet last night, which was a surprise since she had been in the car while we ate. I picked her up and let her lick the peanut butter off my finger. After she finished, and wiggled down, I led her to her bowl and poured some kibble into it. She squatted down and ate. I peeked in her litter box and noticed that she'd used it a couple of times. *That's a relief.* It's nice that she traveled well and adjusted to her surroundings quickly. I didn't realize how crazy my life was going to be when I first got her.

I drove over to my mom and dad's and shared a fruit platter with them. Dad asked if I had bought a trailer for the pontoon yet and I told him no, but that I would get one before the weekend. I made a mental note to do that. Mom and I agreed on a menu for the barbeque, and I invited them to stay overnight if they wanted to. They said that was fine, that they'd be there sometime Sunday afternoon and stay 'til Monday morning. I wasn't on the schedule at Lost and Found for next week, and was going to try to cut down my hours so that the staff could get the hours they wanted. I liked the work, but I wanted to keep it very part time.

After I gave Mom and Dad a hug and kiss goodbye, I headed over to Applebee's. Kat was in a booth, diet coke in hand, when I walked in.

"Hey, girl!" she said standing up to give me a big hug. "Oh, I miss you, country girl! Look at you, the rural life is good to you," she said.

I laughed, "Yeah, all two weeks of it? Puhlease. I miss you too, though. It does seem like we're in different countries sometimes."

The waitress stopped by and asked, "Can I get you a drink?"

"A beer is fine," I said.

"So what brings you to town today?" Kat asked as we took our seats. I smiled.

"Derek. We had dinner last night at Fogo De Chao."

"Really? And then you . . . slept over?" she pried.

"Yes. Me in his bed, him on the couch."

"Girl, you're killing me! You two are really taking this 'let's take it slow' thing to the extreme!" she said, frustrated.

"I know, but it's good. I really like him. We've been through a lot of stressful stuff together, and I like this pace. It's nice that he's such a gentleman and not just after one thing. I know he really likes me since he's taking his time to really get to know me."

"So, are you exclusive?" she asked, putting her elbows up on the table and resting her chin on her folded hands.

"Umm, good question. I don't know. We never really discussed it, I guess. I don't know that I want to be though. I mean I *am* newly single and I'm not sure I should shack up with the first guy I meet, ya know?" I said, wondering what Derek's answer would be to that question.

We talked a while longer and ate our lunch. Kat had to get back to work, and I needed to go trailer shopping. We parted ways with a hug and a promise to get together soon.

I googled pontoon trailers on my phone and found a dealership named Boats Trailers and More nearby. I drove over and parked in the lot. The trailers were all outside. I reached in the back seat, grabbed my winter coat, and put it on. The sun was peeking out, but it was breezy and only forty-two degrees. The lot was filled with all different kinds of trailers, so I decided that it would be best to head inside and get someone to help.

I opened the door and went straight ahead to reception. The young woman said that she would page someone to help me. While I waited, I scanned the small building's inventory. They had five really nice boats with steps and platforms next to them. I was tempted to go over and look at them when I heard steps coming my way.

"Bart Williams, ma'am. Nice to meet you. Thanks for coming in," a man said, shaking my hand fast and firmly.

"Hi. Sara Martin. Nice to meet you too."

"So, you're looking for a pontoon trailer?" he asked, rubbing his hands together.

He was short, in his late sixties, and round all the way to his feet. He had a lot of fluffy, gray hair and full gray beard. His eyes were bright blue. He reminded me of Santa, only shorter. His black suit was of nice quality, and he wore loud, black, shiny shoes. "Most of our trailers are outside. Looks like you're dressed for a tour, so let's go out the back here and stop by my office for my coat," he said turning on his heels and waving for me to follow.

He asked me all kinds of questions about what I'd be doing with the pontoon, how often I'd be traveling with it, where I'd store it, and what my budget was. We looked around the lot and decided on a Yacht Club bunk trailer. We went back into the building, did all the paper work, and then I paid for it. I asked if they were open this weekend and if I could pick it up then. They were and had no problem with that. I didn't know if I could park it in Derek's lot and, since I was just a visitor, I didn't really want to ask.

When I got back to Derek's it was 3:30 p.m., so I grabbed a pop out of the fridge and curled up on the couch with the blanket and pillow by the coffee table. Faith and I watched cable until 5:00 p.m. when I finally got up and touched up my hair and makeup and straightened up the couch.

At 5:30 Derek came through the door with a hot pizza and a case of beer. We spent the rest of the evening on the couch. It was nice and relaxing. Derek reached for his third piece of pizza and turned to me.

"Will you stay Friday and Saturday night with me too?" he asked sweetly, with puppy-dog eyes.

I didn't really have anything going on so I agreed. "Sure."

"I have to work a half day on Friday, and then when I get off at noon I want to head to Morris and check out this Cory guy, and check in on my sister." His jaw was clenched tight.

"Would you want to come with and help me investigate?" he asked.

"Investigate is a big word, " I said with a wink.

"Not when it comes to you, Sara. You might not realize it, but you possess natural skills that many investigators train for years to perfect and never grasp," he said.

"Oh, geez! I highly doubt that! I had a crazy dream, or four or five, that helped find a friend, but that's it. I'd never before experienced that, or anything remotely like it, and I haven't since," I said defensively.

"I know, Sara, and I know that you don't like to talk about it either. That's not what I was referring to. I meant that your instincts are good, like when you felt like you needed to go back to the cabin. You didn't have a reason, you just needed to. And it's a good thing you did. You have a good head on your shoulders, and it works very well in stressful situations. It doesn't work like that for most people. If you don't want to, you certainly don't have to. It's just I could use the help and . . . someone to talk to," he said seriously.

I put my hand on his thigh. He looked so worried. "Sure, I'll go with and help," I said, then leaned over and kissed him on the cheek.

He looked at me and gave me a closed-lipped smile. He put his arm around me and pulled me closer to his side and fixed his eyes back on the TV. I was pretty sure his eyes were watering. He was really worried. *I knew he was close to his family, but I didn't realize he would be this affected.*

Friday morning I got up when I heard Derek turn the shower on. I went into the kitchen. The coffee was started and, looking into the living room, I could see that the blanket and pillow were already folded on the side of the couch again. He was neat, for a guy. I made scrambled eggs and toast and had it ready when he got out of the shower.

"Wow. Good morning, beautiful," he said and gave me a kiss on the cheek.

"Good morning," I said, plating his food and handing it to him. "The juice and butter are on the table."

"So what are your plans for the morning?" he asked.

"Well, I was thinking I'd go to my office and clean out my desk so they can give it to someone who actually works there," I said.

"Really? So you're done for good?"

"I think so," I said with a sigh. "Moving forward, right?" Derek just looked at me and didn't say anything. "I mean, I don't need the money, and it's kind of a far drive. And I don't like doing living wills, but I don't have the time commitment for a big case, so I guess that leaves . . . done."

"Well, if you're sure," he said, looking at me over his coffee cup. "Are you going to keep your apartment?"

"Yeah, I think I'll keep that for a while yet. I like to come here to visit people, and I don't always want to intrude on them."

"You're not intruding on me. I asked you to come. I want you to stay with me when you come here," Derek said. I just smiled back.

"Well, sweetness, I'm off. Thanks for breakfast," he said standing up. He put his plate and cup in the dishwasher, and I followed him to the door. "See ya at noon. Maybe you want to throw a change of clothes in a bag in case we stay overnight in Morris," he said.

I nodded, then he put one arm around my waist and pulled me to him. He kissed me, winked, and walked out the door. I was left standing there in awe once again. *Dang that guy!*

I turned on my heels and used my new energy to clean up the kitchen. Then I got ready for the day, taking extra time on my hair, but it wouldn't quite cooperate with me. When the hair went south, I added extra blush to highlight my cheek bones. If I couldn't make the whole look work at least I could distract him. I dressed in my favorite jeans and a dark-blue, screen-print t-shirt, and grabbed a gray zip-up sweatshirt for later. I put on my white tennis shoes and packed my bag. I was excited to be going away with Derek, even if it wasn't under the greatest circumstances.

I dropped Faith off at Jamie's, who was the landlord at my apartment. She made me promise to call her to cat-sit if I ever needed it. After I left Jamie's, I ran up to my apartment and ran water in the sinks and shower and flushed the toilet just to keep it from getting rusty. Then I checked the fridge and freezer and collected some stuff for the dumpster. I dusted quickly and locked back up. My apartment was really nice. I wished I could take parts of it with me sometimes, but the location of the cabin was unmatchable. *I will own that until I die.*

I tossed the bag of smelly food in the dumpster and angled into the Jeep. After gassing up at the Super America, I went inside. I grabbed a pop and some snacks for the road. At the till I was offered a free car wash with the purchase of one. I looked over the guy's shoulder and out the window to my dirty Jeep, and decided that I should take it.

Once in the Jeep, I tossed the bag of goodies in the back and drove to the car wash entry. The door was closed and I could see a car inside, so I pulled up next in line, opened my window, and punched in the code I'd been given. After I rolled my window up, I had one of those happy moments when you think about how great your life is and you smile inside and out. I was in heaven: free from money problems, man problems, job problems . . . everything. Everything was going great. I sighed and smiled bigger when I noticed the door to the wash bay rise.

I pulled up to the entrance and watched the shiny black Mustang in front of me dry. As it slowly drove away I drove in and both doors went down. When the pre-wash began I looked at my phone. It showed 11:00 a.m. I threw it back in my purse and turned on the radio. When the song ended, I realized that the pre-wash was still soaking. It seemed like it was taking longer than normal. I looked at my phone again and it showed 11:03, just like the clock on the dash. *What the heck?* I turned the window wipers on and could see the spray bar in front of me off to the right, front side of my Jeep. It was twitching like it was stuck. *Great. Now what?*

I figured that they had cameras in there, and was sure that someone inside was keeping an eye on things, and that someone had to be in line behind me waiting to get in. I looked at the clock again, 11:05. I was sure that boy at the till would be out there soon to reset it. I waited. At 11:08 I started honking. No one came. I rolled down the passenger window to clear the foam and saw a door leading into the building. I rolled the window back up and I honked some more.

At 11:11 I decided to get out and walk to the door. Just as I got to the back bumper, it occurred to me that I should probably grab my purse. I opened the driver side door, grabbed my purse, hit the lock button, like I always do, and shut the door. *AHHH!* I gasped. *Shit! Shit! Shit!* I'd just locked my keys in! I heard a loud hiss and turned to my left. Water was spraying full bore out of the sprayer bar! The twitching had stopped and it had started moving across the hood of my Jeep. *AHHH!* I grabbed for the driver door, but it was locked! *Duh!* I reached for the back one. The back one was locked too. *I knew that!* I couldn't think. I didn't know what to do. *The door!*

As I ran to my right, around the back bumper of the Jeep, the sprayer followed close behind me! I picked up the pace, then slipped in the soap and landed flat on my back. I hit my head. Hard. I lay there stunned for a second then scampered to my feet. The sprayer was only a foot away and chasing me around the back of the Jeep to the passenger side. The spray was hitting me, and I was getting really wet. I ran, the best I could, in the slippery soap to the door. Panicked, I slammed my body up against it. I was soaked from head to toe and covered in foam. I turned the knob and it was locked! I started pounding as hard as I could and screaming as loud as I could. I looked over my shoulder and the sprayer was coming back around again. I pounded harder and yelled louder.

Finally the door flew open and I fell flat on my face, spread eagle, with purse still in hand into the coffee and hot snacks area of the Super America. Quickly I tried to get to my feet, which proved a challenge since I was covered in pink and blue foam and the floor was tile. The young guy from the till rushed over and tried to help me up, asking over and over if I was okay.

"No, I am *not* okay," I said out of breath, trying my best to straighten my outfit and fix my wet and foamy hair. "The car wash thingy was stuck and no one came to help. And, well, now it's not stuck, and I'm locked out of my vehicle!" I told him as I hastily shoved my purse back onto my shoulder. I looked around at the four people who were drop-jawed staring at me. I turned to the guy and asked, "Could I get a towel, or three, please!" in a not-so-friendly voice.

"Of course. I'll be right back," he said nervously and ran to the back of the store.

"Ah, no. I'm coming with you to a back room, somewhere out of sight," I informed him.

Then I heard another voice, "Ma'am, oh ma'am! I'm so sorry!" I turned behind me and saw another employee frantically following me. "I'm Calvin, the day manager. I heard about the situation. I am so sorry. Are you okay? Please let me help you. What can I do?" he asked.

He was out of breath and looked extremely nervous. I almost felt bad for him. "You can make sure my Jeep's clean and you can get someone to unlock it for me for starters . . ." I said and took a few more deep breaths to calm myself.

A half hour later I walked out to my freshly washed Jeep, which was unlocked and pulled around to the front of the store. I was wearing a Super America Employee polo shirt, and my hair was a combination of pink and blue and stiff. I had no makeup on, wet jeans, and wet shoes. I put a few plastic bags, which the store so graciously lent me, down on the driver's seat and drove back to Derek's. I waited in the Jeep until I didn't see anyone moving in the lot, then I ran up to his apartment. I was just unlocking the apartment door when it swung open.

4

"Sweetness . . . dare I ask?" Derek said, holding the door open, with a half freaked out and half amused look on his face.

"Please don't," I said very calmly. "I'll need to take a quick shower before we leave, if you don't mind."

"Be my guest," he said swinging his arm toward the bathroom and stepping aside.

I took off my dripping wet shoes and socks and handed them to him.

I tipped my chin up, whispered, "Excuse me," and sauntered confidently to the bathroom.

I avoided the mirror and got into the shower with my clothes on and thirty minutes later we were in Derek's Jeep and on our way to Morris. He never asked what had happened, and I never offered until we stopped about half way there and got a bite to eat at a Pizza Hut. That's when his curiosity got the best of him.

"Okay, I gotta know! What the heck happened?" he asked.

He looked like he was fighting off a giggle. I stared at him, straight faced for a couple seconds.

Then, tipping my chin in the air a bit, I told him, "I've earned a lifetime, unlimited pass for free car washes and coffee at any Super America in Minnesota."

And I left it at that. I saw the corner of his mouth twitch and his eyes narrow as he lifted his glass to take a drink. I was pretty sure he was trying to hide the laughter.

We got to Morris at 5:00 p.m. Derek pulled off at a Super America for gas and asked if I wanted a coffee. I slapped his arm and exited the Jeep. He pumped gas while I went in and used the bathroom. When I was finished I got a pop. I wasn't sure if my coffee card was activated yet. Derek also used the bathroom and grabbed a pop. He paid and we walked back to the Jeep. Once inside he pulled out a manila envelope and looked through the papers inside. He handed me one with a picture of Cory. *It must be his driver license picture.* Cory Deltone age thirty-one, six-foot-one, 190 pounds, green eyes, no glasses. The address was listed as an apartment in Morris. Derek punched it into the GPS and off we went.

"So do we know anything else about him?" I asked.

"No. The guy doesn't have a criminal background on file, so nothing showed up in our database."

"What's the plan then?"

"Well, I think we'll go and check into the hotel, and then we'll stop over at Kendall's to see if she's seen or heard from them, and if she knows Kelly's work schedule. Then we'll go stakeout the house and see if they come or go from there at all," he said shrugging his shoulders.

"All right, detective." I said.

We drove past Cory's address first. It was an apartment in an older part of the city on the west side. The building was plain, with very basic construction. There were two buildings. Both were two stories and had sixteen apartments each, eight up and eight down. There was no landscaping at all. The cars in the lot were mostly rust buckets or older models. It was far from charming. My lip curled at the sight of it. I glanced over at Derek and he looked angry.

"She's better than this," he said.

We drove around both units and figured out which one was his. He was in number 104. It was on the ground level and had a small patio and sliding glass door that faced the street. The curtains were drawn. On the patio there were two resin chairs and a large coffee can on the ground, I imagined it was full of cigarette butts. Derek took a left onto Main Street and drove to the Holiday Inn. We walked in and went straight to the reception desk to check in. The guy started typing and looked for available rooms.

"One king or two queens?" he asked.

"Two queens," Derek said.

"Smoking or non?"

"Non," he answered.

Derek covered the room cost. I tried to pay, but he said I was his guest. We got two key cards and headed back to the lot. After pulling around to the door that was closest to our room, we grabbed our stuff from the trunk. We each had one bag, and Derek had a pillow. He said he was "pillow picky." The room was nice. We were on the ground floor, near the hot tub. There were patio chairs and a table outside the sliding door on the pool side. The big pool was down about eight rooms and to the left. There were kids there, but the hot tub was empty. Derek came up behind me and peeked over my shoulder.

"The hot tub looks inviting. We'll have to make sure we use that," he said.

"Um, I didn't pack a suit," I told him, completely bummed.

"What? You didn't? Too bad for you," he winked.

We drove over to Kendall and Kelly's apartment. Derek had told Kendall that we were coming. I was a little nervous to meet her. Derek parked in the lot and we walked into the building, which was not secured. We went down one hall, took a right, and went half-way down the next. Derek knocked on the door. He looked at me, smiled, and grabbed my hand.

"She's gonna love you," he said and gave me a quick peck on the cheek.

The door opened. There was Derek, in a woman's body. The resemblance was incredible. She was tall and thin with tan skin. Her thick, long, dark hair shone in the light and was curled up at the ends perfectly. The makeup on her eyes was tasteful, with dark shades of browns and some black eyeliner and mascara. Her lips were painted a nude color that went great with her outfit. She had on black dress pants and a tan shirt that was a rayon mix and had buttons down the front. She looked great.

"Hey!" she said and gave Derek a big hug. "I'm so glad you're doing this." She looked at me, and Derek made introductions.

"Kendall, this is my friend, Sara. Sara, this is my sister, Kendall." I was about to extend my hand when she wrapped her arms around me.

"Ohhh! It's so good to finally meet you. We've heard so much about you. You're even prettier than he described," she said.

"Oh, gosh. Thanks. You're gorgeous. Is this what you always wear to school?" I asked.

"Oh, heaven's no. I had an interview for an internship earlier. I just got in. In fact, I'm going to go change right now. You two make yourselves at home. Derek there's drinks in the fridge and snacks in the cupboard if you're hungry."

We both said thanks and watched her disappear into the back room. Derek asked if I wanted anything. I said no, so he got a pop for himself. A few minutes later, Kendall returned to the room in jeans and a UMM sweatshirt with her hair in a pony. She still looked gorgeous. We sat down at the table, and she and Derek talked about what they thought they should do about Kelly. Kendall tried to text Kelly again, she didn't respond. Kendall said that she had not heard from Kelly, or seen her since she stopped by to get her things that night nearly two weeks ago. Then Kendall decided to tag along with us on our stake out.

When we parked across the street from Cory's, it was a little after 7:00 p.m. The lights were on inside and the blinds were only twisted part way open, but we could see pretty well between the slats. Kelly was laid out on the couch and the TV was on. We watched for a few minutes. Then Derek tried to text her. She looked at her phone and set it back down. Derek hit the steering wheel in frustration. I'd never seen him lose his cool, until then. *I wonder if that was all of it, or if that was just the beginning.*

Cory walked into the room, stopped at the end table, and looked at her phone. He threw it down on her stomach and said something to her. She shook her head no, then he slapped her legs and she sat up. He plopped down on the couch next to her and said something and pointed across the room. She got up and returned with two bottles of beer and handed him one.

We were intently staring out the window. After Kelly sat back down on the couch, Derek turned and looked at me, and then at Kendall. We all exchanged worried looks but no one knew what to do or say.

"Why don't we just go knock on the door and tell them we're in town and want to take them out to dinner and see what happens?" I suggested.

Derek and Kendall exchanged glances and shoulder shrugs.

"I guess we could try to make contact . . .," Derek said.

"What if he goes crazy, or beats her?" Kendall asked. "I don't want to piss him off."

We sat there and listened while Derek devised a plan. Cory didn't know me, and neither did Kelly. Derek wanted to keep it that way for a while. He told me to stay in the Jeep and watch, and if anything looked bad to call 911. Derek pulled down the street, u-turned, and placed the Jeep as close as he could to their patio door. I climbed in the back where the window tint easily hid me. I had my phone on the seat next to me with nine and one already dialed, just in case.

I watched nervously while Derek and Kendall exited the vehicle and walked up to the patio door. Kelly sat up when she noticed them at the door. The street was only about thirty yards from the road so I could see clearly. I saw Kelly point to the door and say something to Cory. Meanwhile, Kendall and Derek smiled and waved. Cory sat up and twisted the blinds shut. Derek pounded on the door.

"Kelly, it's us! Open up!" Derek said, loud enough for me to hear through the cracked window.

They were both leaned up against the glass trying to hear. Kendall and Derek waited a few more seconds, and then Kendall knocked again and called for Kelly. Derek lost his patience.

"Kelly, open the damn door or I will!" he shouted.

The door slid open and Kelly stepped out, forcing Derek and Kendall to step back. Derek pushed past her through the door. My heart started racing. It was very unnerving. Kelly tried to pull him back out, but he got in.

Once inside he pulled the blinds open. *Thank you, Derek!* Kelly followed him in, who was followed by Kendall. The patio door was still open and I could see Cory inside frantically picking stuff up off of the coffee table. Derek stood over him and watched, asking him questions and pointing at the coffee table. Cory walked to the kitchen, which was straight back in my line of sight, and dropped a bunch of stuff on the counter. Then there was a lot of yelling and angry gestures. Derek got right up in Cory's face. They were about the same height, but Derek was definitely stronger. Cory had less muscle tone than I did. He looked frail and weak, but also looked pissed and was standing his ground talking back to Derek with authority.

Kendall grabbed Kelly's arm and led her to the right where I couldn't see them anymore, but I noticed a light come on in the next window. A few moments later, Kendall pulled Kelly through the patio door, with a bag in tow, and started towards the Jeep. Kelly looked like she was crying, but she seemed willing to go with Kendall.

They got to the Jeep, and Kendall pointed for Kelly to go to the driver side. They both got into their seats and Kendall introduced us. Kelly was crying and saying that it was a bad idea. I turned my attention back to the patio window. Derek had his hands up in defense and was shaking his head no. I moved my eyes to the right and saw that Cory had a gun pointed right at him!

"Oh, my God!" I screamed and grabbed my phone. I quickly hit one and the call button.

"Oh, shit!" Kelly screamed. "See he's crazy. He'll kill him!"

"Fuck! What do we do?" Kendall screamed. "I gotta go help!"

She threw her door open and ran towards the patio. Kelly opened her door and followed. I yelled our situation into the phone, and jumped over the seat and checked the address on the GPS. Then I hung up and checked the glove box to see if Derek had a gun in there. There wasn't one. I didn't know what to do. I got out and ran to the patio, but stayed to the side of the door frame and listened. I tried to stay out of Cory's sight, but got close enough so that I could still see in.

"Just calm down. We just want to take her out to dinner," Derek said.

"No! I know you're a cop! You're gonna steal her from me and take me to jail! I'll die before I let that happen! She's mine! She's MINE now!" Cory screamed.

Kelly stepped through the patio door and into the room.

"Okay, okay, Cory I won't go with them. I'll stay here with you. Just put the gun down. This is crazy," Kelly pleaded.

"Cory, I'm not here for you. I'm out of my jurisdiction. I just wanted to visit my sister is all," Derek pleaded. His voice was surprisingly calm. "Just put the gun down and let's talk like adults. I hear there's a wedding coming up. Let's go have a nice dinner and talk about it."

"Fuck the wedding!" he yelled.

His voice was getting more and more irate. He was obviously high on something, he was pacing and sweating and completely out of control. Kelly stepped closer to him.

"Cory, just put the gun down and let's talk. This is my brother. He just wants us to be happy," Kelly cried. "Please just stop!" she begged through sobs.

Come on! Where are the police? I gripped the brick wall I was pressed up against as tight as I could.

"No! No! No!" Cory said, pacing and completely irrational. "He's gonna take you away from me, and turn me in for the drugs, and I'll be alone again. I can't be alone! Kelly's mine! You hear me? MINE!"

His face changed as he looked at them. There was a frightening look in his eyes. His voice dropped and turned cold and vicious.

"All of you can go to hell! I'll destroy her before I'll let her leave. If I can't have her . . . then no one can!" He turned the gun toward Kelly and fired.

"NOOOOOOO!" Kendall screamed.

Derek jumped for him as he took off running for the open door. I pressed myself back against the building and held my breath. He ran past me, down the street, and took a left. I was pretty sure he hadn't seen me. Finally I could hear sirens in the distance. I ran to the Jeep and grabbed my phone off the back seat. I redialed 911 and demanded an ambulance. I told them the street name that Cory had run down and gave the operator a description of him. Then I ran back into the apartment.

Kendall was pacing around screaming and crying. Derek was leaning over Kelly, who was lying on the floor. He had his shirt off and pressed onto her abdomen. There was a lot of blood. It was on the floor, both of her hands, Derek's hands, and already soaking through Derek's shirt. Kelly's eyes were wide open and blinking, but she wasn't moving or saying anything. She was very still. Tears were running down her face with each blink. Derek kept telling her to stay awake and not to go to sleep.

"If she's stays awake she'll be fine," he said when he looked up at me. "Just stay awake, Kelly. Just stay awake," he kept repeating to her.

There was a bruise on her cheek and one of her eyes was black. These both looked a few days old.

"I called 911 when I saw the gun, and I called again for an ambulance when he ran out," I told Derek.

"Thanks. Can you go outside and flag them down? I can hear they're getting close."

"Yes," I said and ran out. Kendall was still pacing around crying, and holding her head in her hands.

A police car raced down the street. I stood in the middle of the street, jumping up and down, waving my arms high in the air. When it got closer I pointed and ran towards the patio door. The cop parked in the middle of the street sideways. He left the lights on and bolted to his trunk, where he grabbed a first aid kit and an AED machine, and then ran to the patio. I followed him in, yelling that she was shot in the stomach and the guy ran off.

Sirens screamed from every direction. I stayed outside so that I wouldn't be in the way. One cop car went down the street that Cory had run down and two more parked on the street. A couple of minutes later the ambulance showed up, and two paramedics, pushing a gurney and equipment, ran through the door. Then Kendall came out and fell into my arms. She was much taller than I was, and her frantic hug knocked me back. We ended up on the ground—me sitting on my butt with my back propped against the building and she curled up, almost in a ball, with her head in my lap bawling. We could hear the EMTs talking about vitals and blood pressure and doses of medications. I hadn't cried up to that point, but now that she was in my lap the tears came flowing down.

A crowd had started to gather around us. Everyone was holding their hands over their mouths and shaking their heads. The EMTs rolled the gurney out the patio door and hurried towards the ambulance. When Derek came out of the doorway and saw us, he knelt down and rubbed Kendall's back. I quickly wiped away my tears.

"Kendall, I need you to be strong and go with her in the ambulance. I need to help out here for a bit. I'll meet you at the hospital in a while, okay?"

"What do you want me to do?" I asked trying my best to be calm.

"Did you see what direction he went?" he asked me.

"Yes, he went down Eighth, to the left," I said, pointing to the sign on the corner. "I told a cop and 911 that too."

"Excellent. Can you go with Kendall and Kelly?"

"Yes."

"Make sure Kendall has her phone and that she calls my parents to let them know."

"I will." He quickly kissed me on the cheek and turned to the EMT.

"These two are going with," Derek told him.

While they were loading Kelly in I grabbed mine and Kendall's purses and jumped in the ambulance. I had to sit in the cab with the driver because there wasn't any room in the back. The ride seemed to take forever. The driver was talking with the hospital on the CB. He updated them on Kelly's current condition, which he labeled a "life-threatening, gunshot wound." That's when it hit me. My stress and emotion went straight to my stomach, and I needed to throw up. Now. I looked around for something to hold it. The driver hung up the CB.

"I'm not from around here. How much further is it to the hospital?" I asked in a panicky voice and one hand over my mouth.

"It's about another two minutes from here . . . oh, man, are you gonna hurl?" he asked as he looked over at me.

"Umm, yes! Right now!" I said and started flapping my hands up and down. I opened the glove box and found a large plastic zip lock with gloves in it.

"Yeah, yeah, that's good. Use that!" the driver said, glancing over. "I can't pull over and stop for you."

"I know. Just keep going." I said, as I dumped the gloves onto the seat between us and threw my head forward.

I dry heaved more than I actually puked. It was a good thing we hadn't eaten in a few hours. Nonetheless, pizza was ruined for me for a while. When I finished, I rolled the window down for fresh air. The driver rolled his window down too. He turned the corner and we pulled into the emergency bay.

Already nurses and doctors dressed in gloves, robes, and masks waited. By the time the driver had thrown the ambulance into park, they were already unloading Kelly from the back doors. The EMT from the back shouted Kelly's name, age, and vitals. Both EMTs ran into the building with the gurney and told the doctors what medicines they'd started in her IV. I stood there holding my purse, Kendall's purse, and a bag of puke. Kendall stood next to me, still crying. I looked through the glass doors and saw a garbage can.

"Let's get inside and call your mom and dad," I said.

"Oh, my God, they're going to be so upset!" she said and started bawling all over again.

We walked in and I carefully tossed my puke bag in the trash can. Then I asked Kendall if I could use her phone. She nodded. To our right was an emergency room waiting area, so I escorted Kendall over and sat her down. I walked over and grabbed a box of tissues from the coffee table and paged through the contacts on Kendall's phone until I found "Mom." *This is not the way I wanted to meet Derek's parents, but here it goes.*

5

"Hello?"

"Um, hi, is this Kathy?" I asked.

"Yes, who is this?" she asked.

"My name's Sara Martin. I'm a friend of Derek's . . ."

"Oh, yes. Hi, honey. We've heard so much about you. It's nice to meet you," she said, all chipper.

"Thank you, it's nice to meet you too," I said strained.

"What is it? What's wrong, dear? Why are you calling me from Kendall's phone?" she asked with concern in her voice.

"Kendall's right here with me. She' okay . . . but there's been a terrible accident."

"What? What happened? I want to talk to Kendall. Where is she? What kind of accident?" she stammered, her voice filled with anxiety.

"Kendall fine, she's just too upset to talk. It's Kelly . . . she's been shot," I told her. I didn't know how else to say it.

"WHAAAAT? Oh, my God!" she screamed. I thought she'd dropped the phone because her voice got further away. I could hear a man's voice in the back ground.

"Kathy? Kathy, where are you?" I heard him say. *That must be Derek's dad, Doug.*

"Kathy, what is it?" he asked her, his voice closer now.

"The phone," she managed to say in between sobs. It had now occurred to me that I hadn't mentioned that Kelly was alive. But she really hadn't given me the chance.

"Hello?" an angry man's voice said. "Who is this? What's going on? Tell me right now."

"Hello, this is Sara Martin. I'm Derek's friend. I was with Derek and I'm here with Kendall. There's been a . . . incident. Kelly was shot. We are at the hospital in Morris," I managed.

"What . . . who . . . why?" he stuttered in shock, suddenly sounding breathless.

"She's alive, but in critical condition. It was her boyfriend, Cory. We went to visit her and he was drugged up. He went crazy and shot her."

"Oh, shit! What about Kendall and Derek? Where are they?" he demanded.

"Kendall and I came to the hospital with the ambulance and Derek stayed back at the scene to give a statement and help get the search started."

"What? Cory got away? The son of a bitch shot my little girl and got away?" he yelled at me furiously.

"I'm sure they'll find him, sir," I offered.

"She's alive," he said to Kathy. "Kelly's alive, but not good. Go get dressed and pack a bag. We have to go now! Give me the address of the hospital," he demanded.

I went up to reception and grabbed a pamphlet from the wall display and read him the address.

"Call Kendall's phone when you get on the road. I'll try to have an update for you. And I'll call you if anything changes. I'm so sorry, sir. I'll talk to you soon."

After I hung up, I put our purses down on the chair next to Kendall. She was still sobbing. I plopped down next to her and leaned back with my legs stretched out in front of me. I felt like I had been holding my breath and could finally get air. As soon as that air hit my lungs, I started shaking and tears came. I'm good at holding it together when it's my job, but when the distractions come, or it's in someone else's hands, I lose it.

I leaned forward and put my face in my hands and sobbed. I didn't know Kelly at all, but my heart was broken for her. *What a horrible situation.* The trauma of being in an abusive relationship was bad enough, but to be shot was beyond comprehension. I hurt for her sister, and her mom and dad, who were on their way, and for Derek. I couldn't imagine what he must have been feeling. *He's a cop and his sister was shot right in front of him.* I had no idea what his reaction to this would be. I tipped my head up and dried my face with a tissue. I looked over at Kendall and noticed that she was quiet and staring into space.

"How you doing, love?" I asked, rubbing her back.

She looked over at me shook her head no and laid it on my shoulder. I embraced her and held her until she calmed again a few minutes later. We sat there for another half hour waiting, watching people come and go. After an hour had passed, a nurse came walking toward us. She sat down next to me and asked us a few questions about Kelly. Kendall had to answer most of them. She said that she needed to get the information into the computer, and then she'd ask a doctor for an update and let us know.

"Please hurry," I said as she walked away. My phone rang. It showed Derek on caller ID.

"Hey," I said breathless.

"Hey, any news on Kelly?" he demanded in a rushed, police voice. I could hear a lot of commotion in the background.

"No, a nurse just went to check. She was conscious all the way here though. I called your mom and dad. They're on their way now."

"Okay. We have a team set up and every cop in the state looking, but we haven't found the son of bitch yet." I could hear him take a deep breath.

"I'm so sorry, Derek." I said tearing up again.

"I'll be there soon," he said and disconnected. Kelly's phone rang. I looked at the caller ID: *Mom and Dad*

"It's your parents," I said to Kendall. She shook her head at me, so I answered it.

"Hello, this Sara," I said when I answered.

"It's Kathy, dear. We're in the car driving right now. Have you heard anything new?"

"No, a nurse just went to go check. She should be back soon. Kelly was conscious the whole time, and they say that's really good," I told her.

"Is Kendall doing okay? Where's Derek?" Kathy asked.

She put me on speaker phone and I updated the both of them on the whole situation. As I was finishing, the female doctor came through the emergency room door and walked toward us. I held the phone up so Kathy and Doug could hear what she had to say too.

"Okay, I was just in the operating room. Kelly was shot in the abdomen and the bullet lodged in her liver. It pierced her spleen and broke a rib in the process. She's lost a lot of blood, but her pressure and vitals are holding. That's all the update I have for now. The surgeon will come out and talk to you as soon as he's done," she told us, then turned and walked away.

"Did you hear all that?" I asked into the phone.

They had, and said that they would contact Travis, Derek's older brother, to let him know too. I told them I'd call if we heard anything else. I put Kendall's phone in my purse and leaned back in the chair. I noticed the coffee station set up across the room, so I got up and grabbed two cups. I added a bunch of cream and sugar to mine so that it didn't taste like coffee. I still needed to get the puke taste out of my mouth. "Coffee will warm you up," I said, noticing that Kendall seemed tense and was shivering. I was worried about her. She wasn't saying much at all. I sipped on my coffee and sat quietly next to her. A few more tears escaped. I just wished Derek would walk through the door.

A few minutes later the entry doors opened and Derek rushed in. He was wearing an MPD t-shirt. I ran across the room and threw my arms around him. He looked awful. His hug was tight, and his heart was beating so hard and fast that I could feel it on my chest. He didn't let go when I started to, but instead held tighter and bent over and buried his face in my neck and cried quietly. A few moments later he straightened up and wiped his tears on the back of his hand.

"Sorry," he said. I shook my head and half smiled. He walked over and hugged Kendall for a long while too. She didn't say anything and just sat back down when he let go. "Have you heard anything yet?" he asked.

"Yes, and your mom and dad are updated too. They said they'd call Travis."

I reiterated everything the doctor had said. Then we sat there and waited. Derek told Kendall and me about what had gone on back at the scene of the shooting. It was all police talk, but I got the gist of it.

About an hour later, Kathy and Doug arrived. They came rushing over and everyone hugged. Derek introduced me. I thought to myself, *this is not the way I wanted to look when I met them.* My eyeliner was everywhere, and my clothes and hair were a mess. I was completely stressed out. It was 11:00 p.m. I was tired, but then I thought, *they are in the same boat.* I reached out my hand and got a big hug instead from both of them.

Kathy was beautiful. She was tanned and had the body of a twenty-year-old. I wasn't sure how old she was, but she looked about forty. Her long, thick, black hair was shiny and pulled up into a messy bun on the back of her head with soft curly tendrils falling perfectly all the way around her face. She didn't have any jewelry on, but she had been pulled from home in the middle of the night. I didn't notice any makeup, although with her perfect skin and dark lashes and eyebrows she didn't need any. She was amazing. It was easy to see where the kids got their beauty from. Doug, too, was a handsome man. He was lighter skinned than Derek, and tall and fit. He had a full head of black hair and a five-o'clock shadow that was very appealing. He was an older Derek. *Nice to look at.* They both seemed really sweet.

About a half hour later, the doctor came out and gave us an update. Kelly was heavily medicated and in recovery. The surgery went well but she was still critical. We could go in and see her, but she would not be awake for a while.

When we walked into recovery, all we saw were tubes coming out of Kelly everywhere. We stayed for a few minutes and watched as Derek's mom talked to her as if she were awake. She was so strong. She was trying not to cry and told Kelly that she would be fine. After that we all went out into the hall. Derek's dad pulled him aside and asked him about the black eye and the bruise. They had a few minutes of man talk, and Derek's dad did not look happy. A nurse asked to speak to us at the desk. After giving the nurse all of our contact information, Derek and I went to the hotel, and Kendall and her parents went to an overnight room that the hospital provided for the families of critical patients having all agreed to meet for breakfast at 9:00 a.m. the next morning. On the drive back to the hotel I reached over and patted Derek's thigh.

"What are you thinking?" I asked.

He sighed and said, "That I'm lucky to have you." I wrinkled my brow and looked over at him. "Really," he said, "if you hadn't been there, 911 would have gotten there a lot later, and the direction Cory ran wouldn't have been known. Kendall would have been lying on the ground crying not knowing what to do, my parents wouldn't have gotten there as soon . . . and I wouldn't have had anyone to hold me."

I didn't know how to respond, so I didn't. I just squeezed his thigh. He looked over and gave me a closed-lipped, half smile. When he parked, we walked hand-in-hand into the hotel. And when we got inside the room he pulled me on to the bed with him and whispered, "Hold me."

In the morning I woke up with a crick in my neck and realized that neither of us had moved all night. We were still on top of the covers, and still dressed in yesterday's clothes, some of which had blood stains on them. Derek started moving around after I got up. It was only 7:00 a.m., but I knew I wouldn't fall back to sleep. I called the hospital, said I was Kelly's sister, and asked for an update. Nothing had changed since last night, but the doctor on call said that they'd be slowing down the drip on her sedative later that morning to help wake her up. Then they would know more. I told her that the family would be in around ten and hung up. Derek was sitting up and leaning back on the headboard, looking at me and smiling.

"Thank you," he said.

I told him what the doctor had said. He looked at me with sleepy eyes and patted the bed next to him. I went over and curled up in his arms. We lay there for a bit watching the TV. There was a story on KARE 11 about the shooting. I picked my head up and looked in his eyes when I heard him whisper, "I love you." He smiled and tightened his arm around me, then turned his attention back to the TV.

6

We arrived at Perkins just as Derek's parents and sister were walking through the door. We ate while they talked about the previous night, but no one had much of an appetite so we didn't order much, mostly coffee and muffins. We talked about Kelly's condition and the fact that it hadn't changed. We couldn't decide if that was good or bad. She wasn't getting worse, but she wasn't improving either.

Derek's mom and dad were both retired and planned to stay with Kendall as long as they needed to. Kendall wasn't scheduled to work until Tuesday, so she planned to take at least Monday and Tuesday off of school. No one really knew what to say or do. I told Derek that I would head back to my apartment later that day. I'd left Faith with Jamie, but I needed to get back to her soon.

Upon our arrival at the hospital, we learned that the doctors had stopped Kelly's sedative medication, but that she was still not waking up. They didn't seem overly concerned since she responded slightly to the pain tests. We stayed in the room with her for about an hour then Derek, and I went down to the cafeteria to get a drink.

They had one of those old-fashioned coffee machines that filled the cup for customers. I hadn't seen one of those in years. *Fun!* I put my change in the slot, pressed cream 1 and sugar 2, and stepped back and waited to be entertained. Down dropped a cup and coffee started to fill it up. I watched with a smile on my face . . . because I'm easily amused. The coffee stopped, and then a spurt of cream dropped in and some powder that looked like sugar. I'd just put my hand out to reach for the cup when the machine made a loud noise. I instinctively pulled my hand back. The noise got louder and the machine started to shake. I took a step back and thought, *This can't be normal.* I glanced over my shoulder and Derek was looking at me squinty-eyed. He grabbed a bottle of pop out of the bottom of his machine, never taking his eyes off me. He opened his pop and took a drink, still carefully watching me. I gave him the "What'd *I* do?" look, complete with a palms up shoulder shrug. He smiled and shook his head. A few more new noises started, and I took another step back. Derek came over and stood a few steps behind me.

"You gonna take your cup out?" he asked from behind me. I shrugged. He took another sip of his pop as he stared at me.

I slowly reached for it and gently squeezed my fingers around the cup and slowly lifted it. As soon as I did the machine noises changed and more coffee started pouring out. I pulled my cup toward me and backed up again. The coffee spilled out all over the floor, since a new cup had not dropped down.

"I didn't do that!" I said quietly. I looked around the room and was glad to see that we were the only ones in there. "Just walk away with me," I whispered to Derek as I passed by him with my chin up. He turned and followed behind me.

We got out to the hall and I saw the gift shop. I walked in, found a travel mug with the hospital logo on it, and brought it up to the counter. I pulled a ten out of my purse and paid for it. When I turned to leave, Derek was leaning on the entry door with one leg crossed over the other. Quickly, I dumped my coffee into the travel mug, tossed the Styrofoam cup into the trash can by the door and took a sip. Eyebrows lifted, I confidently looked at Derek.

"Ready?" I asked, with a smile and passed by him again.

"Sweetness," he said, "getting rid of the evidence?"

"What?" I asked him, acting totally confused as I kept walking. We went down the hall towards Kelly's room.

"I'll take a cab back to the Cities in a bit," I told him.

"No, I'll drive you back. I need to get back to work anyway," he said. "We'll go back together."

We went up to the room, said good bye to Derek's family, and then went back to the hotel to collect our things. After we had the Jeep loaded up, I angled into the driver seat. Derek called the Morris Police detective, who had been on the case the night of the shooting, to see if they knew anything yet. They didn't. I could tell that Derek was really frustrated. He made a few more phone calls, then reclined the seat. He sighed and closed his eyes clasping his hands behind his head.

"I don't understand how someone can do that," he stated.

"Drugs make people do crazy things," I reminded him.

He just shook his head. I asked him more about Cory, and he said that they didn't have much on him. Derek admitted that the family knew nothing.

"The police are questioning his parents and the neighbors in the area, but no one's seen him since before last night. He has four different credit cards—all maxed out—no job, no car, no history. His parents kicked him out about two years ago because he was using, but they haven't talked to him since, so they were no help. He has an older brother who lives in Morris too. Rumor has it, they don't get along. Rumor also has it his brother doesn't get along with anyone. The police searched his brother's house, but he wasn't there and his brother claims he's hasn't seen or talked to him in six months," he said. "But the police think he was lying about that."

"So, with no money or job where would a criminal go?" I responded. It hung there for a while.

The drive was really long. I'd filled up in Morris, so we went all the way to Derek's apartment without stopping. Derek slept most of the way. When the Jeep was unloaded, he gave me a quick kiss and went off to work. He wasn't scheduled, but wanted to use his connections to work on Kelly's case. I took all of my stuff and went back to my apartment.

I dropped by Jamie's downstairs and picked up Faith. I'd missed her so much. I also ran into the resident hottie, Jared, in the hall. We only passed with a quick "hi," but he remained in my mind for hours afterward. When I opened my apartment door, I felt a sense of comfort and reassurance I hadn't had in a while. I kicked my shoes off and flipped the fireplace on. Then I grabbed a blanket and the remote before I settled on the couch. I lay there enjoying the cozy warmth until my phone rang. It was Derek. I looked at the clock and realized that I must have fallen asleep because two hours had passed since I'd walked in. *Crap! I need to pick up my pontoon trailer before they close.*

"Hey, sweetness," he said.

"Hi."

"Sorry I was a bore on the way home. I'm exhausted."

"I understand."

"What are your plans? Are you gonna be there when I get home?" he asked.

"No, I'm at my apartment now. I'm just leaving to go get the pontoon trailer. They said a guy in maintenance would be there until five to help me out. Then I'm going to head back to Nisswa. My parents are coming up in the morning to help get the dock out."

"Shit, that's right. I said I'd help," he remembered.

"No, Derek. Seriously, don't worry about it. We'll be able to handle it. I'm tougher than I look," I reminded him. "You have a lot going on right now. You need to focus on Kelly and be there for your family."

"Okay, but I *am* sorry. Please let your dad know why I can't be there and tell them both hi for me. I gotta go but I'll call you soon," he said quickly and hung up.

I figured someone had just walked into his office. He was really busy already, and with this added to his plate I wasn't sure when I'd see him again.

When I got into my driveway in Nisswa a few hours later, I backed the trailer up and left it attached to the Jeep. After Faith and I were unloaded and comfortable in the house, I grabbed my phone out of my purse and called Mom. She said she and my dad would be here about 9:30 in morning. I told her we'd get breakfast in town first, and then work on the dock and pontoon. After the work was done we planned to grill. I also informed them that Derek wouldn't be able to join us and filled them in on that situation.

I made myself a quick sandwich and headed to the grocery store to get some ingredients for tomorrow's dessert. When I got back I made apple pie—completely from scratch! I was pretty proud of myself. When I was finished with clean up, I took a glass of wine to the bathtub and soaked for a bit before heading off to bed.

Sunday morning, I got up early and went for a run, which was short because I sucked at it. I really would have loved to be able to get up every morning and run for miles, but I got about two hundred yards and I couldn't move or breathe. But dang it, I kept trying. I've always loved food, but food always loved to hang on to my belly. It was a fight every day to keep a slim figure. *Maybe if I lay off the carbs . . .*

In the morning Mom's call woke me up. She said that she and Dad were about an hour away. I told her to meet me at Morning Glory and jumped into the shower for an express wash and dry. I figured why bother if I was going to be waist deep in lake water in a couple hours. It was a jeans, sweatshirt, and ponytail kind of day. I added a quick swipe of mascara and was out the door.

I got to Morning Glory just as my parents were pulling in. I gave them a hug, and we walked in together. The place was pretty busy. We found a booth across from the bar area and sat down. I looked around for Tannya, but I didn't see her, which was good. I didn't want to talk about Ms. Kitty today. That conversation had been on my mind and I was curious but not interested. I mean really? I don't have any skills that would help her or anyone else for that matter.

A waitress came over for our order. She was young and pleasant and seemed efficient. I only saw two wait staff working even though the place was almost full. I would've thought on a Sunday it would always be busy with the church crowd and they'd have more staff on.

"So, Sara, tell me about the pontoon trailer," Dad said.

I told him about the one I got, and he agreed that I'd gotten a good deal on it.

"My next concern is the dock. That's a pretty big dock. Without Derek's help, I'm not sure we can handle it. Your mom can't help with her back. I know you're strong but we could use a third person. Do you know anyone in this town who'd be able to help us today?" he asked.

"No, not really. I mean I've talked to a couple people but I don't have contact information or anything. You really think we can't do it?"

Great, if we can't do it alone, then what? It has to come out soon or it could get damaged. Ice was already starting to show in thin sheets here and there, especially in the early morning. I looked over my Dad's shoulder when I heard the bells on the door clang. In walked Rex, Officer McHottie, in full uniform. I couldn't stop the smile from growing on my face. I tried to hide it by taking a sip of my coffee. My dad turned in his seat to see what I was looking at.

"Friend of yours?" he asked with a grin.

"Um, uh, no. I mean I met him a few days ago but we're not . . . friends."

"He's very easy on the eyes isn't he?" my mom chimed in.

Rex stepped through the door, then stopped and scanned the place looking for a seat. He locked eyes with me, smiled, and started walking over towards our table. My heartbeat took off at full speed. It was beating so hard I was sure my chest was visibly pounding. I took a deep breath and revealed my smile in return.

"Good morning, speedy," he said as he stopped at our table.

I laughed out loud as I set my cup on the table.

"Good morning, Officer Dalton," I slyly responded.

"Officer Dalton? Please, Sara, call me Rex," he kindly requested.

I paused, bit my lip. "Rex, these are my parents, Jan and Will Lewis. Mom, Dad, this is Rex. He's a Nisswa police officer, as you can tell. I met him a few days ago when he pulled me over and politely reminded me of the posted speed limit," I told them.

"Sara Martin, you were speeding?" my mom scolded. Her tone was stern. I suddenly felt like a naughty fifth grader.

"It's okay, Mrs. Lewis. I gave her a warning and she has been good ever since," he said winking at me. Dad extended his hand towards Rex, receiving a friendly shake. Then Rex reached for my mom's hand and shook hers too.

"Please, we'd love for you to join us," Dad said as he slid over. He looked at me and nodded. "We just ordered," he told Rex and patted the seat. Rex was a little taken aback, I thought as I tried to read his reaction. My dad was not normally so . . . outgoing. Rex looked at my mom, and then at me.

7

"Ah, sure . . . if that's okay with everyone else," Rex replied.
"Yes, please. We'd love for you to join us. Right, Sara?" my mom said, elbowing me in the ribs.

"Of course," I answered and shot my mom a quick look as he sat down.

The waitress came over and filled up his cup and took his order. Dad started drilling him about his job and life. I learned that he'd grown up in Fargo, North Dakota, and had gone into the police academy right after high school. He had gotten a job offer here upon graduation ten years ago. I did the math and that made him about thirty, although he looked twenty-five . . . and his body even younger. *Ahem!* I gave myself a mental head slap to refocus.

"So, Rex, are you just starting your shift or are you on a break?" Dad asked him.

"No, sir, I worked the night shift, so I'm just getting done for the day. I thought I'd grab a good meal before I went home," he answered.

The waitress delivered all of our meals and left. We all turned our focus to our food. Dad grabbed the pepper and started shaking it over his eggs. He looked up and shot me a raised eyebrow look that I didn't understand.

"Rex, if you have a little time today, I could use some help with something," he started. *Oh no, I know where this is going. Bad idea. Well, actually it's a great idea . . . but a bad idea too. Oh, boy.* "Ya see, Sara just moved here and she doesn't know many people. She owns property on Lake Hawsawneekee that has a dock and pontoon, both of which need to come out today," he informed Rex.

Rex was eating and nodding and looking back and forth between Dad and me with a smirk on his face.

"Sara's friend had a family emergency and wasn't able to help us today. So I was wondering . . . maybe if I paid for your breakfast here, then you might spare an hour or two and help us out today. What do ya say, Rex?" he asked him, not leaving him much opportunity to decline.

I opened my mouth to say something, but just as I was about to speak I got another elbow to the ribs from my mom. Instead, I forked some food into my mouth and uncomfortably waited for his reply.

"Of course, I'd love to help you out," he said, looking at me.

I smiled, chewing my food with raised eyebrows.

"And I love a free meal, so how can I say no?"

"Great. Thanks, Rex, I . . . we really appreciate that," Dad said. "Do you know where Sara lives?"

"Yes, sir, I do," he answered and looked at me again.

I was frozen and had no idea what to say. *This guy really has an effect on me.*

"There are only three homes on that lake, and everyone would love to be out there," he added.

I suppose that's true. It's a nice, clean lake with tons of trees and land. It really was perfect, and I was glad it was mine. "I'll head home and change and meet you out there," he said with a grin.

We finished our meal with a bit of small talk and parted ways. Mom rode with me and Dad followed in their car. We got back to the cabin and changed. I put on some tight leggings to wear wet-suit style, and a thermal long sleeve t-shirt, it was not a great look but we had to get wet. Dad had put on some waist-high waders he'd borrowed from a friend. Mom decided to stay in and prepare the food for later, and "keep Faith company." Dad and I walked out to the trailer. He walked me through what the parts were called and how we'd load the boat onto it.

"Do you know how to back it up?" Dad asked.

"I backed it up to where it is now," I told him, not including the fact that it took ten attempts to get it there.

Details, details.

I grabbed the keys out of my pocket and backed the Jeep up to the trailer. Dad had hooked it up just as a Black 1500 GMC pickup pulled into the driveway. Rex parked close to the house, near Dad's car, and walked over. We said, "Hi," and the boys shook hands again.

"Thanks again for your help," Dad told him.

"Yes, thank you," I added.

"All right, we'll meet you at the dock," Dad said, as he and Rex started walking towards it.

This meant that I had to back the trailer into the makeshift landing next to it, or yell to my Dad that I couldn't do it. Now I have never been the kind of girl to say I can't, and would do anything that proved my strength and independence as a woman, so what choice did I have?

After fifteen attempts, and ten long minutes later, Rex jumped up into the passenger's seat. *Dang it.* I'd tried and tried, but no matter what I did the trailer never went the way I wanted it to go.

"Hello, speedy!" he said with a big grin. "How about if I walk you through this?"

I sighed. I narrowed my eyes at him and nodded solemnly, my only other choice was to keep making a fool of myself.

"Okay," he said. "Pull forward enough to straighten it out." I did, then looked over at him with a "what next" look. "Now instead of using your mirrors, which makes everything backwards, turn around and watch out the rear window. Move slowly and make your turns very slight. The trailer will way overreact to your steering moves. Watch the back of the trailer to determine if you need to make adjustments, and if you do, a tiny bit goes a long way."

I put it into reverse, turned around, and started backing up. I zigzagged slightly but got it in, and straight in, in one try. I kept going until I saw my dad put his hand up to stop, then I looked over at Rex with a huge smile.

"Oh, my gosh I did it!" I said proudly, putting in it park.

"Nicely done! I knew you could," he answered as he gave me a high five. We exited the Jeep and walked towards the towards the trailer. My dad was on the dock.

"Nice work, Sara! Now let's see you put this boat on it," Dad said and tossed the keys at me.

I caught them and argued, but lost. Rex stood on the trailer facing the water and Dad stayed on the dock. After he untied the pontoon, I backed it up and maneuvered it to the other side of the dock. I straightened out, and prayed to God to help me get this on my first attempt. I stood up so I could see the carpeted boards on the trailer better and slowly moved forward as straight as I could. Rex had his hand up giving me the "come here" motion. I drove slowly towards him. All I could hear was my dad saying, "Good, keep it straight" over and over. When I got it up onto the trailer I was straight, and a bit surprised. I let off the throttle.

"All the way, Sara," Dad said.

"Come more," Rex said, still moving his hand to come closer.

So I gave the throttle a little nudge and she sped fast, sliding all the way up the boards, and slamming into the stop bars. At that point the motor was on top of the water and making all kinds of noise.

"Kill it!" Dad yelled.

I was so busy being proud that I got it on in one try I'd forgotten to shut the engine off. I quickly turned the key back. Rex secured the pontoon on the trailer and Dad jump into the Jeep's driver seat. Rex and I walked back over to the shed where Dad was backing up the trailer. We spent the next fifteen minutes trying to figure out how to get the cover on, which proved to be pretty easy when all the snaps started matching up.

Mom came out the back door and stood with her arms crossed over her chest. "How's it going?" she yelled.

"Good," I yelled back. "Almost done."

"Sara, your cell phone rang so I answered it. It was a girl named Tannya asking if she had the right number for Sara Martin."

"Yeah, what did she want?" I asked, wondering how she got my number.

"She didn't say. She just asked, said thank you, and then hung up."

"Okay," I said.

I looked at Rex. He had an amused looked on his face, but he wasn't looking back at me. My dad and Rex were taking their waders off so I said I'd be right back and ran in the house for a quick shower. I threw on jeans and a sweatshirt and a quick swipe of mascara. I walked into the kitchen, which smelled heavenly. Mom was busy getting stuff together for our barbeque. I walked past her and grabbed three cold beers out of the fridge. Outside Dad and Rex were sitting on the tailgate of Rex's truck talking like old friends. I walked up and handed them each a beer.

Dad said, "Thanks, but I'll take mine inside and check on your mother."

Which I knew meant "I'll be on the couch asleep if you need me." Dad turned to Rex, shook his hand, and again thanked him for the help.

"It was no problem at all, sir. Anytime," he said.

As Dad walked away, Rex took his beer and patted the tailgate. I hopped up next to him and let my feet dangle.

"Thanks for the beer," he said.

"Thanks for the help," I said. We clinked bottles and took drinks. "Is it too early for beer?"

"No, not when you're at the end of your shift. After this I'm going to head home and go to bed."

We sat there and talked for another twenty minutes or so. I asked him to stay for dinner but he declined.

"So how do you know Tannya?" he asked

"I really don't. I just met her at the diner."

He informed me that she was the town gossip and had a crazy ex-husband who liked to get into mischief.

"She's a good person, but I wouldn't tell her anything you don't want everyone in town to know."

"Duly noted."

"Well, thanks for the beer," Rex said as he jumped down from the tailgate.

He offered me a hand. I took it and jumped down too. "I'm around if you need me," he said, and slipped me one of his business cards. He put my number in his phone too. When he turned to get into his truck I went into the house. Dad was on the couch watching TV with one eye open and Mom was in the kitchen.

Three hours later I was waving goodbye to my parents as they drove away. I settled on the couch for a bit with Faith and thought about Derek and his sister. I decided I should call and get an update.

"Hello," Derek answered, sounding tired and mad.

"Hey. Wow, you sound . . ."

"Irritated? I am!"

"With work, or the investigation, or what?"

"Both . . . I'm sorry. I don't mean to take it out on you, but I'm glad you called. I have a favor to ask you," he said in policeman mode.

"Okay . . ."

"The investigation with Kelly's case is going nowhere, and I'm trying really hard not to get into trouble with their jurisdiction, but they have a couple of rookies on the case, and I can't stand here and twiddle my thumbs while my sister fights for her life and this guy gets off."

"I know Derek. I'm sorry . . . how's Kelly doing?"

"There's no change. She's still unresponsive and the tests aren't telling them much. They really need her to wake up so they can do more tests. There's brain activity but not much. They won't give much information because they just don't know anything yet. My mom and dad said they are staying as long as it takes. Kendall's going to continue working her scheduled shifts at Applebees and will be at the hospital whenever she can. That way someone's always there in case she wakes up."

"I'm so sorry. Let me know if you want me to go down. I don't really know her, but I'll help in any way I can," I told him.

"Great. There is something you can do," he said, "but let me ask you this first. When Cory ran out of the apartment building did he see you?"

"No."

"No, for sure? Or there's a chance he may have?"

"No, for sure." I said with confidence.

"Okay, then I think this may help. He has a Facebook page. There's not a lot of activity on it, and it was just opened a couple weeks ago. I want you to be his friend," Derek told me, "but I want you to do it under a new, made up alias. I want you to get a new yahoo email address and open a new account. Use a fake name, but put up a real picture of you. And make it look like you go to college at the University of Minnesota-Morris. Get some other friends first. Just friend everyone you can find that goes to that school, male and female . . . about twenty or so. Then go to his page and request a couple of his friends. After that, friend request him too. Then just play on it to make it look real. I'm hoping that he'll be your friend and show an interest in you and you can get close to him," he said with a questioning sound to his voice.

"So you want to use me for bait?" There was a beat of silence and then Derek's tone changed.

"Yeah," he said slowly. "Kind of . . . is that okay?"

"Umm, how close are we talking?"

"I'm not sure. But no matter what, I'd never put you in danger. I'm just hoping he gets comfortable enough and talkative with you that he slips up and gives you his location. If you don't want to do this, you don't have to. It was just a thought. I'm running out of ideas and time is ticking. I really want to bring this guy in."

"I know. I do too . . . I'll do the Facebook account and let you know if anything happens. I can do it right now. I have nothing else going on."

"Thank you, Sara. Just be really careful about what you put on there—fake date of birth, fake home town, and fake job. And if it gets uncomfortable, just let me know and we can end it as easily as hitting delete. Okay?"

"Okay." I said. I wasn't really bothered by the idea.

It would be easy enough, and if I could find his sister's shooter it would be worth it.

"Did you get the dock and pontoon out okay?"

"Yup!" I said proudly.

"Really?" he sounded surprised, which offended me a tiny bit. "Just you and your dad?"

"Well, no. Rex helped."

"Rex?"

"Yeah, he's a Nisswa police officer. I'd met him once before and my dad asked him if he'd help."

"Older guy?"

"Late twenties? I didn't ask his age."

"Oh, well that's nice," he said in a weird tone. "Well, I got work to do. Thanks for your help. I'll call ya soon."

I hung up with Derek and pulled out my laptop. An hour later I had an account, and eight new friends. All of them were from the University of Minnesota–Morris. My fake name was Katie Johnson. I said I was born and raised in Fargo, North Dakota, and was going to college as a freshman with a major in psychology. I didn't friend request Cory yet, but I did look at his profile. He had an "everyone" security setting so I could see everything on his profile. His information wasn't fully filled out, but he did have a picture up. He wasn't a bad looking guy. I closed down my laptop and headed to bed.

In the morning I got up as soon as my alarm went off. I dressed in dark-blue jeans and a fitted brown, light-weight sweater. I threw on some matching jewelry and tan heels and headed to the kitchen. *Monday . . . I think maybe I should change the schedule so I don't have to be the one to open.* Faith was on the counter when I shuffled in to start coffee.

"No, Faith. No cats on the counter," I scolded, as I moved her to the floor.

She did figure-eights around my feet and purred. After I filled her bowl and changed her water, I grabbed a cold bagel and a "to-go" cup with half hot chocolate-half coffee and headed out the door. I jumped in my Jeep and drove to my store. I was scheduled until 3:00 p.m today, Ginger had asked for a later shift because her husband had fallen ill and she wanted to go with him to the doctor. They were both in their sixties, so I hoped it was nothing serious.

I spent the morning reorganizing the jewelry section. The previous owner's daughter made all the jewelry by hand. When I bought the place I called her and offered to continue the agreement she'd had with them and she was thrilled. She was a thirty-something, stay-at-home mom who did it for extra income in her free time. The products were always new and fresh, and they sold like crazy. Once a month she'd ship a supply, and once a month I'd send her a check for half the retail price. It was a win-win for both of us.

It took a couple hours to take down, deep clean, and set all the jewelry displays back up, but it looked great when I was done. I didn't have one customer the whole time. The slow season was starting. Lost and Found normally stayed open all year, but a few of the stores and restaurants on the strip closed for the winter. November was just beginning and I didn't know yet what I was going to do for winter hours. The previous owners had closed the store on Wednesday's and Sunday's and shortened all the other days of the week. I guessed I'd play it by ear.

When I heard the bells on the door ring I looked up and saw Rex come through the door in full "Officer McHottie" uniform, sans hat. He smiled when he caught my eyes.

"Good morning," he said.

"Hi," I said feeling butterflies. I mentally told myself to knock it off. "What brings you in?"

"I need a gift for my sister," he said.

"Really? What's the occasion?" I asked not knowing if I should believe him.

"It's her thirtieth birthday. My parents are throwing her a surprise party this weekend, so I thought I'd drop in and see if you had anything a girl might like," he said with a grin.

"I think I can help you with that. Would this be an older sister or younger sister?" *Yup, I snuck it in there.*

"Older," he said with a sly smile, "I'm only twenty-eight."

"Well, we just got some nice jewelry in," I said leading him over to the display. "Does she wear jewelry?"

"I think so," he said looking at the different pieces. "These are nice." He moved a step closer to me and closed the space. I felt his heat move through me. He smelled good. Really good.

"Yup," I said catching my breath, "Those are one of my favorites."

We stood there making small talk about jewelry for a few minutes then moved on to scented candles. When he'd picked out enough items, we went to the counter. I checked him out and offered our free gift packaging service. He accepted, so I got out a gift bag, tissue, and curling ribbon and started in. When the bells on the door chimed we both turned our heads to see eight loud, older women coming through the door. They were all dressed in obnoxious red and purple outfits. It was the Red Hat Society! We had a few Red Hat items in our store, so I recognized them as that group right away. It was clear that they had been drinking by their volume and giggles. The group ranged from tall to short, from fat to thin. Some were colored and some were gray. All were dressed in red and purple polyester outfits each differing a little from the next. Two had huge hats, the rest had headbands with things sticking up on them or big bows on top of their heads. Large pieces of purple and red plastic jewelry serenaded their wrists, necks, and ears. You couldn't help but smile at the sight.

"Wow," Rex said under his breath.

"Oh, boy, there's a huge bus outside. It looks like there's more of them on it!" I said through a huge grin. "What? You've never heard of the Red Hat Society?" I asked.

"The what?"

"The Red Hat society!"

"Ah, no," he said, looking concerned.

I looked down and continued to bag his purchase. Then I overheard them talking from the scented candle area.

"Oh, gee, look at the nice one up by the counter," one said.

"Oh, yeah, he's a looker," said another.

"Where? Oh, wow! Look at him in that uniform—nice and tight in all the right areas," said a third. By this time they had all stopped looking at merchandise and were staring in our direction. I looked up at Rex and tried not to bust out laughing.

"So, Rex," I said quietly, "what's your sister's name?"

"Amanda," he answered.

His face was beet red. He was trying his best to not make eye contact with them. One of the ladies gave another shove and said, "Lorretta, why don't ya go over there and ask him to join us on the bus?"

"Oh, yes. That'd be great! Maybe he'd dance for us," said another.

"Oh, shit!" Rex whispered. He looked at me, his back to the women and asked, "She's not coming over, is she?"

His eyes were wide with fear. I looked past him. "No, not yet," I said with a giggle.

"That there's probably his girlfriend," one said.

"Oh, yeah, I bet it is. You could cut the sexual tension in here with a knife," said still another.

I finished his bag and handed it to him.

"You're all set!" I said with a smile. I couldn't help it.

"It looks great," he said, smiling like an apology. "Thanks for your help. This was fun. Next time I need a gift, I know where to come. Have a nice day."

"Thanks, you too," I said back as he started walking away.

The women all shushed and turned to pick up items they pretended to look at as he passed.

"Ask him, Lorretta! He's gonna leave!" one said to another with an elbow jab.

"No way! You do it!"

Rex gave them a small nod in passing, "Ladies." Then he stepped out the door.

All the ladies were giggling and chatting about how good looking he was. Some were fanning themselves after he walked past. It was a hoot! I laughed with them and then walked over to see if there was anything I could help them find. One announced that she'd found the Red Hat stuff, and they all moved over in that direction. The bells chimed and about twelve more women dressed in red and purple came through the door. They really lit the place up.

About a half hour later I was around $1,000 dollars richer, and in need of more Red Hat items on the shelves. They'd about cleaned me out. The rest of the day went pretty fast and at 3:00, when Ginger showed up, I realized that I hadn't eaten all day and was starving, so I walked over to Morning Glory.

When I came through the door everyone in the place looked at me, like they do at everyone. I grabbed a booth and sat down. The menus were on the tables, so I picked one up and was trying to decide what I wanted when I heard a familiar voice.

8

"Well look what the cat done dragged in! Hey, sugar!" Tannya said. "Ya want coffee?"

She was holding a full pot of coffee in one hand and the other one was on her hip. She had the face of a twenty-year-old but the voice of a fifty-year-old. Today she was wearing dark-purple eye shadow and red lipstick. It reminded me of the ladies who'd been in the store earlier. She had her hair up in the usual high pony with pen stuck through it. Her roots were getting bad. She was a brunette trying hard to be bleached blonde. Her pony was holding the dead, dry hair that looked more like fuzz.

"No, no coffee. Just a diet pop," I told her.

"All right, hun. What do ya want to eat?"

I quickly scanned the menu and chose a French dip with fries.

"I'll put this order in, and check on my other tables, then I gotta talk to you about something," she said, lowering her voice to almost a whisper.

"Okay," I said a bit unsure that I was ready for what she had to say.

After I'd paged through the weekly paper I'd taken off the abandoned table next to me, I looked up to see Tannya buzzing around. I was nervous. I wondered what she wanted and couldn't concentrate on anything I was trying to read, so I folded the paper up and set it aside. Finally, Tannya came over and sat across from me.

"Okay, I got your phone number and gave it to Miss Kitty. I wanted to give you the head's up. She'll be calling you soon to discuss . . ." she looked over her left shoulder and her right. Then she leaned into the table more and lowered her voice, ". . . her needs."

"Her needs?" I asked, leaning forward with tightly wrinkled brows.

"Yes. She has some things that she needs you to look into and thinks that you're the girl to do it."

"What? What needs? Why me?" I asked kind of panicky. "I don't know Miss Kitty. I don't think I've ever even seen her before."

"Miss Kitty is smart. She knows stuff, and she thinks you'll be perfect for the job." Tannya said with a hushed voice.

"What job? Who is she?"

I had a million more questions and felt like I had two minutes to find them all out. My heart was beating fast and I didn't even know why.

"She knows who you are and says it's for her to discuss with you. She just asked for your phone number. She said if I got your number for her I'd be thanked for my time and discretion."

"How *did* you get my number?"

"I went over to the shop when you weren't there and asked Ginger for it," she said with a look on her face like "duh."

"So how did she thank you?" I asked curiously.

"Money. She has lots of it. She told me to meet her at Amoco and bring the number with. I called first to make sure it was right. I think I got your mother."

"Yeah, she mentioned that you'd called."

"When I got there," Tannya said, "Miss Kitty pulled up in her Mustang convertible and got out. She walked over to my car and leaned in. She took the number and handed me an envelope. Then she blew me a kiss, gave a finger wave and a wink, and got back in her vehicle. I looked in the envelope, five hundred dollars!"

"Five hundred dollars? Holy crap! How would she even know that *you* could get my phone number? It's not like I've known you very long."

"Honey, I know everyone and everything in this town," she said snapping her fingers as her hand moved in a Z formation. *Seriously?*

"Well, then tell me what she wants."

"Okay, well, I don't know everything, but it's just a matter of time before I find out."

"Tannnnnya! Order up!" a voice shouted from the kitchen area.

"I'll be back," she said and got up.

I really just wanted to go home and rake leaves, or maybe call someone about raking leaves. I didn't want to get involved in Miss Kitty's problems.

Tannya returned a moment later with my order. She set it down on the table then went to the other tables, coffee pot in tow, to check on the other customers. I saw her give out a few bills to those who were almost finished and refills to those who weren't, and returned the pot to the warmer. She walked back over and sat down again across from me.

"So like I was sayin', she knows who you are, read about you in the newspaper. She knows about your 'special abilities' and investigative skills. Her words, not mine."

"I don't have special abilities or skills! Tell her that!" I demanded.

"I tried but she wouldn't listen. And what Miss Kitty wants, Miss Kitty gets.

"Who *is* she? Does she live around here?" I asked dipping another fry.

"She grew up here, but has more than one property. She's only in town a few months a year. She made her husband buy her a nice property on a lake so she could feel at home once in a while. She married up. Way up. She has a lot of money and spends it on anything and everything she wants."

I took a gulp of Pepsi and secretly wished I'd packed a flask. "Who's her husband? Is he from around here?"

"Vincent Alburgus. Wealthy man. I have no idea where he comes from but he's not from here. But he has money and a lot of it! He's old too, like seventy or more—too old for Miss Kitty if you ask me. Eww! But that's just me," she said with a curled lip.

"How old is Ms. Kitty?"

"I don't know. And I'm sure she's had a lot of work done, too. But she's got to be at least forty or more."

"Tannya! You workin' or talkin' today?" the guy from the kitchen yelled across the restaurant.

"Yah, Yah. Don't get your undies in a bunch, Marv! I'm coming!" she bellowed back. Then she turned back to me. "I gotta get back to work. Watch for her call. I'll talk to ya soon," she said and walked away.

My mind was wondering and my stomach turning. I did my best to finish eating. Tannya was busy with some newcomers, so I left cash on the table to cover my bill and give her a nice tip. I waved to her as I walked out. She looked up from her note pad and gave me a wink and nod. I walked back to my Jeep, which was parked behind Lost and Found, and climbed in.

When I got home I turned on my computer. While it booted up I grabbed a phone book and looked up a local landscapers. I looked up a few of the ones with bigger ads on the Internet. One had a really nice web page and large ad in the phone book. I figured that they must be run well and have lots of customers if they could afford a big ad in the phone book. I thought I'd give them a shot. I dialed the number to C.S. Landscaping.

"Yes, who is this?" a voice answered.

"Um, hi. Is this C.S Landscaping?" I asked, confused and taken aback by the abrupt greeting. Maybe I dialed wrong.

"Yes, Yes. What you need? Mow? Rake? What?"

Geez! The man sounded like he was Mexican, and in a huge rush.

"Uh, yes . . . rake," I said. Now I felt rushed. This was weird.

"Okay. Where you live?"

I gave him my address.

"You wait," he said. I heard him put the phone down on the desk. Then I could hear him typing. When he got back on the line a minute later he was still in a hurry. "Okay, I Google Earth you. You have many tree. Will be much work. I send men on Thursday. They rake and mow and weed whip and blow and clean up all leaves too. It be $250 for whole yard. You have big yard, yes?"

"Yes," I said.

"Okay, Thursday. You have cash or credit card, bye-bye," he said and disconnected.

Well, all righty then. That's done. Not like I had much say in the arrangement, but at least I can check it off my list. It's kinda funny. No wonder he had such a big ad—anyone calling is booked. I felt kinda suckered, but I guessed I'd wait and see what kind of job they did before I complained. I wrote LANDSCAPING on Thursday's square on the calendar inside the kitchen cupboard then went back to my computer.

I checked my fake Facebook page I'd set up to help Derek out. I had fifteen more friends, both male and female. I played some dumb games to make it look active and wrote "Doing homework again. Does it ever end?" as my status. I searched and made a few more friend requests, a few being friends of Cory's. After I checked my real email, I shut the computer down. I was just headed out to the patio with a hot chocolate and book when my cell rang. Derek.

"Hello?" I answered.

"Hey," he said exhausted. "What are you doing?"

"Just relaxing. I have a few new friends on the fake Facebook page."

"Okay. Let me know when you request him, maybe wait a day or two."

"I will. I requested a few of his friends so if they bite then I request him next. Any change on Kelly?"

"No, nothing. Her vitals are good but no change. They told my mom they're going to put in a stomach tube tomorrow to feed her. Hopefully some nutrition will help," he said sadly.

"Oh, man . . . I hope it helps. Are you at home?" I asked.

"Yes, I'm going to go to bed. I can't think straight anymore and I'm getting more angry every second this guy remains out there. I needed to take the night off and recharge. I'll give you a call tomorrow or Wednesday. If you don't hear from me, feel free to call me too. Okay?"

"Okay, get some sleep. Good night."

"Good night," he said and disconnected.

I lay in bed wondering what I could do to help. I felt so bad for Kelly and her family. I tried to close my eyes, but every time I did I envisioned what had happened on Friday night. It was hard to relax. I got my book out and read for a bit to take my mind off it. I said yet another prayer for healing and peace for Kelly and her family, and for guidance for Derek to find Cory. Then I drifted off.

I woke up Tuesday morning to my phone ringing. I ran to the kitchen where it was plugged in and answered. It was Derek. I looked up at the clock noticing it was still dark out. 5:10 a.m.

"Hello?" I said with a raspy voice.

My mind went straight to his sister.

"Hey, sorry to wake you. I wanted to tell you that my mom just called and said that Kelly is moving her hands and body a little bit. She still hasn't opened her eyes, but they are turning her pain meds way down to see if it will help her be more alert and maybe wake up."

"Oh, Derek, that's great news!"

"I know. I'm heading there this morning. I want to be there if she wakes up. I'm hoping she'll be able to give me some information on Cory I can use. The Morris Police Department isn't getting anywhere. I wanted to let you know right away."

"Thanks for that. Do you want me to come with you?"

"If you want to meet me there you could. I'm not really sure there's anything you can do, but I'd love to see you if you don't have anything else going on. But, I understand if you can't or you're busy . . . You don't have to. I know you have the store to hold down . . . But if you want to, great."

"I'm scheduled to open today, but I bet if I call Ginger she'd come in. If she will I'll call you back and let you know. If she can't I could still head out of town about 11:00 when I get off."

"Okay, well, let me know. But don't feel any pressure. I told work that I'd be back on Thursday at the latest, so I plan to stay overnight. You're welcome to join me," he said his voice getting higher at the end of the sentence. Almost like a "pretty please" mom tone.

"Okay, let me figure things out, then give you call later," I told him with a sweet voice. Now I was really missing him and wanted to see him again.

"Thanks, sweetness. Talk to ya soon," he said and disconnected.

I hung up the phone with some new energy, and decided to use it for a run. I threw on a t-shirt and old sweat pants. After I laced up my tennies, I threw on a light fleece sweatshirt, as it was only fifty degrees out according to the weather channel. I opened the front door, and Faith came over and peeked out the side window. She meowed.

"Yes, I'm going for a run," I told her.

"Meow," she taunted again.

"I'll try to make it more than a block! Thanks for the confidence, Faith! Sheesh," I told her.

I gave her a quick rub on the head and shut the door behind me. The cold, crisp, fresh air that one only get in the country hit me, and I inhaled deeply. *Ahhh.* I loved the smell. I threw my arms up and stretched out my sides then started a slow jog. It was just starting to get light out, so I could see where I was going. It was a good thing because I wouldn't tempt running in the dark. I ran about two miles and returned home. When I got inside I tossed my shoes in the closet, sat on the living room carpet, and stretched while I watched the morning news.

At 6:00 I jumped in the shower and was feeling pretty proud of myself for running so far. *I envy people who get out of bed every morning and run.* I thought that I could get used to that proud feeling, but I knew the consistency would never happen. *I'm not a get-out-of-bed-earlier-than-necessary kind of girl.* I dressed casually, knowing I'd go to Morris later. I had nothing else to do and could easily get someone to work my shift or, if not, just close the store. *I love my life—freedom, flexibility, and never a worry about having enough money.* I looked up at the ceiling and thanked Nana and Papa for the inheritance.

I grabbed a small suitcase from the closet and packed it for three days, just in case. I wheeled it out to the Jeep and loaded it in the back. Then I went back for Faith. I didn't really know anyone in town yet who would be willing to watch her, so for now I was taking her to work and to Morris. I could easily sneak her into a hotel.

I stopped at the gas station on the way to work, filled up, and grabbed a large coffee. Once at work I looked at the clock. I was still running twenty minutes ahead of schedule, and was starving, which I blamed on the run, so I headed over to Morning Glory to get a caramel roll. Tannya was working.

"Hey, sugar!" she said with a wink.

Today she was sporting two ponytails with ribbons around each. She looked like she was dressed up for a costume party. Her blonde hair was the usual dry-dead look and her blush was red like the hair ribbons. If she'd been in a checkered shirt and overalls she could have past for Raggedy Ann. Instead she had on the usual khaki pants, two sizes too small, and polo shirt that said Morning Glory on the left upper corner.

"Hi," I said trying hard not to wince at her appearance. "I need one of those caramel rolls," I said pointing at the bakery case.

"Sure thing. To go?" she asked.

"Yes, I have to get back to the shop and work for a few hours."

She reached for a bag and the tongs, "Did ya get the phone call yet?"

"No, nothing yet."

"Sara, girl, I can't wait to see what this is all about. You have to tell me as soon as she calls. I gotta know what's going on!" she said. "Here, this is my cell phone number. Keep it handy. Don't look in the phone book for my number 'cause you'll just get my crazy ex. Put this into your phone and make sure you call me."

I took the napkin she wrote the number on and put it in my purse.

"Sure thing," I said. "I'll call you if I hear from her."

I took the bakery bag and handed her a five. While she was getting my change, I looked over and saw Officer McHottie coming through the door. I smiled when he made eye contact. His face lit up. He smiled back and turned to walk in my direction.

"Here's your change. I'll look forward to your call," Tannya said with a wink, then turned her gaze to Rex. "Well, good morning, Officer Dalton," she said. "Mmmm Mmm," she said a little quieter under her breath but so I could her. "Can I show you to a table?" she asked, fanning herself with the menu she'd just picked up.

"Sure, Tannya," he said with a wink. "And good morning to you, Sara," he said with a gorgeous smile.

"Hi," I said with a dorky wave.

"You on your way to work?" he asked.

"Yup, for a little bit anyway."

"Well, I'll see you later then. Have a great day," his voice was deep. *Rich like butter and caramel . . . and mmmm . . .* I had to shake my head to snap myself out of it.

"Sara?" I heard.

"Huh? Oh, yeah, thanks. You, too, have a great day," I said and turned to walk out the door.

Sheesh. He was nice. So nice.

I gave Faith a bit of my roll when I got back to the store and put her litter box behind my desk in the back room. She spent the morning exploring the place and seemed perfectly content. I left her water and food out for her too. When she was all situated, I did some much needed paperwork and the schedule for the next week. I scheduled Maureen and Ginger for the whole week since I was unsure of how things were going to go with Kelly and Derek and Cory. I wanted to be flexible in case something came up. I sent Derek a quick message, telling him that I was coming in a couple hours and asked where to meet him. He said he got a room for us again at the Holiday Inn and that I should call when I got close so he could let me know where he was at.

An hour later I'd already had a handful of customers and had most of the paperwork caught up. I heard my cell phone ringing in my purse and, since the store was empty at the moment, I went to the back room to get it. Normally, if the store was open I'd turn the phone to vibrate. I looked at the screen and saw "Number Unavailable" before I connected.

"Hello?" I answered.

"Hello, darling, is this Sara Martin?" an unfamiliar voice asked.

"Yes, it is," *Darling? Oh no, this must be Miss Kitty.*

"Hello, love. My name is Eleno . . . never mind that. Ha ha, it's not important. People call me Miss Kitty. Did your friend Tannya tell you I'd be calling?"

Her voice was twangy with a hint of Southern accent. Her laugh gave me goose bumps, not the good kind. She had a take-charge tone that was instantly intimidating. I shrunk two sizes just listening to her over the phone. I already feared her.

9

"Um, yeah, she mentioned that she gave you my number."

"Good, good. Well then let's get straight to it. I need you to investigate something for me. I can't discuss it right now, but I'd like to meet you sometime soon to go over the details. When works for you? Tonight? Tomorrow? What?"

"Um, Miss Kitty, I think you've got the wrong person. I'm not a private investigator. I can't help you," I told her firmly.

"Miss Sara, love, you underestimate the womanly skills you have been blessed with. You found your ex-friend, and the missing girl's remains, *and* discovered your husband was having an affair, not to mention your spiritual skills. Girlfriend, you've got it all, and I need your help. Don't you even think about backing out. You're the best, and I want you! Now when works for you?"

"But I, I don't possess any skills. It was dumb luck that I found those two. I don't know the first thing about investigative work," I pleaded.

"Nonsense! If this is about the money . . ."

"It's not, I don't need the money."

"I'll talk to you about the money on Monday then. We'll meet at 7:00 p.m. at Morning Glory and go over all the details. Thank you, darling. I'll see you then."

She disconnected before I could argue anymore. *Sheesh, she had power. How do I get myself into these things?* When I hung up I noticed Ginger walking through the door. I asked her about her husband. She said the doctors were running some tests but he'd live for now, although he said he didn't want to if they were going to put him on the low cholesterol diet. I laughed and handed her the schedule for next week. She said it looked good to her. With the medical bills, she wanted all the hours she could get. She didn't notice Faith wandering over until she had rubbed on her leg and scared her half to death. After she fully recovered from the panic attack, I packed the Jeep and went back in for Faith. The bells rang turning my attention to the front door. It was Tannya.

"Hi," I said to her. She was still in her work uniform, sans apron and pencil in the hair.

"Hey, sugar," she said looking me over. "Glad I caught ya here. It seems I almost forgot about my mother's birthday this next weekend and thought I'd buzz on over and get a gift for her."

"Great. I was going to call you, too, and tell you that I spoke with Miss Kitty," I informed her.

Her face lit up like Christmas Day. "She called? Well, what did she want?"

I feel bad disappointing her. "She said she wanted to meet me on Monday to go over details," I said with a shrug. "I tried to tell her that I wouldn't be able to help her but she wouldn't listen."

"Yup. Once Miss Kitty's made up her mind, there's no changing it. She could tell a diesel mechanic to bake a Boston cream pie for her and he'd end up doing it. God love her, that woman is a piece of work." Tannya said.

I tossed my purse over my shoulder. "Yeah, can't wait to see what she wants from me," I said sarcastically.

"Are you leaving?" she said as Faith went over to check her out. "Ooooh, whose kitty?" she asked as she bent over and petted her.

"Mine."

"Oh, wow! She's a beauty. Aren't you? Yes, you are. Who's a pretty kitty?" she said in a high voice as she picked her up and rubbed noses with her.

My first thought was, *Faith is going to have pink blush on her cheeks.* My second thought was, *I wonder how many cats Tannya has.* My third thought leaped to, *I wonder if she cat-sits.*

"Is she always here at the store with you?"

"No, I'm just headed out of town for the weekend and didn't have anyone to watch her so she's coming with me."

"Well I'll take her! I love cats! Scooter done took my cat when he left. He hated that cat, and I cringed thinking about whatever happened to her. I haven't seen her since the day I threw him out. I didn't notice him take her, but there was a lot going on with all the police there and what not. After they left, and Scooter had his things, I couldn't find Clarice anywhere. I called the cops, and Rex went over and asked him about the cat, but he said he didn't do anything with it."

"That's terrible. I'm sorry," I offered.

"That's nothing. Scooter's done much worse, I'm sure. That man went from a nice country boy to a drug-addicted alcoholic overnight. He turned on me and the world for no reason at all, well, except the drugs I guess. Anyway I threw him out and had the police there for protection when I did. They all knew him on a first-name basis, so it went pretty good that day, but he shows up on my doorstep every once in a while on something demanding some money or other item he thinks he left behind. The man's crazy. I keep my distance from him."

"Wow, that's terrible too. Geez, sorry," I said. She looked back at Faith, who had loved the rub down she'd gotten while Tannya told her story.

"Anyways, if you need someone to watch your cat, I'd love to do it. I aint got nuttin' goin' on this weekend anyways," she said.

I thought about it. Faith would probably have more fun with a lonely cat lover than locked in a hotel room for the weekend.

"Really? Are you sure? That'd be great if you could," I said with a smile.

"Oh, yeah. It's no problem. I'm headed home right now, and I plan to paint the kitchen this weekend so she can wander around while I do that."

"Okay, well thanks, Tannya. That's very nice of you. I'm sure that Faith will have a great time." I said.

"Sure, no problem at all. I'll just look around quick for a gift and then we'll head home," she said, turning around with Faith in her arms scanning the room.

"Great. I'll go get her box and food and supplies out of my Jeep and be right back," I said setting my purse down.

Twenty minutes later, I was on the road to Morris, and Faith was with Tannya on the way to paint her kitchen. I was not looking forward to the drive. It was going to be long and boring. I had the radio cranked up and was singing at the top of my lungs, when I heard my phone. I stopped singing and was a bit embarrassed, even though I knew that the caller couldn't hear me. It was silly, but I still felt it. I dug in my purse with one hand, the other on the wheel, and I wished I'd had a bluetooth. Finally, I found it and looked at the caller ID. It was my friend, Kat. *Geez, I haven't talked to her in a while.*

"Hello!" I sang.

"Hey, girl! You're still alive! I was getting worried," she said with a laugh.

"I am! I know I've been busy and been meaning to call you."

"Well, I think that it's time we get together again. We need to catch up. You still seeing that Derek guy?"

"Yeah, although he's been busy too. It's a long story, but I'm headed to meet him now."

"Oh, so you're going to be in the Cities this weekend?" she asked.

"I'm not sure yet. I'll call ya after I meet with Derek and find out what the plan is. If I can, we'll meet for drinks somewhere, okay?"

"Okay, but make me a priority! I need someone to talk to, and dance with, and have fun with."

I laughed.

"Okay. I'll call you later and see what we can do. I'll talk to ya soon."

"Mmm,'kay, bye," she said and hung up.

It was only Wednesday so I hoped that by Friday or Saturday I would be able to get together with her. It occurred to me that it was the last Friday of the month. That meant I was supposed to meet with Blake. Blake was my new financial adviser. He was a gorgeous man. He could fill out a suit like an angel food cake could fill out a pan: all the curves were perfect, the overall shape was appealing, and the smell was heavenly. I picked my phone up off the seat and looked through my contact list. I took a deep breath and dialed his number. After his secretary answered and put me on hold, I waited for a few minutes, listening to elevator music and thinking about him. He was single, and I could tell from the last time we met that he liked me. I liked him too.

"Hello, Sara!" he said, and as always, I could hear the smile in his voice.

It gave me goose bumps.

"Hi, Blake," I said trying to hide the sigh in my voice. "I was just calling to see if we were still on for Friday for our monthly meeting."

"Absolutely! I'm looking forward to it," he said. "Do you want to meet at Applebee's again or try somewhere new?"

"Applebee's is fine. So Friday, at 7:00 p.m. at Applebee's," I said to clarify.

"Sure thing! I'll see you then."

"Is there anything that I should bring with me?" I asked, new to this whole investment thing.

"Just yourself. I'll have a few documents and some reports for us to go over but you don't need to bring anything," he said.

He had a really sexy voice. After I disconnected I wondered how many clients he had that he did dinner dates with. Oh, well, why should I care anyway? I called Derek because he never replied to my message. I got his voice mail. *Weird*. I left a message saying that I would be there around 3:30 p.m.

I stopped for gas at Super America and was offered a car wash, but decided to pass on that. I did get a large coffee, doughnut, and some Fun Yuns. I was half expecting a disapproving look from someone, but the young guy at the counter just looked at me and asked if I had gas. I showed him my free coffee card, and he took off the charge for the coffee. *Yay*. Walking out of there It felt just like when I was a kid and would sneak up to my room with extra dessert.

As I approached Morris, I began feeling a rush of adrenaline.

10

I was suddenly overwhelmed by emotions. I was about to see Derek, which was great. I missed him terribly. I was about to see his sister lying in that bed, unable to move or speak because of what that loser Cory did to her. Then there was the fear of knowing that Cory was loose in this town. I guess he could be in another country by now, but with his lack of funds and intelligence I doubted that. And who knew what kind of drugs he was on. I wondered if he even cared about what he'd done.

I heard a story once that was told at a meth-awareness conference by a retired police officer. Dispatch had him go check out a location along a highway where there were reports of something being thrown out the window. Three calls had come in about a car driving erratically on the highway and a male driver throwing something into the ditch out of the passenger side window. When the officer arrived at the location he found a young man's head. Cut off at the neck.

The police officer went in pursuit, looking for the car matching the description of the three callers' reports. He found it, and pulled the middle-aged man over and asked him what he was doing. The officer then noticed blood on the passenger's seat. The driver told him that while he was driving, the voices were all fighting and making too much noise, and that *he* said to throw him out, so he threw him out of the car.

He immediately arrested the driver. They went to his home and found the headless body of his seventeen-year-old son, still sitting upright on the couch in front of the TV. A sword that was once on display on the wall was now lying on the floor next to the body. The next morning, when the drug was out of his system, the officer went in to see the man.

"The man looked tired and confused," he told the audience. "He asked what he was doing there and why he'd been arrested." The officer, fighting his rage with everything he had, said, "Why don't you tell me about your day yesterday."

The man hung his head and admitted to buying and trying meth for the first time. He said that he was building a new house while working full time and just needed something to get rid of the stress. He apologized to the officer and asked how it was going to affect his record. He was concerned because he was a top business man at his job and worried that it would reflect poorly on him if corporate found out about it.

At that point the officer asked if he remembered what he did last night. He told him no, and that he only remembered going home after work and into the bathroom to light up. He lay down on the tile floor, closed his eyes, and then woke up in the jail cell.

The officer told his audience that he had felt sorry for the guy, and that telling him what he'd done while he *thought* he was asleep was the hardest thing he had ever had to do: "How do you tell a father that? How do you tell his wife, who's out in the waiting room that? How do you tell a man who makes six figures, wears a suit and tie to work every day, has three kids, a beautiful wife of nineteen years, and is near the top of the ladder in his career, that last night he cut his son's head off, put it in the passenger seat of the car, went out for a drive, and threw it out the window going down the interstate at seventy miles per hour. How . . . do you tell someone *that*?"

Meth is a crazy drug. If that's what Cory's on, I fear for anyone in his path. My phone rang. It was Derek.

"Hey," I answered. "I'm pulling in to town now."

"Okay, come to the hospital. I'll meet you in the entry. Just park on the street if there's room."

"All right, I'll see you in a few minutes," I said and disconnected.

I found parking on the street, tossed my bag over my shoulder, and headed to the double doors. Through the glass I saw Derek. I walked up to him and threw my arms around his neck. He looked really happy to see me. I asked about his sister, and he said that she was finally awake. He had a huge smile with tears in his eyes. I sighed in relief and hugged him again. He buried his face in my neck for a few extra seconds. When he pulled back I could see was crying. I smiled a closed-lipped smile and rubbed his back.

"Is she talking? Is she okay?" I asked.

"Her eyes just opened a few minutes ago. So I don't know. We should go up there," he said and took my hand.

We walked towards her room and saw Derek's family outside her door.

"The doctor's in there running some tests," Kathy told us. "Hi, hun. How are you?" she said to me with a hug. "It's good to see you again."

"Oh, you, too," I said. "I'm so glad to hear she's awake."

I gave Doug a hug, too. Derek put his hand at the small of my back and nudged me further down the line of people.

"Sara, this is my brother, Travis, and his wife, Deb," he said. I shook both of their hands and said hello. "This is my nephew, Mich," he said gesturing to a young man leaned up against the wall with ear buds in.

I smiled, and he nodded. His mom elbow-jabbed him in the ribs and he pulled one bud out and said, "Hey," and shook my hand, then stuck his ear bud back in. Derek shook his head in apology. Travis was a lot taller than Derek and was heavier set. He didn't really look like Derek. His hair was medium brown and cut short, and he had a goatee. Deb was around my height and weight but a little softer looking. She had short hair, too, almost a pixie cut. She was dressed in jeans and an oversized sweatshirt and tennis shoes. Mich had his dad's face and his mom's smaller frame. He was wearing oversized jeans that hung low on his hips and a black-and-white printed t-shirt with skulls and daggers on it. His extremely white tennis shoes were thick and fluffy looking, and the laces looked really loose. He looked like every other teenage boy I'd seen lately.

Kendall was there, too. I smiled at her, and she smiled back and put her head down on her mom's shoulder. She looked bad, like she hadn't slept in days. She had minimal makeup on and her hair was in a pony. Not the beautiful girl I saw last time. I felt so bad for her.

"It's nice to meet you all," I said.

"It's nice to meet you, too. Derek speaks fondly of you," Deb said with a smile.

"Aww." I shot a sweet smile at him. He shrugged and turned a little pink in the cheeks.

"He talks about his family fondly, too."

The doctor came out and said, "We're taking her to run some more tests, so if you could make your way to the waiting room, I'll send a nurse for you when she's back in her room."

"Is she talking?" Kathy asked. "Can we see her before she goes?"

The nurses started coming through the door, pushing her bed. Her eyes were closed and she was still hooked up to a lot of machines. Kathy grabbed her hand and made them stop the bed for a second.

Kathy leaned over her and whispered, "I love you baby. They're going to take you to run some more tests. We'll be right here when you get back. I love you so much. You're going to be fine."

She pushed her hair back and kissed her gently on her forehead. She held her lips on her, softly crying without breaking contact until Doug gently pulled her back. I, of course, started crying, too. No one cries alone in my presence.

"We'll bring her right back," one of the nurses assured her.

Kathy rolled into Doug's chest and hugged him for a moment. Kendall stepped up and joined in. Derek reached out a hand and put it on his mom's back. After a moment, Travis said we should go to the waiting room and slowly led the way. We sat down on the various chairs and couches. Everyone was pretty quiet. Derek excused himself to take a call. Travis offered coffee but I wasn't interested, not after last time. When Derek came back he said that it was the Morris Police Department on the phone.

"They had a lead on Cory. He was spotted at the gas station on Fifth last night, around midnight. There are wanted posters that have been handed out to all the local gas stations, grocery stores, and hospitals. They're hung out of the public's sight, so hopefully it doesn't scare him out of town. They're reviewing the security footage now. They'll call back if it leads to anything. But I think I'll go down there in a bit and see what I can find out."

After a very long hour, a nurse came into the waiting room and said that the CT scan, x-rays, and ultrasound were done, and that she was back in her room resting. We could go in a see her but we couldn't stay very long. When we walked into the room she was lying almost flat and all the machines were placed back by her bed. Kathy and Kendall went over to her.

"Kelly? It's Kendall. Can you hear me?"

"Kelly, can you squeeze my hand?" Kathy asked.

We all looked down at her hand, it took a moment but you could see a small squeeze.

"She did it! Did you see that? She squeezed it!" Kathy looked around at us excited. I smiled and nodded.

"That's great Kelly! The doctor says you're going to be fine," Doug told her as he stepped closer.

"Kelly, everybody's here! Dad, Travis and Deb, Mich, Kendall, and Derek and Derek's friend Sara. Can you open your eyes and see us, Kelly? It would make our day. We're all so worried about you."

All of us leaned in and watched closely. A moment later her eyes wiggled and squeezed, and she opened them ever so slightly and then squeezed them shut again. I wondered if it was too bright in the room, so I went over to her bed side and flipped the light switch that was on the wall behind her bed. The two recessed lights above her bed went off. Derek gave me an approving look. We watched and she tried again. This time she held them open for a few seconds and looked around quickly before she closed them again.

"Good, Kelly! That was good," Kathy said and teared up.

Deb and Travis put their arms around each other. Even Mich looked like he had a smile. We stayed in the room a little longer, then Derek announced that we were going to go to the police station to check on the situation with Cory. We gave hugs to everyone then Derek leaned over Kelly's bed. "Be back later, sis. I'm gonna go get the bad guy. See you soon," he said and kissed her forehead. I teared up again.

The police station was about a five-minute drive. When we'd parked Derek told me that I should go in with him. I felt a bit awkward but followed him in. He spoke with the officer at the front desk and was told to "go on back." I followed Derek through a large room that was sectioned off by cubicles with a hallway down the middle and a hallway around the perimeter. There were window offices along the two side walls and the back wall. Derek looked like he knew exactly where to go.

It was 6:50 p.m., so the office was pretty quiet. We walked down the middle hallway to an office along the back wall. The door was open, so Derek walked right in. There were three men gathered around a TV looking at security tape, and another was on a laptop. All of the men were in plain clothes. Two were older, in their late fifties both in great shape and the one on the laptop was young, maybe twenty three or four, also in great shape. They all looked up when we walked in. One of them stood up and walked towards Derek.

"Detective Richards, come on in," he said extending his hand. "This is Detective Jacobs," he said, gesturing to the other older man, who also shook Derek's hand. "And Officer McHann." Derek nodded and shook his hand too.

"Nice to meet you both," Derek said.

"Detective Richards works out of the St. Paul Police Department and is a brother to the victim. He witnessed the crime," he informed the others.

"Sara, this is Detective Jensen. Detective, this is my friend, Sara," Derek said. "She also witnessed the crime and is your 911 caller."

We exchanged greetings and handshakes. Detective Jacobs gave us the rundown on the tape. As soon as it started Derek looked at me.

"That's him, for sure!" I nodded in agreement.

On the video he was driving an older model Chevrolet Chevette. He filled his tank, paid cash and walked back out of the store. There wasn't much to go on. The officers were working on zooming in on the license, but that's all they had. I asked for the ladies' room and excused myself. When I returned, they were searching the database for information on the car. The vehicle was registered to Cory. The tabs on it were over a year old.

"That'll help if he leaves the city," Officer McHann said.

"Yes it will. Let's get an APB out on that car now and wrap this up. McHann, you can go back out on patrol for the rest of your shift," Detective Jensen replied. He closed the laptop, and left.

Derek asked, "Do you still have extra patrols around his residence?"

"We do. There hasn't been any activity though. I'm glad to see that he's still in town. Now we just need him to think he got away with it, and keep showing up in public." He shook his head, "We should have had him by now. I'm sure this is very frustrating for you. How's your sister?"

"Showing improvement. She opened her eyes and squeezed our mother's hand today. The doctors ran some tests a little bit ago but we haven't heard anything back on them yet . . . Thanks for asking."

"You bet. And please keep us informed," he said.

"I will. We will let you get back to finding the bad guys. Please let me know if anything turns up. We're at the Holiday Inn in town for tonight. I'll be in touch tomorrow," Derek said and shook his hand again.

I said goodbye as well, and followed Derek out the door. We talked in the car and decided to go out to eat.

There was a Perkins on the main drag so we decided on that. It was pretty empty since it was after 8:00 p.m. Derek and I got a table in the back so we could talk about Cory and Kelly without having to worry about anyone hearing. The waitress came over, and we placed our order right away. We both got a sandwich with fries and a diet pop. While we sat there, across the booth from each other, I noticed how quiet

Derek seemed. He leaned back and interlaced his fingers behind his head. "It's so frustrating, you know? I just want to get out there and get this guy."

"I know," I said. "You're doing everything you can though. Your hands are tied. It's not your jurisdiction. Everyone understands that. I think it's nice that Morris PD is letting you be involved as much as they are."

"I know. Most detectives would tell a guy in my position to go home and let them do their job."

"Well, we know he's in the area and he *was* getting gas so he must be planning to drive somewhere soon. Hopefully it's somewhere around here."

"Right. And he's hooked on drugs and out of hiding already, so hopefully he'll keep up with the public appearances and you can bring him in."

My hands were folded on the table in front of me. Derek unlaced his fingers, leaned forward and cupped his hands over mine. I looked into his eyes and my heart softened. I had to inhale deeply to make up for the sigh I'd quietly let out. I smiled gently and tipped my head. His eyes were so tired, so loving, so full of pain. I wished I could make him feel better.

"Thank you, Sara," he said. "I'm really glad you're here. I know you didn't have to come and I know how long the drive is. I just want you to know how much I appreciate it. It means the world to me that you came. Just seeing you and being next to you makes me feel stronger."

My eyes filled up.

I blinked and told him softly, "You're welcome."

He leaned over the table, and I met him halfway for a kiss. It was a little awkward because I could hardly reach, but when our lips gently touched it was like the world stopped for a moment, and I didn't care who saw. When we pulled apart, our eyes opened and met one another's. He gently winked one eye and sat back. He made me happy. Every time I saw him he made me happy. I loved him. I *really* loved him.

Feeling a presence, I looked up to the waitress, who was holding our plates of food. She placed the items on the table and we dug in. I was hoping the butterflies in my stomach would settle quickly so I could eat. They did and when the bill came I got it. Derek tried, but I insisted. We loaded ourselves into his car and went back to the hospital.

When we walked into her room, Kelly was sitting in an upright position on her bed. She was leaning back with her head on the pillow. Her eyes were swollen closed. All of the family was still there.

"How is she?" Derek asked his mom.

"The doctor just left," his mom told him, glancing in my direction. "He's very optimistic. Her CT scan didn't show any further damage, and the x-rays and ultrasound didn't find anything new either. Everything seems to be healing the way it's supposed to. So that is great news. She's awake on her own and they are going to lower her meds so that she can start being awake more often. She still has weeks of recovery left, but if there aren't any new complications she'll be okay."

"So it's just a waiting game for her to heal and get her strength up?" Derek asked.

"Yup, she's going to be fine. Praise God!" Kathy said.

"You two smell like food," Travis said as Derek passed him to get closer to Kelly.

"We went to Perkins after the police station and grabbed a bite," I told him.

"The police have surveillance tape footage of Cory gassing up in town. Sara and I took a look and it's definitely him. We have an APB out on his car. Hopefully he's planning on driving more."

"Boy I hope so," Doug said.

Kathy said that they were just talking about going to get some food. They all agreed to leave and find something to eat. Travis and Deb said that after they ate, they would head back to the Cities. Derek and I gave both of them hugs goodbye and, after they said goodbye to Kelly, they stepped out into the hallway. Derek moved over to the side of the bed opposite his mom.

"Get some rest, baby. We will be back in the morning," Kathy said and kissed Kelly's forehead.

"I love you, Kelly. Get better. We miss your sweet smile," Derek said, his voice cracking.

He lifted her hand and kissed it. She squeezed it. We all noticed and looked at her face. She opened her eyes a fraction and a tiny smile formed on her lips.

"There it is," he said. "We'll be back tomorrow. Get some rest."

We quietly stepped out of the room and walked down to the parking lot with Doug and Kathy and Kendall. After we all exchanged hugs and said see you in the morning Derek got into his Jeep and I got into mine. I followed him to the hotel. While helping with the bags, he asked where Faith was. I told him that I'd found a cat sitter in Nisswa. He'd never met Tannya, but I explained on the way up to the room who she was, and what she looked like. He gave me a look with a head shake as he opened the door for me. I slid past him and into the room. It looked like the mirror image of the room we'd stayed in last week.

I walked across the room and set my bag down. It was 10:00 and I wasn't really that tired. Derek grabbed the ice bucket and liner and said he'd be right back. I plopped down on the bed and lay there until the door opened again. When Derek walked in, I rolled to my side and watched him. He was so pretty. If there was such a thing as a perfect ten he was it.

"Are you tired . . . or do you want to stay up for a while?" he asked.

11

"I'm okay for a little while yet," I said.

Derek went to the dresser where the TV was, and inside there were two wine glasses. He set them out on the desk, then reached into the mini fridge and pulled out a bottle of wine. He glanced my way and his eyebrows went up and down quickly. I smiled back. He walked past the bed to his bag and after he'd rooted around a little he came up with a corkscrew. When he was finished pouring the wine, he brought a glass over to me and sat on the bed next to me. I thanked him and picked my head up enough to take a sip. It was good, and wine was so relaxing.

He nudged me a little, so I scooted back giving him room to lie down too. We were both on our sides, one hand holding the glass and the other propped up under our heads facing each other. He smiled softly at me. I smiled back.

"I'm sorry I haven't been calling you as much lately. I've missed you and your voice," he said quietly.

"Me too," I said.

He slid his hand along my cheek, under my hair, and to the back of my head and firmly pulled me to him for a kiss. The kiss lasted for several minutes. When we broke he took my glass from me and set it on the night stand between the two queen beds. He stood and got more wine to refill our glasses. My mind was spinning. *I want him so bad, but not yet. Not in a hotel. Not when he's so upset about his sister and finding Cory. When we're ready, I want it to be perfect.*

"You're dangerous," he said from across the room. "I've had a hard time being close to you and behaving."

I laughed out loud. "I know," I whined, "I feel the same about you."

He sat back down on the bed.

"I want to be with you, just not in a Holiday Inn. And not here in Morris while I'm looking for my sister's shooter."

"I totally agree," I told him. "We'll have our chance," I said with a wink.

We spent the next hour talking and sipping wine, then agreed on bedtime. After I finished my bathroom routine, I came out and climbed into bed where Derek was patting the spot next to him. I had on cotton shorts and a tank.

"Cute," he said.

We slid under the covers. He moved over and pressed up against my back with his arm lying softly across my belly. It was so warm and cozy. He felt so good. Moments later we were asleep.

The next morning was Thursday. Derek woke me with a kiss on the cheek. "Good morning, beautiful," he said.

"Mmmm, morning." I mumbled back.

"I'm going to get in the shower, then I was thinking we should go to the hospital, check in with the family, and then I want to do a little mini-investigation around town with the information I have."

"Okay," I said. "I'm going to check my email and Facebook."

When Derek disappeared to the bathroom, I slouched in the chair at the desk. I logged onto my email account finding nothing important there I logged into Facebook. I had a bunch of new friends. I searched for Cory's page. He had some recent activity on it. I friend-requested him. *Boy, he's a real idiot. Maybe logging onto Facebook and getting gas in your car is not a great idea when you're wanted by the law for attempted murder.* I left the page up and walked across the room. Derek had just come out of the bathroom with a towel around his waist.

My blood was flowing again. After I caught my breath, I walked quickly past him with my clothes in my arm. I grabbed my makeup case and didn't come out until I looked fabulous, or at least as good as I got in jeans and a sweatshirt. My hair was its usual look. There wasn't much else I could do there. Derek was sitting at my computer when I came out.

"Come here," he said urgently.

"Cory accepted your friend request," he told me.

"Really? I friend-requested him just before I showered."

"Yeah, and he came up on chat and asked how you knew him. I'm chatting with him now."

I looked over his shoulder and watched their conversation.

Cory: Hey, Katie, how do I know you?

Katie: You don't. I just saw you on a few of my friends' pages as a mutual friend. I thought I'd check you out.

Cory: So you're a student?

Katie: Yup, and a stressed one at that. I have way too many classes. It was a dumb idea. I get home and just want to hang, ya know?

Cory: For sure.

Katie: I need to drop some classes. I'm failing most anyway 'cause I don't get the work done. But I don't care. It's my parents' money, not mine, and there's more where that came from.

Cory: Wow, well maybe you and I should hang out together sometime.

Katie: Sure, sounds great. I heard through the grapevine that you might have something to help with the . . . stress, ya know?

Cory: Yeah, we'll see if I can help. Who gave you my name?

I looked at Derek and he looked disappointed. I think he was hoping for a meet up.

Katie: I don't remember the guy's name off hand. Real cool though! I'd love to meet up with you sometime soon. When are you available?

Suddenly the chat box showed him "offline."

"Damn it!" Derek said slapping the table.

"Okay, we'll give it a day or so. He knows I'm interested and knows I have money. He may come around," I told him. "You did great."

Derek slipped into his jacket and I followed suit. We jumped in Derek's Jeep and drove to McDonald's for a drive-through breakfast and coffee. After that we stopped at the hospital, but Kelly wasn't in her room. She had been taken for more testing. We told Derek's parents and Kendall that we would be back later. We climbed back into the Jeep and looked at the paper that Derek had with addresses on it. He handed it to me, then unclipped the GPS from his dash and handed that to me as well. I was instructed to get us to the three places on the list. The first one was Cory's apartment. It appeared empty. Crime scene tape was still over the door.

The second one was Cory's parent's house. I went up and knocked on the door. An older woman answered. When I asked if she knew where Cory was, she said she hadn't heard from him in years and hoped she never would again. Then, she slammed the door in my face. *Duly noted.*

The third was Cory's brother's apartment. It was an old four-plex on the outskirts of town. And Kyle, Cory's brother, was living in the unit on the left side of the building. There was only on-street parking, and I didn't see Cory's old blue Chevette anywhere. I went up to the door and knocked. A gross, smelly, drugged-out man in his late twenties answered.

He reeked of pot and b.o. He was missing a tooth, two back from the middle, and the rest of his teeth were small and yellowish-brown. His hair was brown and dirty and needed a haircut about four months ago. He was unshaven and shirtless. He had on long blue shorts that looked like they'd seen better days, and that was it. He was large. About six-foot-four and about 280 pounds of fat.

When he swung open the door, his angry face spooked me a bit. I had to remind myself why I was doing this and that Derek had a loaded gun with him and was sitting in the Jeep across the street. I knew that Derek had my back, so I wasn't too worried. Still this guy was creepy.

"What?" he bellowed before the door was even all the way open.

Then he looked me up and down like I was a 2:00 a.m. Taco Bell nacho platter.

"I mean . . . heeeelllo," he said sliding his slimy eyes across my body.

"Hi, I'm looking for Cory. I was told I might find him here. I really need to talk to him," I said, trying to sound desperate, like I needed my next hit.

"He ain't here, but you can come in. I can help you out with anything you need. In fact I insist," he said opening the door wider and reaching for my arm.

I jerked away from his grasp and took a step back.

"No, that's okay. Just tell him that Katie stopped by. When do you think he'll be back?" I asked, hoping he'd tell me that he was staying there.

"Girl, if you come in, we can talk about it. I ain't giving you anything until you give me something first," he said grabbing his crotch. His face was angry again. "Get in here, so we can talk!"

"Thanks, but just tell him that Katie stopped by, okay?" I said and walked away quickly.

"Whatever, bitch!" he yelled and slammed the door shut.

I jumped into the Jeep and Derek drove away. I told him our exact conversation and that I couldn't see whether Cory was in there or not.

"That guy was scary," I told Derek. "His eyes were evil, and I have no doubt he would have hurt me, had I gone in."

"Thank you for doing that. You've been a big help in this. I appreciate it. And remember you can tell me if you aren't comfortable doing anything okay?"

"Okay. I wasn't too scared. I knew you had my back," I said with a weak smile.

We went back to the hospital and spent a couple hours in Kelly's room with the family. Kelly had opened her eyes a little longer and a little wider today. Everyone was so grateful. She tried to say, "Hi," but her voice was really hoarse. We cheered for her efforts and told her not to push herself. The nurse came in and told us she needed to rest for a while, so we left for lunch. We all met at Pizza Hut and decided on the buffet. Derek and I told his parents and Kendall about our meeting this morning with Cory's brother Kyle.

"Be careful around him," Kendall said. "Kelly told me that he scared her the first time she met him, too. Kelly never talked a lot about Cory and what they did together. She closed right up after they met, and she was never home anymore. I do remember her saying that she'd met his brother, though, and that he was scary."

"Did she ever say anything else about him or any other friends that he had?" Derek asked Kendall.

"No. I told you everything I know, which isn't a lot. After she met him she was always gone. That's why I called Mom and told her that we needed to get her away from him. Everyone on campus knows he's into meth. He buys, uses, and sells it. But that's all I know."

"Okay, but if you remember, or hear anything, even the tiniest detail, I want to know about it. Every little bit helps," he said, reaching out and rubbing his sister's back.

We all finished eating and parted ways for the day. Derek told his mom that we probably wouldn't be back to the hospital tonight, but he would be there first thing in the morning. After we got back in the Jeep, I asked Derek what his thoughts were for the rest of the day. He leaned back in his seat, and stared out the window, gently shaking his head.

"I don't know. I really want to go searching for this guy, but I'm crossing a lot of lines and I don't want to get caught by the Morris P.D. I just can't sit here and do nothing though. I'm going to swing by the department quick and see if any new information has come through, then we'll go from there."

He put the Jeep in gear and pulled out of the lot. When we arrived I told him I'd wait in the car. I needed to call my landscaper and reschedule or let him know that I wouldn't be around. Derek went in. I scanned through my contacts until I found the number for C.S. Landscaping.

"Yes, who is this?" The same rushed, Mexican voice from the first time answered.

"Hi, this is Sara Martin calling. I had an appointment to get my yard done. A family emergency came up, and I'm not home. I'll be out of town for a few days, so I need to reschedule," I told him.

"No, no! You don't need reschedule lady. You out of town, not your trees. Ha ha ha! I send my men to clean your yard. You pay me when you get back to town. You pay in cash or credit. Yes?

"Ah . . . okay. Yes."

"Ha, ha. Okay, lady, bye," he said and disconnected.

I was laughing too by the time I hung up the phone. He was funny. I couldn't wait to see what he looked like. I sent a text to Blake to confirm our dinner meeting and told him I'd have to be done by 8:30 p.m. He immediately responded: "Yes, that's fine, looking forward to it." Then I called Kat and told her to pick me up Saturday at Applebee's and I was hers for the evening after 8:30 p.m., but I didn't get a response back from her. Derek jumped back in and seemed annoyed.

"Well, nothing's happening here. It makes me so mad. They got three guys in there talking about the case, but only one officer out there actually looking for Cory." He threw the Jeep into drive and swung a left out of the lot. "I don't know what else to do besides go look for him. My ideas have run out, so we're going to sit outside his brother's apartment."

"That's fine with me, I'll do whatever you want to help out," I said. We drove to the neighborhood and circled the block. Derek parked the Jeep adjacent to the apartment and shut it off. The blinds on the patio door were open and the lights were on inside. The TV was flashing pictures. "I don't see Kyle," I said.

"Me either. Someone's there, though."

"What are you going to do if he shows up?" I asked.

"Sit here and watch him until the cops get here. The most I could do, legally, is a citizen's arrest, but I'd want the force here for back up anyway if he showed up. If he and his brother are on meth, I'm not taking them on alone," he told me while staring out the window.

About two hours later, Derek looked over to me and slapped my leg, waking me up.

"Well, sweetness, this isn't doing it for me. How about we go get some dinner and head back to the hotel and check out the hot tub."

"Yeah, that sounds great," I said wiping my eyes. "Sorry. I didn't mean to fall asleep."

"It's okay. You didn't miss much," he told me with a smile.

We went back to the Holiday Inn to change into nicer clothes and freshen up. Then we went to Chili's and ate some really good Mexican food and drank margaritas. While we were eating, I told Derek about my conversations with the Mexican landscaper. He got a kick out of it. The food was great, but I was a little concerned about my swim suit fitting after the big platter I'd finished.

Back at the hotel we changed into our suits. Derek grabbed the room key and two towels, and we headed to the hot tub. There was an older man and a young couple with a lot of piercings in there already. Other than that, the place was pretty quiet. Derek tossed the towels on the table to the right, where we also dropped our flip flops. Derek stepped in first and slid onto the bench under the water. I stepped down two steps and had to wait a moment and get used to the hot water.

Everyone was looking at me. The older man was smiling sweetly, and the Goth couple were just staring. I looked over to Derek who gave me a come-here head nod. I smiled, and went to take another step towards him, and completely missed the step. I went under with a huge splash. A few seconds later, I found my footing and came up for a breath, trying not to look panicked. I was mortified! I thought I'd make it look like I'd planned it, so I came up with my head back and smoothed my hair out, then I squeezed the water out and fluffed it up quick.

"Awww, feels great," I said to Derek as I sat down.

He looked at me in shock, then smiled a close-lipped smile and looked away. I couldn't see his face but his shoulders were shaking. I looked around the pool and everyone's eyes were huge.

"Nice try, sweetness," Derek said and everyone busted out laughing. I shrugged. "Only you," he said.

It was true. I was an accident waiting to happen. We stayed in there for about an hour, then stopped by the bar for a night cap to bring back to our room. When the drinks were gone, we snuggled into bed and talked about the next day's plans, then fell asleep.

Friday morning I woke up and went with Derek to the hospital. Kelly was sitting up and trying to talk. She was alert and recognized us when we walked in. Derek went up and gave her a big hug. She said hi in a rough voice. Derek introduced us, and she waved a small wave. Derek's parents were both there too.

"This is Sara. She was there that night and saw the whole thing happen. She called 911," his mom said.

I looked at her with sympathetic eyes.

"I heard. Thank you," Kelly said to me, strained.

"No thanks needed. I'm just so glad you're alive and that you're doing so well. You look great today," I told her. She smiled.

Kathy told us that the doctors were going to take the feeding tube out in a little while, and that they said her vitals looked great and if they stayed that way, tomorrow they would start physical therapy. They expected a full recovery, but weren't sure how long it would take until they see what she can do on her own. The numerous wounds from the bullet entry were healing nicely and there was no sign of infection anywhere in her body.

We left around 11:00 a.m., so that Kelly could rest, and went to Perkin's for lunch with Doug and Kathy. Kendall was at work all day so she wasn't there, and Derek's brother and his family weren't coming up until the next day. Doug told us that he was driving back that night to sleep in his own bed for a couple nights because his back was really acting up. Kathy was going to stay a couple more days and then just stop in for visits as Kelly got stronger. They had no idea if it would be days or months. Everyone was kind of in the same boat, and it was a long drive back. At least Kendall was close by so she could stop over daily and keep us posted.

When we were done eating and had said our goodbyes, I drove with Derek back to the Holiday Inn and packed my things. My plan was to go to my apartment, do some cleaning, and then get ready for my meeting with Blake and my night out with Kat. I told Derek goodbye, loaded all my stuff into my Jeep, and drove back to Bloomington. The apartment looked the same as when I'd left it, but it needed fresh air. I went from room to room and opened the windows all the way, then turned the heat up. It was sixty-two outside, and sunny but windy.

I turned the radio on and got out the cleaning supplies. The place wasn't dirty, but things needed to be wiped down and the toilet scrubbed. After I finished with that, I jumped into the shower. As I was toweling off, I heard my phone ringing in the dining room. I wrapped a towel around me and ran and answered it.

"Hello?"

"Hey, girl! It's Tannya. How are ya, love?" she asked.

"I'm good," I said nervously.

"I'm calling 'cause Faith keeps throwing up. Every time she eats, she pukes. It's doesn't bother me none, but I wanted to be sure that I shouldn't be concerned about her health. Does she normally throw up a lot?" she asked.

"Oh, no! No, she's never thrown up. There must be something wrong with her. Is she still playful or does she seem weak?"

"I wouldn't exactly call her playful. She walks around but mostly just wants to lie on my lap and be petted."

"That's not like her at all. I think I need to bring her to the vet to be looked at. Shoot! I'm in the Cities and just getting ready to go to a meeting and out with a friend. Man," I whined, "how am I going to do this?"

"Well, honey, I've got nothing going on for the next two days, including tonight. If you give me a place to stay tonight, I'll bring your cat down to ya," she told me.

"Really? You'd drive all that way?"

"On one condition," she said in a sly tone.

"Anything. You name it."

"You bring me with you on your outing tonight, and buy me one of them fancy drinks in the martini cups."

"Ha, ha, ha. You got it! I will buy you all the drinks you want. You can stay with me here at my apartment and I'll pay for your gas here and back. Thank you so much, Tannya! This means the world to me! I'll call the vet and get an appointment first thing in the morning."

I gave her directions to my apartment and told her I'd leave a key with Jamie, the manager. I told her I'd come pick her up after my business meeting and take her out with me and Kat. She was very excited. *This will be interesting,* I thought as I hung up.

I called an after-hours vet and got a Saturday appointment for Faith. I felt bad for her, and wondered if she was scared and missed me and that's why she was throwing up.

After I finished my hair and makeup, I dressed in a satin, v-neck, sleeveless shirt and strappy, black high heels. I added jewelry and a wide belt to complete the look. I threw my purse over my shoulder and ran out the door. I was running late, so I hoped Blake was too.

12

I heard my phone ring and picked up to Derek's voice. "Hey. Kelly's doing fine. The family's all heading home for the night. I'm going to come back to my apartment for the weekend. There's not much going on here, and I need to show my face at work. What are you doing tonight?" he asked.

"I'm headed to a meeting right now. Then Kat and I are going out."

"A meeting? What kind of meeting?" he asked in his cop voice.

"A monthly meeting with my financial adviser," I said.

"Oh, yeah, I think I remember that from last time. You were three martinis in by the time I saw you back at your apartment."

"Yuppers, that's the one."

Awkward.

"So are you staying out all night?"

"I don't know yet. Tannya is bringing my sick cat to me as we speak, and she's going to join Kat and me, too."

"Tannya?"

"Yeah Tannya from Morning Glory. She's the frumpy waitress I told you about from Nisswa. Remember I told that she was cat sitting? Faith has been throwing up so she's bringing her to me so I can get to my meeting. She's going to stay overnight here and wants to come out with us and learn about martinis the hard way. I have an appointment for Faith in the morning," I told him. *He sure is full of questions tonight.* "You could meet up with us later if you want," I offered.

"Mmmm tempting, but no. I'll just wait to hear how that goes down. I'm looking forward to my own bed and a good night's sleep before work in the morning. But, hey, why don't you give me a call sometime tomorrow and maybe we can get together for dinner or something."

"Yeah, sure. Sounds good. I'll do that. Talk to you tomorrow. Drive safe."

"You too. And stay out of trouble," he said and disconnected.

I pulled into the Applebee's lot fifteen minutes late and hoped that Blake hadn't been waiting long. I would have called him, but I'd had Derek on the phone. I threw the Jeep into park and quickly walked in. There was a huge crowd in the doorway which was typical for a Friday night. I looked at the bar and didn't see Blake anywhere so I walked up to the hostess and gave her my name. I told her that I was meeting someone.

"Oh, yes. You must be Sara. Mr. Conner is waiting for you. Right this way," she said and led me to him.

He was already seated at a booth in the back. He was on his phone when I walked up. I thanked the waitress and ordered a Vodka Collins. I could see that Blake already had a tall beer at the table. He looked up and smiled and gave me an "I'm sorry I'm stuck on the phone" face with a finger point at the phone by his ear. I waved my hand at him. *No big deal.*

A few moments later he disconnected and set his phone aside. "Sara Martin, you look amazing as always," he said and took a drink of his beer.

"Thanks, so do you," I said, noticing that he was in jeans and a button down shirt that had a thin pinstripe and a design on it. It was casual, but sexy at the same time. "Work just never ends, eh?"

"You got that right! Can I get you a drink?" he asked.

"I got one coming already."

We spent the next thirty minutes going over the details of my account, which was already making some nice returns. I learned how to read a monthly statement and what all the abbreviations meant. After looking at the account and discussing the market we decided not to change anything. We ordered dinner and made small talk while we waited. Conversation was easy with him. I'd mentioned that I'd seen him at church. He said that his sister had joined a couple months ago and was always trying to get him to go. He said he wanted to get involved but didn't have the time.

When our food arrived, Blake asked the waitress for another round. After we ate, and the waitress took our plates, he ordered after-dinner drinks for us. Brandy Alexanders. *Oh, my gosh! Where have these been all my life?* It was the first of many Brandy Alexanders. A few stories and a lot of giggles later, my phone rang. That's when I realized it was almost 9:00. It was Kat.

"I'm so sorry," Kat said. "I had to wait for my stupid landlord to make a repair on my oven. Anyway, I'm almost there. I'll pick you up at the door in ten minutes."

"Okay, I'll be there," I said and disconnected. "I'm sorry," I said to Blake. "I lost track of time. I'm supposed to go out with a couple friends tonight. That was one of them. She's picking me up here in ten minutes." I took one last gulp of my drink. "Thank you so much for dinner," I laughed.

I'd had a great time. We both were feeling it, and everything seemed funny for some reason.

"So you're dumping me again . . . on a Friday night," he said with a pouty lip. "I was kind of hoping I didn't have to be home alone at 10:00 p.m. tonight. It *is* a Friday after all."

"Well, I suppose you could come with," I said with a smile. "We're heading to Flash, so you better be able to dance."

"Oh, I can dance!" he said with a smirk. "You're in for a treat tonight!"

I busted out laughing. The waitress came and took the payment folder and said goodnight. I told him to follow me.

I sent Kat a text: *Minor change in plans.*

She replied: *At the front door.*

Blake followed me to the car. Kat currently drove a 2010 tuxedo black Dodge Charger, but that changed as often as her hair color. I called shotgun and giggled as we walked up to the car. Blake giggled, too, and said something about fairness. I pulled open the passenger door and poked my head in. "Kat, this is Blake. Blake, my BFF, Kat."

They exchanged salutations as I climbed in the front. Blake plopped down in back. Kat looked at him and raised her eyebrows in approval.

"Blake and I had a meeting and kind of lost track of time, and count of our drinks," I said with a giggle.

"It's all her fault," Blake said to Kat pointing at me.

"Yeah she's fun like that," Kat told him. "So . . . are we bringing him home or taking him out?" she asked me as my phone rang. I put up a finger and dug through my purse.

"Hello?"

"Hey, girl, it's Tannya. Faith and I are at your apartment. Nice place by the way."

"Aww, thanks. How's Faith?"

"She only threw up twice today. She's curled up on the pillow on your bed right now," she told me.

"That's her favorite spot! Well, get yourself ready. We'll be there in ten minutes to pick you up for a martini to remember!" I said with a laugh. "Lock up behind you and meet us downstairs."

"Sure thing," she said and disconnected.

"Okay, another minor change in plans. We have to swing by my apartment and pick up Tannya, my northwoods sidekick. This one's in her mid to late-twenties and never been to a big city, *and* never had a martini," I said biting on my lip.

Kat put the car in gear and started towards my place.

"Oh, boy," Kat said.

I heard some giggling come from the back seat. I turned around and Blake's shoulders were shaking and he was waving his hand like "never mind." I started laughing too because he looked funny trying hard to control his laughter. My head was slightly spinning, so I was sure his was too.

"This is the one from the diner?" Kat asked.

"Yup. Hopefully she wears something besides her work shirt," I said.

"You ladies are a hoot! You should take her out and treat her like she's twenty-one. If she doesn't know a martini, there's lots she doesn't know," Blake said excitedly.

"Where do you live, Blake?" Kat inquired.

"Forest Lake."

"Ha! Well, then you're in luck," Kat said. "It's after nine already. The bars close at 2:00 a.m. I don't have time to run you home, so it looks like you're coming with us!"

"Oh, boy," I said.

"Saaaweeet," Blake said, his head nodding.

His professional look was gone. I giggled again.

We arrived at the front doors of my apartment and out came Tannya. She was dressed in what looked like yellow skinny jeans, although I wasn't convinced they were, and a small, gold, sequin tank that tightly embraced her belly rolls, and calf-high black heeled boots that were challenging her walking skills. I exited the car and waved.

"Hey, Tannya, hop on in," I said.

She smiled. When she got a couple steps closer, I noticed her bright gold eyelids, neon pink lipstick, and huge gold shoulder bag, with huge gold earrings to boot. She was a sight! I tried to contain my laughter.

"Thanks so much for bringing Faith back to me. That really helped me out."

"Girl, you have no idea how long I have wanted to wear this shirt out. I ordered it online one night after a few drinks on a one-person-stay-at-home pity party and haven't gotten the chance to wear it yet. I'm so excited to see what this is about! I watch movies about girls going out and drinking martinis in the big cities, and well, it's always been a dream of mine," she said with a huge smile as she approached the car.

Blake had slid over and opened the door behind my seat for her.

"Hey, ya'll!" she said leaning into the car and waving at Blake and Kat.

She picked one foot up to step into the car and THUMP-UFF! She went down like an elephant on roller skates! Her other leg kicked out from under her, and she fell straight back, one leg in the air and one hand still on the door. I quickly maneuvered over to her and tried to help her up. She looked like a turtle on its back, wriggling and wriggling but not getting anywhere. Then, she kind of leaned to one side, and built up momentum, rolled to her other side, and on to all fours. From there she was able to stand.

"Are you okay?" I asked sincerely, but holding back laughter.

"Ohhhhh, aaaahhh," she moaned while she climbed up to her feet. "Goodness me! I can't believe I just did that! How embarrassing! I'm fine," she said looking down at her pants. "Am I dirty?"

"Nah, nothing to worry about," I said.

She had dirt stains on both her knees from rolling over on them when she was trying to stand. She also had dirt on her back and a few sequins had popped off. But she didn't need to know that.

"We're going to a club. It'll be dark. No one will notice anything in there, especially on the dance floor with all the lights spinning," I lied.

I didn't want to wait for her to change or see what else she might come up with to wear.

"Are you sure you're okay?" Blake asked, leaning toward the open car door from his seat.

"Yes I'm totally fine," she said brushing off what dirt she could.

"That's go-oo-oood," he said and then completely lost it.

As he was laughing really hard, Kat and I started laughing too. Blake and Kat went on and on . . . gasping for air, snorting, the whole shebang! Then, finally settling down a few moments later, both of them were drying tears. Tannya stepped into the car, but this time actually made it.

Kat put the car in drive and we sped away. I made introductions on the way to the club. We arrived at Flash at 10:00 p.m. It was filling up with the usual Saturday crowd. There were lots of twenty-something's at the bar doing shots, a few ugly, single men sipping drinks and scanning the crowd, and a handful of various others. Being it was me, my single forever-young friend Kat, Blake-the hottie—clean cut, sharp dressed business man—and Tannya—dirty knees McSmall Town—we fell into the "other" category. So, it was no surprise that when we walked through that door, people looked our way. I headed straight to the bar with Kat in tow and bought the first round of martinis for everyone.

Tannya watched in amazement while the bartender shook, not stirred, and poured them in the glasses with much flair! He was pretty good, I'll admit, so I left him a nice tip. Tannya was in awe watching him.

"A toast," I started, as we each reached for a glass, "To my new friend, Blake, who's going to be a great financial partner, and to my other new friend, Tannya, who's out in the big city and drinkin' her first martini!"

After a few "Woo hoo's," we clinked glasses and took sips. Kat, Blake, and I, all had our eyes on Tannya. She took a drink, and I mean drink! Her eyes opened as wide as they could and she spit it out full force all over the older guy sitting right next to me. The whole right side of his face got wet, as well as his shirt. I got a misting but that was all.

"Holy Mother!" she screeched. She grabbed a bar towel from the counter and gave it to the guy. "Oh, geeze, sir, I'm so sorry! That was an accident. Here let me help you," she said grabbing a few drink napkins and dabbing his face.

Kat and Blake were doubled over in laughter. I stood in shock expecting a bar fight, but he remained seated and uncommonly calm.

"Good grief woman, don't you know you're supposed to sip martini's?" he said in a mean tone.

"No, sir. That was my first one. I . . . I . . . I'm not from around here. I'm so sorry. I'm so embarrassed. I didn't mean to."

He grumbled as he dried himself up.

"Please, let me buy you a drink. What were you drinking?" she asked looking at his empty glass.

He turned on his bar stool to face her and looked her up and down, stopping for a moment at her dirt-stained knees. He squinted his eyes and the corners of his mouth curled a bit. His face changed, and so did his tone.

"Well, all right," he said slyly. "You can buy me a drink, and I'll accept your apology . . . on two conditions."

13

"Yeah! Sure! What are the conditions?" she asked with a smile.

I don't think she has any idea what she's getting herself into.

"One, you have a drink with me, and two, I get a dance later to the song of my choice," he said with confidence.

He was sitting, so it was hard to tell how tall he was, but he was at least fifty-five years old and as round as a beach ball. He was clean cut and nicely dressed, *and he didn't come up swinging when he got spit on, so how bad could he be?* I cut a glance at Kat and Blake. They were both still trying to compose themselves.

"You got it. Now what are you drinking?" Tannya asked him.

"We," he said, "are having a brandy coke. It's much smoother than that martini you just tried." She ordered two and pulled herself up on the stool next to him. "So what's your name, pretty lady?" he asked.

"Tannya," she said and put her hand out. He took her hand and shook it.

"I'm Greg. Nice to meet you."

We took that as our cue to give them a little space. We went across the room and got a stand-up table near the dance floor. Tannya peeked over her shoulder and spotted us. We all raised our glasses, and she smiled big and gave us a thumbs-up. The DJ was on the stage getting set up. I felt my purse vibrate, and heard my ring tone. It was Derek. I excused myself and took the call in a quiet corner.

"Hey!" I answered.

"Hey you," he said with a sigh. "What are you doing?"

"Well I had that meeting, and then Kat picked up me and Tannya and Blake, and now we're at Flash. We'll be here the rest of the night. Why? What are you doing? Wanna join us?"

"Who's Blake?"

"He's my financial adviser, remember?"

Awkward. The line was quiet.

"Hello?" I finally said.

"Yeah, no, I think you've got more than enough company, so I'll pass. Have a good night. I'll talk to ya later," he said and disconnected abruptly.

Well, geez, someone's cranky. I went back over to the table and chatted with Blake and Kat who were getting to know each other.

"So, do you have a girlfriend?" she blurted out.

I almost choked on my drink. Leave it to Kat to get straight to the point.

"No, I don't," he said, then looked at me and smiled.

Oh, crap! I hope that smile meant he was interested in Kat and not me. The music started, and I heard a long scream from across the room. I whipped my head around. It was Tannya! She was off her stool and headed in our direction.

"Yes! I love this song!"

She grabbed my arm and pulled me to the dance floor, which was fine with me. I reached out and grabbed Kat on the way, who reached out and grabbed Blake. We were the only people on the floor. The song was "Last Friday Night" by Katie Perry, and Tannya knew all the words. *Her drink could not have kicked in already! She must just be very excited to dance.*

"This is so cool. I can't believe I'm here! And I met a great guy already! This is going to be a great night," she screamed in my ear.

"Glad you're having fun," I yelled back at her.

We stayed out there and danced a few more songs, and then when the music changed to a slower song, Greg came shuffling out with his and Tannya's drinks in hand. She took hers and thanked him, then he took her hand, turned her around, and pulled her in close. She didn't seem to mind. The three of us headed to the bar. We slowed down the pace by switching to beer. After the bartender brought me my change we walked back over to the stand-up table.

Kat asked Blake what he did for fun, and if he was looking to meet anyone. I listened and watched the conversation, and hoped that those two would hit it off. He was so hot, but I liked Derek. Not Blake. I mean Blake was nice, and handsome, and successful, and easy to talk to, and fun to hang out with, and smelled so good . . . but, I liked Derek. *Yup.*

"Sara? SARA?"

I heard my name but found myself staring at Blake while I was thinking and not at all paying attention to what they were talking about.

"Huh?" I asked snapping back to attention.

"I said," Kat said, "that you were one tough cookie and have been through a lot lately, but are the strongest I've ever seen you. Does Blake know about your interesting past?"

I shot Kat a warning look and then turned to Blake. "Yeeees, I told him about my divorce and my land purchase. I left out all the boring details, but, yes, he's up to date."

"Okay," Kat said with raised eyebrows and took a drink.

"So are you a baseball fan?" Kat asked Blake. "I love baseball," she said as she leaned over the table towards him.

Oh, the flirt was working the area now. I excused myself to go to the bathroom and gave them some space. I took my time, secretly wishing Derek was there with me. Maybe I should call him or maybe not. I was pretty tipsy. I checked my phone. It was almost midnight and I had a facebook message. I looked at the message. It was from Cory:

I got what you need. My brother said it was urgent. Come over and get it, text me first to make sure I'm here. Come alone and don't give out my name. Bring cash.

Oh geez, here I am on a Friday night, drunk, and we finally get a break on Cory. My heart was beating fast, which caused the room to spin a bit. I exited the bathroom and walked out the side door to call Derek. It was just as busy and loud outside because all the smokers were pressed up against the walls by the entry getting their fix. I walked to the other side of the crowd and dialed.

"Yeah," he answered sounding upset.

"Hey, it's me," I said trying not to slur. The seriousness of the situation and the cold night air was helping with the effects of the alcohol. "I got a facebook message from Cory," I told him.

"What? What'd it say?" His voice had become more alert and the TV noise in the background disappeared. I told him word for word what it said.

"Do you think I should respond?" I asked.

"Ummmm, not yet. Let me think," he said with a sigh. "Geez, this guy is dumb. Why would he post his whereabouts to a stranger on Facebook when he knows damn well that the police are looking for him? I want to get the MPD involved and ready for a sting since we know he's going to be at his brother's. Crap! It's like midnight! By the time we get there it's going to be after 2:00 a.m. He'll probably be asleep. And I don't trust the MPD. They've screwed this case up from the beginning."

"I could respond and say that I'm in for the night, but that I could come tomorrow," I suggested.

"Yeah, you could. Why don't you do that and see what he says. I don't want to frustrate him or lose him, but if we can find out when he'll be home that'd be huge. Where are you? I think I should come and pick you up and stick with you for the night. Maybe we can head up there now and be on our way if he says it has to happen tonight," he was in detective mode again.

"I'm still at Flash, but that's fine—you can come pick me up. I'll have to stop at home and pick up some clothes," I said thinking about Faith's appointment in the morning. "Do you want me to respond now or wait for you to get here?"

"Go ahead and respond. Let me know if he gets back to you before I get there," Derek requested and then disconnected.

Logged back into Facebook and responded: *"Hey! That's great news! But I'm down and out for the night. Can I catch ya tomorrow? When's good for you?"*

I went back into the club. I noticed that Tannya was still dancing with Greg. They looked like they were having fun, but neither knew how to dance. It was entertaining. They did actually look cute together despite the age difference. I swung by the bar and ordered two large waters. When they came I slammed one and left the glass on the bar. The other I took with me over to the high-top table where Kat and Blake were still talking.

"I just got a call. I have to leave. It's kind of a family emergency, but not really an emergency. I don't want you guys to worry but I have to go out of town for a day or two to help clear something up. So I'm sorry, but I'm going to have to cut out early tonight."

Just then Tannya swaggered up to the table.

"Hey, yah!" she said, and set her drink down on the table.

She reached back to feel for the bar stool behind her. As she touched it she moved to sit, but misjudged the height of the chair and completely missed. She ended up on her ass on the floor! It was a hard thump. Kat and Blake immediately started laughing. I gasped and asked if she was okay, trying not to laugh myself. She jumped up as fast as she could and said, "Yes," and looked toward Greg's directon across the room. He hadn't noticed. She was red-faced and relieved.

"Yes, yes I'm fine," she said. "What the heck is my problem today anyhow? Must be these stupid boots. I bet the heel is loose on one of them! Dang boots!" she said.

"Tannya, I was just telling these two that I have to go out of town for a minor family emergency. It's nothing to worry about, but I have to leave soon. My ride'll be here in a little bit."

My phone beeped. The text was Derek saying he was going to jump in the shower first and pack then he'd come get me. I responded okay.

"What's going on?" Kat demanded.

All three of them were staring at me. Knowing them like I did, I knew that I was not getting out of there without an explanation. So, I spent the next ten minutes telling them everything about Derek's sister and Cory, all the way up to the message I'd just sent to him.

"You'd better be careful," Kat said. "Meth heads may be stupid when they're high, but they're just as crazy in between hits, especially if they need money. Don't mess around with him."

"Cory and his brother both sound scary," Blake said. "I wouldn't get involved."

"I'll be careful, plus Derek has my back," I said.

"Who's Derek?" Blake asked.

"He's the detective in charge of the case. I'm helping him out, as a friend."

"Ha!" Kat said. "Is that what we're calling him now?" she smiled and took a drink.

I ignored her and turned to Tannya. "Do you have to leave right away tomorrow?"

"No. I don't have to work until Monday morning. Why?" she asked.

"I was hoping you'd still stay overnight at my apartment and bring Faith in for her appointment tomorrow," I said hopefully.

"Oh, sure! No problem. I can stay with her as long as you like. And if she needs to come back with me on Monday that's fine too. Whatever you need. It's no big thing," she quickly replied.

"Thank you so much. That means the world to me. And, Kat, if you need to stay at my place tonight you can too."

"Okay, we'll see how the night goes," she said with a wink.

I looked down at my phone again. There was a new Facebook message from Cory: *Tomorrow, 7:00 p.m. At my brother's. You know where he lives apparently. I know things too . . . I know I like that shirt on you. The color is great!*

What the fuck?! My eyes about popped out of my head. *Is he here? Oh, my god!* My heart was pumping blood so fast that I could hear my heart beat in my ears. I tried not to over react. *He's bluffing. He's playing with me. I don't know what to do. Why is he doing this? Is he mad that I found his brother? Does he seriously know what I look like?* My mind was spinning a hundred and thirty-five miles an hour. *Did he follow me? Does he know I'm with Derek? That I'm helping Derek? What the hell does he want? No. No. He's just playing with me. What if he's not? What if he knows what I look like and that I made a fake Facebook page.* I couldn't stop my mind from racing!

"Hey who's the message from?" Blake asked with wrinkled eyebrows.

"Um, no one. I . . . ah . . . I . . . I got to take this. Excuse me for a second," I said to everyone at the table.

I walked around the corner of the bathroom wall to block out the noise to try to figure out what I should do. I couldn't decide if I should respond or call Derek or ignore it. My eyes darted around the filled room, unsure if I'd even recognize him. I knew his size and shape but never really got a good look at his face. He could have dyed and cut his hair too. *Shit!* I was scared. As I was rereading the message Blake walked up to me.

"Hey, so you're leaving us for the night?" he asked with a smile, leaning his arm on the wall.

"Um, yeah," I said, trying to regain my composure and act normal. "You'll be in good hands though. You guys'll have a blast and close the place down I'm sure."

"Yeah, well I'd prefer to close the place down with you," he said.

Then he took my face in his hands and kissed me. It was a firm, passionate kiss. It put me into shock. I didn't see it coming. My eyes were wide open and I was stiff, but it felt really good. And dang-it he smelled good. I had to admit I liked it. I relaxed after a moment and kissed him back. A few moments later he pulled back.

"I want you to stay here with me," he said. "I don't want you to spend any more time with that Derek guy."

I closed my mouth when I realized it was still hanging open and swallowed hard. "Umm, I, I, I . . ." *Holy crap. I'm never drinking again! What is going on? Hot cop is on his way, hot investment man is kissing me and crazy meth head is stocking me.*

"I can't do this," I finally managed. "I'm seeing someone . . . I think. And I . . . I got a lot going on right now."

I stumbled over my words while staring at his soft lips.

"I'm sorry. That wasn't fair of me to do that. I shouldn't have done it. I'm sorry. I just wanted you to know how I feel," he said apologetically. "It's the drinks. I guess they made me braver than I normally am.

I really don't want you to leave. I hate when you have to leave. But that was really unfair. I'm sorry."

He was rambling and embarrassed.

"It's okay. I like you too . . . It's just that I . . ."

"You got a lot going on right now. I heard," Blake said with a wink. "Forget it. I'm sorry. I was in the wrong, please forgive me . . . and excuse me," he said and gently rubbed past me to the men's room.

I stood there for a moment in shock before finally replying to Cory: *What? What shirt? You're funny! See you tomorrow at 7pm.*

As I walked back to the table I took a few deep breaths. Kat and Tannya were still standing there talking.

"Hey, girl! Where did you and Blake disappear to?" Tannya asked.

"Nowhere, I was taking a call and he went to the bathroom."

"And you smeared your lipstick how?" Kat slyly asked. I instinctively wiped my lip. And Kat burst out laughing. "Seriously! How do you do it? You got Blake and Derek and there was a guy at the bar asking about you too. I have been all over Blake tonight and he can't look past you for a second."

"I'm not interested in a relationship with him. You go for it, Kat!" I told her.

Blake walked back up to the table and smiled at everyone. "I got the next round," he announced and walked away.

"None for me!" I said to his back.

We all stood there watching the dancers on the dance floor until Blake returned with bottled beer for everyone and another water for me. Tannya and Kat walked off arm in arm to the dance floor. After they were out of ear shot Blake slid over next to me, touching his shoulder to mine.

"Again, I'm sorry. I was way out of line. I shouldn't have done that, I hope it doesn't ruin our friendship or our business relationship. I feel awful. I just . . . I just couldn't help myself anymore. I know now it was too soon," he said.

I could tell he felt awful, his eyes and face were so hurt.

I smiled gently, "It's o . . ."

"Sorry for what?" came a voice from behind.

I turned around to see a straight-faced Derek.

"Geez, Derek! You scared me!" I said taking a deep breath. "Hiiiii!" I said with a forced smile. "Derek, this is Blake O'Connor. Blake this is Derek Richards." I wondered how much of the conversation he had heard. "Blake's my financial adviser."

They shook hands. From the look of it, Derek's grip was nice and firm. Neither said anything but both nodded.

"You ready to go?" Derek asked, as he kissed me on the cheek.

I was sure it was more for Blake than for me.

"Actually, I need to talk to you about something. Blake will you excuse us?" I said taking Derek's arm and walking toward the bathroom with him in tow.

I paged to the text and handed him my phone. He read it and looked at me shocked.

"Is there anything else besides these three texts?" he demanded.

"No, and I scanned the room a little, but I don't know if I could pick him out of a line up? Do you think he's here?" I asked. "Do you think he knows who I am?"

"I don't know, but I want you to go back over to your table and stay close to your friends. But not too close," he said in a mean tone. "I'm going to go talk to security, and take a look around. Stay here."

"Okay," I said and walked back to the table where Blake was still standing.

"Hope I didn't get you into trouble," he said.

"Oh, please. Derek's a really nice guy. He's just got a lot of work stress right now," I told him.

I watched as Derek went over to a bouncer at the back door and started talking to him. I saw him flash his badge from his hip and the bouncer straightened up and listened intently. I glanced back when I heard Tannya laugh from the dance floor. Greg, it seemed, was off his stool and back out there dancing and Kat was talking with a young guy.

I told Blake I'd be right back and went to the bathroom. There were two very drunk girls wobbling around by the mirror trying to touch up their makeup. I went into a stall and sat down. It took a while. I'd drunk a lot of water. It seemed to be working too. My buzz was wearing off. I heard the door open and close, and the girls giggled and walked out. All was quiet. I pulled up my jeans, fastened my belt, then took my phone from my purse and stuffed it into my pocket to make sure that if it rang or buzzed I'd feel it. I flushed, threw my purse over my shoulder, and exited the stall as the entire room went dark. I'd heard the switch flick, so I knew someone did it. I froze. *Shit!*

"Hello! Turn the light back on. Someone's in here!" I called out.

Nothing.

I quickly felt around in the dark for the stall door. At least I could lock myself back inside there. I pushed the door open, stepped in fast and pushed the door shut. But something blocked it. I pushed harder but it wouldn't close. I was struggling. Someone was trying to open it as I was trying to shut it. I could smell whoever the person was. They stank like they needed a shower. *This isn't good!*

"HELP! HEEEEELP!" I screamed, hoping someone would hear me.

I knew that was almost impossible because the walls were vibrating from the music in the other room. No one would hear me.

14

If I can just reach my phone! With one hand on the door and my shoulder pushed up against it, I grabbed it out. It lit up. I managed to hit a button or two, but I was being banged around so bad that I couldn't make out anything on the screen. And I couldn't hold still enough to touch the right buttons.

"Help me!" I screamed again, out of sheer terror.

What if it's Cory? What if he's high? He's crazy! He shot his girlfriend. He won't think twice about shooting me. I pushed as hard as I could on the door, and it finally shut. I quickly felt around for the lock and turned it. It seemed too easy, like the person gave up and let me shut the door. I heard shuffling outside the door.

"What do you want?" I asked with a shaky voice.

No response.

My heart was knocking hard on my ribs. I tried to take a deep breath and slow it. I listened at the door. I put my ear right against it and tried to breathe quietly so I could hear. It was quiet, but I sensed a presence. I turned to my phone again and it lit up. When I pressed the green phone button it beeped. BANG! The door burst open, hitting me in the head.

It was dark. Really dark. I'd always hated and been afraid of the dark! It took me a second to realize that my eyes were open. It was so dark. It was noisy and bumpy. That's when I figured out that I was no longer in the bathroom of the Flash, but in the trunk of a car. I did my best not to panic. I wanted to scream and kick, but I knew it would only waste energy. I tried to feel around for an emergency pull to open the door, but from the sound of the motor, and the smell of the interior, I knew it was an older vehicle and probably didn't have one. I felt around to see if there was anything else in the trunk with me—another body, a tire iron, my phone. I couldn't find anything.

I wondered how long I'd been out, and if anyone had seen me carried out of the club or knew what trunk I was in. I started crying. It felt hopeless, and by the speed of the car I didn't think the driver was trying to outrun anyone, which probably meant that no one was following him. It was cold in the trunk. *What if it's Cory? What if we're going back to his brother's?* That was more than a three-hour drive. I was terrified. *Who will take care of Faith? She needs me. She needs to go to the vet in the morning! Will Tannya remember that?*

I cried some more, this time more for Faith and less for me. She wouldn't understand where I'd gone. She'd always wonder what had happened to me. *My parents don't like pets. Will they send her to the pound? Oh, God, I have to survive this! This isn't fair! I'm tired of people trying to ruin my life!* I was pissed. I promised myself that whoever took me would be sorry when they opened that trunk. *They got the wrong girl on the wrong day! You don't mess with Sara Martin. Not after the shit she's been through.*

I prayed hard. It had been a couple of busy weeks and I hadn't been to church, but I was pretty sure God would understand. I asked him for safety and protection from the evil people who had me, and I asked him for someone to find me. *Where's Derek? Does he know I'm missing yet? Is this a blue Chevy Chevette I'm in? God help me!*

The ride seemed to last forever. The adrenaline had taken over the alcohol, so I least I could function and think straight. I was moving emotionally from scared, to pissed, to scared, and was trying to decide if I should jump out of the trunk and make a run for it, or if I should stay calm and try to escape later, when I knew where I was and which way I should run.

Ahhh! It was hard to know. I just knew that my mom always said, "If someone ever tries to take you, scratch and bite and scream and yell for help. Try with everything you have to get away, because if you don't get away fast you may never get away." *Yup, I'm gonna make a run for it as soon as I have the chance! That's better than spending any time with Cory and his creepy brother. If both of them were on meth, they could be capable of doing anything to me.* I was afraid of what they might be planning to do with me and didn't want to hang around to find out.

The car was slowing. We made a turn, and then it got really bumpy. *Gravel road.* I was trying to think of where there was a gravel road anywhere. The problem was I didn't know how long we'd been driving. I was unconscious for part of the trip. I had no way to know our speed either. *Gravel isn't good. It's far away from main roads and the city.* There were three more turns, and then the car shut off.

I could hear voices, at least two. I heard two of the car doors slam shut. *Crap. Two against one. This is no good.* My heart rate was up again in anticipation of the trunk opening. I tried to maneuver my body to get ready for a quick escape. I heard mumbling but couldn't make out what they were saying. I knew it was two men for sure though.

I heard a key go into the trunk lock. *CLINK!* The latch released and up went the lid. I looked up to two men. One was Cory's slimy brother Kyle, and the other had to be Cory. Same size and shape, and he hadn't cut or dyed his hair. He looked just like he did in the gas station video, but this time I could see his face. He was nice looking, unlike his brother. His eyebrows were nicely shaped and his skin was clear and clean shaven. He was dressed nicely, too. *He must have cleaned up to get into the club.* Kyle on the other hand was not. He looked as gross as he did last time, and I could smell him from where I lay in the trunk. It was the same smell from the bathroom.

We were far from the city. It was dark, but there must have been a light on nearby. I could see, but not very far. The area behind the men looked heavily wooded. The trees had lost the majority of their leaves but it was still looked like a really thick forest. I didn't notice a house or anything, but still being in the trunk I could only see in the direction I was facing.

The thing I did notice was the pistols pointed in my face. *There goes the run-for-it idea.* I was afraid, but severely pissed off too! Part of me wanted to attack them, the other, the smart part, wanted not to get shot.

"Well, hello, bitch! How was your nap?" Cory asked, in a snide voice. "Did you like riding in my trunk?"

"Cory, I presume." I said with a bitchy tone.

"You got it. Nice to finally meet you, Katie Johnson. Or should I say . . . Sara?"

Then I was really freaked out. *How does he know my name? This guy is smarter than I thought. He'd done some homework.*

"You can call me Katie," I told him with my pissed-off voice.

I looked to Kyle who was undressing me with his snakelike eyes while pointing a gun at me.

"I guess you already know my brother," he said, turning to Kyle.

"Yeah, you remember me, right? I'm the better looking one, unlike this guy," he said half joking.

As he spoke he pointed the gun at Cory in gesture.

"Fuck! You idiot! Don't point that thing at me!" Cory said and smacked Kyle on the back of the head.

"Heeey, asshole!" Kyle whined, rubbing his head. "That hurt! It's not even loaded!"

Hearing that, I jumped out as fast as I could and ran down what looked like a dirt driveway. I ran like I've never ran before, praying to God that the gun really wasn't loaded and that I wouldn't fall over in the heels I was wearing.

"Hey!" I heard Cory yell. "Stop!"

"Bitch, I will shoot you! You better stop!"

From the sound of their voices, and the rustling I heard, they were in pursuit. I veered left into the woods hoping to lose them, turning my fear to what might find me in there. There were animals roaming around in the woods at night. *And spiders.*

"You're an idiot, Kyle! You just told her the gun wasn't loaded! She's not going to stop, and I ain't chasing her! You're on your own. You go get her."

Cory was yelling, so I assumed that he wasn't running, but that Kyle was. I doubted he was in shape, but if he was high on meth or adrenaline that didn't matter! I was trying to concentrate on breathing and not crying. I knew from experience that I couldn't panic and cry at the same time. I'd run now and cry later. I was going as fast as I could but the woods were thick and the undergrowth was even thicker and caught on my clothes, what little I had on. My arms and the tops of my feet were bare and scratched to heck from all the branches. I was dodging trees branches and stepping on leaves and mud and sticks.

The farther I got, which wasn't very far, the darker it got. I could hardly see my hand in front of my face. Fear and logic took turns controlling my thoughts. *I'm going to freeze to death out here. I won't be able to get very far in heels, a thin, sleeveless shirt, and jeans.* The lows had been in the thirties lately. And it was about that now. The voice of an old friend, who went to school for real estate, was sounding in my head: "You're never more than seven miles from a Walmart." *But can I even make it seven miles?*

I stopped and turned around for the first time to look behind me. I couldn't see Kyle. I couldn't hear anything behind me either. I could see tiny bits of light through the trees but was unable to tell if there it was a house or cabin or any other structure. There was a driveway so I assumed that there was *something* there, a house or a shed at least.

I had no idea which way to go. The moon was obviously hidden by clouds because I couldn't see anything. I was frantically waving my hands in front of my face to feel for branches as I slowly moved forward. I stopped when I heard a car engine turn over. I could hear Cory and Kyle arguing and yelling in the distance, but between my loud heart beat and my quickened breathing I couldn't make out what they were saying.

Then the car engine revved and the headlights lit up the area I was in. I turned to see Cory about forty yards behind me coming my way. I started running again and now that I could see a little better I could pick up the pace. The branches were easier to see but the ground was really unstable. I kicked a small fallen tree and tripped. With my face down on the ground I tried to get my shoe back on when I heard Cory.

"Bitch, the more you make me run, the sorrier you're gonna be!"

I scrambled to my feet again. Cory was right on me. *Shit, he caught up fast!* I stumbled along as fast as I could. SMACK! A stick hit me on the back. I went down hard. It knocked the wind out of me. I was coughing and gasping and trying to get back up.

"Stay down! Fuck, I need to catch my breath. I hate running! Now you've pissed me off. You think you're in charge here? You're not!" Cory yelled at me while he bent over, panting.

I used the time to get in a few breaths myself. *Shit, now what?* A few moments past and he stood up straight and ordered me to my feet. I stood up and made sure my shoes were on good.

"What do you want with me, Cory?" I asked.

"What do you want with me, Sara?" he yelled back in my face. "You're the one following me around. You're the one trying to get in my business."

"Why do you keep calling me Sara? I'm Katie. Someone at school told me I could get some meth from you. That's all. I needed some. I was all out, and I'm new in town, and school is adding a lot of stress to my life. I was going to pay you cash! And I would never tell anyone!"

"Cut the shit! I know that your name is Sara, and I know that you're dating the cop," he said. "You must really think I'm stupid!"

I did up until a minute ago. Now I didn't. He'd figured it out. How he did, I didn't know. Unless he'd been following me, I didn't know how he would have put two and two together.

"Ya know, my brother might look stupid but he's very resourceful. It's amazing what you can learn when someone comes knocking on your door. I went out the back window and walked a half block away. I saw you talk to Kyle and then get into a black Jeep. The Internet is wonderful for searching things like a plate number. A few hours of following you and your friend Derek and a couple Internet searches and you can learn a lot about a person. I knew you and Derek were planning to come and get me. I just beat you to it. Ha ha ha ha," he laughed. "Your friend at the bar was helpful too, when I asked her your name. That's when I knew I had you for sure."

"So what do you want?" I asked. "I'm no good to you. Why kidnap me?"

"'Cause with you out of the picture, Derek won't know where to look and he'll be too busy looking for you to be looking for me. Now get moving! We're going back to the cabin."

I started toward the light with Cory right behind me.

"Whose cabin?" I asked trying to collect some useful information.

"Mine. Well at least it's mine now." He laughed again.

"So you own it?" I asked.

"Not exactly, but that's not your business either. Walk faster!"

"What's your plan, Cory? You gonna kill me, or hold me hostage for ransom, or what? What exactly do you need me for?" I pressed.

"My brother likes you. He's been on my back for money I owe him and I don't have the money. You're in my business and pissing me off, so if I give you to him I'll kill two birds with one stone."

Oh crap. I didn't want to walk through the cabin door to see his brother.

"Why don't you let me help you get the money for him? I have money. I can get it for you. I just need to get to a bank," I said. He grabbed my shirt from behind and turned me towards him. He stared at me, his face inches from mine. "I do! Seriously! I have lots of money. How much do you need?

"Seven hundred dollars, Bitch! Do you have seven hundred dollars in the bank?" he asked sarcastically.

"Yes, I do! You can have it. I promise. Just drive me to an ATM and I'll get if for you. We can go back to the car and drive to town now, and you'll have it instantly. Heck, Cory, if you're nice enough to drive me there now, I'll even give you another seven hundred for your time and gas. I have fourteen hundred exactly in my savings. You can have it. But I don't want to go anywhere near your brother. Is that a deal?" I asked, sticking my hand out. He stared at me hard in the eyes, which was challenging in the dark. "I promise," I drew a cross over my heart for emphasis.

"Deal," he said with a shake. "But we're not going 'til morning."

"WHAT? WHY? No, no deal then! You'll have to kill me now then," I said and took off running again.

I got about three steps before my heel broke off on my left shoe and I fell. *Dang it!* Cory laughed, grabbed my arm hard, and yanked me up.

"Fuck, you got a lot of energy! Stop running away from me. It's starting to piss me off. Now walk nicely back to the cabin," he said shoving me forward. I did the best I could hobbling on my heel. My body was burning from all the cuts and scrapes. "We'll go back to the cabin for tonight. It's too dangerous to go back into town right now. I'm sure your boyfriend is out looking for you. Then in the morning we'll go to an ATM. When I got the money in my hand, you can get out. If you try anything stupid between now and then, I'll give you to my brother to pay the debt. Got it?"

"Got it. But are you going to stay by me the whole night so your brother doesn't do anything?" I asked, terrified.

He may be decent now but what if he takes another hit? He could change his mind at any second. I didn't trust him. *Where's Derek?*

"Yeah, we'll see."

When we got closer to the cabin, I could see that it was small and there was a large shed on the property too. There was a small section of yard that looked mowed and a ton of trees, but there wasn't much for leaves on the property, so someone must have taken care of that recently. I knew it couldn't have been Cory or his brother.

The car was still parked facing the woods and its lights were still shinning on us. The engine was off, and I didn't see Kyle anywhere. I looked around the property as we approached the car, but I couldn't see much in the dark. I strained to look past the car but couldn't see if the drive led to a road, and I couldn't see through the trees completely surrounding the cabin either. *Who knows if there are neighbors nearby, or how far town is.* I could see lights on in the cabin. My guess was Kyle was in there.

"So, did a relative leave you the cabin in an inheritance?" I asked Cory.

"Ha ha. Yeah, like any of my family actually cares enough to leave me anything. No. Bitch! Sometimes people have to go out and get what they want. Not everybody gets everything handed to them on a silver platter," he said. I didn't like his tone.

"I've never had anything handed to me either! I've studied and worked very hard to get where I am. Life is about choices. It's not *easy* to make the right choices, ya know. There are days where I'd like to sit on my ass all day, and do nothing, and skip work, and just play video games, and drink beer, ya know? But that doesn't pay the bills does it? No! It doesn't! So I force myself to get up and shower and show up for work! Easy? No! But I do it anyway! But never, *never* has anyone just handed me anything on a silver platter!" I lied. But I wasn't going to tell him about my inheritance. I was pissed! What a loser! As if his welfare check wasn't just handed to him! "So, tell me, Cory, whose cabin is this?" He shoved me forward.

"Wow! You're a nosey one! Like I said lady, it's none of your business! Now walk!"

I was freezing. I was almost glad to be entering the cabin when we walked in. My whole body was trembling. I really needed to sit and I really needed water. Cory opened the door and shoved me in. It was warm and lit. I took in my surroundings, noting things like the light switch locations, doors and windows, and where the locks were on them. The cabin was newer, built within the last ten years for sure. It was well maintained and smelled nice. It wasn't a log cabin, more like a smaller house. It had dark-brown, vinyl siding, tan double-hung windows, and a simple, open floor plan. The whole cabin was probably the size of my apartment. The colors were up to date and the decor was tasteful. The counters and floor were clean, which told me these two losers hadn't been here very long.

I stood in the kitchen and noticed the knife block on the counter. *May need that later.* The dining room consisted of a small, four-person table off to the right. Past the kitchen, the rest of the cabin was the family room, which ran the entire length of the back of the cabin with the bedroom and bathroom on the right.

Kyle was sitting on the couch watching TV. He looked tired. The smell of pot floated over to me, and I noticed the paraphernalia on the coffee table in front of him. *Good. Pot relaxed people. Hopefully he'll take a nap soon.* There were windows in the living room, but the door I was standing by seemed to be the only exit.

"Found her, huh?" Kyle said slowly, looking over at us with heavy eyelids. He nodded in approval, and smiled slyly.

15

"What the shit, Kyle? Stop with the pot! I need you alert. Dude, you've been here five minutes and you couldn't wait, or come and help? You're fucking worthless! Did you at least check on . . . things?" Cory asked him.

"Huh?"

Cory walked over and smacked him on the back of the head. "I said, did you check on the things you needed to check on? Is everything as it was when we left?" Cory asked him sternly.

"Oh, yeah, yeah. All is good," Kyle said and rested his head back on the couch.

There were two over-stuffed recliners on either side of the couch. The coffee table was in front of the couch, and two small end tables with lamps were on either side of the recliners. I had no idea what they were talking about, and had no intention to stick around long enough to find out. Cory told me to sit pointing to one of the chairs. I did. I took a good look at my arms and feet. They burned. Some of the cuts were bleeding and at least two were deep enough to possibly leave scars. I was glad to be able to rest a bit, but relaxation was completely out of the question. *At least the violent shaking has stopping.*

The TV was an older model. Some game show played loudly. Kyle seemed happily lost in it. Cory was rummaging through the fridge. He pulled out some chip dip and then went rummaging through the cupboards. The way he opened each one and shut it quickly told me he had no idea where anything was, another sign he was not a regular guest here. I wondered if this place was abandoned, or if he and his brother did something to the owners, or if the owner would in fact show up at any minute. I looked at the clock on the wall, it was 2:30 a.m. I prayed that Derek was looking for me and would find me soon. Cory finally returned with a can of pop, dip, and an unopened bag of chips.

"Hungry?" he asked.

"Ah, no. But can I use the bathroom?" I asked.

He thought about it while he squinted his eyes at me.

"Hold on," he said. He got up and went and looked in the bathroom. "There's a window in there. You can go, but the door stays open. If you try to escape I'll kill you this time," he warned.

I didn't know if I believed that, but I did really have to pee. I went in and peed. The bathroom was clean and had fresh towels and soap. I washed my hands and looked out the door to the living room. Cory was sitting on the other recliner leaning forward slightly to see me. I shot him a fake, sarcastic smile. He glared back. I stood at the sink and used the soap and water to wash my sliced up bloody arms and then threw a foot up one at a time and cleaned them good, too. *Hopefully they won't get infected.* I grabbed a few tissues from the box and held them over one of the wounds that had started bleeding again, and returned to the living room and sat back in my chair.

"We're staying here for the night. Tomorrow we will go to town and get the money," Cory said.

I nodded at the TV but didn't look at him. I had my eyes focused on the TV, while my head spun with escape plan options. Then I heard my ring tone. Cory reached in his pocket and pulled out my phone.

"Who is it?" I asked, as if he'd tell me.

It occurred to me that my battery had to be getting low. I had been getting warning beeps all evening.

"Derek." Cory informed me.

Oh, gosh. I hope he knows I'm kidnapped and doesn't think I just left without him. No, Derek's smart. He's trying to find me. I needed hope.

"Are you going to answer it?" I asked.

"Fuck no! You really think I'm an idiot, don't you?" he snapped.

Then he hit a button and tossed the phone onto the coffee table. *Yup. You're an idiot. A smart kidnapper would have smashed the phone or at the very least put it back in his pocket. Will Derek still get a tower location if he didn't answer it?*

The noise from the phone ringing and from it being thrown on the table woke Kyle up. "What the fuck?" Kyle said, glaring at Cory.

"Get up, asshole. Why should you get to sleep?" Cory asked him. "We got company to keep an eye on, ya know."

"Oh, yeah," Kyle said and looked over at me.

My blood pressure suddenly skyrocketed. I wondered if he could see my heart beating from the outside of my body. Kyle sat up straight on the couch and helped himself to some chips, then he stood and went to the fridge.

"Hey, there's eggs and bacon in here! You know how long it's been since I've had a good breakfast?"

Cory degraded him by saying, "Yeah you wouldn't know the first thing about how to even make eggs and bacon, Doofus!"

"Shut up! That's what a woman's for. Fucking and cooking!" *Oh no! Please no.* "Woman! Get in here and make me breakfast," he demanded. I looked fearfully at Cory, and he nodded and jacked his head toward the kitchen. *Seriously?* "NOW!" he screamed.

He rushed over to the chair where I was sitting, grabbed me by the hair and pulled me to my feet. He dragged me to the kitchen and threw me towards the stove.

"OKAY!" I yelled.

I started opening cupboards and digging out pans. I grabbed the eggs, bacon, and milk and began. Kyle sat at the table and stared past me to the TV in the living room. *If only I had a vile of poison in my pocket.* Twenty minutes later I announced it was ready. Cory and Kyle dished up and even left a little for me. I wasn't hungry, but I thought it might be a good idea to put something in my stomach to keep my strength up. I had a few bites of eggs, but that was it. I grabbed a glass out of the cupboard and drank a glass of water.

When Kyle was finished eating he came back into the kitchen, threw his plate in the sink, and grabbed my hair again pulling me to him. I grabbed my hair below his hand in defense, it hurt so bad I thought my scalp might literally rip off.

"That was good. Now for dessert," he said and yanked my head back hard and bit my neck.

I shoved his face away as hard as I could, but it wasn't helping, he was big and strong and fat. There was no way I could fight him off.

"Cory! Help!" I yelled.

"Just play along, and I'll be gentle," Kyle said in a gross, guff voice. "Cory can have his after I get mine."

I could smell him. It was so gross to have his hands on me. I tried to bend down and get out of his grip but instead he just shoved me hard onto the floor. I quickly flipped on my stomach and tried to crawl away, but he grabbed my ankle and yanked me back towards him. I clawed, and squirmed but he lay on my back crushing my pelvic bone on to the linoleum floor. He was so heavy I couldn't breathe.

"Give it up, bitch! You ain't gonna win," he said, his mouth touching my right ear.

He licked my cheek and reached around and grabbed my left breast. I screamed out of frustration, then tipped my chin down and bit his hand as hard as I could. He pulled back and sat up on his knees still straddling me.

"OWW! You stupid bitch!"

I scrambled to get away, but he swiftly yanked me back. He flipped me over on my back and lay on me again. He was fumbling with his pants and trying to hold me down at the same time. I looked over to Cory who was sitting on the couch watching. He was high and not caring.

"Help, me! What kind of person are you?" I said looking at him.

He was lighting up, doing meth this time. I started to cry and let my body go limp.

"That a girl," Kyle said. "It won't hurt as much if you lie still."

He pushed his pants and underwear down to his knees. Then, while straddling me, he grabbed my jeans on both sides and started tugging. I punched him in the nose with all the strength I could muster. Secretly hoping it would break, shove into his brain, and instantly kill him. But no such luck. He let go of my jeans and grabbed for his nose.

"Fuck! You bitch!"

While he had his hands on his nose, I slid out from under him as fast as I could.

"You broke my nose!"

There was blood pouring out both sides. I scrambled to my feet and reached for the first thing I could find, which was a kitchen chair from the dining room table behind me. I hit him over the back as he stood over the sink bleeding, his pants and underwear still around his ankles. He leaned forward and slid down the counter to the floor. He looked unconscious. Shocked it actually worked, I looked at Cory expecting retaliation, but he was laying down on the couch now and appeared to be dead, or passed out . . . he hadn't noticed anything.

Shit! I was sweating and shaking from fear. I quickly lept over Kyle and went into the living room.

"Cory?" I whispered.

No response. I looked over to Kyle and he was still not moving. My heart was pumping hard and I wasn't sure what to do first. I slowly and quietly made my way to the coffee table and carefully picked up a gun. I wasn't sure if it was Kyle's or Cory's. The gun hadn't been loaded earlier so I doubted it was then either, but I took it anyway. I tip-toed through the kitchen and grabbed a large knife from the block, then went to the closet by the entry way door. I was hoping I would find some tennis shoes close to my size.

I quickly, but quietly, turned the knob and looked down. There was a nice selection of men's and women's shoes. I could tell by the styles that this home belonged to an older couple. I made a quick scan and grabbed a pair of tennies off the floor. *Thank God!* I threw them on as fast as I could. They were men's, and a bit big, but would work better than my heels. I looked up and noticed a selection of jackets too. I grabbed a woman's large, black, hooded winter coat. *Yes! Maybe I'll sur-*

vive the night. After I tossed it over my arm, I closed but didn't latch the door, and reached for the knob on the entry door.

Just as I had stepped out and closed the door behind me, I noticed Kyle stirring. *Craaap!* I quickly and quietly ducked down so he wouldn't see my head through the window. *I need to hide. Fast!* I turned around and quickly scanned the property. *The shed!* I ran as fast as I could.

The shed was pretty big, probably enough for about six cars. It was tan with tin siding on all sides and the roof was green tin. There was a large automatic door that was tall enough to pull a big truck or camper through. Off to the right side I could see an entry door with a window. I sprinted towards it and prayed that it was unlocked. There was a window in the middle of the shed wall on that side. It was small and high up off the ground. It looked to be for natural light, and not actual use.

I frantically reached the door and twisted the knob. It spun and the door swung open. I frantically shut it and turned the dead bolt on the inside. I stepped to the side of the window and peeked back towards the house to see if anyone had seen me or was following me. I didn't see anything, but I knew I didn't have much time before they came looking for me. I heard my cell phone make a funny beep. *What was that beep?* I pulled it out of my pocket and looked at the screen: LOW BATTERY.

I quickly dialed Derek. I put the phone to my ear and waited. The phone was banging against my head, which made me notice how much I was shaking. *Pick up, pick up! Grrr! What's taking so long?* I pulled it away from my ear and looked at the screen. It made a beeping sound and said: *Call ended. Oh, no!* I tried again. It said: *Cannot connect.* I didn't have any lines of service. It must be the tin roof.

I turned and looked around the shed. It was so dark. There was a tiny bit of light from the security light outside shining through the window but I couldn't see very well. I was hoping my eyes would adjust soon and that would help. I could make out a few things. The shed wasn't heated but felt much warmer than outside. Under my feet I noticed the floor was poured cement. Off to the right there was a large pontoon boat with a playpen cover on it. Behind that was a riding and push lawn mower. There was an older, collector pickup in multiple pieces on the right side near me. I was next to the door still, and I could see a light switch on the wall but didn't want to turn it on.

Scraaaaap, thump thump thump.

"Huuumph!"

What was that? I heard something move! Then I heard whining and a rustling around. I froze with fear, and starred hard into the darkness.

"Mmmmmm! Mmmmmmm!"

Oh, my God! Someone's in here with me!

16

I looked towards my right. About half way down the shed, sitting on the ground between the pontoon and the shed wall, I saw two people tied back-to-back with tape over their mouths. I gasped! I carefully walked over to them with my hands cautiously in front of me.

"Oh, my God! Are you guys okay?" I asked as I knelt down by them.

It was an older man and woman. Their age was somewhere in their late sixties. They were wearing long-sleeved shirts and pants but had to be freezing. They were both very nice looking. Both were clean cut and dressed nicely and both in good shape for their age. I gently removed the tape from the woman's mouth first.

"Oh, thank you! There are two men in the house! They did this to us! Are you the police?" she asked in a panic.

"No, ma'am. I was kidnapped and brought here. I just escaped from the house, but they could come out here at any time. So be quiet and stay down."

"But you have a gun," she said referring to the one I'd just set on the ground next to her. I had forgotten I'd had in my hand. "Why do you have a gun?"

"Oh . . . I took it from them, inside, before I escaped. It's their gun, but it's not loaded. Or at least I don't think it is," I said removing the tape from the man's mouth.

He took a deep breath.

"Those bastards are never going to get away with this! What's your name?" he asked me.

"Sara . . . Martin," I said reaching between them to see how they were tied together.

It was duct tape.

"I'm Sam Hilland and this is Betty," he said a bit winded. "Is there anyone else in the house with you?"

"Who can help us? No. Both of the men are high on drugs right now. I just hit one pretty hard with a chair. He wasn't moving much," I informed them.

"Were there any other cars in the driveway or did you see anyone else?" Sam asked.

"No. Is there a knife or scissors around here I could use to cut the tape?" I asked Sam.

He looked at me confused and Betty spoke up.

"There! Check on the counter over by the lawn mower," she answered.

I went over and felt around and found a scissors. It was actually more like a tin snips, but it would work. I went back to them and told them both to lean forward so I could see and feel what I was doing. They obeyed and after a moment I was able to free them. They both sat there and rubbed their wrists for a second.

Out of nowhere Betty gasped, "Shhh, I hear someone coming."

We all froze and I heard the house door slam shut followed by voices. I quickly grabbed the gun and tucked it into the back of my pants.

"Stay here!" I said shoving their shoulders back together.

I put the tape back over their mouths and ran to the door. Quietly, I unlocked the deadbolt and stepped back into a dark corner and ducked down. Immediately, the door swung open and Cory stepped in. He flipped on the light. I could see I wasn't very hidden so I side-stepped behind a large barrel and ducked down.

"They're still here! Everything's fine in here."

He did a quick scan of the shed and then looked at Sam and Betty. He shone a flashlight in their faces.

"Did you see anyone come in here?" he shouted at them.

They both shook their heads. *What? He expects the truth?*

"Good," he yelled, "stay here!" he slammed the door and walked out.

Outside the door, I could hear both men talking. Cory sounded pissed.

"She's not in there! You let her get away! You get your ass out there and find her!" Cory yelled.

"No way. I ain't going out in that woods! I didn't *let* her get away! She hit me with a chair and knocked me out. *You* should have been watching! You go get her," Kyle demanded.

"Go get your flashlight, moron!" Cory yelled.

Then there was mumbling and a door slammed shut. A few seconds later I heard a door slam again. The mumbling got quiet and then I couldn't hear anything. *Good. They're gone.* I peeked out the window and noticed two flashlights scanning the area across from the house. They were headed deeper into the woods. I didn't expect them to be out there very long. I ran back over to Sam and Betty who were standing up and dusting off.

"Do either of you have cell phones on you?"

"No. They took them," Sam told me.

"Do you have a land line in the house that works?" I asked Sam.

He looked at Betty.

"Yes, unless they cut the line. But it worked earlier," Betty answered.

"I think we should run to the house and try to call for help quick before they get back," I suggested.

Sam offered, "Maybe they left the keys to the car."

"Yes, we can check that, too." I said. "We need a plan. Sam are there any guns in the house?"

"Uuuhhh," he looked at Betty again, and she again answered for him.

"No, there aren't," she told us both.

Weird, why doesn't he answer me?

"The phone's in the corner of the kitchen by the door. There are knives on the counter. That's all I have that might work for defense."

"Okay, okay, okay," I stammered, trying to think fast. "Um . . . Okay, here's the plan. We'll open the door and run to the house. If they see us we're screwed! So be quiet and fast. I'll go first, then Betty, then you Sam. Sam, you make sure you shut this door . . . quietly. And you shut the house door quietly. That way it looks the same in case they happen to glance back. As soon as we get in the house, Betty, you get on the phone and call 911. Sam you grab knives or anything else we can use as a weapon, and then both of you grab jackets to keep you warm in case we have to make a run for it. Sorry Betty I'm wearing yours, and I borrowed some sneakers. I was barefoot. Grab any waters and snacks from the fridge that you can fit into your pockets, too. I'll look for the car keys and try my cell again. It worked in there earlier. We need to be in and out fast and get to the main road. We can meet the police there. Anything else you two can think of?"

"Ummm, no. Do you know what time it is?" Betty asked.

"Not really. Around 3:00 a.m., I think. Why?" I asked annoyed.

Why the hell would she care what time it is?

"No reason. I was just curious," she stated then looked at Sam's face.

Sam shot her a shut up warning look. I had a feeling they weren't telling me something, but I didn't have time for it.

"All righty then. Are we ready?" I said beckoning to them and moving close to the door. I peeked out the window and didn't see the boys, so I slowly turned the knob and whispered, "GO!"

I took off running as fast as I could to the house. Betty was right on my heels, and Sam a moment behind. I swung the house door open and stepped out of the way. Betty flew in right behind me and Sam jumped through the door and quickly and carefully shut it and locked it. Betty went straight to the phone on the wall but the cord had been ripped from it. I tried my cell but as soon as the light came on it went back off again and said low battery. I tried to dial 911 with it anyway. But it kept shutting off. I doubted that the signal went out. *Dang it.*

We all grabbed warm stuff from the closet and each took bottled water from the fridge. Betty grabbed a bunch of weight watchers meal bars and shoved them in her pockets. Sam ran to the bathroom quick and then checked the living room for car keys. There was nothing there. I left the heavy, useless gun on the counter. We each grabbed a knife from the block and held it in our hands. We all gathered around the door, near the kitchen window. We peeked out the window, looking in all directions. We were all terrified but held it together pretty well.

"Okay we really need to get far away from this house quickly," I said. "Those jerks will be back soon. Let's go out the door and get a ways into the woods so that we are not easily spotted and then head to the main road and follow along that. Are there any neighbors around here that we can head towards?" I asked them as they stepped up to the door with me.

Betty answered, "The closest one is a mile from here. I've never met them. We just moved out here a couple months ago ourselves."

"How far from town are we?" I asked Betty.

"About twenty miles."

"Ooooh, shit." I said, thinking that we couldn't make it that far in this cold. I thought that heading towards the neighbor's was a better idea. "Well, which direction is the closest neighbor?"

"To the main road, then go right. They're down the first driveway approach on the right." Betty answered again.

"All right, let's go far enough into the woods that we're hidden, then run to the main road. Don't make noise, and don't get hurt! Okay?"

"Okay," they said in unison.

I unlocked the door, and carefully and slowly opened it. "Wait! Do you guys have any flashlights?" I asked.

Betty said, "Maybe in the basement," and ran down quick to look. She returned empty handed. "I don't know where else to look. I didn't unpack those."

I looked to Sam. He shrugged. I shook my head in frustration and opened the door. We took off running to the right and followed alongside the house. When we got to the end of it I stopped and put my fingers to my lips. We listened quietly. I didn't hear anything.

"Okay, when I say go, you two follow me into the woods."

I looked at Betty and she seemed ready to get out of there. Sam looked concerned and seemed to be just following along with us like a lost puppy. I could tell who wore the pants in that marriage.

The rusty, blue Chevette was about twenty yards further down the driveway. I gave them a "let's move" hand gesture and darted into the dark woods. We went opposite from where I'd seen the lights from the men earlier. My spine was tingling. I didn't like the woods. Something caught my eye and I whipped my head around to the left. *No freakin' way!* Was that the car keys dangling from the trunk lock?

"Oh, my God! You guys, look!" I whispered loudly. "The keys are in the trunk lock!" We all squinted in the darkness and agreed. "Yes! Let's go! Get in the car!" I yelled and took off.

I ran to the back, grabbed the keys out of the lock and then launched myself into the driver seat. Betty climbed in the front passenger seat and Sam was approached the car on my side, a bit slower than us, and reached for the handle.

"There they are!" he spat out while opening his door.

He was pointing over the car roof to the woods on the passenger side. Sure as shit, you could see two figures bumbling through the woods.

"Get in!" I yelled.

I fumbled with keys and tried two before the third key fit into the ignition. Sam reached around and locked all four doors.

"Hey! Hey! That's my car!" We could hear them yelling from the woods. "Stop, get out! Get out or I'll shoot!"

"Aaagh! Let's get out! I don't want to get shot!" Sam cried.

"They're running! Hurry up!" Betty screamed. She covered her head and ducked.

"The gun's not loaded. They're bluffing!" I yelled hoping that was true.

I turned the key and the engine rumbled and shook the whole car but wouldn't fire.

"SHIT!" I screamed and tried again. "Come on, come on, come on!"

The engine again vibrated and tried and tried but was struggling. I pushed down the gas pedal a few times and it finally started! I looked to my right out Betty's window and they were only ten yards from the car. I quickly shifted into reverse, looked over my shoulder, and floored it.

I turned forward again to see if they were still coming at us. They were! I was still flying backwards when BANG! The car stopped suddenly! I hadn't made it more than twenty yards. We were still plenty close to the house. The light was still strong enough to see the area a little.

"What the heck? What did I hit?"

I was still on the driveway, so it couldn't have been a tree. I whipped my head around to see another car behind me.

"Are you guys okay?" I asked Betty and Sam.

"Owwww! Aaah! Betty said holding her neck. "What happened?"

"I hit another car," I told her.

"I'm okay!" Sam announced. "I'm going to have whiplash, but I'll be fine."

I looked at him and nodded. The car behind me was smoking and I could smell the stench of radiator coolant. I looked out the front windshield and saw that Cory and Kyle stopped, standing there staring in shock. *Crap! Now what?* Sam turned and looked out the back window.

"Oh, shit! It's Joe! I-I-I gotta go," he said and opened his door.

"No, Sam. Don't leave! Where are you going to go?" Betty asked him.

"I don't know, but I'm not going to stay here!" he opened the door and got out.

"Get outta da cha, you cheat'n broad!"

What was that? The unfamiliar voice was coming from behind me, from Sam's open door. Sam slammed his door shut, locked it and moved over behind Betty. I looked out my side mirror to see an older man holding a rifle pointed at our car, stumbling towards us.

"Get out, woman! You ain't gonna leave with him!"

I looked at Cory and Kyle and they were still standing there staring in our direction. I was so scared, I was panting. Now I was stuck between two groups of crazies, both with guns, one that might in fact be loaded. And all of them were pissed off at me, or someone in my group. *Why do these things happen to me?* I didn't know what else to do, so I exited the car.

"Hi, I'm Sara. Not sure we've met." I said extending my hand.

Dork. I guess I don't work well under pressure. This man was short, balding and had a huge beer belly. He was dressed in a button down, flannel shirt and baggy jeans. His shirt was half pulled out and had a couple of stains on the front.

"What? Who the hell are you?" he slurred. "Tell Betty to get out here!"

"I'm Sara," I repeated. "How is it you know Betty?"

Over my shoulder I noticed a car door swing open. Sam jumped out and bolted towards the woods. He made it maybe twenty yards when BANG! The stranger fired at him. I grabbed my mouth, and shot my eyes to Sam. He'd dropped to the ground and didn't move.

"OH, SHIT! DON'T SHOOT!" I screamed and held up my hands at the guy.

He looked stunned, shocked that he'd actually shot him.

"OOOOH! OOOOH! Oh, no he didn't!" I heard Kyle yell. "SHIT! That was a great shot!"

"No, no! I didn't mean to hit him! I was just trying to scare him," he cried. Then he lowered the gun and looked at me with worried eyes. "It was an accident. I didn't mean to," he told me like I was the one he had to explain things to.

He started crying and shaking his head.

"Saaaaam!" Betty yelled. "NOOOO!"

She leaped from the car, ran around the rear of it straight up to Joe and punched him in the stomach. He dropped the gun, and grabbed his stomach with both hands. He folded in half at the waist and collapsed to his knees. Betty was bent over him screaming and pointing in his face.

"What the hell are you doing? You crazy drunk fool? This is exactly why I'm leaving you! You're drunk and stupid every day of the week! I can't believe you killed him! I hate you, Joe! HAAATE! YOU!" she screamed fiercely then she kicked him.

I stood there with my mouth hanging open in utter shock. The puzzle was coming together. Joe and Betty were married and Betty and Sam were having an affair. That would explain why Sam was so unfamiliar with the property, and why Betty was wondering what time it was. She knew Joe would be home from the bar soon and wanted to get Sam out of there in time. *Woozers! Not only did those idiots pick the wrong woman on the wrong day, they got the wrong property on the wrong day too!*

Betty ran to Sam's side and knelt down by him. She put her head on his chest and started bawling. *Poor thing.*

"Who are you?" Joe demanded, holding his stomach and standing.

"I'm Sara. Those two idiots over there kidnapped me," I pointed to Kyle and Cory, who were still just standing there staring at us. "They're wanted by the law. This was their hide-out of choice. It's a long story. Can I borrow this," I asked referring to the rifle I was picking up of the ground. "And do you have a cell phone?" I asked quietly.

"Yes, in the car," Joe answered.

"Go get it and call 911 before they kill us all," I told him quietly.

I turned around, pointed the gun at Cory and Kyle and started walking towards them.

"HE'S ALIVE!!" I heard, Betty announce from the edge of the woods. "He was just faking because he was scared. He's not even hit!"

That is a relief. But now what? I had the gun pointed at idiot one and idiot two and knew that I could not let them out of my sight until the police got there.

"You two, sit!" I said walking towards them.

They looked at me and then at each other. Cory rolled his eyes and looked annoyed. Kyle sat. It was funny because he's such a big guy, and if he would have said no, I have no idea what I would have done. I was faking my bravery. I tried to look tough and sound tough but I was completely scared on the inside.

"Sit, Cory! Now!" I screamed. "I'm in no mood for your shit right now!"

I clicked the safety off the gun, and he sat. I pushed the safety back in place and lowered the barrel. They were sitting side by side. Cory still looked annoyed, and I didn't trust him. Kyle had his head down and looked like he might be crying. *Seriously? He'd better not be! If he is, I'm demanding a psychiatric evaluation upon his arrest. An hour ago he was on top of me in complete control, and now he's crying?!* I heard mumbling behind me and took a quick glance at Joe who was talking into the phone.

"Hey, lady, what did you say your name was?"

"Sara Martin," I yelled back to him. Then I called to Betty and Sam, "Hey, you guys, come over here," I yelled.

Betty and Sam slowly walked toward me. When they got close enough, I asked Betty to go to the shed and get some rope or duct tape. Sam stayed next to me. I didn't trust Joe and him together. I kept the gun pointed in Cory and Kyle's direction. When Betty returned with duct tape, I instructed Betty and Sam to secure their feet and hands. They taped their wrists behind their back and their ankles together in front of them. When they were done Betty slapped them both across the face.

"Shame on you two! Your mother will be so ashamed of her boys," she told them with a finger point.

Cory looked pissed off, as usual, and Kyle looked sorry. I almost laughed at the child-like fear on his face when she mentioned his mother.

"Suck it, old lady!" Cory shot back, and then spit at her. He missed, but now I was not happy. I took the tape from Sam's hand and slapped a piece across his mouth.

"Respect your elders!" I scolded. Then I took the duct tape and wound it around both of their chests and arms bundling them together as tight as I could. "There, get comfy, boys. The police should be here soon."

"They're on the way," Joe announced, walking up to us. "They asked about you," he told me.

His eyes were still bloodshot, but he seemed to be sobering up a bit.

"Who the hell is this guy?" Joe asked Betty, pointing at Sam.

"He's my boyfriend, Joe," she said proudly, as she put her arm around Sam's waist. Sam's face filled with shock at the word boyfriend. His mouth hung slack as he fearfully looked at Betty.

"Boyfriend? Boyfriend!"

Joe reached for the gun in my hand and I pulled it away from him.

"Stop!" I yelled.

I put my hand on Joe's chest and stood between him and Sam.

"Yeah, that's right," Betty said. "You don't come home until after 1:00 a.m. every night of the week! You go to work, to the bar, and fishing. I never see you! You never talk to me or make me feel loved or appreciated, so I got a boyfriend. I need to be loved Joe, and you don't show me lo-lo-lovvvee!" and with that, Betty put her face in her hands and started sobbing.

"Awww, she just needs some love, man!" Kyle said to Joe.

I put my hand over my mouth to keep from laughing. *What an idiot.* Joe dropped his shoulders and stepped closer to Betty.

"Oh, now, honey bun. Don't cry. I didn't know ya felt like that. I love you. I thought you knew that. I don't mean to drink so much. It just sort of happens. And when I do come home, you tell me you like it better when I'm not here," Joe told her.

"Well, that's because you go right to bed when you get home and leave me with dirty dishes and laundry," she said in a whiny voice. "What I really need is my Joey Pooh to hold me and love me," she said through sobs.

Wow. I am not hearing this!

"What?" Sam said loudly. I shook my head at him and he got quiet.

"Ahh, man, you need to hug her. She just needs a hug." Kyle chimed in with a soft baby-like voice. I looked over at him.

He had puppy-dog eyes and was sporting a soft smile. *Puuleeeze!* Cory was not feeling the love. His eyebrows were smashed together and he mumbled something sounding like, "Shut the F up" from under his duct tape, then leaned over and head-butted Kyle.

I let out a quick snort of laughter and then pointed the gun back at Cory and told him, "Knock it off!"

"Haaaaaaaay! Cut it out, man, that hurts!" Kyle cried.

"If all you needed was a hug, you shoulda just said so Betty Boo," Joe whimpered.

Seriously? Kill me now!

"Commere, Boo Boo. I'll give you hug. I didn't know that's what you needed. You just have to tell me."

"Ooooh, Joey pooh," Betty said and stepped towards him.

I moved back, so I was out of the way. They embraced. I noticed Sam's eyes roll and Kyle's head tilt. Then Joe and Betty kissed. It was a quick peck . . . then another . . . then another. Then they started moaning and smearing their faces against each other.

"Ah, for the love of Pete! I'm standing right here!" Sam yelled.

But they kept going, arms rubbing backs passionately. I turned away and did a loud "AHEM!" cough. They finally parted and both were out of breath. *Seriously what's taking the police so long! I can't take anymore of this insanity!*

"I'm so sorry, Boo Boo," Joe said. "I won't drink anymore. I'll quit, just for you, honey bun."

"Ohhh, Joey pooh, you'd do that for me?" Betty asked in a voice like she was talking to a two-year-old.

I was gonna puke if I had to hear anymore of it. The whole situation was bringing back bad memories. "I promise, if you quit drinking, I'll stop sleeping with Sam . . . and Larry . . . and Earl," she said. Another quick snort of laughter escaped me.

"Earl? Who's Earl?" Joe asked.

"It's not important, Pooh. What's important is we're back together and in love again!" She kissed him again. He seemed fine with that.

"How *you* holding up, beautiful?" Sam asked me.

I felt his breath on my ear he was so close.

"Ahhhhh! Nah uh! No! Step back," I snapped at him.

Betty and Joe were whispering in each other's ears and giggling with their arms around each other. Finally, I could hear sirens in the distance. *Thank God!*

17

The sirens got louder and louder. I turned to look up the driveway at the approaching cop cars when I heard a stick crack in the woods.

"Ooow!"

And there was Joe, in the woods, trying to make a run for it. He was sitting down holding his ankle. There were four police cars in all, and an ambulance. The sirens silenced and all the cars quickly angled in at different directions. Spot lights and high beams illuminated the area. *Wow!* The place was really lit up. Joe was in the woods up and running again. An officer took off on foot after him.

"Stop or I'll shoot," the cop yelled.

Joe stopped and threw his hands in the air. I scanned the crowd of police faces looking for Derek. They were all male officers and they were all standing behind open car doors with their weapons drawn. I supposed they didn't know the good guys from the bad guys and needed a second to figure it out.

The bull horn buzzed, "DROP THE WEAPON!"

It suddenly occurred to me I was still holding a long-barrel rifle, which was pointed in their direction. *Shit!* I quickly set it down, and put my hands up in surrender. *Oops!*

"Stay where you are and nobody move!" he yelled again.

"Don't shoot. I won't move," Joe yelled from the woods.

Another car raced into the driveway and Derek bounded out almost before it came to a full stop. I saw him right away. He was scanning the area and noticed Joe and the officer in the woods right away. He swung his head in my direction and noticed me. I tilted my head a little and gave him a half smile, but as soon as I did I got all mushy inside and suddenly felt really weak.

Now that he was here, I wanted to collapse in his arms and cry, but there I stood helpless in front of what was beginning to feel like a firing squad, with my hands still in the air. When Derek and I locked eyes, he put his hand on his chest. I could see it rise and fall with a breath of relief. He ran over to one of the officers and they spoke for a moment. Then Derek and the other officers lowered their guns and approached. Two officers went to Cory and Kyle. One grabbed the gun I'd just put down and walked towards the squad car with it.

Derek ran to me and wrapped his arms around my neck and held me tight. It was as if the world stopped. He was warm and smelled so good and felt so safe. With his arms around me, I felt like there was a cement building surrounding me, protecting me from everything. I didn't have to fake being brave anymore. I broke down and cried.

"You're safe now," he whispered. "It's okay . . . you're safe. Thank God, you're safe." He pulled his head away from mine and moved my hair out of my eyes. "Did they hurt you?" he asked in his police voice.

I shook my head. "They tried," I said, regaining my composure, "but I got away."

I wiped my tears and sniffed. I heard chuckling and looked over to see the officers trying to decide how to get idiot one and idiot two separated and into the squad car.

"Is that your handiwork?" Derek asked me with a grin.

I half smiled, and looked at Sam and Betty.

"It was a joint effort," I told him.

"Is anyone hurt?" one of the officers asked loudly.

Everyone shook their heads. Except Joe, who was being escorted from the woods and overheard the question. "I am! I think I twisted my ankle."

The officer pushing him along from behind and shook his head. They sent the ambulance on its way.

"You'll live," the officer told him.

"What's the story with the two smashed cars in the driveway?" Another officer asked.

I looked at Joe.

"That was my fault," he confessed. "I had too much to drink and I drove."

Wow, that's big of him. Then he waddled over with his hands still cuffed behind his back and kissed Betty on the mouth. I held my breath hoping this wouldn't get ugly again. It didn't.

He stepped back and said, "Betty Boo, Pooh has to go away for a little while, but I'll be back, and when I do I'm going to take care of you good. Real good, baby! We've got to make up for our lost time, don't we?" he said in a whiny voice.

"Yes, Pooh. I've missed you these last eight days. I promise to wait for you," Betty said.

Eight days? Lost time? Good lord! The officer escorted him to a car. Derek shot me a look and I smirked back.

"Isn't that sweet?" I sarcastically whispered.

The other officers looked like they were going to puke too.

After they cut the duct tape off Cory and Kyle and cuffed them, they transported them to separate squad cars. Derek said I could ride with him to the station, while Betty and Sam went with another officer. A few officers stayed on the scene to collect evidence and take pictures. The rest of us met at the St. Paul Police Department. We all went into separate rooms and gave our accounts of what happened. Two hours later, I'd had two cups of coffee and needed two quarts more. I was so exhausted. I signed my statement, and Derek took me home. I just wanted to see Faith. He left me at the door but waited until I got in.

When I got there, Kat and Tannya were on the couch and floor half asleep. Derek had called them when he found out what was going on, and then again on the way to the station. He'd told them that I'd be home in a couple hours and I was okay.

I quietly closed the door behind me and they stirred. Faith meowed and came bounding over. She stopped short and threw up. *Sheesh! Nice to see you, too.* I grabbed a rag with soap and water and cleaned it up quickly, then I picked her up. She seemed lighter, like she'd lost some weight. Kat opened her eyes, saw me, and jumped to her feet. After whipping the blanket off herself but accidentally onto Tannya's face, she ran over to me and wrapped her arms around me.

"Shit, girl. We were so worried!"

Tannya threw the blanket off her face and sat up.

"Ohhhh! You're back! Are you okay? Man you had us scared!"

Tannya wrapped her arms around both of us and made it a group hug. Faith meowed and jumped down. I assured them I was okay and went to the fridge and got a bottled water for me and Tannya, who also wanted one. We sat in the living room and I told them the whole story. We talked for a while about it, when it hit me that I had been in serious danger. Not that I hadn't thought that before, but to hear about what happened after I was discovered missing—the way the bar was locked down for over an hour, the interviewing everyone had to go through, and the huge search effort that went on for me. It was very surreal. I was exhausted and wanted to sleep, but the adrenaline was still there. *I'd probably be able to run my best mile right now if I wanted to.*

"So, Tannya, tell me about the rest of your night. Did you and Greg exchange numbers at least?" I asked her with a smile.

Kat socked her in the arm, bit her lip, and smiled at her.

"Well . . . yes," she said, with a school-girl grin. "After you took so long in the bathroom, me and Kat went in to check on you .When we saw the door had a big dent and you were not in there, we ran to get Derek, and he put the place on lock down. They shut off all the music, turned all the lights on, and stopped serving."

"Oh! Ooooh! No, they didn't!" I gasped holding my mouth. "Ugh. What did everyone look like? I bet the bright lights were not their best friends!"

"Ohhhhh! They, ah, we, were at our worst as you can imagine," Kat announced. "It wasn't a pretty sight, and they wouldn't let anyone in the ladies room because it was a crime scene."

"Wow. It's the low lighting we depend on to look our best!" I said.

"Yes it is, and lots of people needed low lighting!" Kat said.

I was pretty sure she was referring to Tannya and her rather loud outfit of the evening, along with the dirt stains on her knees and butt from falling earlier.

"Yeah, so anyway, there we were stuck with nothing to do but worry. When Greg realized it was my friend who was missing, he came over and talked to me. I was really upset for you, Sara," she told me tearing up.

"Ohhh, thanks, honey," I said, reaching and putting an arm around her.

"So anyway me and him went over and sat on a couch in a quieter corner and talked. And about a half hour into that he kissed me."

"Ahhh!" I high-fived Kat. "Score!"

Tannya laughed.

"He's a nice man. I like him. Kinda goofy and silly but I like him! And yes, we exchanged numbers. He said he'd call me."

"Oh, Tannya, that's great!" I said. I looked at my watch and it was 7:00 a.m. Faith's appointment was at eight. "Well, girls, Faith's appointment is in an hour . . ."

"We'll come with you!" Kat interrupted. "We already talked about it. She's sick and needs to get in today. We already said that if you couldn't bring her, we would. And if you could, we'd go with you anyway. You shouldn't be driving until after you've rested anyway."

"Oh, okay, thanks! That's sound like a good idea. I'm going to take a shower and then we'll go."

The shower was nice and hot. I was still a bit chilled from being outside so long. A few tears came while I was washing and thinking about the assault and how much worse it could have been. I was glad to be home. Something simple like a fluffy towel made me feel so blessed to be alive. I knew I was being overly emotional, but I'd had a rough night.

I dressed in jeans and a t-shirt and threw a Vikings sweatshirt over the top. Then I put on some face lotion, two coats of mascara, and Chapstick. I didn't really care much at this point. To finish, I threw some mousse in my hair, and shot it quick with a blow dryer. When I got out to the kitchen, the girls were ready to go, with the exception of bathroom stuff. They had made orange juice and toast for me too.

"Thanks you, guys. You two are amazing friends," I told them.

We shared a group hug.

Saturday early morning traffic was nothing in the Cities, so we left fifteen minutes before the appointment, as it was only a few miles away. Kat drove, and Tannya rode shot gun so I could be with Faith in the back. Faith paced the car the whole way. She didn't seem to be slowed down much by whatever was wrong with her. I had packed a wet rag and paper towels and a garbage bag just in case she got sick on the ride, but we made it. Kat parked the car as I threw my purse over my shoulder, then I grabbed Faith. I'd brought a large bath towel to wrap her in because it was so cold, that and I had no idea how she would react to the vet's office environment. We entered the building and Faith was acting excited.

"It's probably the smell," Kat said. "When I was a kid we had a large dog and I swear that dog could smell the vet two blocks away. It would take two people to shove that dog out of the car, and two more to get him into the building." We all laughed.

Faith was trying her hardest to escape my arms. I held tight but didn't want to hurt her. It appeared we were the first appointment of the day. The staff was still getting settled, and the lights and computers were still warming up.

"Good morning," said the young women in scrubs standing behind the counter. "This must be Faith." She reached out to pet her and I almost dropped her. "You can let her explore if you want. You're the only other appointment besides Pepper, and he's a really gentle dog that wouldn't harm a flea."

"Okay," I said and set her gently on the floor.

She took off pouncing around and jumping onto all the displays of toys and pet accessories that were lining various shelves throughout the room.

"Looks like Faith has a lot of fans," she said smiling at Kat and Tannya.

"Yes. These are my very good friends, Kat and Tannya. I had a very rough, very long night and they came to help me, and drive for me," I informed her.

I was started on paper work when I heard the door chime ring. I looked over my shoulder to make sure that Faith wouldn't run out. She was busy chewing on a ball-on-a-spring in a toy box on the bottom shelf. In through the door walked a great Dane. It was huge! The dog was almost as tall as the kid walking it. The little girl was probably ten or eleven years old, and the dog was up to her chin. It looked like an adult walking a pony around. The dog was very calm and simply strolled in.

"Good morning, Pepper!" the receptionist said from behind me.

My eyes shot open as Faith turned to see him. I didn't know what to expect. That dog could eat my entire four-month-old cat in two bites easily.

"Fear not," the receptionist said holding my arm. "Just watch."

Kat and Tannya looked concerned too when Faith pounced over to Pepper. Pepper kept walking the length of the room, with a bit of a limp, towards the desk as Faith caught up to him and was meowing and jumping and pawing at him. Pepper stopped and sniffed Faith. She looked up to him and they were nose to nose. He licked her once. His tongue was as big as she was and knocked her on her back. The room erupted in laughter and Pepper continued on, nose in the air, sauntering to the front desk like he didn't have the time.

"Oh, cute," the girl said. "Is that your kitten?" she asked me.

"Yes, that's Faith."

"Pepper loves all animals. He won't hurt her," she told me. "My mom is on the phone in the car. She'll be right in," she said to the receptionist.

"Sure, have a seat, Hailey. The doctor will be in shortly."

Hailey sat and so did Pepper. Even seated they were about the same height. Faith was on her feet again and back over by Pepper. He bent his head forward as she pawed at him playfully. He again licked her and knocked her on her back. We all laughed. It was really fun to watch. Then Faith stood up on her back legs and put a paw on each side of his jowls and they stayed nose to nose for a second, staring into each other's eyes, both so very still. It was like watching two people fall in love at first sight.

"Awww," Kat said.

"I know, right?" I said with compassion.

The whole room including the two ladies behind the desk all stopped and watched with tilted heads. *Bing!* The door chimed again and in walked a woman with a purse in one hand and cell phone and keys in the other. Pepper's owner.

"Hi, sorry. My mother . . . she's having some issues."

"No problem, the doctor is just getting set up, so have a seat," the receptionist told her. "You can enjoy the love story unfolding between Pepper and Faith."

"Oh, wow, she's cute. Is she yours?" she asked me.

"Yes, and she seems to really like your dog."

"Everyone and every animal likes my dog," she said, patting Pepper on the head."

Then she turned to her daughter and told her that grandma was not doing well and they might need to go there. Hailey seemed upset and asked about missing school. Pepper lay down and Faith curled up next to him. The mom told her they would have to do what they needed because from the sound of it, Grandma wouldn't be going home from the hospital but rather into a nursing home. The drive sounded long, and from what I got from the conversation she was a single mom with an only child.

"Okay, Sara, the doctor is ready for you," the receptionist announced.

I gave Tannya and Kat the "come with me" head nod, then I went over to Faith and peeled her away from Pepper, and we walked back into an exam room. The doctor walked through the door, and Kat elbowed me.

"Mine," she whispered.

He came over and introduced himself and shook our hands. He was around our age and thin with light-blonde hair and blue eyes. *Very nice looking.* He was clean shaven and sported a white jacket, stethoscope, and clip board.

"Hello, ladies. I'm Doctor Rittgers, but please call me Wes. This must be Faith? Sweet baby girl, what's upsetting your tummy?" he asked Faith taking her from my arms. I heard Kat exhale and shot her a look. She was behind him fanning herself. "Which one of you is the owner?"

"I am. Hi, I'm Sara. These are my friends, Kathrine and Tannya."

"Nice to meet you. So tell me, Sara, what's been going on with Faith?"

I explained to him that she was four months old and that over the past week she had started throwing up. Tannya and I both told him that it was a clear fluid and, other than the puking, she seemed happy and she was eating and voiding normally.

"Did you get her at a breeder?"

"No she was a gift, from my friend Kat here," I said gesturing to Kat.

"Her mother and I got her at the humane society here in town." Kat told him with a lingering smile, and slow blink.

"And did they tell you that she had gotten her shots?" he asked her.

"Yes. They said she'd gotten her first shot, and was de-wormed." Kat told him.

"Shot? Not shots? Did they give you any papers about that shot?" he asked.

"Um, I'm not sure if they said shot or shots . . . and no paperwork other than a receipt for adoption."

"Okay. I'm going to have my nurse see if she can get hold of anyone over there. That place has been known to lie to people about shots to increase adoption rates and keep their fees down. Maybe we can find out if she had the necessary shots. I'll be right back," he said.

He handed Faith back to me and excused himself.

"Oh . . . my God!" Kat said. "He's perfect! And no ring! Did you guys notice that? No ring," Kat excitedly announced.

"Yeah, a fellow that nice looking without a ring . . . he's gotta be gay. Sorry, sista," Tannya said.

The door opened and Wes walked in again.

"Okay while she's on the phone I want to do an exam and take some blood from her."

He took Faith up on the table and looked in her eyes, mouth, and ears. He worked his hands over her entire body, and then listened to her heart.

"She looks good. Let's get some blood and run a couple tests," he said then poked her with a needle and sucked some blood out. Faith meowed, making me cry too.

I didn't like seeing her hurt much. Plus, I was so tired I could've cried at the drop of a hat. Wes tipped his head and gave me a tight-lipped grin.

"Do you have kids?"

"No."

"I heard that's even worse," he told me with a head tilt. Kat and Tannya giggled. "I'm going to get this to the lab. I'll be back in a little while. Have a seat, ladies."

We sat in the room, me and Kat on the two chairs and Tannya stood. We talked about Wes and how Kat should go about getting his number or giving him hers. In the hall I could hear the nurse bringing Pepper and his family to a room. I thought I may fall asleep sitting up, but when the doctor finally returned twenty minutes later, I was back on my feet.

"Well, just as I suspected, no one was at liberty to say," he told us with air quotes. "If the kitten had any shots there isn't any record of it. So, just like I thought the blood test proves she has a condition called Dirofilaria Immitis, otherwise known as heartworm." I put my hand over my mouth.

"What does that mean?" I said scared.

Wes put his hand on my shoulder, "It's curable," he told me. "It means we need to give her medicine to treat her tummy and a stronger drug to kill the worms. If we caught it early enough, which I think we did, she'll be fine. I have already written her prescriptions, which you can fill here if you'd like, then you will take her home administer the meds as directed and we will see her again in a week. We'll check her blood again then and hopefully all will be well. In two weeks, if she's better, we'll vaccinate her too. Keep her indoors and avoid contact with pets that are not vaccinated. And as always wash your hands. Lots!"

"Okay, thank you, Doctor." I said, scooping up Faith.

"You're welcome. Ladies . . ." he said holding the door for us. "So Kathrine, you're a cat lover huh?"

Kat stopped and talked to him while Tannya and I scooted to the lobby. I filled the prescriptions there. Then Tannya and I sat down to wait for Kat. Faith wanted down and went off exploring again.

"Aww . . . she misses Pepper already," the receptionist said.

"I think you're right," I said. "Was Pepper here because of the limp?" I asked.

"Yes. Unfortunately he needs a very expensive surgery, very soon. The doctor is giving them the news in a minute. It's not good. Kerry, the dog's owner, just recently divorced and was left with the house and the dog, neither of which she can afford. And now her mother, who lives in Iowa, is sick. Kerry needs to sell that house and get her mother moved out a.s.a.p. The poor woman. And on top of it, she has Hailey, who's in school. Kerry moved here from Iowa when she married. She doesn't have any friends here and only has an entry-level job."

"Oh, no. Can't her ex-husband help with Hailey while she's in Iowa?"

"Her husband took off to New Mexico with his secretary," she divulged.

"Oh, geez."

"Yeah, not good. Kerry loves Pepper, but she doesn't have the time or money for him. She's been trying to find him a home, but who wants a great Dane with a bad hip?"

18

After a few moments, Kat came strutting into the waiting room with a huge smile on her face.

"Ready?" I asked.

"Yup! Sure! Ready!" she said and skipped out the door to the car.

She was pretty stoked all the way back to my apartment. They'd both exchanged numbers, and Wes told her he'd call her later. He had a group of friends, along with their wives and girlfriends, going out that night and thought it would be great if she joined them. From the smile on her face it appeared she planned to.

"He told me to extend the invite to you guys too. It's just a big group thing. I think you should both come. Maybe Derek and Greg can join, too?" Kat said with puppy-dog eyes and her hands held up in prayer form begging please.

I laughed, which took a lot of effort. "I need sleep, lots of it, and so does Derek. So it's a distant maybe for me. Tannya, you're welcome to stay tonight again if you want to go with. I won't be much fun today and I'm not sure about tonight, but if you want to go with, you sure can, and still crash at my place. It's totally up to you."

"Well, I don't know. Go out clubbing two times in the same week? Gosh. Well . . . sure! Why not! You only live once, right?" Tannya laughed.

She was very excited, but her face suddenly changed to fear as we approached our parking spot. I tossed Kat the keys and went to the back door.

"I only brought one nice outfit with. If I ask Greg to join me, he'll see me in it two days in a row."

"Ah, plus there're a few stains on it," Kat added. "Well, I guess then you'll have to spend the day at the Mall of America with me!"

"Wow, really? I've never been there. Is it far?" she asked as we loaded into the car.

She rode shotgun again, and Faith stayed cuddled in the towel with me in the back. She'd had a big day and the receptionist said that she might be sleepy from the meds. Kat pulled out of the lot.

"No it's minutes from Sara's apartment, and they have a huge food court so we can grab lunch there too."

So it was decided. I'd go home to sleep and Kat and Tannya would spend the day at the mall. Later they'd go out and I'd play it by ear. Going out didn't sound appealing to me after what had happened the night before. My phone vibrated. It was Derek.

"Hello?"

"Hey, sweetness, how you doing? Did I wake you?"

"No, I'm just heading home from the vet with Kat and Tannya." I told him.

"That's right. I forgot about her appointment. Did they find anything?" he sweetly asked.

"Yeah, heartworm. She should be okay though, we caught it early. She's on meds for a week and then she goes back for a re-check. Are you still at work?"

"I'm just leaving, I need to get some sleep. They gave me the rest of the weekend off to catch up. I was just . . . missing you. I was really worried last night. That was scary. I . . . I didn't like not knowing where you were," he said.

He sounded emotional. It put me right to tears. I wasn't able to handle anything at that point. I just wanted sleep.

"Can you come over?" I asked through tears. "I don't want to be alone."

"Yes. I'm on my way, sweetness," he said and disconnected.

Kat shot me a sympathetic look from the rear-view mirror. I wiped my tears away and looked out the window. Ten minutes later, we pulled up to the building and went into my apartment. Tannya jumped in the shower and got ready for shopping, and Kat and I sat and talked some more about last night. A little while later, Derek buzzed and I let him up. Tannya was dressed in black spandex pants stretched to the max and a bright pink oversized hoodie. At least it covered her butt. Tannya walked over to the door and slipped on some white-and-blue tennis shoes. Kat looked at me and rolled her eyes. I smiled and mouthed, "Good luck." Tannya popped to her feet and announced she was ready. We agreed to call each other about 5:00 p.m. I bid them farewell and shut the door behind them.

"Hi," I said exhausted, turning to Derek and hugging him. He took a long time to let go. "Are you hungry?"

"No, I just want to curl up on that couch with you and sleep," he told me and kissed my forehead.

I noticed that he'd changed into Minnesota Gopher sweatpants and a maroon t-shirt. He must have run home first.

"Sounds perfect," I told him.

I went into the bedroom and grabbed a bunch of pillows and some blankets from the hall closet and joined him on the couch. When I returned, I noticed he'd flipped on ESPN and was settled in. I curled right up next to him, covered up, and reached over and turned my phone off. Derek turned his to vibrate.

I wondered what was going on with Cory and Kyle. I was comforted knowing they were behind bars and would remain that way for a long time. But I didn't want to talk about it. I just wanted to close my eyes. Faith came over, climbed onto the top of the back of the couch, spun in three circles, and lay down. Derek put his arm across my stomach and pulled me in nice and close.

He leaned in close to my ear and whispered, "Thank you."

"For what?" I asked him.

"For helping me find the man that almost killed my sister . . . and for your bravery. I couldn't have done it without you, Sara. So, thank you."

I smiled gently and pressed my face into his chest and closed my eyes. He gently kissed my forehead, leaving his lips there for an extra second.

Then he whispered, "I love you."

After I squeezed him softly, I snuggled in deeper and fell asleep.

I woke up a couple hours later. Derek was wriggling away. He got up and went to the bathroom then went back to sleep, on the floor this time, with the extra pillow and blanket we hadn't used. I stretched out on the couch happy to have some space. My body was achy. I was pretty beat up, scratched up, and I was really beginning to feel it.

I fell asleep again until 4:30 p.m. After I woke up and lay there for a minute, I went to the kitchen and drank a glass of water and used the bathroom. I looked at myself in the mirror and was disturbed. The little makeup I'd had on was gone, and my hair was a disaster. I stood there trying to decide if I cared or not. I stuck my tongue out at my reflection and went back to the kitchen. I was starved.

I looked through the cupboards and fridge and freezer and was not surprised to find that there wasn't any food. I hadn't been here long enough to go grocery shopping in a while. So, instead I grabbed my laptop and put in an order to Domino's Pizza. Derek was stirring a little on the floor. Tip-toeing quietly, I grabbed my phone and sent a text to Kat: *Slept some, still tired, not going out tonight. Derek's here, pizza ordered. How's it goin'?*

A few seconds later I got a response: *Good. Two new outfits, ones that are in style, three new pairs of shoes, lunch, and hair did!!*

Hair did?

Yup. Now all blonde, not blonde with black root. Plus a conditioning treatment. She's never used conditioner!

Wow.

I'm gonna take her to dinner and then she and Greg are going to a movie and out for a drink. He'll drop her at your place later. I'll meet up with Wes and friends.

Okay. Have fun, Thanks!! I typed then set my phone down. Derek rolled over and grabbed my ankle.

"Hey, you," he said to me with a sleep voice.

I looked down to him and asked, "Are you hungry?"

"Yes, starved. Now that you're okay, and Cory's locked up, I feel like I can stomach some food," he told me.

"Agreed. I ordered pizza. And I have a bottle of wine in the freezer chilling. I also have some dessert pizza coming. This here is a five-star apartment," I said with a nod.

He rolled his eyes and laughed. My phone buzzed, it was a text. I looked at the screen as Derek reached for the TV remote.

"*Hey, Sara, just checking in. Rumor round these parts is that you and Tannya have gone missing. LOL. You two okay? Rex.*"

I laughed quietly to myself and I responded.

"*Ha, fine here. Well, at least now I am. Tannya's visiting me here in the Cities at my apartment. We should both be back in a day or two. Thanks for checking. :)*"

Good to hear. Coffee when you get back? My treat . . .

Sure, I'll let you know when I'm back! I responded, then set down my phone.

I slid down to the floor and curled up in Derek's warm blankets while he flipped through channels.

"I plan on doing this the rest of the night. You're welcome to stay as long as you want," I told him.

He looked me up and down twice.

"Okay, thanks. I'll for sure stay through dessert pizza and wine," he said with a wink.

The buzzer rang, and I let the pizza man up. When he knocked on the door I answered and traded the money for the pizza. I always felt like I was doing something wrong when I took a box from a bag, and handed a strange man cash and walked away. *I live a dangerous life!*

Derek and I ate pizza and drank pop and watched movies for a couple hours. We drank wine, ate dessert pizza, and watched another movie. When that movie ended, I stood up and picked up our carpet picnic. He stood and helped me. I was loading the last of the dishes into the dishwasher when he walked up behind me and wrapped his arms around my waist. Then he leaned in and kissed my neck. Heat rushed through my body. I turned around and faced him. He pressed me back against the counter with his body, and we kissed. His kisses were sweet . . . like dessert pizza frosting. *Yummo!*

When we parted, I took his hand and led him to my bedroom. He locked eyes with me and stepped into me again. He kissed me intensely as he slid my shirt over my head. The shirt hit the floor as we slowly lowered to the mattress. The rest of the night consisted of well . . . we didn't talk much!

In the morning, I woke to pots and pans banging and the smell of bacon, which was strange since I knew I didn't have any food in the house. It brought me back to the first night Derek stayed at the cabin with me. He had been there on business, and I didn't know him very well. We didn't share a room, but in the morning he'd made a delicious breakfast. I was pretty sure I'd fallen in love with him that morning.

I rolled over and looked around the room as I thought intently about the day before. It had been a crazy couple of days. I knew Derek loved me. And I loved him too, but I wasn't sure how to go about saying it with meaning. *I should have done it last night. Last night was amazing!*

I got up and sauntered into the kitchen. I looked in the living room. I saw a purse and stilettos lying on the floor. *Tannya must be in the guest bedroom. Shit, I didn't hear her. I wonder how she got in.*

"Good morning," I said with a yawn.

"Hey, glad you slept well," Derek responded. "You didn't even move when Tannya buzzed at 2:30 this morning. I got up and let her in."

"Oh, my gosh, thank you. I know. I slept like a rock!"

He looked me up and down.

"I'd like to take some credit for that."

He gave me a smug look and turned back to the stove, smiling. He was pleased with himself. I couldn't really argue.

"Hungry? I've got bacon and cheese omelets, and strawberry French toast going. It's almost done."

I picked Faith up off the floor and gave her medicine, then put food in her bowl. She went over to the bowl and ate. I hadn't noticed any puke piles, so I hoped she was getting better. I looked around. The table was set, juice was made, and breakfast was almost finished.

"You must have been up really early."

"Yeah, I woke up at 2:30 and then again at 7:00. I couldn't get back to sleep, so I ran to the grocery store and got a few things," he said taking the French toast out of the oven and placing it on the table.

I grabbed the juice, mashed strawberries, and the Cool Whip from the counter and set them on the table then sat down. It was nice to be spoiled! Derek put an omelet on each of our plates, set the pan back on the stove and sat down next to me. He grabbed my hand, kissed it, then held it as he said a quick thanks to the Lord for everyone's well-being and the food on the table. He released my hand and winked.

"Dig in!" he said.

"Thank you. This is so nice, Derek."

We ate and talked a little about last night. He told me that Cory and Kyle were both wanted on multiple charges and that they would both be going away for quite a while. He said that I would probably have to go to court at some point to testify. Derek assured me that it would be an open and shut case, so I would be in and out. We finished eating and cleaned up the mess, leaving a plate in the fridge for Tannya. Derek grabbed the dish towel from my hand and set it down. He led me to the couch and guided me to sit next to him.

"I want to ask you something, just between you and me. I didn't want to ask you Friday night, when the other officer was there getting statements but..." I knew what he was going to ask. "Did Cory or Kyle sexually assault you?"

He looked very serious and very concerned. I closed my eyes and took a deep breath. "Yes. Well, Kyle tried, but I got away," I said nervously.

"What did he do?" he pushed.

I really didn't want to go into it, but I understood his concern, and maybe his fear, after our being together last night.

"Cory got high on meth and passed out. Kyle grabbed me in the kitchen, threw himself on top of me, and started to touch me. I fought like crazy and was able to flip to my stomach. I tried to crawl away. He pulled me back, flipped me on my back and pulled his pants and underwear down. He was sitting on me, straddling me and was trying with both hands to pull *my* pants down, so I punched him as hard as I could in the nose. He got off me and went to lean over the sink because he was bleeding. I picked up a chair and hit him on the back with it. He fell down, and I ran away to the shed. The rest you know."

Derek's eyebrows were pushed together and I could feel his anger. He nodded and took a deep breath.

"You're so brave, Sara. Good for you. You did everything right. You have to fight for your life or the bad guys will steal it from you," he said, then sighed and kissed my hand." I'm so glad you got away. I was so scared for you. We were doing everything we could, and I was going crazy not knowing where you were."

I looked down at my arms. One of my scratches was itching.

"Look at you, you got really beaten up. You have a bite mark on your neck too."

"That's from Kyle right before he pushed me on the floor."

"He'll get everything he's got coming to him. That jerk will make lots of friends in prison. The boys down there will take good care of him. When the guards know that a man has assaulted a woman, they tend to let stuff slide, so justice can be had, if ya know what I mean. I don't condone it, but I don't work there, and I don't hear all the bragging about how they've harmed women."

"Geez. Don't ever work there," I requested.

Derek stood and stretched, "Well, I'm going to go home and shower. It's Sunday. Are you heading back to Nisswa today?"

"No. I'll probably go back on Monday morning. I'll see if Ginger or Maureen can take my shifts Monday and Tuesday, so I can have a little break. I have to stop by my parents and catch them up. Then I want to do some shopping . . . maybe get a massage." I said and stood up.

"I can help you with that. I won't even charge you." Derek said eagerly.

"Aww, thanks. Aren't you sweet?"

I shoved him towards the door. He pulled his tennis shoes on and stood close to me.

"Thanks for last night," he said an inch from my lips.

"Thank *you* . . . I love you," I finally told him.

Faith came over and rubbed on Derek's leg. She loved him too.

19

Derek had a smile from his eyes to his lips. He gave me a quick, passionate kiss.

"See ya, sweetness," he said, then disappeared out the door.

I took a deep breath and walked back into the living room and sat on the couch. I called my mom and dad and told them that I would be over at about 4:00 p.m. It was already noon now. I wanted to shower and hit the mall first. I grabbed my robe from my room and went into the bathroom.

When I got out, I dressed in dark, denim jeans and a long, fitted, dark-orange sweater with an over-sized collar, and rider boots over my jeans. I went into the kitchen and saw Tannya grabbing some juice out of the fridge. She was still in the clothes from her second night out, which were a lot more tasteful than Friday night's apparel. She was all wrinkled, but looked pretty good wearing a polyester/rayon shirt with a small triangle print on it that was blue, black, and white. Her oversized bottom was covered in dark, denim jeans that were a straight leg fit, and made her look a lot lighter than she was. She looked really good.

"Hey, girl!" she said with a big wave, as if I'd just walked through the doors of Morning Glory.

Her energy was insane.

"Hi, I'm so sorry I didn't hear you come home last night. I apparently slept like a rock," I told her. "Love the hair color by the way, it looks much healthier."

"Thanks," she said. "And no problem. Derek let me in," she said with a smile and raised eyebrows. "I'm glad you're feeling better."

I went to the fridge and pulled out her plate.

"Compliments of Derek!" I said handing it to her.

"Oh, wow! He's a keeper! Thank you." She took the plastic off and put the plate in the microwave. "So what's your plan for the day?"

"Well, I'm going to head to the mall now. I need to do some shopping. And then I told my parents I'd be there at four for a visit and probably supper. I think I'll go back to Nisswa on Monday morning. If you want to come shopping with me you can. You're welcome to stay as long as you'd like."

"Oh, thanks, but I'll probably head home after breakfast . . . or lunch," she said with a laugh. "I need to finish that painting project and get my kitchen back in order. But thanks for the offer."

I sat with her at the table and we talked while she ate. I told her about my night, and she told me about what happened after I disappeared. Tannya said I should call Blake. He was drunk and confused and worried about me when they dropped him off. She put her plate and cup in the dishwasher and went to the guest bedroom to get her things together. While she did that I called him.

"Hello?" Blake answered.

"Hey, Blake, it's Sara. Just wanted to give you a call and let you know that I'm home and fine. Tannya said you were kinda worried."

"Oh, thank God," he said with a big breath. "Yes, I was worried! I just got off the phone with Kat. She promised to call me and finally did this morning, How are you holding up?"

"Oh, I'm fine. I'm glad she called you. I didn't really think about it 'til now. The last two days are kind of a blur," I explained. "But, I'm good, and I'll pencil you in for our meeting next month. Same time and place?"

"Sure. Sounds great, Sara. Thanks again for calling. You take care."

"Thanks, I will," I told him and hung up.

That wasn't as awkward as I thought it would be. At least he didn't bring up the kiss again. Tannya came out of the room with her two bags in hand. She had changed in to bright Zubaz pants and a sweat shirt. I laughed, accidentally out loud, when she came walking out. She noticed and stopped in her tracks.

"What? You like my pants?"

"Oh, my gosh! How long have you had those? I remember those from middle school!"

"How long? How long? One day, girl! I got these yesterday at the Mall of America!" she proudly announced.

She very confidently put her tennis shoes on and tossed her bag over her shoulder.

"I can tell you where I got them if you want to get a pair," she said.

I waved my hands at her.

"Oh, no, that's okay." I told her. "I've got lots of pants already."

"Suit yourself. These here pants have personality, and probably need a certain type of person to wear them," she told me.

I felt kinda insulted. *What? She thinks my personality is not big enough for Zubaz. Huh!*

"Right. They are a little much for me," I agreed. I handed her some money. "Here's for cat-sitting and delivering Faith to me. I really appreciate it," I told her.

"Oh, thanks. It was no problem at all. I had more fun and excitement this weekend than most people should be allowed to have."

She took the money, put it in her purse and then opened the door.

"Bye. Drive safe," I told her.

We shared a hug and I closed the door behind her.

I arrived at the mall at 1:15 p.m. I'd called my gay hair-dresser, Stephon, on the way. He's tall and large framed, but in good shape and very fashionable. We had been friends for a while. He's the guy I call if I need advice on anything from handbags, to hair, to clothes. *I love him!* Plus, he was always super fun and made me laugh. The receptionist told me that he had had a cancellation, so I took it.

I called my mom and asked if we could make our visit more like 6:00 p.m. She was fine with that and said to bring dessert and a date. I texted an invite to Derek. *We'll see if he responds.* Rounding the corner of the salon entrance, I heard a familiar squeal and clapping. Stephon came galloping over in his smock and threw his arms around me.

"Ahhhh, Sara! Darling! So good to see you! Look how beautiful you are. You've really learned how to work this hair doo! You're fabulous, love!" He gave me a kiss on each cheek. "Here you go," he said handing me a complimentary glass of sparkling champagne. "If your life's anything like the last time I saw you then you need this. And if it's not, I'll drink it. My life's never as exciting as yours."

"Aww, Stephon, my love. So good to see you, too," I said removing my jacket.

He took my jacket, which distracted him for a moment.

"Tweed, multicolor, double-stitched, satin lined, double breasted. Sara? . . . very nice!" he said with one hand on his hip.

"Thanks, did that all on my own!" I proudly declared.

He slapped me a high five, then escorted me to the station. He draped me and fingered through my hair.

"Lovely . . . healthy . . . beautiful! Do you like the look?"

"I love it! I just need a trim and the roots done," I told him. "And then if there's time you can put me in the books for a massage."

"Ohhh! Day of Beauttttty!" he sang. "I love it! Hold on, my lady, I'll check the massage schedule."

He skipped over to the front desk, threw his body over the counter, and looked down at the receptionist as he spoke to her. She smiled and looked at the computer, then nodded and typed some more. Stephon clapped his hands, blew her a kiss, and bounced back over to me.

"Okay my dear, you're on the books for a massage in an hour and thirty minutes. We have got to get going!"

He got the colors all mixed up and started on my roots. I was going to be a light-brown with golden-caramel highlights. He started painting and asked for the life update. I first told him about my newly purchased lake property and Lost and Found. Then I asked for a refill on the champagne.

"Ooooh, girl! Hold on, I cannot wait to hear this." He took my glass and quickly tippy-toed off to the back room. He returned with a refill and two bottled waters. "This must be good if you need a second glass," he said as he handed me my glass and opened one of the waters for himself. He took a drink with one hand, pinky up, and placed the other hand on his hip.

"Well, let me start by saying, Friday night I was kidnapped and thrown in a trunk." Stephon spat his water out all over the mirror in front of him!

"Saaaay whaat? Good Lord, woman! You never disappoint! Excuuuse meee," he said taking a towel and wiping the mirror clean. "Girlfriend, I need to hang out with you more. You're the olive to my martini!" He put the towel down and went back to painting my hair. "Kidnapped? Do tell."

I recounted the whole story while he worked. He listened intently adding a "tsk" here and a gasp there. When Stephon had completed my color, he set a timer and sat down in the neighboring station's chair. I continued giving him all the details. When the timer beeped, he checked me. After an "ooh la la," he led me to the sink for a wash and condition.

We went back to the chair. Stephon let out bouts of laughter here and there when I described Betty and Joe's relationship. By the time I finished my story, Stephon had finished my hair. After checking in the back, he said that Pinota was ready for me. He walked me back to the massage room.

"Sara," he said in introduction, "this is Pinota. She's the best we have. Trust me! She got her training in the south of France and let me just say, the French know what they are doing, honey! Mmmm mm," He added a head slide and finger snap. "You two enjoy each other. Sara, love, I'll catch you later!"

He gave me a kiss on each cheek and sashayed away. Pinota and I shook hands and said hi. She led me into the room with instructions to undress and lay face down on the bed then she left the room.

An hour later I felt amazing. I paid, tipped, and walked out of the salon with some new products. I felt on top of the world. I swung through a couple of stores and tried on some new clothes. I got a couple of things but nothing was jumping out at me, so I left and headed to my parents instead. Derek sent a text saying he would meet me at my parents at 6:30 p.m. He had a few things he had to take care of.

It took longer than normal to get across town to my parents because of road construction. Minnesota was busy replacing and repairing bridges, so I had to take the long way to avoid one of the bridge roads. Ever since the 35W bridge collapse the state had been looking hard at repairs and replacements everywhere. I guess they didn't want to be making the news again with a story like that. Since that day, I'd gotten butterflies in my stomach every time I crossed a bridge. *You really just never know when it's your time.*

I followed the curvy road to my parents' driveway and went inside. Dad was in the recliner. He stood up and gave me a hug. It was longer than usual. I wondered if he knew what my weekend had been like. I hadn't call them, and as far as I knew Derek hadn't either. There wasn't any time when it was going down, and afterwards I just wanted to sleep. I knew my mother would have been at my side in a second if she had known, but I hadn't wanted her there just then, and Saturday was sleep, and well, Derek, so there hadn't been time for her then either. I knew she was going to be mad that I hadn't called, and I wanted to tell them the story before Derek got there so that he didn't take any heat for not calling either.

Derek had only met my parents one time at the cabin, the day after I'd closed on it. They had gotten along well, and conversation had flowed easily between them. I knew that the night was going to tell me a lot about their places in my life and the respect level they had for each other, because of the situation.

"Hi, Dad. How are you?" I asked.

"Good, honey. I'm good. Thanks for coming. Your mom really wanted to have you over. She's been talking about you since Friday. On and on she goes! 'We should have her over for dinner. She should stop and visit us. Maybe we should go visit her.' Oye! I'm glad you're finally here. Now she can shut up!"

Strange, must be her spidey sense.

"Well, I'll go in and help her with the food and put her at ease. There's something I want to talk to you guys about together, so I'll be back with her in a minute," I told him.

"Careful, your aunt Val is here," he warned.

"Oh, really? When did she get into town?"

"Yesterday and she's staying a week or two, she says. I may have to live in your apartment for a while."

He winked, but I knew he was serious.

My aunt Val was one of a kind. She was my dad's younger sister. There were four kids on my dad's side. Aunt Val had always been the free spirit of the group. She bounced from city to city, switched jobs like seasonal purses, and had been married and divorced three times. She had no kids, and no intention of having kids. In fact, she didn't like kids. Kids or dogs. She always said, "They're dirty and slobbery, and if they poop you have to take care of it." Val liked to have a good time and no responsibility. She was loud and funny and drunk pretty much every time I saw her. I liked her . . . a lot.

I could smell something Italian as I approached the kitchen doorway. I secretly wished for lasagna. I stepped through the door just as Aunt Val was throwing back the rest of her martini.

"Well, butter my buns and call me a biscuit, look who's here!" she screeched and came running over. Her arms flew around my neck and she squeezed me hard and tight. "Dang, girl," she said, stepping back and looking me up and down. "You're beat up! What happened?"

Well, that's one way to start the story. My arms were still looking pretty rough, and I had a small bruise on my face that my faded makeup was now showing. And the bite mark was still there.

"Well, hi, Aunt Val. How are you?" I said.

"Hi, nothing. You tell me what's wrong! Come on, sit down and tell me," she demanded. "You look really tired. Why? Aren't you sleeping? Is it your boyfriend? Your mother said you got a new boyfriend. Is he keeping you up late into the night? Huh? Huh?" she asked elbowing me and grinning.

She shook her eyebrows up and down and nodded.

"No," I told her. "Well, yes. I mean no." *Ahhh*, I was stuck. I laughed out loud. "Hey, Mom," I said, in an effort to change the subject. She walked over from the stove and hugged me. "Dinner smells amazing."

"Hi, Sara. It's your favorite. Lasagna! Where's Derek?" she asked looking over my shoulder to the living room.

"He'll be along in about an hour. He had some things to finish up." I looked behind me when I heard a strange rattle. It was Aunt Val with a martini shaker. She filled two glasses and set them on the table.

"Jan, are you sure you don't want one?" she asked.

"No, thanks. I'll be in bed by seven if I do," Mom replied.

"All right, chicky, spill!" Aunt Val said, patting the chair next to her at the kitchen table. "I wanna know what your story is. Those scratches didn't happen in bed, or did they?" she said with a wink. Smiling at her enthusiasm, I sat down and took a big sip.

"Sara! Yeah, look at your arms and your cheek! Is that a bruise?" my mom asked.

Dad came into the room.

"What is this I hear about scratches and a bruise?" he asked in his serious voice.

I took another deep breath. My heart rate increased three-fold. I felt like a teenager in trouble all over again.

"Mom, Dad, please sit down. I do need to tell you something." Dad pushed his eyebrows together and looked angry, like he wanted to kill someone. Mom looked scared as she studied my right arm. "As you know Derek's sister was shot . . ."

I studied their faces as I continued on and told them the whole story. They listened intently as their only daughter told them a story of menace, horror, and terror. It was like something out of a movie. Aunt Val made it even worse by constantly interrupting and asking for more details. About twenty minutes into the story, the oven timer buzzed and my mom, who was hanging on my every word with her mouth hanging open, jolted to attention.

"Sara!" she said angrily as if she was scolding me.

I looked over at her. She was startled and confused by her own voice. It took her a second to realize it was the oven timer that buzzed. She got up, turned the oven to warm, and sat back down at attention.

"Go on," she said, reaching for my glass and finishing my drink. Dad was just staring, waiting for me to continue.

Over the next ten minutes I wrapped up my story, with an apology for not calling them. I sat back in my seat fully prepared for angry words and punishment. No one said anything for a whole minute. Finally Aunt Val pushed her chair back and stood. Her eyes where huge and, for the first time ever, she was speechless. She reached over and grabbed my glass from in front of my mother and went to the counter to make some more martinis. She made four. In silence.

When she returned to the table she set one down in front of each of us. Mom threw hers back in two swallows, and Dad pushed his towards Mom. She reached out and pulled it closer.

I took an awkward sip from mine while looking over at them and said, "I'm okay. I'm fine . . . I'm sorry. I should have called."

"You should have called," my dad said. He stood up, patted me on the back, and walked back to the living room.

"Ah, Will!" Mom said. He stopped in the doorway and turned to her.

"What? Jan, she's an adult. She didn't need us involved. If she did, she knew she could call and we'd be there." He winked at me and walked out.

"I understand," Aunt Val said. "I mean really, Jan, what service would you have provided? A lot of crying that's what! That's the last thing Sara needed, you sobbing on her shoulder. Sounds to me like she had a man to comfort her. Am I right?" she asked, with a smile, raising her cup towards me. I picked mine up, clinked hers, and took a sip. Val winked and took a sip of hers too. "Jan, your baby's a grown woman now. She doesn't need her mommy as much anymore."

"I do need you, lots and lots!" I said leaning over and giving her a hug. "It's just that the whole night flew by, and when I got home I had to bring Faith in, and then I just wanted to sleep. I didn't want to talk about it. Just sleep. I couldn't even think clearly. But I'm here now, and I'm rested and better, and ready to talk to you about it. And Cory and Kyle are in jail, and will be for a long time."

"Look at your arms!" she said with tears.

"My arms are fine. It was just the tree branches. They're just scratches."

"What about your face?" she whined.

"It's a small bruise. I don't even know what it's from, probably the bathroom door that knocked me out."

"Exactly, you don't know what they did to you while you were out!"

"Jan!" Aunt Val said, "She would know if she were . . . harmed in anyway."

I nodded and took my Mom's hand. "I wasn't," I assured her.

The doorbell rang and startled us. *Derek.*

"I'll get it," Dad yelled from the living room.

I stood and walked over to my mom's chair and hugged her. "I'm fine," I said quietly and walked away and went to meet Derek. Aunt Val stood and followed. When we got in to the living room, I heard Aunt Val say, "Oh, wow," under her breath.

"Hey, beautiful," he said, and kissed me on the cheek. He had flowers and a bottle of wine in his arm.

"Hi," I said, with a one-arm hug. "Derek, this is my Aunt Val. Val, this is my boyfriend, Derek."

Derek extended his hand and Val wrapped herself around him.

"Very, nice to meet you."

"Oh," Derek gasped at the strong hug. "Ah, nice to meet you, too."

My mother came into the living room, said hello, and hugged Derek too.

"Jan, sorry I'm late. These are for you," Derek said, handing her the fresh, fall-colored flowers and the bottle of red wine.

"Oh, Derek, you didn't have to do that. But this will be lovely for tonight," Mom said, and returned to the kitchen.

We all followed her in, and she yelled to my dad that dinner was ready. We gathered around the table and my father said a quick prayer, which was mostly praise about my safety. Derek looked at me. I nodded slightly to let him know that I'd told them. Aunt Val announced to dig in and we all passed the food.

"So, Derek, I understand you had a scary weekend," Aunt Val said.

Derek continued loading his plate as he spoke. "Yes, I did," he said as he looked at me with loving eyes. "It got kind of hairy there for a while. We had the entire force on the situation. Thank God Sara is as strong as she is. She not only saved her own life, but the lives of three others."

"What?" my mother asked.

I shook my head, "Not really."

"Ah, yes really! I personally interviewed those involved. They all agreed that if Sara had not been there the situation would have been way worse. She held Cory and Kyle at gunpoint until the police got there, and she had them duct taped nicely for us when we arrived," Derek said with an amused smile.

"She did? Thatta girl!" Val said.

"She did," Derek continued. "She found and untied the hostages in the shed, and got them warm clothes and protected them as well!"

"Anyone would have done the same thing," I said, and I meant it. I was no hero.

We finished our meal and retired to the living room where we focused the conversation on my Aunt Val. She was off work for two weeks and planned to stay with my parents for one of them. After that, she wasn't sure where she'd head. After dinner, clean up, and dessert, we got ready to leave.

"I may stop up at your new cabin and see you," Aunt Val announced as Derek and I were walking towards the door.

"That sounds great," I said. Derek and I exchanged hugs with everyone and left. Outside we stopped by our vehicles and talked. "Do you want to come over and stay?" I asked him.

"Sure, I'll swing home first and grab a bag. In the morning I'm going to head to Morris to see Kelly. Do you want to come with me?" he asked.

"Yeah, sure. I can come with, but then I'll leave from there for Nisswa. I need to check on things at the store and get some paperwork done."

"Okay, that sounds perfect. I don't have to work until Monday night," he informed me. "I'll meet you at your place in a few minutes then." He kissed me and left.

I drove home. I turned on a couple lamps and the TV, then checked on Faith. There didn't seem to be any puke piles, and her food was gone, so I thought that she must be doing better. When I heard my phone beep I went to my purse to check it. It was a text from Tannya:

Hey, girl! Thanks for the fun and excitement this weekend. BTW Miss Kitty was asking about you, so was Rex, and I've only been at work for an hour! LOL, C U soon.

Miss Kitty. I'd almost forgotten about her. I did tell her that I would meet with her on Monday. I wished she'd lose my number. I didn't need any more drama. And, she seemed like the kind of person who would like to stir up drama. *Dismiss it*, I thought. *Derek's coming over. That's all I want think about. If I can get a replay of last night, I'll be a very satisfied woman.* I went in the bathroom and put some lotion on my arms. The scratches were starting to heal so they itched like crazy. After that I picked up a bit and wiped off the counter and mirror in the bathroom.

I went out to the living room and lit a candle. The Twins were playing, so I turned it to that station and sat down on the couch. It was close to nine, but it felt like midnight. I was still very exhausted, both physically and emotionally. The couch wrapped its warmth around me and I closed my eyes.

20

BUZZZZZZZ!
"Ah! I'm awake!"

I walked to the door on weak, half-asleep legs and glanced at the clock. It was 11:00 p.m. *Wow, he's late.* I swung the door open, and there stood Derek. He had a duffel bag over his shoulder, a paper bag in his arms, and a six pack in the other hand.

"Hi, sorry I'm late. I . . . I got stuck taking care of something. I brought snacks!" he said raising the beer.

"Come on in."

I wondered if it was too early to give him a key. My heart was still racing. I stepped aside so that he could enter. He set the bag and beer down and I helped him unpack.

"Thanks for picking this up. I have close to nothing here. I'm really not hungry for snacks, but I'll have a beer," I said and pulled one out of the plastic ring.

Derek unpacked Fritos, chocolate Chex mix, and butter-pecan ice cream. It looked good, but I was still full from dinner.

After the groceries were unpacked, I saw Derek reach for his cell phone on his belt. He looked at the screen, then tipped it away from me and pushed something on it. When he glanced back up, his face was weird.

"I'll take a beer too," he said with a strange voice. My guard went up. I had that uncomfortable feeling in my gut. "Is the game on?" he asked.

Glancing back to the TV, I informed him, "Nope, it's over."

"Did they win?" he asked.

I took a pull on my beer, "I don't know. I fell asleep watching, while I waited for you." He looked like he didn't have anything to say. "So what thing were you stuck doing?" I asked, hoping I wasn't being too nosy.

After another sip of his beer, he set it down and took a moment to collect his thoughts. "When I got back to my apartment there was a friend there who needed someone to talk to. This friend is going through some tough stuff right now and needed to bend someone's ear. Sorry I was late."

"Oh . . . it's no problem . . . you just looked stressed, and I thought I'd ask. Do you want to talk about it?"

"No, I think the situation will work itself out. I couldn't do anything for them but listen, but I think it helped them, so it was time well spent, hopefully. I just hope that your nap gave you a bit more energy for us tonight," he said stepping into me.

"Well I *was* sleeping . . . but you have my attention."

He tipped his head down and kissed me. When we parted he handed me his beer.

"Save me a spot on the couch, sweetness. I'm going to use the bathroom," he reached behind me and set his wallet and phone on the end table by the couch, then removed his coat and shoes.

Just after he'd shut the door to the bathroom his phone vibrated. I looked down at it. It showed an incoming call from Jodi. *Huh, I wonder who Jodi is.* I set his beer on a coaster next to his phone. I sat on the couch and flipped through the channels. There was nothing on. Derek re-entered the room and plopped down next to me. His phone buzzed again.

"You missed a call when you were in the bathroom too," I said nonchalantly. He looked over at his phone and turned it off. "Do you have to get that?" I asked.

"Nope, it's nothing. Sorry. It's off now." After flipping through the line up three more times, I looked over to Derek and told him I was tired.

"Sorry I just can't keep my eyes open anymore. I'm going to head to bed. Do you want to watch TV for a while, or join me?" I asked him.

"I'll be in a few minutes," he said.

I walked into the bedroom and changed into a shorts and t-shirt and climbed into bed. I just couldn't shake the feeling that he was hiding something. After about twenty minutes I heard Derek's voice quietly talking. *He must be on the phone.* I strained my ear to hear but could only make out a few mumbled words: *No, had, chance, call, anymore, I'm serious.*

When it got quiet I heard him sigh loudly. The TV clicked off and I heard empty cans fall into the garbage. Derek walked into the bedroom dropped all his clothes, except his boxers, on the floor and slid into bed. I didn't move and pretended to be asleep. He scooted over and threw his arm around me.

"Good night, beautiful," he whispered, then kissed my cheek softly and fell asleep.

I woke up to Faith licking my hand. Monday, my least favorite day of the week. Derek was out of bed already. The shower was on, so I knew I wasn't too far behind him. I moaned and rolled over to look at the clock—7:03 a.m. I threw the covers off and waddled into the kitchen. There was some juice and some breakfast food left in there. I drank the juice, but didn't feel like making anything else. *Derek must think that I'm really lazy, or that I don't know how to cook. I do know how, I just don't enjoy it that much. Plus I have the money to eat out, so why not do that? Someday soon I'll cook him a nice meal, just to show him.*

I noticed his phone on the counter. I really wanted to look at it, but I felt I shouldn't. But I wanted to. *But it's wrong. But I can't stand it. But it's an invasion of privacy. But he is my boyfriend. But . . . Ahhhh! Screw it! I'm looking!* I reached for the phone and heard the shower shut off. I quickly turned it on and hit the green phone button for recent calls. My adrenaline was pumping. I quickly scrolled the list. It showed the last seven calls were from Jodi. The latest being an outgoing call to her at midnight, which was about when I had gone to bed and heard him talking softly. *What the heck? I'm sure it was work, or a cousin wondering about Kelly.* I put it back to the main screen and set it down exactly where I'd found it. The bathroom door opened and out walked Derek.

"Mmm, good morning," he said, taking my face in his hands and kissing me.

"Oooh, good morning," I said with a smile. He smelled good. *Fresh, soft, clean-shaven face. Mmm, Mmm.* "What time do you want to head out?" I asked.

"Soon, I was thinking we could grab something to eat on the way. The faster we get there the faster we can leave. I want to get a few hours of sleep in before my shift tonight."

"Okay, I'm going to take a quick shower and we can be on the road in thirty."

I went to my room, picked out my clothes, and went to the bathroom. After a quick shower, I dressed in jeans, a cute fall shirt and half sweater, and casual brown shoes. I put some mousse in my hair, brushed my teeth, and did a few swipes of mascara on my top lashes. I took a moment to put some extra lotion on my arms. They'd begun itching in the middle of the night again. Next, I scurried to the bedroom and packed up everything I needed to bring with to the cabin and set it by the door. Derek took my keys and said he'd start running stuff out to the Jeep. I put some food in a small cooler to take with, then got Faith's meds, food and litter box. Back in the bathroom I shot my hair quick with a blow dryer and put the finishing touches on it. After closing all the blinds, turning down the heat, and shutting off all the lights, we headed to our Jeeps.

I followed Derek in my red Jeep all the way to Morris. *I still get a kick out of the fact that we have the same vehicles.* The drive was long, but it felt much better going there knowing that Cory and Kyle were behind bars. I passed the time by calling Kat. We chatted about my new situation with Derek and her date with Wes. Her date went well. They were seeing each other again later this week. After I got done talking to her, I had an incoming call.

"Hello?"

"Yes, this is Sara? Sara Martin?"

"Yes, this is she . . ." The voice sounded familiar.

"Yes, lady. This Rocko Sanchez. I in C.S Landscaping. You owe me money. Your yard is cleaned up, yes? You back home now, yes?"

"Oh, hi! Um, no I'm not back home yet. Later this afternoon I'll be back in town."

"Oh, oh, okay. You pay me when you back. Sorry. When you back here, you stop in a pay me, or I send you bill instead. One is easy for you? Si? Yes?"

"Yes. I'll stop in and pay you. That's easy for me. How late are you open today?"

"Five. We close five. No close five oh one . . . five oh twoooo . . . No! We close five! Okay, lady?" he asked.

"Okay. I'll be there before five. Thank-you."

"Yes, yes. Good bye," he said and hung up. I smiled and shook my head. *That guy cracks me up!*

Looking out the window, I noticed that Derek was talking on his phone, too. I wondered if it was Jodi—who was this Jodi? I was sure I didn't need to worry about it. I usually wasn't the jealous type, but the situation with my ex-husband and my late, ex-bestfriend had caused me to have my guard up and my trust of people way down.

I called my mom to help clear my mind. I thanked her for the meal and told her, again, that I was sorry about not telling her what had happened sooner. We talked about it for a while and I let her go. I really didn't want to re-live that horrible situation. I just wanted a break from it. I tossed the phone on to the seat next to me and noticed Faith walking on top of the bags of stuff in the back. She was very curious and getting so big. I was kind of sad that she was looking more like a cat and less like a kitten.

I turned the radio on and just drove for a while. My mind was busy and I was trying my best to not stress about anything. I enjoyed the time in the car, but there weren't any good songs on, so my mind went back to wondering. Rex popped into my mind. He was gorgeous and I was missing his face. It felt wrong to think that, but it was true. I liked Derek's face too, but there was something about Rex.

RING! RING! My ring tone filled the air. While reaching for the phone I went out of my lane and hit the rumble strips. I corrected quickly and straightened out. I saw Derek shaking his finger and looking at me in his rear view mirror when I looked down at my screen. I didn't recognize the number.

"Hello?"

"Hello, darling! It's Miss Kitty! Just making sure we are still on to meet later today. Is that going to work for you, love?" Elenore Kitstoff asked.

Oh, man. I was hoping she'd lost my number. "Ummm, I, well . . ." I stumbled trying to think of an excuse not to meet her.

"Stop, my dear, you're babbling," she insisted. She made me feel like I was a nerd and she was a high school bully. "What are you doing right now?" she demanded.

"I . . . um, I'm driving to Morris to visit someone in the hospital, and then heading back to Nisswa."

"Okay, so let's make it a dinner date at that shabby diner on main street," she said.

"Morning Glory, or Ed's Bar-B-Q Pit?" I asked.

"Morning Glory. There are not a lot of choices, but I try not to frequent the Pit," she told me. "Let's make it 6:00 p.m. That'll give you enough time," she said, as if she were in charge.

I wanted to say, "You're not the boss of me," and stick my tongue out at her. I didn't. "Ah, yeah, sure, that's fine," I obediently answered. "See you then."

"Oh, and Ms. Martin . . ."

"It's Sara. You can call me Sara."

"Fine, Sara, come alone. Later, darling," she said and disconnected.

Oh boy, now what? She thinks I'm psychic. I can't read minds. My dreams were a total fluke. I haven't had one since Carrie and Lily were found. I have no abilities whatsoever that would be of any benefit to her. I don't know why she is even calling me.

My phone rang again. *Sheesh!* It was Derek.

"Hello!" I said.

"Hey. Hungry?"

"Yes."

"We're almost there. How about Perkins in Morris before we go to the hospital?" he asked.

"That's fine. I'll follow you."

I threw my phone down and dug in my console for the car charger and plugged it in. We pulled in to Perkin's and walked in together. Faith had a nose up against the glass quietly meowing. I made a mental note to bring her a treat on the way back. The only bad thing about traveling back and forth between the Cities and Nisswa was hauling her around. She had to spend a lot of time in the Jeep. Besides being active in the Jeep, she did travel well, and I always left her litter box on the floor in the back seat, just in case. She was such a good cat. We placed our orders and both went to use the bathroom. Derek was back at the table when I returned.

"So . . . you were on your phone a lot," he said. "Lots of people, or just a long chat?"

"Well, four different calls actually. There was Kat, my mom, C.S.Landscaping, and . . . Miss Kitty," I said and quickly took a drink of my juice.

"Miss Kitty?"

"Yes."

"Is that a nickname?"

"Yes, her real name is Elenore Kitstoff."

I wasn't giving him much but I didn't really know what to tell him. That, and I knew he probably wouldn't like me to get involved in her issues, especially since last Friday night.

"And . . . this is a friend of yours?"

"Umm, no. More like a friend of Nisswa. She has called me a few times and wants to meet me and chat."

He looked me up and down with squished eyebrows. "Oh, so she's a reporter," he concluded.

Maybe I should let him have that. Nah, with my luck, he'd ask for the article next week. "Not really. I'm not sure what she wants. Tannya said she's an older lady, who married rich and is a diva. She seems to think that I can dream the future, or the past, and I possess some special ability that she needs the service of."

Derek was drinking his pop and almost spit it out with a laugh. "What did you tell her?" He squinted his eyes at me. "You can't . . . can you?" he questioned.

Oooh, this could be fun . . . I better not. "No, of course not. And I did tell her that, but she refused to listen, and basically demanded a meeting with me tonight."

"Just tell her no." It seemed like a simple concept.

"I tried. This woman is used to getting what she wants, and she's actually very good at getting it. She wouldn't listen, and told me where to meet her and when."

The waitress brought our food and we dug in. After a few bites it was my turn.

"You were on your phone too. Any crazies bothering you?" I asked.

"None I can't handle," he said with a wink and a smile.

He offered nothing further, and I wasn't sure that I wanted to push it.

We finished eating and I said I'd cover it. Derek tried to argue, but I reminded him that he brought more than enough food to my apartment this weekend, so it was my turn. On our way back to the Jeep, Derek's phone rang, but he ignored the call. *Seriously? He never ignores calls.* It was beginning to really bother me. I mentally scolded myself, knowing that it shouldn't.

Through the window of my Jeep I could see Faith lying in the sun on the dash board. I hoped she wasn't cold. The temp was in the low forties. We were only in the restaurant for about forty-five minutes, so I figured she was fine. I followed Derek to the hospital and parked next to him in the lot. I jumped down from the Jeep and locked it behind me.

"I can't stay very long. Faith will get cold," I told him.

"I don't plan on staying long either," Derek said.

He took my hand and we walked into the building together. In the elevator he pressed me up against the wall and thanked me for coming with him. I kissed him to say *you're welcome*. When the doors parted, we walked out and down the hall to Kelly's room. Kendall was there with Doug and Kathy.

"Hello, everyone," Derek said as we entered the room.

His mom and dad were both on the far side of Kelly's bed and Kendall was closest to the door. They all came over to us and hugged us. I had shared more hugs with people in the last year than I had in my entire life. Kelly was sitting up and looked really good.

"Hey, sis," Derek said. "You look great!"

"Thanks," she said, her voice sounding good too. "Kendall brought my makeup. It feels good to know I have it on, as silly as that sounds."

"Whatever works," Derek said shaking his head.

I leaned over and gave her a hug. I always felt a bit weird hugging her because I didn't know her outside of the hospital. "Well, your brother doesn't get it, but I understand completely," I assured her.

"Thanks. It's good to see you guys. Thanks for coming. The doctor was just in a little while ago and said that I should be able to go home tomorrow. I still have a lot of follow up visits and physical therapy but at least I won't be stuck in here anymore," she told us.

"Wow, that's great!" I said. "How are you feeling?"

She tipped her head side to side and said, "Pretty good. When I get up and go for walks down the hallway I have some pain in my stomach, but nothing too bad. It feels like a lot of work just to walk, but that's because my muscles haven't been used for so long. The nurse said that it will take a few days to improve. Since I tire very quickly I can't go back to work or school for at least two weeks, at which point the doctor will see how things look and let me know if I'm cleared."

"That's great news, Kelly!" Derek said. "I have great news too.

21

"Did you find him? Did you find Cory?" Kelly anxiously asked.

"We did! And when I say *we* did, I mean *we* did!" he said pointing a finger back and forth between him and me. "I couldn't have done it without Sara. She basically used herself as bait and led us to him."

"No, that's not true," I told her. "I helped where I could, and then it was out of my hands."

Derek told the entire room the story of Friday night and made me out to be some sort of hero. The whole family seemed grateful and said that they were extremely thankful for what I'd done. Kathy was really upset about the kidnapping, and so were Doug and Kendall, but Kathy was full of rage and hated the jerk for what he'd done, not only to her daughter, but to me too.

"Jesus, who the hell do these guys think they are?" she demanded.

Derek put an arm around her, "Well, they're in the slammer now and will be for a long time. They're being charged with multiple counts of kidnapping, burglary with intent to harm, attempted rape, possession of stolen goods, drug possession, grand theft auto, trespassing, driving while under the influence, failure to appear, and for Cory, attempted murder, and fleeing a police officer. And that's just a start! I'm sure there'll be more. Those two jerks will be in there a long time."

"Good! Let the bastards rot!" Doug said.

Doug was a man of few words, but I always liked what he had to say. He thanked me for putting myself in danger and doing what I did to help catch them. I again shook my head. I really didn't feel that they needed to thank me.

We sat there and visited for about an hour, and then Derek announced that we had to get going. It was about 1:00 p.m., so I was fine with that. We said our goodbyes and walked back out to the lot. At my Jeep I unlocked the door and tossed my purse in and started it. It was cool and Faith was awake. The sunny spot I parked in had become shaded already.

"When can I see you again?" Derek asked, leaning into my window.

"Whenever you want," I told him. He tipped his head. "I don't really know what my schedule looks like, but it would be nice to just hang at the cabin for a few days and be drama-free. I need to be at Lost and Found for a couple of days, for paperwork, but other than that I'm flexible."

"All right, well, when I know *my* schedule better I'll give you a call and see if I can come out there or you can come to my place. Okay?" he said and kissed me.

"Okay," I replied when we parted.

"Drive careful, sweetness," he said and headed to his Jeep.

I turned towards home. The drive there was long . . . and boring. The trees were no longer pretty and everything including the grass was brown. I found a talk radio station and listened for a while, but that got boring too. *Does it really matter that another celebrity is getting a divorce? Ugh!*

I played with my GPS while I drove and typed in C.S. Landscaping. *Apparently they like to get out of work on time. Can't say I blame them, but I've never quite been told like that.* I wouldn't say they had bad customer service, just a blunt, straight-to-the-point approach. *Hopefully they did a good job, because I don't have time to go home and check first.*

My GPS led me through Nisswa to the outskirts of town just past the Jefferson farm. It had a newer aluminum-sided building, tan with a green roof, and had three white, automatic doors on one side. There was a nice brick entryway with windows and an office area near the front. It was pleasant. There was a large, hand-carved, log sign that read, C.S. LANDSCAPING, with the phone number. I slowed and made the left turn. There were three vehicles in the lot and the lights in the office were on. After exiting the Jeep, I tossed my purse over my shoulder and walked in. The place smelled like new carpet and was very clean. When I'd passed the entry way door, I heard Mexican music playing. It seemed appropriate. Then I heard a familiar voice: "Hello, lady!"

"Hello," I said with a smile.

"Come in office. What your name, lady?"

He briefly looked at me, then got up from the desk and walked over to the wire file basket on top of the credenza behind him. He was Mexican, short, petite, black hair, black eyes, and in his mid to late thirties. He was donning dark-blue, denim jeans with cool designs on the back pockets and a perfectly fitted, red, Ed Hardy polo with a graphic that wrapped over his right shoulder and down the shirt sleeve. He was clean cut, clean shaven, and very nice looking.

"I'm Sara Martin."

"Haa haaa, yes, yes, I remember you. You the funny one!" he laughed and shook his head while digging through the large pile of files. *Apparently they run a large, successful business here.* "You the one that call to reschedule the fallen leaves! Ha ha ha. Lady . . ." he said shaking his head. "One thing I tell you. When leaves on the ground, leaves not going anywhere. Leaves no go out of town with you, no?" He shook his head, amused.

After pulling my file he walked back up to the front counter.

I think he's mocking me. "No," I said. "That's not what I meant. I just didn't know if I needed to be there when you came," I tried to explain.

"I just joking with you, lady. Relax, relax," he laughed.

I smiled at him. His teeth were really crooked. He was much better looking when he didn't smile. I was trying not to visibly cringe at the sight. "You need us grass, or leaves, or snow, or even till garden or move dirt, anything, you not need be there. We know how to do it! You go do you stuff, we get you work done while you gone. Is okay, yes?" he looked up at me awaiting my response.

It felt funny to keep responding yes, but I did. "Yes."

"Is you cash or card? We no allow check."

"Card," I said and handed it to him. A quick swipe through the machine, and signature later, and he was paid.

"Lady, we see you have large driveway. Snow coming! They say this week, snow! You have plow and truck, yes?"

"No," I said. I hadn't thought that far ahead.

"You need us do that? Here, I show you how it work," he said and went to a drawer. After flipping through a few folders, he pulled out a sheet of paper and laid it on the counter in front of me. "This is contract for snow. It snow two or more inches, we come and plow it out of way. We bill you each time we come out. If you want us take snow away, it cost more. You have big yard though, you can leave snow on side by trees. It melt. You want that? We come as soon as we can. Can't be everywhere at once, but we get done fast! Yes?"

"Yes. Yeah, that sounds perfect."

"Sign here, and we add you to route. You get bill next day after we plow. You send card info, or stop by, or pay online or auto pay. No mail check. Okay?"

"Okay."

I reached over and signed the paper. He had written in ninety-five dollars each time in the blank. That seemed reasonable to me. I told him to do the auto pay so I didn't have to worry about it every time it snowed two inches.

"Okay, here is where we put it."

There in the file was a Google Earth print out of my property. He drew with a yellow marker where they would push and pile the snow.

"That looks fine to me," I told him. "Thank you."

"Yes, yes. Thank you for business. Much appreciated. Have good day."

"You too. Bye." I tossed my bag back on my shoulder and walked back to the Jeep.

There was only about an hour before my meeting with Miss Kitty, so I drove home. When I pulled in the driveway, I noticed what a great job they did on the yard. There was not a leaf anywhere. I unpacked my Jeep and got Faith all set up inside. I looked out the deck door and noticed that they had even gotten the leaves that were piled up around the grill. *Very nice!* I unpacked the cooler and my clothes, and then loaded myself back into the Jeep.

The drive to Morning Glory was nerve racking. *I just need to stand my ground, tell her that I have no special abilities, and that she needs to find someone else for whatever she needed. I mean really, did she think that I was going to read her palm or tarot cards?*

I made my final left and pulled into a space in front of the entry door. It was a few minutes before 6:00 p.m. I turned the key and jumped out. When I opened the door, I saw Tannya right away. *Good, at least I have a back-up if things go crazy.*

"Hey, girl!" Tannya yelled from across the room when I entered.

I waved and smiled. The place was pretty busy. It was mostly older couples who had already finished eating. The daily special sign said, MONDAY MASH AND POT ROAST SPECIAL, and that's what was on almost everyone's plates too. I scanned the place for a booth near the back where people wouldn't be able to overhear us. Tannya came over with a pot of decaf as I sat down.

"Coffee, hun?" she asked me.

"No, just a diet Pepsi."

"How's Faith doing?" she asked.

"Great. She stopped throwing up, and has even more energy, so the medicine must be working."

"Oh, that's great! She is such a sweet cat. I'll watch her anytime!"

"Thank you. I'll probably need you again. Ya never know."

She leaned closer to me and quietly asked, "So how are you doing since the whole incident? Your arms healin'? Your face looks good."

"Yeah, I'm fine," I said quietly. "The bruise on my face is completely gone and the scratches are healing nicely."

"Oh, good. So are you here for dinner?"

"Kinda, I'm meeting Miss Kitty here any minute."

"Oh! Really! Tonight? You changed your mind?" she said excitedly.

"No, but she wouldn't take no for an answer over the phone, so I had to meet her. I guess I'll just take the pop for now, and see if she is going to eat or not when she gets here. So, how will I know it's her? Will you give me a signal or something when she comes in?"

Just talking about it made my heart beat faster. I didn't know why she made me so nervous.

"HA! Oh, honey, you won't need my help. You'll know when she arrives. The girl practically arrives with her own theme song," she laughed and walked away.

Tannya returned a moment later with my pop. I couldn't help but notice that her pants were new and fit her much better, and her hair was much healthier looking. Her makeup was still very loud though.

RING, RING, TING! The bells on the door chimed and in walked Miss Kitty. There was no mistaking her. And I was pretty sure that I actually did hear theme music! She was tall, about six foot and all legs. She was wearing a bright pink, velour sweat suit. The bright pink pants had rhinestones in a line down the outside of each leg. Her white tank showed about a foot of cleavage said, SEXY, also in rhinestones, right across the girls. The suit included a matching bright pink, front zip hoodie. And, of course, the hoodie had rhinestones on it too. The pants were elastic at the cuff and skin tight so they looked more like leggings. She weighed only about 120 pounds and had no fat anywhere.

Miss Kitty was in silver, spiked stilettos with pink toenail polish with rhinestones on her big toes. Over her shoulder was a huge purse that may or may not have contained a small dog. Her hair was a yellow-brassy, fake blonde color that was pulled up into a sloppy pony tail with loose curly pieces falling around her face. She was pretty, but it was way too much! She stopped and scanned the room. I glanced at Tannya, She was just smiling back at me nodding. When I looked back to Miss Kitty, she was already wiggling her way over to me.

"Sara, I presume," she said in a valley-high voice.

"Yes. You must be Elenore," I said extending my hand.

She took my hand, but had her hand palm down and her wrist bent as if wanting me to kiss it. I shook it quickly and let go. Her scent was overpowering. *She must have bathed in perfume.* It made my throat scratchy.

"Please have a seat," I offered. She sat and set her purse gently on the floor. I noticed it did have a vent in it and wondered about its contents.

"Please call me Miss Kitty. I hate the name Elenore, makes me sound old," she said with a wink. "Did you eat, dear? Regardless of the interior design of this . . . this place, they do have pretty good food," she said with a lot of hand gestures. "It'll be my treat of course!"

"Um, okay sure. I'll eat." Tannya came over with a tall glass of iced-tea and set it in front of Miss Kitty.

"Hello, Miss Kitty. How are you today?"

"Fine, fine. We'll take the special and whatever she wants," she said in a pleasant but hurried tone.

"I'll have the special too," I told Tannya.

"Thank you, gals. You can go to the salad bar when you're ready. It's unlimited visits, just take a clean plate every time," she said and picked the menus up and walked away.

"Let's go now, Smoochy Poo is starved," she said.

"Smoochy Poo?" I questioned.

Miss Kitty put her finger to her lips, "Shhh, she's in the purse. Come on let's get some food."

I followed her to the buffet. When we returned to the table I noticed that she had mostly chocolate pudding on her plate, along with a few bread sticks and a large scoop of the mystery salads. I had a large lettuce salad with no dressing and I skipped the bread stick. *So how is her ass half the size of mine?*

While we ate she asked me about myself. I told her the basics. Then she asked about the situation on the lake a few months back. I told her a brief story and emphasized that, while I did have dreams that led me to two dead bodies, I had not had any since, or even before that.

"I really don't have any special skills. I'm not sure why you think I'm the girl to help you . . . What is it you need help with?" I asked, just as Tannya returned with our plates.

Tannya wiggled her eyes brows at me from behind Miss Kitty and set the plates down. I ignored her gesture and thanked her as she walked away.

"Sara, darling. I'm perfectly aware that you're not psychic. If you were you would already know what I want. Ha! Ha! Ha!" she said as she laughed at me. When she calmed herself, she stuck some more food into her purse vent and continued on. "Love, the reason I need your help is because you are a woman scorned."

"What?"

"Your husband cheated on you, and with your best friend no less. You're a girl who understands what that's like. I, too, think that something's going on with my husband. Not just with another woman, but there's something going on with his business," she told me as she stuck more food through the hole. *Whatever breed it is, it's very quiet.* "I don't work, so all my money comes from my husband's business, and lately I've noticed that the numbers are down. He doesn't know that I look at his computer at night when he sleeps, but I have noticed that there are a lot more withdrawals lately, and the money's not being given to me. I've been trying to pay attention to where it might be going, but I can't find anything. I don't want to ask because I don't want to be cut off or cause a fight. You see, my husband and I aren't exactly close. I love him . . . but more like a father than a lover. The money's satisfaction enough for me. I'll stay with him until he croaks, as long as I continue to get my allowance for making him 'happy' once in a while," she added air quotes with her fingers. "If you know what I mean." I wished I didn't.

"So you want me to spy on him?" I asked.

"Yes! Would you, darling? I'll pay you whatever you want. This will be a good start and, depending on your time and efforts, I'll pay you more when you are finished." She pulled a fat envelope from her purse and slid it across the table to me. "It's ten thousand. Is that enough to get started?" she asked.

Gasp! I choked on the food in my mouth and coughed. After taking a sip of pop, I took a deep breath and looked her in the eyes. I had no idea what to say. Suddenly Tannya appeared with a pitcher of iced-tea and another diet pop. She was nodding as she approached the table, but stopped when she came into Miss Kitty's sight.

"Refill?" Tannya asked. "You can never have enough of something this good," she said topping off our glasses. "Even if *you* don't need more, there's some one who might!" she said, all loud and chipper. "Anything else I can get you?" I was sure she was meaning me.

Miss Kitty chimed in first, "No, we're fine, Tannya. Thank ya, dear!" Tannya nodded and left.

"I really don't need the money," I told her.

"Bull shit!" she snapped. "Everyone needs money. You can never have enough. And if you think you do, then give it away to one of those charity thingy's and make someone else happy. You know it's true, money *can* buy happiness. It's the broke people that came up with that bullshit about money not buying happiness."

"I . . . ah . . . I . . ."

"Please, Sara," she begged. "I know we just met, and you don't owe me anything, but you know firsthand how it feels to be cheated on. Wouldn't you have wanted to find out earlier if you could have?" Her tone was serious and sad. I could see hurt behind all that makeup. I nodded slightly. "So you understand what I'm going through? Sick to my stomach every day. Constantly questioning his every move. If someone could've taken that from you, wouldn't you have paid anything for that?"

I thought seriously about that. *Yes.* She begged some more.

"Please, Sara. Please help me to figure this out, so I can stop this icky feeling I'm living with every day."

"I . . . um . . . okaaaay," I whined.

"Thank you so much! I promise to make it worth your while, or if not your while, than someone else you know, or a charity you love! You can decide what to do with the money."

"All right, but I need to know more about this whole situation. Your husband, his work, the address for both, any partners, and suspected lover's names and addresses . . . everything!" I said, sounding all official. I was surprised at my own voice.

"Okay, love! Now we're talking! I have everything you need in here," she said and handed me a manila file folder.

I opened it and quickly paged through it. It contained a picture of her husband, Vincent Alburgus, a complete bio, addresses to the properties he resided at, and a list of the properties he owned. There was also a similar page on a man named Dave Stone.

"Who's Dave Stone?" I asked.

"He's Vincent's assistant. He's worked for my husband for the last twenty years. I don't like him. I *never* liked him, but lately he's really been rubbing me the wrong way. He's mean, rude, and slimy."

The way she curled her lip when she spoke about him made me a believer. There was also a picture of a young twenty-something woman, in a bar, taken from across the room.

"Who's this?"

She threw her hands up and shook her head. "I was checking up on him one night, and I saw her stumble out of my husband's limo and walk into the bar. So, I parked and followed her. I took that picture right before she went into the bathroom, threw up, and passed out. I couldn't even confront her because she wouldn't wake up. I just left and that's when I really started thinking about things."

"How long ago was this taken?" I asked her.

"About three weeks. Around the same time I found information about an Alexa on my husband's computer. Thing is, that's not a picture of Alexa."

I was confused. "So there are *two* women?"

"Who knows? That's why I'm hiring you. You can figure all this out for me. It's all too much! I have to get to the gym, and salon, and shop. I don't have time to figure all this out. There's information on Alexa in the file too."

I paged ahead. There was a printout of a computer screen. The set up was very similar to Facebook, but at the top it said, "Gold Digger Prospects." *Seriously?*

There was a picture of Alexa and a short bio under her name: Likes martinis dry, and skin wet. Loves to have fun—lots of it! *Eww*. She was blonde, skinny, pretty, and had fat red lips. Her boobs were the size of cantaloupes, and the tight tank over them was stretched so tight it looked painted on. In the picture she was leaning toward the camera. Her arms were pushing her cleavage together and she was pouting her lips, with one finger in her mouth. She looked a bit older than I was, but who knew if she'd had work done. The bio stats said she was five-foot-eleven, 120 pounds, twenty-five years old.

"So she wants to marry a millionaire, and your husband has an account with Gold Digger Prospects? Is this like a millionaire matchmaker dating service thing?"

"Yes and he has 300 friends, all girls. This is the one he messages with the most. I've read the messages. I don't think they've done anything yet, but it sounds like they plan to soon. She's from the Brainerd area, not too far from here. The messages alone are cheating in my book!" She looked hurt again.

I paged through the rest of the papers. Most were daily schedules, contact info for her, and daily routines for Vincent. There was also a copy of his planner for the next two months with appointments, lunch dates, and anything else I might need.

"I'll see what I can find out, but I'm not promising anything. I have a business to run too, so if you're on a time line I can't promise *when* either."

"No, I don't care about how long it takes. I'll just keep collecting money and acting like I don't know anything. Just keep in touch every couple days or so, okay?" she asked.

"Okay."

"Well, I have to run. Smoochy Poo has a play date tonight. Thank you, darling, for helping me with this. If you could be discrete about it, I'd appreciate that." She stood and put a fifty on the table. "Have some dessert too before you leave! Bye, bye, darling!" she sang and blew me a kiss.

I watched her walk away and wondered what the hell I was thinking! She got to the door, and it swung open and was held for her. She smiled and stopped to talk. She looked like she was flirting with someone, but I couldn't see who it was because of the reflection on the glass door and the fact it was already dark out. Then she walked away and in came Rex.

22

Lord help me! Rex was just as gorgeous as the last time I saw him, and he was in uniform.

"Hey there, handsome!" I heard Tannya yell. "Take a seat I'll be right with you."

"Hey, Tannya. Thanks," he said.

He scanned the room and caught my eye. I realized my mouth was hanging open, so I shut it quickly and smiled as he approached my booth.

"Hi, Rex," I managed.

"Hey, you! Glad to see you're back and doing well. I caught some of the buzz at the police station about you and your . . . little incident. You had me . . . ah us, pretty worried," he told me.

"Oh, the kidnapping? Ah, that was nothing. All in a day's work!" I said with a hand flip.

"Seriously, I have to hear the story," he said with a serious look.

"All right. Well, what are you doing now? Did you eat dinner? This special is amazing. You can join me if you'd like," I offered.

"Yeah sure," he said and sat down.

Tannya came over with a coffee and a pop. She sat them down in front of him. "Your usual I assume?" she asked.

"Yes, thanks," he told her.

"Do ya know what ya want, hun?" she asked.

"Yeah, I'll have the special," Rex replied.

"What? Oh, yeah, I already knew that! I was talking to Sara," she said with a wink. "You wanna pass some time, tell her to fill you in on the details of this past weekend."

She walked away with a smirk. Rex looked at me and smiled.

"So what do you want?" he asked, narrowing his eyes.

I smiled and squirmed in my seat a little.

"I'm not sure I follow you. I think she meant which dessert, but I haven't decided yet. Anyway, I do have a good story for you," I said changing the subject. Tannya arrived with his order and set it in front of him. While he ate I told him about my weekend. Although he was impressed, he also got a bit parenty. "Aren't girls supposed to go to the bathroom together in places like that?" he asked.

Oh geez, we're all the way back there? "Um, only in middle school. Although somehow I don't think that would've prevented those guys from getting to me. Their plan wasn't exactly . . . well thought out. Idiot one and two were kinda flying by the seat of their pants," I said referring to Cory and Kyle.

"Well that's quite the story, Sara. I'm glad you're okay."

"Thanks. Did I miss anything here while I was gone?" I asked.

"Nope, same old, same old. Which is nice most of the time, but once in a while I'd like some action. Nothing too awful, I'd just like to use my skills someday," he told me with a half grin.

"Sounds to me like you need to move to Chicago or New York. Somewhere that actually has crime. This town is too little for you."

"Nah, I like the small town feel, just need to wake up from the mundane routine is all. That being said, did I see you sitting with Miss Kitty when I parked?"

"Yes." That's all I offered.

"Well?" he said, waiting.

"Well, what?"

"Well I don't want to pry . . . are you two friends now?" he asked.

"Not really. She just wanted me to check on a couple things for her."

"Like her husband?" he pressed.

I wondered if there was more to the story that I didn't know. "Yes."

He finished his last bite and pushed his plate aside.

"I'm going to go get some salad. Do you want anything else?" he asked me.

"No thanks. I'm full." I watched him fill up his plate, studying his perfectly chiseled face.

He must have felt me staring because he looked up and winked at me. *Great, now I'm blushing!* When he'd finished, he walked back over and sat down.

"Well, just be careful with her. With money comes power, and with power comes stupid decisions. Rich people don't respect laws, and they don't think past what they're doing," he paused and took a bite. "Just be careful, okay? And you have my number. You can call me if you ever need anything. Day or night, I'll pick up."

"Okay," I said. All I could think about was what I might need him for at night. Tannya came over to check on us and left two bills. I grabbed for both right away. "My treat!" I said.

"Thanks but it's my turn."

"No, it's not. I owe you a lot. And you can consider it payment on my future needs," I said with a giggle. "Ya just never know what kind of trouble will find me. And when it does I know I can call *you*, 'cause now you owe me."

We slipped on our jackets and walked to the front. After I paid the bills with Miss Kitty's fifty, we headed to the door together.

"Call me, Sara!" Tannya demanded with a wave from the back of the room.

I nodded and waved. Rex walked with me to the Jeep. He thanked me for dinner and then there was an awkward moment . . . and a pause that I finally broke. "Well it was nice to see you again," and loaded myself into the Jeep.

He smiled and winked.

"You, too," he said slowly and returned to his truck.

I was exhausted by the time I pulled into my driveway. It was 9:00 p.m. but it felt later. It had been a very long day. When I got home I fed and medicated Faith. After that I put on lounge wear and fluffy socks and climbed into bed. Faith decided to join me. She circled three times and plopped down on the pillow next to mine. Carefully I reached past her for the remote and turned on the TV, but fell asleep before the second commercial was over.

I bolted awake! *Shit! I didn't set the alarm. What time is it?* I looked at the clock, and it said 5:17 a.m. *Phew!* I needed to open Lost and Found and get some office stuff done. I got up and jumped in the shower. While I was in the middle of rinsing my hair I remembered that I had ten thousand dollars cash in an envelope in my purse. *Not too smart.* I made a mental note to stop by the bank and make a deposit into a new account. I didn't know what I was going to do with the money yet, so I'd just put in there for now and let it grow.

I got to the store at 7:30, which gave me plenty of time to get my paper work done and do a bit of cleaning before I opened. One of the things I was going to do was look at the hours I was open and shorten them. The owner before me had much shorter hours in the fall and winter and I knew now there was a reason for that. Our traffic was way down.

I had left a note for Ginger and Maureen last week to let me know what they thought would be good hours and when they wanted to work. After going over what they wrote down I decided that starting next week we would be open Tuesday through Friday 10:00 a.m. to 5:00 p.m., and Saturday's 9:00 a.m. to noon. They must have talked and said they'd split the hours and had it all planned out, so I didn't need to work at all, but I'd just come in to do filing and paperwork. *That works for me!* I'd just be backup in case either of them was ever sick. At 11:00 a.m., when Ginger arrived, I left for the bank. I opened a new account and deposited the money.

When I was finished, I climbed back up in my Jeep and looked through the file on Vincent. He was sixty-eight years old and looked it. His picture looked like a real estate photo, which, from what I understood, was his official title. He was a white man with hair that was obviously dyed black with it being a bit too dark for his gray eyebrows. He was in a black business suit and smiling. He was a nice-looking man. He seemed to be in good shape at six-foot-three and 200 pounds. He didn't have a belly but he had a bigger frame.

I flipped ahead to Alexa, from Brainerd. I thought I would start with her. She was only a twenty-minute drive, and I had nothing else to do. A quick stop at the gas station for gas, coffee, and a couple donuts and I was on my way. I called Kat and told her what I was up to.

"Are you kidding me? I want in! Dang, girl, I'll take the money and come and help you, then I could get out of this office! It's just not the same here without you."

"Oh, I don't think you'll be missing much. But I'll keep ya up to date. We'll go out again soon, since our last night was cut short," I told her.

"Okay girl. Keep me posted, I'll talk to ya soon," she said and disconnected.

By the time I'd gotten off the phone with her, I was just blocks from Alexa's listed address. I had expected an apartment, but was in a residential area. I slowly followed the commands of my GPS and stopped in front of the house. There was a Buick Park Avenue in the driveway and some white swans that served as flower planters in the middle of the postage-stamp-sized front yard. The swans were full of dirt. The homes were all one levels and all looked almost the same. It was a low- to middle-income area and the houses showed their age. Most still had wood siding and the window paint was peeling on most. The landscaping was minimal and curb appeal non-existent. They were very plain.

I saw someone move inside the house and decided to jump into the back seat. I had tinted windows and no one would be able to see me in there from the outside. I saw an older woman through the large picture window in the front. Inside I could see a couch and TV and a few other pieces of furniture. The woman stood from the couch. I could tell she was in her fifties. She was chubby with short curly hair, and dressed in over-sized sweat pants and a sweatshirt. From where I was she looked bad. I couldn't tell if she had makeup on or not, but she wasn't what I would've called pretty.

She bent over and picked something up off the coffee table and walked towards the door next to the window. She opened the inside door, stuck her foot out the screen door, and lit a cigarette. She stood there smoking it and staring back into the living room, I assumed at the TV. She didn't seem to notice my Jeep, or if she did, she didn't give it a second thought. When her cigarette was done, she tossed it on the ground, pressed it out with her slipper, and kicked it off the front step into a large pile of butts below the front step. *Classy.* She shut the door and plopped herself back on the couch.

It has to be her mom, I thought. I got on my iPhone and logged onto Alexa's page. She didn't have a job listed, so maybe she lived with mama. I looked up her contact page and phone number. I dialed and continued watching through the window while it rang. After the second ring, I saw the woman sit upright, grab the TV remote, and point it at the TV. Then she picked up the cordless phone that was lying on the coffee table.

"Hello?" she said in a surprisingly sweet voice.

I would never have put the face and voice together.

"Hello?" she said again.

"Hi, is Alexa there?" I asked.

Maybe I should've thought this through more. I didn't know exactly what I was going to say.

"This is Alexa. Who's this?" she said. Wait . . . what?

"Um, this is Alexa?" I asked

"Yes, honey. I'm Alexa,"

I watched her speak into the phone.

"Um, hi. My name's Jill, and I'm calling for my boss Gerard. He saw your picture on "Gold Digger Prospects" and wanted me to call you and touch base. He's very busy and would like to know if it's okay for me to set up a date for you and him."

"Oh, well, um usually I like to chat for a bit on the site before I meet anyone—ya know to make sure we have a connection. So, tell him I'd love to chat and I'm on all the time night or day. Then we'll see how it goes, okay?" she told me.

"Okay, Alexa. I'll let him know. I'm sure he'll be in touch. Thanks. Bye."

I hung up, leaned forward, and pressed my head against the back of the passenger seat in front of me. *So she's a player. She's using a fake picture and probably a fake name too.* I sat up and noticed her mailbox next to my Jeep. *I should peek in it and see what name is on the mail. It's a federal offense, but I'm not stealing. I'm just looking, right?* I watched her for another fifteen minutes then she grabbed an empty glass and walked out of the room. *Refill!*

I quickly opened my door took two steps, pulled the door on the mailbox down and slid out an envelope. *Eva Jennings.* I slammed it shut and leaped back into the Jeep, quietly closing the door so I wouldn't alert the neighbors. I wrote down that name on her page in the file. *What the heck?* I punched in the number on my phone again and stored it as *Alexa/Eva*, in case she had caller ID and tried to call me back. Then I could ignore it. After it saved, I hit call and watched through the window. She came back into the room on the second ring, set down her full glass, and picked up the remote and muted the TV again. She answered in the same young, sweet voice. "Hello?"

I changed my voice hoping to throw her off.

"Hi, is this Eva Jennings?" I asked.

"You got her," I watched her say into the phone. I panicked and hung up. That's all I really needed anyway. I looked again and saw her shake her head and set the phone down. *She didn't look at the phone so she must not have caller ID.* I wrote down the make, model, color, and license plate of the car in the driveway on her page in the folder.

A few minutes later, when I saw Eva lie down on the couch and pull a blanket over herself, I climbed back into the driver's seat and drove away. I watched the road ahead as a black Porsche turned down the street coming towards me. *Strange neighborhood for a Porsche.* I took a right and headed towards home. It was 1:30 p.m. and a nap on the couch sounded really good. *I should go home and do that too,* I thought.

Driving along and thinking about Alexa, her motives, and how she was going to get any rich guy to marry her was puzzling me. If she lied about her looks and put up someone else's picture, how would that ever work? She'd eventually have to meet the guy right? I was pondering that when another thought occurred.

The Porsche! I recognized the driver! I know that face! I veered my Jeep on to the side of the next road and stopped. After I threw it into park, I paged through the folder Miss Kitty had given me. *It was Dave Stone! I drove right past him! What was he doing on Eva's street?* I threw the folder down and whipped a U-turn. After a few minutes I was back in front of Eva's, or should I say Alexa's, house again.

I slowly pulled closer and noticed the Porsche parked in the driveway behind the Buick. The living room blinds were pulled down now. *What the heck? Are they sleeping together? What does all of this have to do with Vincent?* I backed up and turned around. *I don't really need to see more, do I?*

I thought about calling Miss Kitty, but I didn't really have any proof of anything and I didn't know what was going on yet either. So there wasn't much to report yet and I was tired. I drove home, made a few notes on some loose paper, put them in the folder, and took a nap instead.

I woke up about 4:00 p.m. Faith was pouncing around on the bed chasing shadows the setting sun cast through tree branches. I sat up and grabbed her and tried to cuddle but she wasn't having it. She went back to hopping about so I got up to eat. I was hungry. I had forgotten to eat lunch. I seemed to be tired a lot still. I wondered when that would go away. I knew I had been through trauma, but I thought I should be recovered by now. It already was Tuesday night.

Then I remembered Morning Glory's Taco Tuesday. That sounded really good and I just loved how the whole place turned in to a Mexican restaurant, if only for a night. I didn't know if I felt like going into town again though. Standing there staring into an empty fridge pretty much settled it. I'd go to Morning Glory to eat, then I'd go get groceries so I didn't have to eat every meal there. I was beginning to look like a regular. I fed Faith, hiked my purse up on my shoulder grabbed a coat and locked the door behind me. My cell phone rang as soon as I got into the car.

"Hello," I answered.

"Hey, sweetness," Derek said.

"Hi."

"What are you up to?" he asked.

"I'm just on my way to get a bite to eat and then to the store to get groceries," I told him.

It was loud where he was. I looked at my dash clock and saw 5:10 p.m.

"Where are you?" I asked.

"Hey, do you still like Barcardi Coke or do you want something else?" I heard a woman's voice say. Then there was a scratching like he was covering the phone, and some muffled words I couldn't make out.

"I . . . ah . . . just finishing up a work report, and then heading home for the night. I thought I'd check in with you."

I wasn't happy.

"So you do work reports at the bar with women and cocktails now?" I asked trying not to sound angry. "Who was that?"

"Uh, no. Well, yes and no. I'm finishing up a report but I needed to get some paperwork for another detective, so we met here at the lounge down town," he said. I didn't know if I trusted that.

"Oh, who's the other detective? Anyone I know?" I asked in a more friendly tone.

"No, it's one from the MPD. They were assisting on a case that involved one of the gangs in the area that we both deal with."

"Oh, okay. Well you two have fun and enjoy yourselves," I said.

"You sound upset. This is a work thing, not a date, Sara. You don't have to worry about anything," he said.

I could hear the smile in his voice, which made me even madder. *But really, he can do what he wants. It's not like we're exclusive, right, Sara?*

"Oh, yeah, of course not! I know that. Sorry, I'm just tired. I just got up from a nap and I'm super hungry. Sorry if I sounded crabby," I said.

"So what else is new? Any plans for the week?" he asked.

"Nope, well I guess I'm kinda helping new friend with a project."

"Really?" What kind of project?" he asked in his police voice.

"She wants me to check up on her husband. He's a little off lately, and she thinks he may be cheating. I told her I'd help her out."

There was a long silence.

"As a friend, right? Is she paying you?"

"Why?"

"Well, because if you're acting as a private detective you need a license. And if you're getting paid to do this, you should have one."

"Whatever!" I said. *Man I hate rules.*

"I didn't hear that. Just keep me informed on the other happenings in your life and I won't know anything about *that* should it come up. Okay?"

"Okay." *I'm not going to get a license for this crap. If anything her husband should need a license to cheat. She shouldn't need one to find out if he's cheating. Sheesh!* "Well, I'll let you get back to your uh, business meeting," I said.

"Okay, take care. I'll call you tomorrow . . . after you've eaten."

"Whatever." I said annoyed and disconnected.

Hmm, was that our first fight? Who cares. I'm going to eat tacos and stock up on wine. I'll be good in a little while. Men! Who needs 'em? Wowzers, I'm crabby. Must be PMS. I pulled up to the door just as a police car did. I threw it into park and jumped down. There was Rex.

"Hey, you!" he said with a smile. "Come here often?"

I laughed out loud.

"I was just going to ask you the same thing."

He stood by his open door and took his jacket off, then tossed it on the passenger's seat. Under it was a tight blue uniform shirt and a belt full of "toys." My mind left for moment, on a mini vacation, to a happy place, that included a cop and a billy-club and . . .

"Sara?" Rex asked.

"Huh?" I snapped to attention.

Sheesh, yup I must be hormonal. There was heat where there shouldn't be heat when one is standing in a public parking lot. "Here for the Mexican Buffet?" I asked.

"Never miss it," he answered with a grin and squinted eyes.

I wondered if he could read my mind.

"You?"

He shut his door and walked to the sidewalk to meet me.

"Yeah, I was going to make something, but I have nothing in the fridge. Bummer too 'cause I was kinda craving homemade food."

"Really?" he said and stopped.

"Really. I've been eating out a lot lately and haven't had much energy since the . . . kidnapping. Man I hate that word."

"Oooh," he said sympathetically. "Then I have an idea, and since you owe me, it's an offer you can't refuse."

23

"Really?" I said. "What's the offer?"

"We are going to get in our vehicles, drive to the grocery store, and you are going to walk with me through the aisles while I get everything I need for my famous Taco Pie. Then we're going to drive to your place, and I'm going to make you a home-cooked meal and plop you down on the couch where you can rest while I clean up. And then . . ." he paused, looking confused, looking for something to say.

"And then?" I asked with my eyebrows in the air, a small smirk on my face.

"And then I'll bid thee farewell, my lady," he said with a slight bow. "But there's one condition."

"What's that?"

"You borrow me some Tupperware so I can take some leftovers to work for lunch tomorrow."

I eyed him up and down. I already knew my answer, but I wanted him to sweat a little.

"You can't refuse. It's my turn," he insisted with puppy-dog eyes.

"Okay," I said, "but I get to pick out dessert."

"Deal!" he said and extended his hand. I shook it. He held onto it and said, "Okay, follow me to the store."

I parked next to him in the grocery store lot and climbed out of the Jeep. He was already standing by his truck waiting. We walked in together. I followed him through the aisles as he explained his recipe.

"My mom taught me how to cook from a young age, and I must admit I *am* pretty good at it."

As we went along our conversation was mostly about foods—what we liked, what we didn't like, and most importantly, favorite desserts.

We both agreed that cheesecake was the best. We stopped by the bakery and I picked out a turtle cheesecake just before heading to the till. He insisted that he pay for the Taco Pie, but agreed that I could get the cheese cake. After we were rung up, we went back to our vehicles and drove to my place. It was really dark already, *stupid time change*, and it was downright cold out too.

I drove the speed limit the whole way home. It took forever. I pulled into the driveway close to the front door and he parked behind me.

"So do you always drive the speed limit exactly?" he asked as he grabbed the bags out of the back.

"As you know, no I do not. Normally I speed but now that I know the cops in this town keep a close eye out, I do more often. I always do when one is following me though," I said with a wink.

Once inside I started a fire in the fireplace and turned on the stereo for background music. Rex started unpacking the food and asked me for a few items like a frying pan and nine-by-thirteen baking dish. I grabbed a couple of cold beers out of the fridge and opened them.

"Here ya go!"

"Aw, thanks!" he said and drank half of it. "It was a long shift today."

We talked some more about his boring work day, and then he taught me how to make taco pie. He plopped a pound of hamburger into a pan and handed me a spatula.

"Here ya go. Brown it up, nice and small."

I went to work on that while he chopped up an onion and garlic. He added it to the pan, and then unrolled a package of Pillsbury crescent rolls and stretched them to fit the bottom of the nine-by-thirteen pan. He opened a bag of nacho cheese Doritos and crushed a few handfuls, sprinkling them on top of the dough. After the meat was brown, he added the Ortega seasoning packet and water like normal and then spooned the meat over the chips. He brushed his arm across mine to reach for the shredded cheddar and sprinkled the entire package on it.

"That's it!" he said and put it in the 350-degree oven.

He finished the rest of his beer and I got him another one.

"How long before it's done?" I asked. I was starving, and the beer was really kicking in.

"Only about twenty minutes."

We cleaned up the kitchen, got plates ready, and sat in the living room and talked for a bit. He asked about my store and if I was going to change the hours for winter. I told him the new hours and he promised to come in and get some help with Christmas shopping.

When the oven beeped we jumped up and went to the kitchen. It smelled wonderful. Rex cut a large piece for me, put it on a plate, and said to add whatever I wanted to it pointing to the counter where he had set out lettuce, tomato, black olives, sour cream, and taco sauce. I piled a little of all of it on top and sat it down at the table. I got two glasses of ice water, and two more beers over to the table and started in. Rex was already two bites into it.

"Mmmm. Oh, my gosh! This is amazing, Rex!"

"And so easy!" he added. "And it's better than the Morning Glory Buffet, at least once in a while."

We ate a few more bites.

"Thanks for coming over and cooking for me." I said.

"You're welcome," he replied sincerely.

After we ate, he did the rest of the dishes and I got him out a Tupperware container, which he loaded up, then told me that I got to keep the rest. I didn't argue that one at all. I heard my phone ring and looked at the screen. It was Derek. I ignored it, but suddenly felt guilt pouring through me, not that I should've. *After all he's at the lounge with little miss Bacardi-Coke.* I set the phone it back onto the counter.

"Don't want to talk to him right now?" Rex asked.

I realized I wasn't the only one who could see the screen.

"Nah, I'll call him back later," I said as I put all the toppings and leftovers in the fridge.

I grabbed the cheesecake out and cut two pieces. We ate that and went into the living room again. He asked me about Miss Kitty, and I told him everything I knew. He seemed very interested in Vincent, but I didn't have a lot of information on him yet.

"The guy seems shady. I've talked to him a couple of times, and he seems like the kind who tries to feel ya out to see if you can be paid off. Just a jerk! No respect for the law. I made it pretty clear I wasn't going to be bought. And he never actually said those words but he was pushing the subject. Anyway, like I said before, be careful. Just watch your back and don't get too close to them. I don't trust them. And remember you can always call me if you get in to a situation you don't like," he told me.

"I know, and I will. Thanks."

I smiled and got up and took his plate from him. After I put the dishes in the sink, I returned to the living room. He looked at me with his soft, dark eyes. Our eyes locked and I wondered again if he could read my mind. Again I felt the guilt wave!

"I should go," he said and broke his stare. "You need your rest and my work here is done."

I laughed.

"Thanks for coming. Supper was amazing."

When he got up to put on his shoes I went to the kitchen and grabbed his leftovers from the fridge and put half the cheesecake in another container for him too.

"This has to go with you, too," I said handing it to him.

"Oh, fine!" he said, and took them. "Thanks. This was fun."

"Yes, it was. Thanks again for the home-cooked meal, and the lesson."

"You're welcome," he said. "I'll see ya soon." He turned the door knob and walked out. He looked back as I closed the door and winked. "Good night."

"Good night."

I closed and locked the door, and tried to control my heart rate and catch my breath. I was suddenly startled by my ring tone.

"Hello."

"Hey, did you get some food in ya?" Derek asked.

Did I ever!

"Yup, I ate Mexican. It was good." I answered. "How was Bacardi-Coke, or whatever her name was?" I asked, surprising myself at the sarcasm. It had come out of my mouth before I knew it.

"Huh," he sighed before answering. "The investigation will be complete once the paperwork I got is added to the file. Then I can close the case. And the cocktail was fine, pretty weak, but fine," he answered.

"That's nice," I said trying to use a nicer tone.

"So what did you do tonight?" he asked.

"I got some groceries and had Mexican food with a friend, and I'm home. What are your plans for the weekend?" I asked trying to move on to a new subject.

"Not sure yet," he said. "You?"

"Not sure yet either. I'm going to go to bed now. I'm still pretty worn out from the events of last weekend."

"Yeah, I'm still having nightmares about it to. It was pretty scary, Sara."

Ahh, now he's being all sweet, and I want to be crabby. Dang him. I exhaled hard. "I know. I'm sorry," I said gently. He was so nice to me, and here I was being mean to him.

"Well, I have to work all week, but I have the whole weekend off. I'd like to see you, if it works for you," he said.

"Yeah, I'm sure it'll work. I'll call you later in the week and we'll set something up," I said.

"Okay, I'll wait to hear from you. Have a good night. Get some rest okay?"

"I will. Good night," I said and disconnected.

I sat there on the couch for a while longer feeling confused. I prayed to God, hoping he remembered me, and asked him to calm my mind. I didn't know what to think about either man. Both seemed to like me but I didn't know what I wanted. I prayed that it was just PMS and would pass. *Derek's my boyfriend right? It was just a business meeting. But what was the Taco Pie about? Ugh!* I grabbed another beer, the last beer, from the fridge and went to the bathroom and soaked in the tub. I read through *Vogue*, then dried off and went to bed.

Faith woke me up before dawn. I shooed her off the bed and tried to go back to sleep again, but it didn't work. I got up, showered, and got dressed. My plan today was to check out Vincent's schedule and see if I could figure some things out. I dressed in dark, comfortable jeans, and t-shirt with a sweatshirt over that. I wore socks and tennis shoes in case I had to run fast. I was kind of excited to spy on someone. I had gotten rushed the day before and I liked the puzzle of it all. *Maybe this is my new thing! Sara Martin, detective at large!* I was drying my hair and laughing at myself in the mirror, while my mind was coming up with all kinds of crazy crap. I mentally designed my super hero suit and cape when my phone rang. I turned off the hair dryer and ran to the kitchen. I didn't recognize the number.

"Hello?"

"Hi, is this Sara Martin?" asked a strange voice.

"Yes it is."

"Hi Sara, gosh I don't even know where to start. Umm, my name's Kerry Vedders. I met you briefly at the vet's office on Saturday. I was with the great Dane and my daughter . . ."

"Oh, yes, I remember. How are you?" I asked.

"Oh, good. I was hoping you'd remember us. I'm . . . I'm really not good. I hope you don't mind that I got your number from the receptionist. She was very reluctant to give it to me, too. Please don't be mad at her. I promise not to harass you. I just . . . I'm out of options. You see I'm recently divorced. I moved to this state to follow my husband. All of my family and friends are back in Iowa. I have a daughter in middle school, that I try my darnedest to keep up with, and a mother who is sick, needs constant attention and is being put into a nursing home. I need to help her with the move and the sale of her house. She's broke and I can't afford to cover any payments for her. I'm the closest child to her, so it's up to me to help with all this."

"Wow," I said.

"On top of that, I need to get her stuff moved to her room at the home and then get her house stuff packed up, auctioned off, and the house ready to sell. But, the real kicker is now there's Pepper. My daughter's pride and joy, her best friend through the whole mess her father caused. Her dad ran out on us, and as much as I want to keep Pepper, I just can't do it right now. I'm going to be gone for a few weeks and Hailey's going to stay at a friend's house from school so she doesn't have to miss classes, but I don't have any place for Pepper."

She finally paused to take a breath, so I jumped in.

"Kerry, if you need someone to watch Pepper, I can do it for a few weeks."

I heard her catch her breath. "Really? Oh, my gosh, are you sure? I know it's a lot to ask. Plus he's huge and he's an indoor dog."

"Really, it's no problem. I love animals, and I know he gets along great with my kitten, Faith. I have room here at my cabin, and I also have the apartment in the Cities which allows pets, so it's fine."

"Oh, Sara, I'd really appreciate it. It'd just be for a few weeks, I promise . . . But there is just one catch. He needs surgery. The doctor insisted I do it a.s.a.p. so I scheduled it for Friday morning, but I was hoping that Saturday I could head to Iowa."

I jumped in again, "So you'd need me to get him from the vet Saturday morning?"

"Yes, it's awful timing I know. Does that work with your schedule?"

"Yes, I'm very flexible, and Faith has an appointment Saturday morning anyway, so I'll just take Pepper home with me after her appointment."

"You're so kind. I really appreciate this. I'll meet you there Saturday, and be there when the doctor gives follow up instructions. You realize that he'll be in a cast right?"

"Will he be able to walk by himself?" I asked trying to picture how I would get him in to the house and back out to pee and poo every few hours.

"Yes it'll be a leg cast, but he should be able to walk for the most part. The surgery's on his hip, but they cast the leg to make him use the other leg more and not rotate the leg while it heals. I'll bring a leash, his bed, food, and his toys to have while I'm gone. You sure you're okay with this?"

"Really it's no problem, and if your daughter wants to come over after school to visit she can, whenever she wants to. Give her my phone number and have her call me. I'll be back and forth between Nisswa and the Cities, but I'll make sure Pepper's comfortable and with me at all times. And if it works out, she can stop by when I'm there."

"Sara, I can't thank you enough. This is a huge help. I have so many burdens, and there's only one of me. I just can't keep up. Then you throw a divorce in there too . . . some days I just feel like giving up, ya know?" she said, sounding like she was on the edge of tears.

"Trust me, Kerry, I know! Really it's not a big deal at all to me. Pepper will be in good hands, and it'll be one less thing for you to worry about. Faith's appointment is at 8:30 on Saturday. I'll meet you at the vet's then and we can work out the rest of the details. Okay?"

"Perfect. Thank you, thank you, thank you! I'll see you Saturday."

"You're very welcome. Bye," I said and hung up.

Well, then, it looks like I'll be having a house guest next week. I plugged my phone in to charge, and went back to the bathroom to finish my hair and makeup. Then I grabbed a bowl of oatmeal and glass of water. Just as I was turning off the lights and putting my phone in my bag, it rang. I looked at the screen: *Miss Kitty.*

"Hello?"

"Hello, darling? How are you?" she asked, not giving me the chance to answer before she started talking again. "I got to thinking, the other day that you don't usually do this, so you may be a bit unprepared. So after Smoochie Poo's play date, I went back to Morning Glory with my laptop and used their Internet. I didn't want to get caught doing it at home. I ordered you a bunch of stuff. I paid for overnight delivery and it came this morning! Meet me at Morning Glory at 10:00, and I'll give you the stuff. Okay, love? See you then. Bye!"

She hung up before I said even one word. *The nerve! What if I was busy and couldn't meet her? What if I had another meeting at that time? Huh? Does she think I have no life of my own and I'm at her beck and call?*

Truly, I had no life and was at her beck and call, so I turned on the TV and sat and waited. I watched the news and *Live with Kelly*. At 9:40 a.m. I hauled myself into the Jeep and drove to Morning Glory. Miss Kitty was there with a big box on the table.

"Hey, girl!" Tannya sang when I opened the door.

She came running over and walked with me to Miss Kitty's table. "Ooh, girl, she got you some nice stuff! I helped her pick out what you needed when she was in the other night. I'm so glad you're on board with this. Ya know if you need help, I'm your girl!"

"Tannya, you leave her alone," laughed Miss Kitty. "I'm sure she can handle this. But if she can't, well, I did order lots!" Miss Kitty held up two black items that looked like binoculars. "I got extras just in case you wanted to share in the fun."

"What is all this?" I asked sitting down in the booth across from her.

"Well, it's just some items to aid your little investigation. The more stuff I get on him, the better job my lawyers can do to get me a fair settlement," she said nodding and smiling.

She didn't look sad like she did on Monday. Now she was greedy and vengeful.

We looked through the box. There were multiple sets of binoculars, some with night vision, and one pair with infrared capabilities. There was a hidden wire set with a receiver and recorder, black face masks, a pen that worked as both a recorder and a camera, a few tiny video cameras that could clip to almost anything, and a flower pin that was also a video camera. There was also a six pack of bugs the size of watch batteries, four walkie-talkies, and black stretch pants and jackets for three people. Two were small sets and one bigger.

"Just in case you need assistance," Miss Kitty said

Tannya stood by the table smiling and nodding.

"Yeah, she said I could be your wing man!" Tannya said, smiling like a kid at Christmas.

"Um, okay. Wow, I guess I didn't know how close you wanted me to get," I told her.

"Oh, close. Yes! I need hard proof of anything and everything and this stuff will help us get that," Miss Kitty said.

"I'm not sure this kind of evidence can be used in court, but I do have some news for you," I said. Tannya gasped and slid into the booth next to me.

"You do? What is it?" asked Tannya.

"Yeah, what?" Miss Kitty repeated.

I held back my smile at their enthusiasm. "Yesterday I went to check out this Alexa girl in Brainerd, and I learned a few things." I went on and told them every detail of my time in Brainerd, finishing the story with the blinds being pulled shut. Then I sat back and waited for their mouths to close.

"TANNNNYA! Get off your butt and get this food out!" yelled the cook.

"Dang it, Marv! I'm coming!" she got up and went to the kitchen.

She got the food and set it in front of the two men on the bar stools, then she grabbed the pot of coffee and topped off their cups.

Quickly sliding back into the booth, she asked, "Did I miss anything?"

"Nope, that's all I know for now," I said. Miss Kitty sat staring off over my left shoulder.

"I'm going to ask him about it," she said. "I'm going to his office and I'm going to ask him."

"We'll be right there with you!" Tannya offered. My eyes darted open and I shot my head over to look at her. "Right? I mean I think she should wear the wire, and we should wait in the getaway car for her, and record everything that's said."

"Perfect!" Miss Kitty said. "Vincent leaves this afternoon for a meeting in Chicago and won't be back until late tomorrow, so Dave will be in the office alone. I'll go there wearing a wire and confront him on it. Yes! It's settled then."

With that Miss Kitty reached in the box and handed me and Tannya the black wind jackets and the black cotton/spandex pants, in our respective sizes.

"Change into these, and we will meet back here at 3:00 p.m. Vincent's flight is *at* three, so he'll be gone by two for sure. Then we'll go to the office and see what Dave has to say for himself. Sara, you can keep these in your Jeep in case we need them later. We'll take that tonight," she said and got up from the table. "I'll see you soon, darlings."

She reached back into the booth and grabbed her big purse off the seat. I assumed it still contained a dog. She carefully placed it on her shoulder and sashayed out the door.

24

"Ooooh girl, am I excited! This is going to be so much fun! We're gonna catch a bad guy and make Miss Kitty richer than she is! How much is she paying you?" Tannya asked.

"Too much. And by the sounds of it, I'm not working alone," I told her. "If you are helping, then I'll give you a cut." I didn't need the money, but I didn't feel the need to tell Tannya my life's story either.

"Sounds good to me! I never have enough to make ends meet. In my world, when it comes to money, the more the merrier. Before I met my ex-husband, I had a nice savings and, well, he smoked all that up in a matter of months while I was out working. The no good piece of shit! And now I gotta mortgage that owns me and an old house that needs more repair than it's worth."

"Well, I'll fix it soon enough! What time are you off work?" I asked her.

"I opened this morning so I'm off at 2:00 p.m. I can change here and be ready at 3:00."

"I think I'll run over to Lost and Found and take care of some things and meet you back here later."

I walked over to Lost and Found and talked to Maureen for a while. She was excited for the new schedule to start and said she really liked working for me. That was good to hear. We talked about her idea to rearrange a few things in the store, and I gave her the go ahead. I liked her idea. I though it would add space to the store for the crowded holiday items.

After that I went into the office and worked on filing and tax preparations. There was a lot to get done and I didn't want to wait until the last minute. A couple hours of later, I got changed into my black outfit, which looked really good on me. The pants and jacket were very slimming, and they were a really nice quality. My hunger kicked in and I thought I'd better grab something to eat first.

I went across the street to get a barbeque sandwich this time. When I was done eating I walked over to Morning Glory. Tannya and Miss Kitty were inside waiting for me. They were both dressed in the same outfit and I suddenly felt like a total dork. I must say though, Tannya looked good. The pants were a straight seam instead of tight to the ankles and they flattered her in that style.

"Ready?" I asked them.

"Lets roll!" Tannya yelled as she threw her fist in the air.

Oh, boy. We all climbed into my Jeep, Tannya in the back, Miss Kitty riding shotgun. Miss Kitty gave us directions to Vincent's office, which she told us was in Brainerd right off of highway 371, in a strip mall running parallel to the highway. When we got there, Dave's car was out front, and we could see lights on inside through the window. The glass door leading to their section of the building read "Aburgus Enterprises." Instead of parking in front of the office I drove past it down a few doors and parked out of sight. I didn't want Dave to look out his office window and see my Jeep in case I needed to do more spying later, plus Miss Kitty wasn't wired yet.

"All right, we'll park here. Let's get you wired up and you can go in and confront him," I said, again sounding all professional as if I'd done this before.

Tannya dug around in the box and handed her a small box with a wire and a tiny mic on the end.

"Is there tape in there?" I asked Tannya.

"Should be. I ordered some," Miss Kitty said.

Tannya found it and passed it up. I handed her the equipment and she taped the mic between her breasts, and pulled her jacket down again. Then she pulled it back up, taped the little box to her lower right stomach area, and turned it on.

"All right. I'm all set," she said and exited the vehicle.

We watched her walk through the door.

When she disappeared I said, "Shit, wait! Tannya, what do we listen with? Quick! Look in the box. There has to be an audio device of some sort so we can hear her. Tannya dug through it and found what might be what we were looking for. She jumped into the front seat with me. We ripped the package apart and tried, as fast as we could, to get it up and running. Thank goodness there were batteries in the box. When we finally turned it on, we could hear what they were saying and the red record light was lit where it said RECORD, so I hoped it was on right.

"Shhh!" Tannya said and turned the volume up.

Geez, I thought, *this is not the job for us! What a bunch of amateurs.*

We heard a man's voice. "He should be on his plane by now. Is there . . . something I can . . . do for you . . . Miss Elenore?"

He sounded really dumb.

"Yes, there is. You can give me some answers! You can start with telling me why you're drunk at four in the afternoon!" Miss Kitty snapped.

"Fuck you! I don't have to tell you shit! I don't work for you! I work for your stupid asshole husband. Yeah, I work for that son of a bitch. He makes me a very wealthy man and fucks with my life. Ya know why?" he slurred. "'Cause the son of a bitch thinks he can."

"What the hell are you so upset about?" Miss Kitty asked.

"Look at you," he paused and made some snorting noises. "You're gorgeous, and as far as we can tell faithful, and he still pulls his high and mighty shit."

"What do you mean 'as far as we can tell'? Are you two spying on me?"

"Us two? No. *I* do the dirty work around here. Your husband does whatever the hell he wants, and sends me to clean up the messes. He thinks if he pays me enough he has control over me. Well that shit's gonna stop."

I looked at Tannya with raised eyebrows and she returned the same look. *This guy is beyond mad.*

"What dirty work? Are you talking about the business?"

"Ha! Yeah there's that, too! Ha ha!" he added with a laugh.

I could hear some noises in the background.

"Yeah, mix another drink! That's perfect, that'll solve all your problems! Who's Alexa?" she finally demanded.

"Alexa?"

"Yes, moron! Alexa! I know about the Gold Digger website that Vincent's been on, and I know they've been chatting with each other. Did he sleep with her?" she blatantly asked.

"Ha! Oh, yes, Alexa. She's another one. Thinks she can play people and get away with it," he said.

"Is he sleeping with her, Dave? Has my husband cheated on me?" She demanded.

"Ha ha ha ha!" he laughed really hard. "Um, no, he hasn't slept with Alexa from the website. He's slept with many women, but not Alexa." He laughed some more.

"What?" Miss Kitty gasped with shock in her voice. "Who? When?"

"Oh honey . . . Little . . . Miss . . . Kitty Cat," he mocked. "You're such a gem. So pretty, so spoiled, so STUPID! Your husband fucks some new girl about twice a week. I can't keep up!"

"What are you talking about, Dave? If you're lying, I'll make sure you're fired!" Miss Kitty threatened.

"I don't need to lie, bitch! Your husband's as low as they come. You want the truth? I'll give you the truth, but you better sit down, 'cause this shit's gonna hurt like nothing your spoiled self has felt before."

He paused and we could hear more liquid pouring. I looked at Tannya. Both of us were hanging over the recorder with our mouths slack from shock. She shook her head at me and I covered my mouth. *This is going to be bad.*

"Your husband's limo has more DNA in it than a hospital lab! Ha ha," Dave said with a sick laugh. "Whenever we're out on the town, which is a lot, and by the way, it doesn't even matter anymore if we're in state or out, Vincent goes into a bar and scouts the place for his next victim. It's become like a game to him now." He hiccuped, then continued. "Late into the night he finds some young, stupid, hot girl that's drunk and keeps feeding her drinks, the last one of course laced with a roofie. Then he invites her back to the limo. He waits for the drugs to kick in, has his way with her, then dumps her back on the curb of whatever bar he picked her up at."

"You're lying!" Miss Kitty snapped.

"Why? What do I care? I'm done working for him! You don't have to believe me. I don't give a shit. But this is the truth! Yeah, and the kicker is once in a while a girl shows up that has figured it out. That's when I get to deal with them and have to figure out how much it's gonna cost to shut her up. You know how much money he's spent shutting women up lately? A lot! More than I make in a year! He's getting stupid, and it's costing him."

"I can't believe this! Why didn't you stop him?" she asked.

"He made his bed. I'm his assistant, not his moral adviser. But I'm done. I've got a plan. We'll see who gets the last laugh. We'll just see who ends up with the money and who ends up in jail," he said in a relaxed, evil tone.

Tannya and I exchanged glances.

"I'm leaving. I don't know what your plan is, Dave, but if you know what's good for you, you'll keep your mouth shut about this conversation. I'm going to pretend I didn't hear any of this. Do you understand me?" she said very seriously.

"Yeah, whatever. Go get your shit in order because after we close the deal on this multi-million dollar manufacturing plant in the next couple days, shit's going to hit the fan! You have until then to do what you gotta do! Then it's my time!" he said forcefully.

"I'll be in touch," she said and walked out.

Tannya and I both looked up and saw her march towards us. She was not happy. Tannya climbed in the back and Miss Kitty opened the door and sat down.

"Let's go!" she said. "Let's get out of here!"

I quickly started the Jeep and backed out. I drove back towards town and parked in the back of a large parking lot. It was sunset and getting colder by the minute. I left the motor running. Tannya was looking at me in the rear view mirror. She was very quiet. I turned to Miss Kitty and reached over and gave her a hug. She hugged back and broke down sobbing.

"I can't believe he cheated on me!" she said through tears.

After a few moments she pulled back and wiped her tears.

"How many do you think there were? That asshole!" she screamed. "What a monster!"

She was fighting hurt and anger at the same time and kept flip-flopping back and forth.

"I love him. I've never cheated on him. Fuuuck! I wonder how many diseases I've been exposed to! And he's paying them off? AAHHHG-GRR!" She screamed at the top of her lungs and punched the dash over and over with both hands until she was exhausted.

"Let's get him!" Tannya said from the back seat. "We need a plan!"

Miss Kitty refocused immediately. "Yeah let's! Excellent idea, Tannya. We need a plan!"

Oh, boy.

"He's in Chicago at a meeting right about now. We could fly there now and follow him tonight and see if it's true. I'm sure he's going out tonight after the meeting. Let's go, Sara! Drive us to the airport!" she said and sat up straight and faced forward, then she ripped off her wire and stuffed it into her purse.

"Now?" I asked in shock.

"Yes, now! We'll take the next flight out. Southwest flies to and from Chicago all day long. I'll pay and buy what we need as we go. Come on. You guys are in, right?"

She had suddenly lost her cute flare with words, and her accent. She was in a whole new mode now. She was a determined, scorned woman on a mission!

"Yeah, I'm in!" Tannya said. "You are too, right, Sara?"

They were both staring at me.

"You have to be!" Kitty informed me. "I'm paying you for this! Now drive!" she yelled.

I didn't feel I had much of a choice, so I backed out and asked for directions to the airport. *I didn't even know there was an airport in Brainerd.*

We parked and grabbed our box from the back. Miss Kitty told me to go to the gift shop and buy a big bag to put it all in, while she went to the bathroom to fix her makeup, and she handed me a hundred-dollar bill. Tannya followed me to the gift shop door, then waited outside with the box.

"Can I help you?" the lady in the store asked.

"Yes, I need a large bag for some carry-on items."

"Right over here," she said leading the way.

I picked out a black-and-white zebra stripped one with a bright pink handle. It had Miss Kitty written all over it, and it was huge. I paid for it and walked out to the hallway. Tannya dumped the contents of the box into the bag and left the box next to the door. Miss Kitty caught up to us and looked like a million bucks again. *I don't know how she did it, but she doesn't look like she's been crying at all.*

We went up to the counter and booked three seats on the next flight, which was scheduled to leave seventy minutes later. It would put us in Chicago at about 8:00 p.m. The lady behind the counter asked if we needed to check luggage, and we told her no. She pointed us to the security check point and handed us the tickets.

We got in a short line and waited until we were waved up. The security officer called us forward and Miss Kitty handed him our tickets. Then he asked for our photo IDs, too. After he looked at them, he instructed us to put our shoes in the tub and to take any electronics out of the bag. My blood pressure went up as I bent over to remove my shoes.

"Shit, Tannya," I whispered, "You take the bag."

"Oh, hell, no! That there's your bag. This is an airport! Don't you know you're not supposed to let others tamper with your bag?" she said, a little too loudly.

I squinted my eyes and shushed her. The uniformed man was looking at me with his arms folded and eyebrows pressed together.

"Ma'am, is that your bag or not?" he asked sternly.

"Um, uh, yes?" I answered with a nervous voice.

I smiled at him to help matters, but he wasn't having it. He made a loud, "Ahem," and waved more officers over without ever taking his eyes off me. *Oooh shit.*

I looked to my left. Miss Kitty was already through the metal detector and putting her shoes back on. I shot her a look. She winked at me. I watched her walk a few steps back and sit on a bench against the wall.

"You! Come through!" A security guard yelled pointing at Tannya.

She pushed her bin with her shoes inside the open door of the exam box and stepped through the metal detector. It was silent, so he waved her to keep going. She put her shoes on and sat down by Miss Kitty.

"Ma'am, take any electronics out of the bag, put them in a bin and then come through the metal detector."

I reluctantly put my purse in one bin, then took another, reached into the bag, grabbed the video camera, and set it in the bucket. Then I reached in and grabbed a pair of binoculars and set them in the bin. I exhaled and looked up at the guard.

He stood there with his arms crossed and asked, "Is that all?"

I reluctantly shook my head no, and reached back into the bag and pulled out another pair of binoculars and set them in a bin, and then grabbed the recorder out.

"What the . . . ?" the guard said.

I looked at him and bit my bottom lip. He walked over and dumped the bag upside down. The bin was mounded with our equipment. He shot me a look of bewilderment. I smiled. He pieced through it and looked at me.

"Care to explain?"

"Um . . . I . . . uh . . . no." I stammered.

He waved me to walk through the metal detector and it beeped. I'd forgotten about my phone in my pocket. I took it out and handed it to him. Then he motioned me to walk through again. I did and passed. He squinted his eyes at me.

"Over here," he said. "Martha, check her!"

A large angry woman with arms folded and lips pursed together stepped towards me.

"Spread your legs and put your arms out," she ordered.

She pulled on gloves and gave me a pat down. I glanced over at Tannya and Miss Kitty, who were smiling and quietly giggling. I stuck my tongue out at them. After I passed the pat down, I got to put my shoes back on, that is after they were thoroughly inspected. Then they dumped everything out of my purse on to a table, handed it back to me empty, and told me I could go.

It took me about five minutes to get my purse and the shoulder bag put back together. I hiked both on to my shoulder and met up with Tannya and Miss Kitty, who were now standing against the far wall.

"Well, thanks for that, ladies!" I said.

They laughed.

I heard the angry pat-down lady's voice, "Excuse me, ma'am!"

Crap! I slowly turned to look at her.

"You forgot your cell phone," she said and handed it to me with one eyebrow up and her lips still tightly pursed together.

"Oh, ha ha. Thanks!" I said and smiled.

"Un huh," she said snidely, still giving me the stink eye.

We stopped at the Starbuck's and got three strong coffees. It was going to be a long night. Then we sat at the gate and made phone calls. Tannya called her work and told them she wouldn't be in until Friday. Miss Kitty called her mom and told her she was going on a short trip and made arrangements for Smoochie Poo. I called Rex.

"Hello?" he answered

"Hi, how are you?" I asked.

"I'm great. And my lunch was great. So was the dessert, thanks! How are you?"

"I'm pretty good. I have a favor to ask . . ."

"Already! Wow, how quickly the tables turn," he said. I could hear the smile in his voice.

"Yes, I know. I'm wondering if you can stop by my house and feed my cat tonight and give her her medicine, and leave her enough food for tomorrow morning, too. I'm kinda going on a last-minute trip and, well, I can't make it back to feed her first."

"Sure."

"Thank you so much! I have a hide-a-key under the mat on the back patio door."

"Wow, how secure. Very original, Sara." he scolded.

"I know, sorry. I'll fix that when I get back."

"So where are you going?" he asked.

"Um," I said, stepping away from the two ladies. "You know that thing I was helping the friend you know with? It's for that. We need to go check on a few things . . . in Chicago."

"Chicago? Is this for Miss Kitty? Who's we?"

"Um, yeah. It's us and Tannya."

"I don't like . . . this has trouble written all over it," he said.

"We'll be back tomorrow sometime. It's just a quick trip," I tried to reassure him.

"Hmm, what's your boyfriend say about this?" he asked.

"Derek? He doesn't know. And it doesn't matter. I'll be back by Friday." *Geez, now I feel like I've called my dad.* "Can you just feed the cat, please?"

"Okay. But call me when you're on your way home."

"Okay, I will. Thanks."

"You're welcome," he said and disconnected.

I hung up and heard the boarding call for our plane.

"You ready to do this?" Tannya asked.

She sounded like a boxing coach, and I was stepping into a ring. I could tell she was looking forward to this. Her mundane life was getting exciting, and she was enjoying every second.

Me, I could do without the drama, but there I went again.

25

After we landed and were off the plane, we went straight to the taxi zone of the airport. We piled into the first one available and looked to Miss Kitty for instructions. She told the driver to take us to the Ritz Carlton Hotel, then was on her smart phone the whole way there. Tannya was telling me how she'd never been to a fancy hotel, just a Motel 6 a couple of times when she was a kid. I'd been to some nice hotels, but never stayed at a Ritz Carlton.

When we arrived, Miss Kitty paid the cab driver and led us inside. She walked us to the lounge, gave us a fifty, and told us to order drinks, so we did. She went to the front desk to get us a room. For as spoiled as she was, she impressed me at how independent she was too. She handled things well, like she'd done it all before. I'd thought I'd have to babysit her, but that was not the case at all. And, now that she was in a serious mood minus her sashay and accent, I kind of liked her. We ordered three long islands and sat down at a table to wait.

"Do you think she'll take us shopping for new clothes?" Tannya asked me with wide eyes.

"I don't know, maybe. I hope she does. I feel kinda silly, all of us being dressed alike."

"Yeah, today didn't go how I thought it would," Tannya told me. "I was hoping for sneaking around outside of buildings and peeking through windows and following his vehicle from three cars back, ya know? This is nice, but not as fun as I'd thought. Still, this is a great hotel. I can't wait to see the room!"

We looked around. Even the lounge was state of the art. The entry area was breathtaking and had a crystal chandelier the size of a car. The floor was marble and the counter tops granite. There were enormous fresh flower arrangements the size of my recliner, and probably cost more than most people made in a month. Miss Kitty walked over and plopped down in a chair.

"All right we got the last suite. And I double-checked, Vincent's not registered here and doesn't have a reservation for tonight either," she told us. "What are we drinking?"

She picked up her glass and slammed it.

"Ah . . ." I watched as the last swallow disappeared. "It *was* a long island tea."

"Mmm, pretty good."

She threw her hand up in the air and snapped her fingers. When the bartender looked at her, she drew a circle in the air above us and pointed down to the table. He nodded and grabbed three glasses.

"Get done, girls, there's more coming."

We sat there and finished our drinks and talked about the plan for the night. Miss Kitty knew which hotel the business meeting was being held. It was about a five-minute cab ride from where we were. She also knew from texting and threatening Vincent's limo driver, that the club he would frequent was called Spice. We needed new clothes to fit in and get in to a club like that, so she planned to take us out shopping for a bit, and then we'd grab dinner. She had the hotel call the club and get her on the VIP list with a reserved section for us. It was $1,500 for the night and included drinks. That was a ton of money, but she didn't want to risk us not getting in. I wondered if we would have gotten in without it. I wondered if Tannya and I would have made the cut. I didn't have fake hair or fingernails, so I doubted it.

We went up to the room and looked around. It was huge! It was bigger than my apartment was, and had a hot tub in the corner of the living room. A seventy-inch flat screen TV hung on the wall with every gaming system ever made below it. The furniture was gorgeous and the beds were super soft. There was a menu on the pillow and chilled champagne in an ice bucket stand, filled with ice. There was also a man standing there wearing a black tuxedo and white gloves. *Apparently, we get our own butler too.* Miss Kitty dismissed him, and he walked out. She informed us that we just had to press a button and he'd come back when we needed him. I knew this worked too because, of course, Tannya had to test it. Twice. She couldn't stop giggling after she excused him the second time and shut the door. Miss Kitty asked her not to do it again.

We left for shopping, and an hour later we all had new outfits for the night, along with new shoes, a collection of makeup and hair products, and pajamas for later. Our bill was over a thousand dollars. And Miss Kitty never blinked an eye. It was kinda of hard for me. It seemed so wasteful. There were starving children out there that could eat for a year on what she spent on a three-quarter-ounce jar of eye cream.

When we got back to the hotel, we took about forty-five minutes to get dolled up, then headed out on the town. We stopped at a restaurant right on the Magnificent Mile. The food was good. I wasn't really sure what I ate, but it tasted great. Then we headed to the club. Miss Kitty had her hair pulled back in a tight, low pony tail and had a big floppy hat on. She didn't want Vincent to recognize her.

We checked in with the bouncer. He opened the door for us and another person led us to our reserved area. It was a round couch against a back wall with a big circle-shaped ottoman in front of it. The area could seat about eight people. There was a hole in the middle of the ottoman with a stripper pole coming out of it. The entire area was surrounded by red mesh netting that hung from the ceiling and draped all the way to the floor. It was pulled back but could be closed at any time. We also had a large silver drink cooler with a few bottles of wine and beer. As soon as we sat down, a half-dressed man introduced himself as Alfonso.

"I'm your personal server for the evening, ladies. Just let me know when you'd like a drink, and I'll get it for you. Would you like your dancers now?"

My mouth hit the floor, and Tannya gasped then covered her mouth to hide the laugh coming out of it. "Personal dancers?" she asked.

"Yes, man or woman? They'll dance for you and when you want them to leave just tell them to go. They'll wait there until you call them back," he said and moved his hand to the right. Lined up along the wall were half-dressed men and women wiggling slightly to the music, darting their eyes from couch to couch.

"No thanks!" I spoke up for the group. "I'll take a diet Coke though."

He pressed his eyebrows together at me and then looked to Tannya. She ordered the same, and Miss Kitty asked for water.

The place was packed, and all the couches were full of people. The club was loud with music and voices. Miss Kitty got up and pulled the red mesh almost closed.

"Try to watch for him, but I don't want him to see us," she said.

My phone was vibrating in my pants so I pulled it out. I'd accidentally hit the accept button when I did. It was Derek. I had no choice but to answer.

"Hello?"

"Wow, where are you at? It's very loud!" he said.

"I'm at a club with a few friends."

"Okay. Which one?" he asked.

"Spice." I reluctantly told him.

"Spice?" he asked. "Where's that?"

This was not going to go well. "Ummm, Chicago."

There was a long silence. "You're in Chicago?" he finally answered.

"Yeah."

"Why are you in Chicago?"

"I'm, ah, helping a friend with a mini-investigation into her husband's recent activities," I told him.

"Really? Who?"

"I'll talk to you about it later." I told him.

"Were you planning on telling me that you were going on a trip and leaving the state?"

He sounded mad.

"I didn't know myself. It was kind of a spur-of-the-moment type thing. I'll be back tomorrow."

"Right. Well, I just called to check in on you and make sure we, ah you, were okay."

I could tell he was annoyed.

"I am!" I yelled into the phone. "I'm fine. And I'll be back in town by tomorrow night. Thanks . . ."

"Yeah, bye," he said and hung up.

Another hour went by, and Tannya had already hit the dance floor. I was on my third diet Coke. Miss Kitty was pretty quiet. I tried to talk to her, but she was trying not to feel anything until she knew the truth. Out of nowhere, Tannya came bursting through the curtain and sat down.

"I think I saw him! He looked just like the picture you showed me," she said out of breath. "He's up at the bar talking to that girl in the blue tank."

We turned and looked to where she was pointing, and sure as shit, there was Kitty's husband, and he was definitely flirting with a girl at the bar. I looked at Miss Kitty. She was red with anger. He was still in a suit, sans tie, and sitting very close to her. He had a highball glass with a gold-colored liquid in it that I assumed was scotch.

"All right, let's just watch him and see what happens," Miss Kitty said through a tightly clenched jaw.

We had left the shoulder bag with all the stuff in the hotel except for a camera we threw in my purse. I took it out and took a picture. I felt like maybe I should be doing my job. We watched him for more than thirty minutes and then, in the middle of their conversation, he pointed to something to the woman's left and when she turned to look, he poured a powder in her drink and quickly stirred it with his finger. Then he leaned close to her and pointed further saying something as she looked hard to where he was pointing.

"Did you guys see that?" I asked.

"Yup," said Tannya.

"Yes," said Miss Kitty slowly. "I see his ring is missing, too," she added in a pissed-off voice.

I looked at my watch, it was 11:40 p.m. We stared at them for a while longer. She seemed to be really responsive to him. They ordered shots and took them.

Looking all sly and sexy, a guy came over and asked Tannya if she was coming back out to the dance floor. She shooed him away.

"Nice, Tannya," I said. "He was good looking."

She winked and gave me a high five.

"Ladies!" Miss Kitty snapped.

We turned our attention back to Vincent and the blue tank girl. He was paying the bartender and standing up. The girl laughed and nodded at what he said, then he pulled her chair out and she stood too. I took another picture.

"Get ready, girls. We have to follow him. If Dave was telling the truth, they'll go to the limo." We grabbed our purses and walked towards the door they'd gone out. "I'll stay in here. You guys go out there and see where they go. I don't want him to see me."

Tannya and I walked out the door. Sure enough there was a limo outside. They stepped into it. I snapped a picture again.

"Tannya, go get Miss Kitty. I'll get a cab," I instructed.

I hailed a cab waiting in a line just outside the doors. It amazed me that there were still people standing outside, in the freezing cold, waiting to get in. The night was pretty much over.

We jumped into the cab. I told the cab driver to follow the limo at a distance. We followed it for about an hour. It was going nowhere, just circling. Then it started heading back to Spice. When it pulled into the lot, the door opened, and blue-tank girl stumbled out and wobbled to the curb. The limo drove away. I took a few more pictures of that too. Miss Kitty made a gasping noise, and I looked over and saw her crying.

I rubbed her back. "Wait here. I'm going to get the girl some help."

I got out of the cab and sat down on the curb next to blue-tank girl. I asked her if she was okay. She moaned and her eyes were rolling around when she looked at me. She was wobbling all over just trying to sit up straight.

"Hey! Get your friend out of here now!"

The bouncer was pointing at me and was not happy.

"Okay," I said to him. Then I turned to the girl. "I know you don't know me, and I'm not sure you can even hear me, but I'm going to take you to the hospital. I think you've been drugged. Come on," I said and helped her to her feet and into the cab.

Tannya jumped up front and the girl sat between me and Miss Kitty. I yelled for the cab driver to drive to the hospital, and he whined about the fare being too high. Miss Kitty threw two hundred dollars at him, and he hit the gas.

The driver pulled right into the ambulance drop-off zone, and we tried our best to get her out of the cab. Tannya ran into the entry way and grabbed a wheelchair that was waiting near the door. We got her seated and two nurses came rushing out and took over.

"What's wrong with her?" one of the nurses asked.

"We think she was drugged," I said.

She glared at me and made a tsk sound, "You think?"

"We assume . . ." I corrected her, sternly.

"What's your friend's name?" The second nurse asked as she started pushing the chair to the doors.

"Um, she's not our friend. We're just helping her," I said, following her through the doors.

Tannya was right behind me, and Miss Kitty was still at the cab. I looked back at her and she yelled that she'd wait there. She did not look happy, which I completely understood.

"We need a tox screen stat!" Tannya said loudly. We all stopped in our tracks and looked at her. "Seriously! This is Sara Martin. She is a private investigator, and this here woman is part of the investigation. We're gonna need a tox screen and a rape kit done, and we'll be waiting here for the results," she said and stopped short of the EMPLOYEES ONLY door.

The nurses looked at her, wondering if she was serious, and then looked to me.

"Stat!" I added. "The faster I get the results, the faster I can take this guy down."

They frowned and exchanged glances.

"Seriously, the guy who did this has done it before. We're trying to catch him and collect evidence. We don't need your names or anything official from you. If you could just let us know if he did it again, that would be enough. Please." I begged.

"Wait here," one of the nurses said. I told Tannya to wait and went to get Miss Kitty. She didn't want anything to do with waiting around. She was fighting back tears, so I told her to go back to the hotel and we would get a cab and be right behind her. She said she'd send back the cab we were using. We worked that out with the driver and then I went back in and sat with Tannya.

Finally seventy minutes later a nurse came out and said that there was evidence of recent sexual intercourse and that she had Rohypnol in her system. They would be collecting DNA and had called the police. We thanked her and walked out to the cab.

Back at the hotel Miss Kitty was lying in bed with a deep pile of used tissues surrounding her. Tannya and I sat on either side of her while she cried, then Tannya pushed the button and ordered pizza and mixed a few drinks. After we ate, we fell asleep, all of us in a king size bed together with the pizza box and tissue mountain.

I woke up with a sore neck at 9:00 a.m. I was the first one awake. I went to the bathroom and hopped in the shower. Two hours later we were all up, showered, and once again wearing our matching black outfits. Miss Kitty insisted that we stop one more time for new outfits, her treat. After fifty minutes in Macy's we walked out in all our own styles.

In the cab on the way to the airport Miss Kitty used her iPhone to get tickets on the next flight. As we stepped up to security and took our shoes off, I set the shoulder bag with all the electronics on the floor by our feet, then rushed to put my shoes in a bin having left the bag by Tannya.

I went through the metal detector just as I heard, "Ma'am, you forgot your bag on the floor." I looked back to see the guard talking to

Tannya and pointing at the bag. She looked over and saw it. She looked up and shot her eyes at me. I smiled and gave her a little finger wave. Miss Kitty of course made it through no problem, so I joined her on a bench while we waited for Tannya's bag search and body pat down and, of course, purse dump. *Ahh, the victorious pleasure of payback!*

We were back in Brainerd by 3:00 p.m. After we paid for parking, we stopped for a bite to eat in town. Miss Kitty was really upset, not so much sad anymore, but angry. She didn't eat much, which concerned me since her weight was about 115.

"So what are you going to do now? Do you want me to keep going with this," I asked.

"I don't know." There was a long pause as she stared at the salad in front of her. "Yes, keep going. I want to know what's going on with Alexa, and what his plans were with that."

"Okay, I will. I don't think he's seen her. I think it's been all computer, which is a little strange."

"Yeah, I wonder why. She lives close enough that he could go and see her at any time. Maybe he was taking it slow because he likes her. Maybe he was planning on replacing me," she said and stared at me.

I could see the hurt in her eyes. I was sad for her. *What an awful thing to see.* We finished our meals and climbed back into the Jeep.

"Kick his ASS!" Tannya yelled from the backseat.

It came out of nowhere and made both Miss Kitty and me jump.

I turned around in my seat and looked at her.

"Sorry. It's just I can't stop thinking about it, and he's really pissed me off. Don't ya just want to kick his ass?"

"Yes, I do. But what good will that do me, Tannya? I need to be smart about this. The only income I have is his. I have no schooling, so if I don't get money out of this divorce, what am I going to live off of? I need to make sure I get as much money as possible from this. I don't want to work the rest of my life."

"What's so wrong with working for a living?" Tannya snapped back.

There was a moment of silence. I put the Jeep in reverse and backed out of my parking space.

"Nothing, Tannya. It just isn't for me. I don't have any skills. No one would hire me."

She put her arm up on the window and rested her head in her hand. She suddenly seemed like a lost little girl.

"We'll figure this out, and make sure we have the evidence your lawyer needs to get you a really nice settlement. We've already got tape of the conversation with Dave and pictures of last night." I said trying to reassure her.

"I still wanna kick some ass! We didn't do any of that this weekend," Tannya said.

The rest of the ride was quiet. When we got into town, I dropped them off at Morning Glory.

"I'll do some more digging tomorrow and let you know what I find out," I told Miss Kitty.

"I wanna come with!" Tannya yelled. "You call me. Don't leave me out!"

I smiled at her and nodded. Miss Kitty looked at the ground.

"Yeah, let me know if you learn anything new. I'm going to go home and try my best to pretend that it was just another day. He should be home soon. I think he was scheduled for a 5:10 p.m. flight."

I gave her a long, tight hug.

"Hang in there," I told her.

I turned right towards home and drove in silence trying to figure things out. It was almost five and dark as night out. When I pulled in the driveway I saw a familiar black Jeep. Derek.

26

I threw the Jeep in park and jumped out. Derek had been sitting in his Jeep waiting for me. I didn't know he was coming, and our last couple conversations were very short, and a bit tense. *This is going to be awkward*

"Hey," he said exiting the Jeep.

"Hey," I said with a smile.

"I . . . uh, wanted to see you. I hope you don't mind that I'm here." He looked sad.

"I love that you're here. Are you staying the weekend?" I asked.

"I did pack a bag, but I don't have to if you have other plans," he said.

"I just have to go to the Cities tomorrow to take Faith to her appointment and pick up Pepper."

"Pepper?" Derek asked.

"Yeah, he's a dog that had surgery today. His mom has an emergency and has to go out of state for a while, so I said I'd help out. He's going to stay with me for a couple weeks."

Derek shook his head and gave me a hug.

"Come on in," I said.

We got our things from our Jeeps and went inside. I told him all about my week. He asked a lot of questions about Miss Kitty and her husband so I showed him the file. He looked it over and said that he looked like a scum bag with a less than legal business and wouldn't doubt if he was wanted in multiple states on drug and rape charges.

"Sara, this is big!" He tossed the file on the island counter and sat down on a stool. "What do you plan to do about this?" he asked in his cop voice.

"I don't know. I think it's worse than we expected. What should we do? We have to make sure that Miss Kitty gets a good settlement. I promised I'd help, and she doesn't want it all over the papers, so I don't think calling the police is the answer. I think that tomorrow afternoon I'll go pay Alexa a visit and see if she has anything to say for herself."

"Well, I'm coming with you," Derek said. I shot him a look. "I'll stay in the Jeep unseen, just in case you need back up."

"Tannya's my back up. I don't know how she's going to react to you stepping in on her territory. She's pretty jacked up about this."

"Fine. I'll wait in *my* Jeep down the road. I don't want you going there without me. We don't have to tell Tannya," he said standing up and walking towards me.

I was leaning back against the counter, and he pressed himself up against me.

"It could be our little secret," he whispered in my ear and then kissed my ear lobe.

"Um, okay." I said trying to keep my focus.

I wasn't sure I wanted him in my business and making decisions for me. He licked my neck and then kissed it three more times. His hands were on the move, too. My eyes closed. I tried to will them open and to get my voice to say something about being in charge of my life when he kissed my mouth and untucked my shirt. *Oh, screw it!* I didn't care. As it turned out, I did want him all up in my business.

An hour later, I was craving a cigarette, but I didn't have any, since I didn't smoke. I lay in my bed, Derek next to me, trying not to think about my crazy life when I heard Derek. "I'm hungry. Are you hungry?"

"Yeah, I'm hungry."

"Do you have any food here?"

I thought about the taco pie still in the fridge. "Yup I do," I said. "Meet ya in the kitchen."

After we ate we curled up by the fire and watched a movie then went to bed. We had to leave really early to get to the Cities by 8:00 a.m.

Saturday morning we got showered and dressed and out the door with Faith by five. We barely made it there in time with the gas and food stops. Faith checked out great and got her shots. Pepper was drugged on pain meds and lying down in the back. I had to fold down the back seats to fit him in. Thank goodness Derek was there. I wouldn't have been able to get him in to the Jeep by myself. Faith climbed over to him and curled up between his chin and neck and fell asleep. They both slept the entire way back. As we were coming in to Nisswa, I got a call from Miss Kitty.

"Where are you?" she asked, her voice still serious and accent still gone.

"I'm in my Jeep about ten minutes outside of Nisswa. Why?"

"I need your help. I've been doing some digging, and I know some things. I need help to spy on a meeting between Vincent and Dave. Dave called Vincent this morning and said he was coming over to discuss the manufacturing plant paperwork and other stuff," she told me.

"Oh, oh. What other stuff?" I asked.

"I don't know, but I want to hear it, and I don't trust Dave. I've never seen him like that, the other day in his office. He scared me. And he said something about having a plan. I think we should be there, hidden of course, to listen and watch and record."

"Um, okay. What time are they meeting?"

"Dave said he was coming over at three and would have paperwork ready by then. So can you and Tannya be here by two?"

"Sure, I'll call Tannya, and we'll drive together. So this is at your house? You want us to just show up?"

"Yeah, I'll tell him I'm having friends over for snacks and girl talk. He won't care, and he'll be in the east wing in the office anyway. We will pre-bug and hide video cameras in the room beforehand. Vincent said he has to run to the office in Brainerd in a bit and won't be back until just before three, so it will be perfect!"

"Okay, we will be there at two," I told her and disconnected.

"Be where at two?" Derek asked.

I repeated the conversation to him and he, again, said that he would like to follow me from a distance, just in case. I reluctantly agreed to that. He suggested that I wear a wire so he could hear me from his car too. I also agreed to that.

I called Tannya and told her the plan. She said she would be at my house at 1:30 and said to dress in my black SWAT outfit. Tannya said she knew where Miss Kitty lived, so she'd give me directions if I drove.

When we got home Pepper was half awake. We carefully carried him in. *Man he is huge.* This had to be harder than moving a dead body. We put him down by the fireplace. He didn't seem to care. I put his three-foot bed on the floor next to him and he got up and climbed in it. He looked around the room then put his head down and went back to sleep.

I made a quick PB and J sandwich for Derek and me. After we ate, I got dressed in my black outfit then changed back out of it thinking it would look suspicious if Vincent walked into his kitchen and saw both of us in the same black outfits. Instead I wore jeans and a long sleeve, black t-shirt and tennis shoes. Derek shook his head at me.

"You can stay here. You don't have to come," I said snobbishly.

"Sweetness, I'm going. I don't like the idea of Barbie and the two musketeers doing this alone."

When Tannya arrived, she said a quick hi to Derek. We went through the bag of electronics and I put the wire on. Derek tested it and warned me about the distance limits and about the fact that it may not be admissible in court either. I knew this and so did Miss Kitty but it was worth a shot anyway. Derek wasn't happy about the whole situation, but he knew he couldn't change my mind.

I climbed in my red Jeep and Tannya rode shotgun. When Derek got in his black Jeep, Tannya made a comment about his and hers. Tannya gave me directions as I drove. We went about three miles down the county road then made a few turns on roads I'd never been on before. After about five minutes I was lost and had no idea which direction we were even headed in. We came to a long driveway. Tannya told me that was it. I flashed my brakes at Derek and turned in. He kept going farther down the road. I wondered if he could hear us if he waited on the road.

The home was on Long Lake. There were other homes but none as big as this. We both made sure the batteries on our phones were fully charged. They were. I wouldn't be making that mistake twice. We drove up to a huge mansion. It was in a big opening in the middle of the woods and was nicely landscaped. There was an attached garage with four doors. The house was white and black and very sharp.

The entry door was huge and had side-light windows and a half-circle window over the top. Pillars went up to the second level where a huge window showed a double-curved staircase and a huge chandelier. The house must have been seven-thousand square feet or more. It was strange to see it in such a small town. Tannya said that they had two other homes besides this one. It seemed like a bit much for someone who just passed through once in a while. The asphalt driveway circled around in front of the house, so we parked nice and close to the front door. Miss Kitty met us at the door.

"Bring the bag of stuff!" she husked. Tannya threw the zebra print bag over her shoulder and we walked in. The house was gorgeous and state of the art. It was like being on *Cribs*.

"Dang, girl! I wanna tour," Tannya said.

"Sure thing, girls, but quickly because we gotta get set up," Miss Kitty said.

She was lit up as she showed us around the home. It had nine bedrooms, six bathrooms, and two pools, one inside and one outside. She ended the tour in the office. Tannya still had the bag on her shoulder so we dumped it out on the desk and dug through it. We hid the pen recorder in with the other pens on his desk, and hid the flower pin video camera on the shelf in a dried flower arrangement. It didn't match at all but I'd doubted he'd notice. Miss Kitty placed a bug under the lamp shade and another one over by the couch across the room.

The room was rectangular with two windows on the back wall and a large desk almost against the wall between them. There were two chairs in front of the desk and a full-size couch against the right wall. The left wall had two tall file cabinets. We shut off the lights and went up to Miss Kitty's spa room. It was pink and blinged out in every way possible. She had a cozy couch and pictures of herself everywhere. It was a woman cave of sorts. We took the rest of the electronics and turned them on. The flower-pin video camera we could watch and hear on a hand-held, four-inch TV screen thingy. The others were recording, but we wouldn't be able to see or hear those until later. We left it all there and went down to the kitchen. Miss Kitty mixed us three martinis and Tannya shot me a look.

"Sip it," I told her. "Little tiny sips."

She nodded, but looked freaked.

We sipped our drinks and munched on Chex Mix for a while. I noticed a tiny dog that looked like a Yorkie, tippy-toeing around the place every once in a while. I was surprised at how quiet it was. It hadn't barked at us when we came in either.

Vincent walked through the front door and yelled, "I'll be in the office. Send Dave in when he gets here."

"Okay," Miss Kitty yelled back. She looked at us and rolled her eyes.

"What, no 'Hi, honey, I'm home'?" Tannya asked.

"No," Miss Kitty said matter-of-factly.

Dave showed up about ten minutes later, and Miss Kitty opened the door to him. Tannya and I turned in our seats to see him. He was in a suit, briefcase in hand, and looking stressed.

"He's drunk again," Tannya whispered in my ear.

She was right, he was drunk, not stressed. *Well maybe both.*

"Hello, Dave. You look like shit." Miss Kitty said to him as he stepped in and shut the door behind him.

"Thanks, bitch. Just what I needed to hear!"

He grabbed her by the hair and yanked her to towards the office hallway. I was in shock. *What the heck was going on?* Miss Kitty was being yanked down the hall, fighting and pulling back on his arm screaming that it hurt and to let go. Tannya grabbed my arm when I stood to get up. I looked at her, and she put a finger over her lips to shush me. Then she moved me behind the island counter and pulled me down with her.

"He doesn't know we're here. Let's go listen and watch in the spa room."

We ran to the room and leaned over the hand-held device. I wished the screen was bigger. We could see the three of them standing there. The view was from behind Vincent's shoulder. Vincent was standing behind his desk, and Dave still had Miss Kitty by the hair. Her arms were behind her. I wondered if she was tied or cuffed. She was no longer fighting, or holding her hair.

Vincent said, "What the hell's going on, Dave? Let go of her!"

"Oh, what's the matter, Vincent. You don't like it when men disrespect your woman?"

Dave laughed and tossed Miss Kitty towards him. She fell to her knees. I noticed a phone fall from behind her. Her hands were free now. She stayed kneeling on the floor half way between Dave and Vincent's desk.

"What the fuck's going on, Dave?" Vincent demanded and slapped the desk. "Get up, Elenore!"

I shot Tannya a look. She looked ready to kick some ass.

"Vincent, Vincent, Vincent . . . today is the day that your life changes," Dave said. "Ya see, Vincent, I'm tired, so tired. Tired of pretending. Tired of pretending I'm your friend. Tired of pretending that what you do to these women doesn't bother me. Tired of cleaning up all your messes."

Vincent shot a look at Miss Kitty and then stared back at Dave.

"Dave . . ." Vincent tried to interrupt.

"NO! No! You don't get to talk. For once in your pathetic life you're going to listen! I've spent the last year of my life planning this day. Yes, Vincent, a whole year. You see 'cause it was a year ago that you fucked my wife!"

I covered my mouth. Tannya's eyes shot out of her head. I leaned my head down.

"Derek! If you can hear me, you may want to come closer. This could get out of hand!" I said into my shirt.

"Dave, I don't know what you're talking about. I didn't do that!" he looked at Miss Kitty and repeated himself. "I didn't do that!"

She just stared at him and stood up tall. Dave snapped back.

"Please! Don't waste more of my life with your lies. I *know* you did! You see my wife, unlike you, confessed to me the next day. Then, even though I told her I wanted to work through it, she couldn't get past it and left me!" He shook his head hard and started pacing the room. "I need to know . . . did you drug her?" he turned and faced Vincent. "Did you?"

"Whaaat?" Vincent asked.

"DID YOU DRUG HER?" Dave screamed.

"No."

"Don't fucking lie to me!"

Dave reached in his jacket and pulled out a gun. He held it point blank at Miss Kitty. She screamed and backed up slowly until she was sitting on the couch. Tannya grabbed my arm.

"What do we do? We should kick his ass!"

"Which one?" I asked.

"Tell me the truth! And I know the truth. You had better have the guts to say it to my face! I deserve the truth! YOUR WIFE deserves the truth! DID YOU DRUG MY WIFE AND THEN SLEEP WITH HER?" He screamed again.

"I . . . uh . . . I," Dave pointed the gun closer to Miss Kitty's head. "Jesus, Dave! Take it easy! Don't point the gun at her!"

"ANSWER ME NOOOW!" he screamed.

"Okay, okay! Yes. I . . . I . . . I'm so sorry, Dave. It was an accident. It just happened. It meant nothing."

Vincent was making a lot of hand gestures to try to calm Dave, but it wasn't working.

"An accident? So you *accidentally* slipped something into my wife's drink and then *accidentally* assaulted her?" Dave asked in a snide voice. "What about my daughter?"

"What?" Miss Kitty gasped and covered her mouth.

"I didn't drug *her*!" Vincent said. "*She* came on to *me*."

"Bullshit!" Dave snapped.

"No, it's true! Kelsey came on to me. I didn't drug *her*."

"But still you slept with your employees daughter? Miss Kitty scolded.

"Dave, she's of age! It was her decision," Vincent stated.

"Really? So now other women get to decide who sleeps with you?" Miss Kitty asked. "Weird because I thought we were married. I thought that would be *your* decision to make, not some seventeen-year-old's!"

"Yeah, and she knows, too," Dave said referring to Miss Kitty.

Vincent looked at Miss Kitty.

"About what? Is there something I should know? I mean beside my husband sleeping with his assistant's wife and daughter," she asked Vincent.

"No, no there's not." Vincent said. "Dave and I have a meeting to conduct. I'll talk to you later about that incident. Dave, lower the gun and let her out of the room so we can talk," Vincent said.

"NO! I am in charge here! And this is how it's going to go," he said.

Keeping the gun pointed at Miss Kitty, he reached in his briefcase and pulled out a file. He threw it down on the desk in front of Vincent.

"Sign where all the red stickers are," he demanded.

"What is this?" Vincent said looking through the files.

"Those are the deeds to two of the lavish properties you own. One is this house. Miss Kitty is going to live here, in her home town, with her dog and her friends. You're signing over the house to her, and don't worry . . . it's already been paid off by the funds in your investment accounts." He smiled at Miss Kitty. "You're welcome."

She stared at him, just as surprised as Vincent.

"The other, is your home in Bermuda. That one you're signing over to me. It too is paid for. Thanks for that! It is, after all, the least you could do. In fact thanks for the substantial transfers to our new savings accounts too. That was nice. Wouldn't you say Miss Kitty?"

Miss Kitty didn't say anything, she just looked confused.

"You really think this is going to work?" Miss Kitty said.

"Oh, yeah it'll work. Won't it, Vincent? You see Vincent will still have a few dollars to get him by, and he'll have the Chicago house. He's not going to give us any trouble in this matter either because he knows if he does, his dirty secret, or shall I say *secrets*, will be out. We wouldn't want those out, now would we?"

"Dave, this'll never work. I'll destroy you! You smug, son of a bitch!"

"I mean it, Vincent. This is your only option, or I go to the cops," Dave said.

"You'll rot too, as an accessory."

"No, I'll kill myself first, before I'm ever brought in," Dave told him. "I don't care either way. You've already taken everything from me. My family included. My wife and daughter won't talk to me and won't even look me in the eye because of what you did and the fact that I still work for you. They wanted to go to the cops, but I told them not to because we'd be broke. She left me anyway. They both left!"

"Yes! And I made you a very wealthy man in the process!" Vincent yelled.

Now he was getting pissed.

"You were involved in all of it! In fact I think it was your idea."

"No, that's not going to work, Vincent. I have records, pictures, and a paper trail of those you've paid off. They'd all be willing to testify, too, since most have spent the money already and are looking for more. And Alexa can help with that part."

"What?" Vincent asked.

"Alexa. The one from Gold Diggers you've been chatting with? She's my new girlfriend. Yeah, how does it feel to lose to me for once? I slept with the woman you wanted."

"She's an ugly, fat loser who's using someone else's profile picture you morons!" Miss Kitty yelled.

Vincent looked at her, in dismay, probably wondering how she knew that, and for how long.

"Shut up, bitch!" Dave warned. "That's not the point. You might say you made us both rich. Remember that one girl, two years ago, the one that didn't make it, the one that died from an 'overdose' they labeled alcohol poisoning? The one that you gave just a little too much of your 'special cocktail' drug to? Her mom, Alexa, was pretty upset about it. You see, her daughter was her meal ticket, and you ruined that for her. So, she did a little digging in to her daughter's death and found out about you and your smug ways. She followed you one night and saw what you did. She found out who you were and started to bait you online. You still have my number as a contact number on the site so your wife wouldn't find out," he said turning to Miss Kitty.

She looked furious.

"Well, she found me. She came to visit me over and over and refused to give up on finding out what happened. She threatened me and my family! So, I finally told her the truth. I'm sick of you and your messed up life destroying mine. I'm done picking up your pieces when all you've done is destroy everything I've ever had." He stopped talking for a minute to collect his thoughts.

"What did you tell her Dave?" Vincent asked him.

"I told her all of it. As it turns out, she just wanted a monthly payment, and she promised to keep quiet. In return I can live there with her since my wife took the house. Did you even know that? Did you know that for a year now I've been homeless because of you! That's part of your problem, no conscience! You don't give a shit about anyone but yourself! You're a condescending jerk! Well this is where your path has led you, my king. With my ideas and her ideas, we put our heads together and came up with this plan. And it's pretty good. We all get a great home and cash and no one goes to jail. You have no other options."

I looked at Tannya.

"He's never going to let this happen," she said.

I shook my head. I didn't think he'd go down without a fight either. *But what am I going to do about it?*

"You're going to sign these papers. Miss Kitty will live happily ever after here, I'll be with Alexa in Bermuda, and you can go on with your life in Chicago. It's win-win. If you try to fight me on any of this, it's just one phone call and you'll go to jail. I have documentation of all of this, in multiple locations, left with multiple people, should something happen to me. You're up against murder one and sexual assault counts of dozens of women, plus drug charges. You'll never get out! If you kill me, the police will know for sure. I've covered all my bases."

"Did you see that?" Tannya asked.

"What?" I looked at the screen harder.

"The shadow, someone else was in the hallway door. I saw a head peek."

"Derek?"

"I don't know?"

"Fuck you, Dave. I'm not going to jail and you're not taking my money. As far as I can tell this is just a blip on the map. All I need to do is get rid of you, and Alexa, or whoever she is, and well . . . my wife. Then I can put all this behind me."

"So your solution is to kill us all?" Miss Kitty asked Vincent.

Vincent looked at his wife.

"Baby, this is not how I wanted this to end. It's just that *someone* got selfish, and now the game has changed."

"Ha! The game? So my life, our marriage—it was all a game to you?"

"Huh, yeah, I guess it was. I mean you can't tell me that you really loved me, can you? You were only in this marriage for the money. We both knew that. You can't even look me in the eye when you tell me you love me," Vincent told her.

"Maybe that's because all I see is evil when I look in your eyes. I did love you. But it was for a short period of time, probably until the first time you cheated on me. I don't love you now, and haven't for a long time. And, boy, am I glad for that! You're a waste of life. And now you're a murderer, and rapist? Where's her body? What was her name? Who is the girl YOU KILLED?" she screamed.

"I DON'T KNOW THEIR NAMES! THAT'S THE POINT!" he screamed.

I could tell he was losing his composure. He knew he was done.

"Screw you both! I'll take care of things my way! I ALWAYS WIN!"

He reached in to his desk and pulled out a gun of his own. He pointed it at Dave. Dave moved his gun and pointed his at Vincent.

"Oh, shit!" I yelled.

I grabbed my phone out of my pocket and called Rex's cell. I was still watching the screen waiting for it to connect. *Pick up! Pick up!*

"Did you see it that time?" Tannya asked. "The head in the door, it was back!"

The next second there was a strange noise and everyone in the office turned and looked at the door.

"Did you HEAR that?" Tannya asked still starring hard at the screen.

I looked hard too. *Oh, shit.*

"It's Rex! I just blew his cover!" I told her and quickly hung up my phone.

Tannya and I took off for the office as fast as our legs would carry us! When we rounded the corner, we saw Rex just stepping in. He had his gun pointed into the office and walked in slowly, out of our sight.

"Oh, my God!" Tannya yelped.

"Shhh!" I said and pulled her back against the wall.

We crept along the wall to the office and waited outside, a little ways down from the door. We listened hard.

"Rex!" Vincent yelled. "Thank God you're here! Arrest this man!"

"Gentlemen, put your weapons down. No one's getting shot tonight. We need to calm down and talk about this," Rex said slowly and calmly.

"No. You put him in cuffs or I'll shoot! We are not *talking* about anything! He's full of lies!" Vincent said desperately.

"It's all true! I have proof, lots of it, and tons of witnesses! Yeah, I helped cover it up, but I didn't do it, and I didn't know it was happening until after the fact. I was never with him! I have proof in lots of locations. I'll show you!" Dave yelled.

"Both of you lower your weapons!" Rex yelled. There was a clanking noise I assumed was a gun dropping. "Good, Dave, now get on your stomach on the floor, and shut up!"

"Miss Kitty is going to leave the room while we figure this out," Rex told them.

"NO! She stays," Vincent yelled. "Sit!"

"Vincent, drop your weapon now! She doesn't need to be here." Rex yelled.

The tension was building. My heart was pounding hard. Tannya's was too. She was panting next to me.

"She's going to get away with my money! It's *my* money! Neither of them is going to get it!"

His voice was panicky and irate. I thought for sure he was going to shoot someone right then. It seemed Tannya thought the exact same thing because we both covered our ears and crouched down. BANG! BANG! Two gunshots fired at almost the exact same time. *There was no way that one gun could have fired again that quickly. Two guns must have gone off.* There was the sound of broken glass hitting the floor. I needed eyes in the room. *Why didn't we bring the hand held screen thingy with? We were such amateurs!*

Miss Kitty screamed and came running from the room. She saw us in the hall, and fell on the floor into our laps. She was bawling and shaking. I moved her more on to Tannya, and carefully walked to the office door way. Dave was still on the floor. Rex was cuffing his hands behind his back. Vincent was on the floor behind the desk. He was moaning, and barely moving. Rex spoke into his radio on his shoulder and said he needed an ambulance. Then he went to the shattered window behind the desk.

"He's alive. Nice shot!" Rex said to the window.

"You too," a voice from the window said.

"Derek?" I asked quietly.

Rex turned around and looked at me. "Yes, Derek. I met him a few minutes ago outside. I got a hang-up call from Miss Kitty and came out here to make sure everything was okay. I found Derek lurking around looking in windows."

I turned around to Derek who was walking into the office door.

"Hey, you okay?" he asked and wrapped his arms around me.

"Yeah, we watched it all on the video thing upstairs. I came down after Vincent pulled out the gun. Tannya and I waited in the hall. We didn't know what to do."

Derek stepped closer to Rex and shook his hand.

"You pompous jerk," Dave said to Vincent from the floor. He was still face down and cuffed. "I'll see ya in hell. The only advantage you have over me now is that you can kiss my ass, and I can't!"

Derek let out a snort. Vincent didn't respond. He just closed his eyes. He was struggling to breathe, but his color was still good, except for the two red spots in each shoulder.

"Shut up, Dave," Rex said and gave Dave's leg a little kick.

Rex went over and was talking to Vincent telling him he'd live, but to concentrate on breathing and not to talk. A few moments later Tannya and Miss Kitty walked in. Miss Kitty was done crying and looked pissed.

"I hope both you jerks enjoy prison!" she said. Then she walked over to Vincent and knelt down by him. "You destroyed your life and the lives of everyone you came into contact with, but you didn't destroy mine. I'm going to be just fine!" she said and kicked him hard in the stomach.

I could hear the sound of sirens through the broken window.

27

Sunday came way too quickly. I woke up to a warm body next to me. It was nice to have him there. I rolled over and put my arm around him. A moment later, a large tongue covered my entire face in one lick. *Geez!!* I shot straight up. It seemed the warm body was Pepper. I'd forgotten about him. He was apparently feeling better, and somehow made it to my bed. I should have set the alarm to let him out. Derek walked in with two cups of coffee.

"Morning!" he sang. "We have four inches of snow, and it's still coming down. There were some Mexicans here this morning, plowing already."

Ugh, he is such a morning person. I really didn't feel much like talking yet, but I smiled and took the coffee.

"Thanks. That's good. Now you don't have to shovel. Did Pepper go out yet?"

"Yup, he woke me up an hour ago with a big, wet kiss. I thought it was you at first."

"Ha, ha. I could say the same to you. I got one of those, too, and it took a second to figure it out!"

"So what are you plans for the day?" he asked.

"I have none. But I can't do too much, I'll have to be here for Pepper. You?" I asked.

"I have to make a stop at the police station, and so do you. Tannya and Elenore said they'd be there about 8:00 a.m. I spoke to Rex this morning, and he said to come in a little later. He's the only one to take statements and can't do us all at the same time. I have breakfast almost ready, so we can go in awhile."

"Sounds good to me," I told him and took a sip.

He was standing at my bedside leaning on the wall, looking me up and down.

"And then, you and I are going to pick up some food, come back here, and lock ourselves in this cabin for a snowed-in, *drama-free* day!" he told me.

"Mmmm, a drama-free day? That sounds nice . . . but what about tonight?" I asked with a flirtatious smile.

"Oh, I got big plans for tonight," he said with a smirk. "Tonight will be *very* exciting," he said. "Tonight, I plan to destroy you for all other men." He winked, turned on his heels, and walked out.

Acknowledgements

A special thanks to:

My husband Jared: for all the love and support.

My writers group: Mollie Rushmeyer, Laura Tangen, and Milissa Nelson for all your help, opinions, and encouragement.

To: Mike Kalmbach, Blair Schrader and Milissa Nelson and all the other beta readers. Thanks for all your feedback and great suggestions as I developed this book.

To the North Star Press staff: for all your help turning this manuscript in to a beautiful, successful book.

Keep up with Danelle Helget on:

Facebook: Author Danelle Helget

www.danellehelget.com